I am afraid. I am a coward. I am sorry for everything. If I had done this a long time ago, it would have saved a lot of pain.

ˌ PEG ENTWISTLE
Hollywood
1932

FUNERAL FOR A QUEEN

THE BODY HUNG at the end of Mulholland Drive where it meets the Cahuenga Pass. There are a handful of trees there, with a few thick branches that jut out over the intersection. That's where the world found her, just above the California 101 freeway, above the crowded passageway to success and failure. It was Thursday, June 13th, 2019.

At 3:21 a.m., a car with a drunk driver heading south down the pass saw what looked like a woman take her final step from a small stool. But because of the drunkenness and his true-crime superstition, the man assumed it was some specter of ancient Hollywood lore and drove on without calling the authorities, swerving dangerously somewhere in the distance. Several other cars also passed the body, but at those early hours, traffic was mercifully light, and no one had time to let an eye lazily wander to the side of the road.

Early morning cyclists on their rides over the hill also paid the body no mind. One saw it and briefly considered calling it in, but because stopping would create an ordeal, likely making him late for work, and because the woman was so obviously dead without hope of being revived, he didn't know what good it would do. It wasn't until 5:33 a.m. that the fifth cyclist to make their way down the pass saw her and called 911.

Authorities arrived and took the cyclist's statement, which was nothing more than a description of her morning ride to the gym, then to work at a vintage apparel store near the corner of La Brea and Melrose Avenues, about four miles away.

A disgruntled detective and their partner arrived, alongside an ambulance and a fire truck. Paramedics cut the woman down and placed her on a gurney, tucking her almost violently into a body bag. The police officers helped direct traffic but mostly talked among themselves about nothing, laughing periodically. Drivers at the front of the line of traffic who could not turn around had no choice but to watch the scene. On his phone, one man took pictures of the body as it was being taken down from the tree. A woman filmed it. Someone else live streamed the confusion. Though they didn't yet know who she was, at least there was entertainment. Meanwhile, the long line of cars stretched down in one direction past the Hollywood Bowl and, in the other direction, past the In-N-Out Burger. Since news of her death would not hit any media outlets for another three hours, drivers had no context as to why they were trapped. There was honking and shouting. It was a fucking outrage.

A reach into the back pocket of her loose denim jeans produced a wallet with identification: a California driver's license.

ROSEANNA MARGARET MANDRIE.

To some, just a body hanging from a tree. But to many, Molly Mandrie, star of *Molly's Messy Life*, better known to fans and viewers as *MML*, the former hit reality show in which she tried and failed repeatedly to get her life together after suffering drama after drama and relapse after relapse, all in the aftermath of being a successful child actor. By that point in her life, to anyone who'd gotten a good look at her, she truly was that specter of ancient Hollywood lore; a ghost of her former self, the firelight of glamor gone from her eyes long ago. Now they were set back in her skull as if pushed in by thumbs, cheeks hollow and sunken, her blonde hair thin and half gray, as if someone had stolen her soul.

Once the announcement of her death was made, rumors began. Molly had been seen drinking the night before, alone, talking loudly to herself on Ventura Boulevard in Sherman Oaks. Four weeks later, a leaked toxicology report revealed there had only been alcohol in her system, but that in the second back pocket of her jeans, police had found a dime bag of heroin with a faded red stamp on it that read *J2Z*.

She was in no condition to drive but had done so anyway, leaving her car a few yards up Mulholland. Inside it there was no suicide note. In the remaining pockets of the jeans, no note. And after a search of her apartment, still no note. The coroner later told authorities that the stool she had used to jump from had not been high enough to break her neck. She had been strangled by the weight of her own body. And, he further pointed out, judging by the shredded, bloodied tips of her fingernails and by the fibers of rope lodged beneath them, it appeared that she had changed her mind. If she could've told anyone anything in any note, it would have been that, in the end, she had wanted to live.

Two weeks later, her funeral. Many former friends and costars made appearances. Although none, not even her father, appeared more grief stricken than her *Molly's Messy Life* castmates. They all appeared appropriately beside themselves with grief. Luckily, most of the cameras had set up on their good sides, except for a young woman named Cyd, who unfortunately had most of the cameras set up on her bad side, which, apart from looking almost identical to her good side, was apparently hideous.

People made speeches and remembered Molly for her childhood stardom as Peggy Whistler on the popular eighties sitcom *The Family That Stays Together*. Friends from rehab clinics told their stories of the trials and tribulations of what it meant to be someone like Molly Mandrie, to never be seen without the emotional scars of childhood celebrity. They shed tears. One of them eventually switched places with Cyd.

The person most noticeably absent, however, was Guy Maker. Guy "the People" Maker. Guy "the Money" Maker, as he had been christened by *People* magazine. One of Molly's oldest childhood friends, he was also the creator and executive producer of *MML*. From her show he had produced two successful spin-offs based on popular costars and friends from Molly's life, *Tamandrea* and *Fievel Goes East*. Additionally, he produced three other shows for the same network. One a cooking competition show called *Simmer Showdown*; another that presented marriage counseling between overbearing women and their meek husbands as entertainment, called *Hard Knock Wife*; and his own, a talk show, *What Happens Here, Stays!* (*WHH,S!*). All were property of what had originally been called the Applause network, later more friendly rebranded as APLZ, which most viewers mockingly referred to as "Apples." The ridicule did not please the network. A PR firm was fired. But the nickname stuck.

People loved to see stars from other Apples shows bicker back and forth on Guy's show as he drew them further into the petty dramas and inconsequential intrigue of what it meant to pretend they were living out their real lives in front of the camera. Only, after so long, these produced lives had become their real ones. The petty dramas and inconsequential intrigue became dense and legitimate, and the stakes were high. Because Molly's show had brought the initial success that had propelled the network into the world of successful reality programming and away from its origin in home-and-garden hell, to the audience she was the godmother of Apples, forever one of two women: one they loved or one they loved to hate.

It was curious that Guy was not present at the service of the woman many argued had given him his career. But his fans assumed he had his reasons.

The stars of *Tamandrea* were there: Tamara Collins and Andrea Bocelli, the latter having spent most of her career ham-fistedly insisting that she was not related to or involved with famed blind Italian opera singer Andrea Bocelli.

Tamara had been a celebrity dancer, choreographer, and eventual co-host of the competition show *Dance Battle*. Each episode, two stars were pitted against each other in a test of skills as they tried to learn the same moves, then a panel of judges determined who had performed best. Her popularity as the most sought-after partner on the show also led to her marrying, and later divorcing, its requisite British judge, Winslow Philips. She had met Molly when she appeared as a guest dancer on the show and had eventually been approached by Guy to join the cast of *MML*.

She had initially seen the opportunity as a vehicle to move her brand away from being seen as strictly tits and ass. It was the chance to present her real life to the audience. But the offer eventually revealed its double-edged nature. When she joined *MML*, Tamara was the only Black cast member on an Apples show. As such, she became a diversity token that the network could cash in when it wanted to reach the coveted "urban" audience.

Despite her enormous success and her popular image as the picture of fitness and health, Tamara and Molly had bonded over empties—vodka bottles, pill bottles, eco-friendly reusable water bottles, and plenty of empty matcha cups with lipstick markings on white plastic lids. For a long time, their problems rode shotgun to their successes. Their inevitable falling out came when, seeing the faltering ratings of a circus past its prime, Guy gave Tamara her own spin-off and Apples pulled the plug on Molly's show a season later.

The other half of the double act, Andrea, had been raised in a strict Lutheran home in Tyler, Texas, the daughter of an Italian father and Korean mother. Sheltered and celebrated for both her beauty and her chastity while growing up, she had a reputation for being overly trusting. She had not had sex until she moved to Dallas and married her first husband. He had just turned forty-five. She was twenty-two.

A personal injury attorney with a penchant for the pricey services of high-end sex workers, he managed to keep this secret for four years until Andrea discovered it and filed for divorce. That the wool could be pulled over her eyes by a man twice her age should not have been a complete surprise, but it did paint a picture of who she would become on television: an endearingly gullible gal who had to work three times as hard as anyone else to be taken seriously. The first thing she did to demand such respect was to make sure that, for as good a litigator as her husband was, she hired an even better divorce attorney. She had pursued a career in cosmetology lightly while in Texas, but when she moved to LA at twenty-six with a hefty pile of fuck-you money and an eye on becoming a makeup artist, she was free to fly.

Having now been on TV for ten years, the innocent girl from Tyler had evolved. In the pursuit of putting a stamp on the world outside of her persona on her show, she had recently published a *New York Times* best-selling diet, fitness, and pseudo-inspirational memoir titled, *B*tch, Your Single Body Is Your Best Body!*, which outlined ways to make the men in your life envious and drive them stark raving mad at the notion of you obtaining your hottest body and strongest sense of self post-breakup.

Sitting beside Tamara and Andrea at the funeral was Fievel Geitman, Molly's ex-boyfriend and star of the second *MML* spin-off, *Fievel Goes East* (*FGE*).

During his and Molly's time together, he had reinvented himself seven or eight—maybe seven and a half—times to fit into whatever new career it was he wanted to master. When he had decided he wanted to be an upscale art photographer, his name had been Fi, although his insistence on taking photos only on his iPhone using portrait mode put an early expiration date on that dream. When he had decided he wanted to be a life coach and the face of success and entrepreneurship for a new herbal supplement brand called You-trition, his name had been B. Well. When he'd wanted to play high-stakes poker professionally, he wore sunglasses at all times, including indoors, because he said he had to "protect his tell," and he'd referred to himself only as Gee.

He'd also dipped his toe into the arena of amateur wrestling, concocting the persona of "Gatman," who was a Gatling-gun-wielding, American-flag-wearing lampoon of a patriot. But when Gatman's fans began chanting, "Gun him down!" as he prepared to crush his opponents, and some started coming to his matches with fake and even sometimes real guns, everyone knew it was time for him to stop.

His occupation at present was as a DJ named Five-El, a moniker inspired in part by Kal-El, the birth name of Superman, who Fievel said was created by two New York Jews and meant to embody the ideal image of the chosen one, come to save the world. Being Jewish himself, he hoped he might be music's chosen one and was scheduled to make his debut the following weekend at the poolside bar of the Tropicana Las Vegas.

Next to him at Molly's funeral sat Elliot Rossi, his best friend and costar, who had begun as his personal driver. Elliot had made a minor name for himself on *MML*, the way Andrea had alongside Tamara. Even though his screen time on *MML* had gradually increased the more producers saw how important his friendship was to Fievel, Elliot worked hard to retain his quiet, shy reputation. But every now and again he would let booze get the better of him, and the traumatic decades of being the son of an overbearing Italian Catholic mother and a physically abusive father would spill out a cupful at a time. But, by and large, he was amiable and affable.

A short fling with Andrea had thrown a wrench into seasons eight of *Tamandrea* and five of *FGE* (precipitated by a major crossover event, when two cast members from each show, Matt and Trisha, tied the knot in the appropriately titled televised wedding special, *Holy Matt-Trisha-mony*). The reception had been one of those rare occasions when Elliot got drunk, and Andrea had told him how she'd always thought he was cute but needed to let go of his shy-guy demeanor, in reply to which he slurred, "I'll show you who's not shy" and kissed her. She responded in kind, and they disappeared to the back of the limousine that was meant to take the couple to their honeymoon suite.

Most noticeably present at the funeral was the actor Hector Espinoza, one of the highest paid stars of the past decade. To most everyone in attendance, seeing him there was like witnessing the second coming of Christ. Many thought it was a poor attempt at grandstanding. Hector and Molly never had any known relationship, which caused wild speculation.

It was rare that celebrities of his caliber crossed over into the world of shows like the ones Apples had to offer. There remained an intangibility to movie stars that even someone like Tamara, Andrea, or Fievel could not reach. While Hector's fame was part of some ancient machine, everyone on Apples had been injected with a fame virus. They were often portrayed as "normal" people who did not know what to do with their fame. But Hector and his persona had been crafted by many hands, his corner of Hollywood having been built, broken, and rebuilt for over a century to gradually come to resemble a new pantheon.

Having recently been outed by an internet tabloid as bisexual and having worked to keep it a secret well into his forties, Hector was making fewer and fewer public appearances as he found it increasingly difficult to keep up with social media and all its criticisms. Across the world its power had transcended frivolous life updates and silly observations about grocery shopping to become a real tool for both justice and injustice. It was the only functioning paradox he knew of.

His caution had also come on the heels of the great wave of reckoning that had occurred two years prior, when centuries of truths about abuses had bled out from social posts and into the streets, marked by two words that fired like silver bullets aimed at aging toxic werewolves: "me too."

Outside of releasing two lackluster films in the two years since, one a needless further installment in an already-too-long-running franchise, Hector had isolated himself. Many of the high-powered men he had grown accustomed to working with and hearing about were now living out their days in conscious or unconscious fear. Things he had traditionally laughed off and chalked up to the old boys' club were now dominoes falling one by one to a female might no man had ever expected in their industry.

Not much farther south, at a home in Murrieta, California, Nixon Bryce and her mother, Samantha, watched the televised funeral. Samantha's eyes were peeled from floor to ceiling while Nixon's fluttered half-open, gradually being weighed down by apathy. Reruns of *MML*, and later *Tamandrea* and *FGE*, had been substantial building blocks of her and her mother's relationship. Impressions of Molly were how Nixon had found a fan base and a rabid following on Instagram. She had been five when her mother started filming and posting her daughter's comedy and impersonations to only a few hundred followers, all family and friends. Now that she was fifteen, her following had grown to more than twenty-five million across all her platforms. And she had only higher to go from there. But despite that, most of the time when any adult spotted Nixon in public, they would shout, "Do Molly! Do Molly!" And she would languidly comply with what had become one of the many catchphrases from *MML* she was famous for quoting: "Let's get lit, hos!"

Though her fame had begun relatively inappropriately with her as a toddler quoting the rated-R language of an addict, everyone knew that videos of children cursing were funny. Followers loved to watch videos of the young Nixon dressed as Molly saying things like, "This bitch is out of *control!*" then throwing a cheeseburger at a wall. Or chugging what appeared to be a glass of rosé and burping before saying, "Life is like a fucking puzzle, and sometimes you just gotta piece that shit together." It was not uncommon to hear the voice of Samantha just behind the camera phone laughing and urging her daughter to say something else or to throw another burger or to chug more fake wine.

Once *MML* had ended and the power of those cute impressions had diminished, Samantha had worked hard to turn Nixon's budding social media stardom into a viable business empire, paying consultants and working with other top influencers to understand how best to monetize @niXMarkstheSpot. Nixon was looking at a clothing line launch, a feature film debut, and an album drop all in the span of a few short months.

Only now, the great inspiration for the young girl's career had ceased to live, her head slipped through a noose, body dangling like a carrot over those who had watched her fall apart for years. The audience had finally taken the bait. The stick on the rudimentary trap she'd set had come loose, and now that they were all trapped inside the box, the real drama could begin.

1.

HECTOR

Two Weeks Later

I DON'T KNOW, CYD," Hector said. "I don't know. Fuck."

"Well, you either do or you don't." She swept her middle finger under her right eye to catch a small tear.

"I'm sorry," he said. "I didn't think this would make you cry."

"Oh, I don't know, Hec," she said. "I'm only dating the most interesting man in the world. You think it wouldn't hurt like hell when he dumped me?"

His face scrunched as he doubted that very much.

She had always called him Hec, as if it were an endearing nickname she could playfully say while she spun her fingers through the hair at the nape of his neck. But he hated it. No one else in the entire world had ever called him that.

"We've been on three dates," he said. "I didn't know if you . . . was this, like, a *thing* thing? Are we dating?"

"What else would you call it?"

"I guess dating. But, like . . . dating around dating. Not exclusive dating."

"What's the difference?"

"There's a big difference."

"Oh, is there?"

"I think so."

They sat silently at their small outdoor table at Figaro Bistrot in Los Feliz.

"God, you're such a fuck boy," she finally said, folding her arms and looking out toward the street.

"I'm a what?" he asked, unfamiliar with the term.

"You're just like everyone else."

"Everyone else is a fuck boy?"

"Yes."

"Okay." A long pause. "But what is it?"

"You'll say anything just to fuck someone, then you'll ghost them."

"Oh," he said. "What did I say?"

"All of it." She wouldn't look at him.

"All of it."

"Yes."

"Okay."

"You've never heard that before?"

"No," he said, not bullshitting. "I don't . . . I usually try to keep to myself. Which I'm now realizing would have been the better call here. Did I . . . give you the wrong impression?"

"You did," she said sternly.

"I'm sorry if it wasn't clear, but I—I told you on our first date that I wasn't looking for anything outside of the . . . you know."

"The fucking."

"Well, it sounds crass when you say it like that."

"How else would you like me to say it? The *passionate lovemaking*?"

"I guess that sounds worse."

"See? So you're a fuck boy."

"Would you please stop calling me that?"

"You have fuck-boy demeanor then, *okay*?"

"Okay." He decided to play along, knowing that arguing wouldn't change anything. After another long silence he stood up.

"You're just going to leave?"

"I mean, I'm not going to stay."

"Fine." She turned away from him again and swept a tear from her other eye.

"How are you doing that?" he asked.

"Doing what?" She flipped her sunglasses down from the top of her head.

"Making exactly one tear come out of each eye at a time?"

"It's not for the cameras, if that's what you're thinking."

"I mean, it kind of is." He pointed to three men with cameras across the street snapping photos of what would no doubt be a trending topic in T-minus ten minutes. "They're right over there."

"I hadn't noticed," she said.

"All right." He stuck his hands in his pockets and started to head north up Vermont Avenue.

"Hec!" she called after him.

He turned back to face her.

"If this is because of that tweet, I'm really sorry!"

He registered the genuine apology in her voice and offered a small smile, then turned again and left.

Hector and Cyd had met on *Splice*, the popular dating app meant primarily for celebrities and the well-to-do. Despite the company assuming most people would think their name was a clever way of saying "two who would be joined," those people actually thought it sounded gross. But their investment capital was high, and the faces of the app itself were an up-and-coming TV actor named Brando Keates and Fievel Geitman. Fievel's catchphrase in internet marketing videos for the service was, "Experience a different splice of life!"—a line he delivered before snapping his fingers on both hands and then pointing them like guns at the camera as a girl appeared under each arm.

A year prior, when his cloud storage had been hacked and nude photos of him with an ex-boyfriend had been leaked, Hector had been forced to come out. Now not only had the select few he trusted seen his penis but everyone else in the world had seen it too. Much as with his films, the reviews were mostly positive, though some critics said they'd hoped for more substance. He'd agonized for days over the notion that he might not have a substantive penis.

Because of his decade-long success in big-budget films, his reps were struck with the sudden panic that America might turn on him. His franchise of films based on the *All That God Allows* book series saw him playing Matt Source, a hyperintelligent codebreaker who, despite being bookish, appeared to lift a lot of weights and have a knack for handling dangerous weapons with relative ease. The fourth film in the series, *Source Wall*, had been released the summer prior and, despite turning a profit, was the least successful in the franchise.

That lack of success coupled with the fact that he was now a queer actor meant both good and bad things. Most concerning to his reps was the possibility that his conservative audience might stop paying to see his movies. After sharing a handful of Instagram posts about his sexuality, the comment sections became littered with former fans saying things like, "I follow you to be entertained, not to be preached at," "You need Jesus," "Why do you have to make this about politics?" and his favorite, "I don't care what you do in private, just don't make it my business." There was also a bevy of people who had clearly been waiting in the wings, gleefully ready to lob the three-letter f-bomb.

All That God Allows had possibly found all of whatever it was that He allowed.

Cyd had been an aspiring model and barista at the café attached to Tamara's dance studio. When cast in *Tamandrea*, she had a boyfriend named Josh who was an amateur music producer. He'd also had a previous relationship with Guy Maker and had been seen with him many nights leaving expensive restaurants and nightclubs. After it was alleged that they were spotted doing cocaine together in the bathroom at Barney's Beanery on Santa Monica Boulevard, Guy had made it clear that he had not been doing the drugs; rather, he had "discovered" Josh doing them and strongly disapproved. Shortly thereafter, he encouraged Cyd to break up with him, effectively kicking him off the show.

Because she was a cast member of *Tamandrea*, dating Hector had seemed like something she was doing solely for optics. Rumors swirled that she was potentially being let go before filming began on the next season, so she had to make some semblance of a splash. After they were caught on camera on their third and final date leaving Craig's restaurant in West Hollywood, Cyd's first statement on their courtship had been made via Twitter. She retweeted and captioned the press photo to say that she was a proud ally of the LGBT community and thrilled to be dating a bisexual man.

Seeing this the following day, Hector got a bad taste in his mouth. Much of social media accused Cyd of being an opportunist, as well as insensitive for leaving out additional letters from the acronym, to which Cyd initially responded that it was always changing, and she couldn't keep track of all the letters and symbols, for which people roasted her further. She eventually deleted the post, but it was too late. Screenshots had been grabbed, and as it was with any social media misstep, what might've once been forgiven was now a meme that would follow her forever.

Remaining in his self-imposed isolation was part of the reason Hector had avoided doing much press for *Source Wall*, a factor in its box office stutter. According to his manager, Murphy Beck, it wasn't wise for him to be seen with floozies. As he returned home, his phone rang.

"What the fuck happened?" Murphy said.

"What do you mean?" Hector asked.

"These pictures of this Cyd girl crying at Figaro."

"That was fast." Hector stopped at his front door.

"Slow by most people's standards, honestly. Why didn't you tell me?"

"It didn't seem like it would be that big of a deal."

"You can't trust these Apples people." Murphy sighed on the other end of the line. "Every fucking human being around you has a magic box in their pocket and is willing to use that magic against you. You're Superman. You hate magic. Remember? Which is why you run these things by me first."

Hector stood quietly, staring at his front door, mocked by the thought of plunging himself back into his spoiled retreat. It wasn't as if he were off the grid in a cabin somewhere doing a lot of self-reflection. He had mostly been catching up on Netflix shows in his lavish home off Benedict Canyon where he could have food delivered whenever he liked.

He took in a deep breath and reached down, touching the ground beneath him as part of a calming exercise he'd learned from his life coach, Essence. Murphy could hear Hector's deep breaths through the phone, in through his nose and out through his mouth.

"What do you recommend I do then, Murph?" Hector asked, forcing calm on himself.

"Listen, I'm not angry. Okay? I just need to know what you're going to say."

"I guess I'll say nothing," Hector said in a monotone. He heard Murphy make a "*hmm*" sound in reply, as if he thought it was a bad idea. "Why do I have to? I went on three dates with h—"

"You should say that you think she's a bigot," Murphy said optimistically.

"I'm not going to say she's a bigot."

"She's insensitive."

"I don't think she meant to come off that way."

"We have an opportunity to spin it in your favor after her dumb fucking comments the other day. We should."

Hector stood slowly and sighed. "What should it be—a story?"

"No. Static post. Do another picture of you and King," Murphy said. King was Hector's dog, a pit bull mix, beloved by all. "Say he's the only love in your life. You have no room for insensitive opportunists—"

"Murphy," Hector said, cutting him off. Then he considered it and sighed again. "Fine. Give me fifteen minutes."

"And read that script from Shelley!" Murphy hung up before Hector could.

Hector stared down at a small sun deck on his property and fell into his favorite daydream, the one about what it would have been like to have met Molly when they were younger. Their impossible childhood friendship. He remembered her as if she had been his best friend down the block who had helped him through the hardest times in his life. The loss of his mother when he was only fourteen. The confusion of his sexuality. He had wanted desperately to be friends with Peggy Whistler.

When he thought of Molly now, he thought of the photos posted by those sitting in traffic. Her body hung out to dry. Inevitably he felt a small sense of guilt and regret at the fact that he had never reached out. Maybe there could have been a real bond. Maybe he had been the thing missing from her life. Maybe she would still be alive. But he knew that was selfish and largely unrealistic. The center of his core began to tighten as the anxiety of his own past trauma surfaced. He touched the ground beneath him again and took another string of deep breaths, but it was too late. He sat down on the driveway and lay back, hands clasped over his stomach, taking deep breaths and chanting, "Fuck, fuck, fuck, fuck, fuck." Essence had told him that a mantra was merely words, and words have only the meaning we give them. So, if saying "fuck" to himself over and over again helped reduce his anxiety, then it was a perfectly suitable mantra.

Why had she done it? Why hadn't she left any kind of note? Why wouldn't she name names?

His body forced him to take a breath. He sat up slowly. He wondered why, given what a good friend he had supposedly been to her, Guy Maker had not been at the funeral. Hector could not wrap his mind around the man's absence. The man who had been responsible for Molly's career comeback, for launching a struggling reality network into an empire.

A week after her funeral, Guy's next episode of *WHH,S!* had been dedicated to her memory. How could he have gone on with his show, Hector wondered, but not been there for her final curtain? All of Guy's social media had expressed extreme regret that he could not attend because of production emergencies with his show. But he claimed she was always in his heart, would always be the core of his being, and always his better half. Hector wondered what that really meant.

It felt like an impossible excuse to expect people to swallow. Apples would've fought hell to get him there. Maybe it was too hard losing a friend like Molly. Maybe it was the fact that he had been having trouble in his marriage. Maybe he had been on another not-so-discreet cocaine binge. Maybe he simply had not wanted to go. Maybe he didn't care. But if anyone was going to have answers as to why she'd done the unthinkable, it was Guy. It was her costars. Theirs was a world of fame and celebrity not even Hector could make sense of. Clearly, Molly hadn't been able to either.

That day was one of the exceedingly rare occasions when Hector had nothing to do. Though he was reading a few scripts, his self-exile meant he turned down projects for fear of letting his secrets slither out into the sun for all to see—secrets that, in this new Hollywood era, shared a similarity with Molly's.

He felt like pressing his palm into the ground wasn't going to accomplish anything other than making him feel like an idiot. He closed his eyes. He could see Molly's trauma and his own interweaving, clawing up out of the shallow graves they had buried them in. He saw her standing there too, his never-was childhood sweetheart, at the emotional graveyard of their industry. She was holding a shovel. She told him to start digging.

IN MURPHY'S OFFICE Hector sat with a cup of tea that Murphy's new assistant, Lyle, had fetched him.

"That's black tea, Lyle," Murphy said as the mug was set down.

"It's fine," Hector said.

"I'm s–sorry," Lyle stammered.

"Black tea is caffeinated," said Murphy, in a corrective tone.

"It's fine, Murph," Hector insisted.

"This is . . . decaf Earl Grey," Lyle said, as if stating a fact he was unsure of. "See?" He indicated the little paper tag on the end of the string, which had a green, highlighted notation saying as much.

Murphy looked at Lyle, then at the tea, sort of glaring at it, resenting that the tag meant he was wrong. Then he looked back at Lyle. "Okay, thanks," Murphy said. And Lyle left the room.

"Why do you still do that?" Hector asked.

"We've been together over twenty-five years; you know why I do it."

"He's new."

Murphy smiled. "Remember when we were new?"

"I think things are different now. Your swimming-with-sharks days are numbered." Hector looked at the myriad awards with his own name on them behind Murphy's head. He didn't like to keep them in the house, and Murphy liked to consider them shared victories.

"Just because a couple of kids got their feelings hurt by some old guys—"

"Don't pretend to be a mean guy. No one has once bought that performance."

"Why do you think I get after kids like Lyle? Fear still has a place here in Hollywood, you know."

"Stop it." Hector laughed, not able to take Murphy seriously. "When are you going to stop playing the part of Murphy Beck and just be Murphy Beck?"

"Please don't fucking Ivana Chubbuck me or whatever the fuck."

"I'm not Ivana Chubbucking you."

"You're in your head about something. I can tell."

"That's an actor's job."

"Well, don't take it out on me." Murphy looked exhausted by him, like a parent who'd been up all night. "Let's enjoy our morning beverages a moment," he said, then popped the top on a can of tangerine LaCroix. "It's only ten a.m., and you've already broken a heart and are apparently having a major personal crisis."

"I want to talk about Guy."

"Maker?"

"Yeah."

"What about him?"

"Why wasn't he at the funeral?"

"Fuck if I know. He's busy. Busy guys don't go to funerals for drunks."

Hector's mouth tightened in frustration. "I would've thought this particular funeral was important to him."

"I'm not going to call him, if that's what you're asking."

"Why not?"

"I just said, he's a busy guy. Why can't we talk about the Cyd thing?"

"Because there is no Cyd thing. We went on three dates."

"That's a lot by some people's standards."

"Three dates over the course of two weeks."

"That sounds like a lot."

"It isn't."

"It is for LA."

"Murphy."

"What did Essence say about all this?"

"Why would I have talked to Essence about this?" Hector said, raising his voice, losing his patience.

"All right, okay." Murphy held up his open palms as if he'd woken a sleeping lion. "I don't know. You talk to her about the emotional things. Why are you talking to me about this?"

"Because you and Guy used to be friends."

"Emphasis on *used*," Murphy said, spinning himself in his oversized rolling chair. "That guy fucked me in the end. So, fuck him. I guess."

"You guess?"

"He's one of the biggest mama bears in television. You think I'm just going to go for his jugular?"

"Maybe."

"No," Murphy said, then peered out his office window. "Listen, why do you care where he was during Molly's funeral?"

"Because it makes it look like he's hiding something."

"Your childhood Hollywood sweetheart killed herself. I understand there's probably a better way to phrase all this, but it bothers you. That much I can ascertain. And although I like the idea that you come to me with problems, because it means you trust me, to some degree, I can honestly say that I am not equipped to deal with your emotions." Hector's face sank, so Murphy added, "On this level." And upon seeing that have no effect, he also tacked on the addendum, "At this time."

Hector pulled on the string of the tea bag, forcing it to bob up and down in the brown leaf water. "I've been thinking a lot, since all this Me Too stuff."

Murphy looked as if an assault of clouds had suddenly cast him in a dark shadow. "If I can give you any real advice, it's to let this all go. You got a lot to be happy about."

Hector had known he would say that. Murphy's advice for the entirety of his career had been to let things go. He was adept at putting himself in a caretaking position to prevent Hector from hearing hard truths and learning how to handle problems with his own two hands. It was the perfect bubble of ignorant bliss that he and everyone else had crafted around themselves that had burst when the leaky pipes to the industry did the same, and all the women's stories flooded the building.

"Did you ever watch her show?" Hector asked.

"My wife did. I watched it with her sometimes. But I wouldn't call myself a fan." Murphy sounded defensive.

"Maybe I should."

"I don't see the point."

"Why?"

"Self-flagellation?"

Hector sat silently, obsessing over the box he had been strategically placed in over the years.

"You've made it, what"—Murphy checked his nonexistent wristwatch—"fifteen years without watching? That should be a source of pride. You're not one of *them*."

"She wasn't one of them at one point."

"Guy Maker is not an easy person to talk to. Okay? Over the years even you have been able to figure out that the universe he created is pumped full of whatever goo it was that Batman pushed the Joker into."

"Please stop talking to me like that," Hector said with the tonality of a little kid. He looked at the awards behind Murphy's head again.

"They're all clowns," Murphy said.

"And that includes the dead one?"

"I'm trying to protect you, pal," Murphy said earnestly. "That's all I've ever wanted to do. I wish I could've seen this coming, but shit, I guess death by misadventure is one of the things I can't."

"It was suicide."

"Yeah well, she signed up for that life. They all do."

Hector had heard that phrase to describe a celebrity's apparent comeuppance more times than he could count. How else would audiences be able to prevent themselves from feeling bad? If tragedy befell them, it had to be their fault.

"Maybe I should talk to them," Hector said.

"People from Apples?" Murphy looked like he was starting to sweat.

"Tamara was probably her second closest friend after Guy."

"What is this? Some gumshoe shit?"

"Don't you remember? I'm her biggest fan," Hector sneered.

"She's not some fucking dame Guy Maker plugged in a back alley,

Bogie. She killed herself. Bad things happen to good people. Life is dark and depressing sometimes. Case closed."

Hector wished someone had written a monologue he could've recited but knew on his own he wasn't great with words, so instead of saying anything, he stood slowly and didn't break eye contact. He had worked with Murphy since the start of his career. He couldn't deny him his part in the accolades and the money, but now he felt belittled, as if Murphy had locked him in a child's bedroom. As if he had been lied to for centuries. All he wanted was to slam his fist on the table to make Murphy admit it. He wished he hadn't been so sheltered.

"If it's shaking you up that much, call Essence," Murphy said calmly, trying to regain some emotional ground with his oldest friend. "I mean it."

Hector left without another word. He walked briskly from the building on Beverly Boulevard to his car out front with the valet, who handed him his keys in exchange for a crisp hundred-dollar bill from Hector's hand. He always liked tipping big, even if, as Murphy said, it made him look like an asshole. He felt entirely without leads, so he begrudgingly took Murphy's advice and called his life coach.

"You made it," she answered, speaking in a serene tone.

"What?" he asked, turning right in his car, heading north up La Cienega.

"You made it," she repeated reassuringly.

"Made it where?" He leaned a little forward in the driver's seat and half yelled into the void of his car knowing the unseen microphone would catch his voice.

"You are here," her voice said through the speakers.

"Essence, I'm . . . I'm driving right now, and it's kind of loud, so I sort of need you to be more clear—"

"Hector, I'm trying to begin our conversation with a reminder that wherever you are, you are there. You are in the present and can be nowhere else."

"Oh." Then, like a kid lying to the teacher about understanding a math problem, he said, "Okay. Yes. Right. Sorry."

"What's up?" she said.

He could hear bustling in the background. "Where are you?" he asked.

"I'm at the Belvedere." Then he heard her hold the phone away from her face slightly and distantly place a food order.

"If this is a bad time, I can call back."

"Hector. This is the only time," she said. "What's up?"

"I'm, uh . . . I'm having a really hard time with this Molly thing."

"Molly Mandrie?"

"Yeah."

"Why, babe?" She had a way of talking to her clients like both their comforting and condescending partner.

"I'd rather talk in person. If you have time. Can I come there?"

"I'm with a few other clients right now."

"I thought you said this was the only time."

"It is. And the only time isn't always the time we share. How about tomorrow?" she asked, and Hector felt like he had to say the alphabet backward in his head to formulate a response.

"It feels . . ." His breathing intensified as he looked up at the gridlocked street traffic now going down Santa Monica Boulevard. "It feels urgent."

"Hang on," she said, then he heard her distant voice say, "Sorry, just one sec." And then, after the sound of her walking briskly to a quieter area, she said, "Okay. I'm all yours."

Hector rolled down his window to get some air, just in time to hear someone yell, "Holy shit, *Hec-tor!*" And he rolled it back up.

"I don't know what to do," he said, rubbing his forehead.

"What do you mean? Don't know what to do about her death?"

"Yes. And no. Also mine." He could feel a knot cinching up in his stomach.

"Also your own death?" she asked, confused.

"No, no. My . . . shit. Some stuff that happened to me." He risked opening a can of worms, events he'd never discussed with anyone other than Murphy.

"Okay. All right. I hear you, okay? Remember that."

"Thank you."

"You're seen and your feelings are validated, all right?"

"Yeah."

"I know how much she meant to you. Does it feel like this is sort of throwing your balance out of whack?"

"I guess so." He pulled the car over onto a side street and parked it at a miraculously available meter. "I want to know why she did it. And why Guy didn't go to the funeral."

"That is interesting, isn't it?" She seemed to enjoy the drama.

"Have you heard anything? Andrea is one of your clients, right?"

"I hadn't thought to ask her. Feels personal. I'd hate to overstep my bounds."

"Right, right."

"Have you worked on your grounding exercises?"

"Yes." He leaned over and pressed his palm into the floorboard of his car and shouted to be heard. "I'm doing it now!"

"Okay. All right. Keep that pressure firm. I'm going to walk you through some breathing exercises, okay?"

"Okay!"

"First, remember that you are—" Then the call dropped.

Hector sat up fast in his seat and looked at his phone. He had full bars. He called her back, but it went straight to voice mail.

"Fuck, fuck, fuck, fuck, fuck," he said, rapidly repeating his mantra.

He tried her again with the same result but hung up before the call went to voice mail. Then his phone buzzed with a text from her that read, "Bad service for some reason. Let me call you back after this meeting." But 2019 was the future, and he knew bad service was a virtual impossibility. Especially at the Belvedere. A fucking *meeting*. She was at brunch.

He flopped back in his seat, took a deep breath, and blew it out slowly. Another text from her buzzed: "Just breathe, baby. We'll make it through."

He felt mocked, as if she had copied and pasted previous advice offered to a pregnant lady. He grabbed his phone and hurled it against the windshield. There was a loud *crack*. He huffed for a moment before leaning forward to grab it, staring at the now-spiderwebbed screen. He regretted having to call Murphy to tell Lyle to get him a new one.

He looked out the window to see people with their phones out, recording him. He smiled, rolled down his window, and said, "No service!" Then he put his sunglasses on, shrugged, made a dopey face as if he were on a sitcom, and drove away like they were all in on the joke.

2.

TAMARA

THE WEATHER APP on Tamara's phone predicted the light July gloom would blow over by late morning. It was going to be a beautiful day.

As she stepped into the bathroom, she caught a glimpse of herself in the mirror. She felt like the recent tweaks she'd made to her diet were paying off. Every day was a battle with her body. It was rare for her to gaze into the mirror and start the day with positivity instead of shame. Typically, she had to work hard to convince herself she was worthy of good things at the end of each day and that the obstacles of her life shouldn't drive her to twist open a bottle of gin. The comforting *snap* of the cap breaking from the metal ring that kept its elixir sealed, pouring out relaxation and devastation. She'd been sober for ten years.

She flexed, exhaling, examining. She decided she was beautiful, after all. She deserved to stay sober.

In the kitchen, a food scale measured out six ounces of tempeh. She tossed it in a skillet with one crushed clove of garlic, one chopped green onion stalk, one quarter of a tomato, and three egg whites. Every day she stuck the landing of her diet to a T. Among all the things in her life she could not control, diet and exercise were the two things she knew she had a tight grip on. The kettle boiled water for the half cup of unflavored instant oatmeal she poured into a bowl. A teaspoon of chia seeds and half a tablespoon of unsalted butter followed, promising blandness. But it was balanced. And balance was all she could hope to wring out of each day. It was always one day at a time.

She was on the fence about going to Andrea's first book signing that night at the Barnes & Noble at the Grove, a lavish shopping mall popular with both the well-to-do and the wanting-to-be-seen. On the one hand, Tamara loved to support her better half, Dre, as she often called her. But on the other, she wanted her friend to shine beneath her own spotlight for once. They had been joined at the emotional hip for the better part of eleven years. Tamara thought it might be best to sit this one out.

Maybe she would send a nice text. She knew Andrea better than anyone. A phone call would stress her out as she was undoubtedly obsessing over what she would say to the crowd that evening. They both had their daily routines, designed down to the letter to alleviate stress, to put them in positions of personal power, and to make them feel like the day belonged to them and no one else, particularly in the off-season. During filming they had enough chaos to contend with.

Anyone who dared get in the way of their downtime had better have a damn good reason, especially when all cast members of Apples' shows waited with bated breath to learn whether they were being picked up for another season. The idea that they wouldn't seemed impossible, but Apples loved to dangle threats over all of them as a way to keep them in their places. Even if shows were renewed, not all cast members made the cut, and every summer someone was dealt a crushing blow. Word on the street this year had been that it would be Cyd. But Tamara wasn't entirely sure; despite the show being named after both her and Andrea, she never could trust Guy when he said he had her and everyone else's best interests at heart. From the beginning, Tamara had known whose interests superseded all the rest.

Her fastidiousness was one of many reasons people considered her a bitch. Early on, she had earned that reputation by being the primary emotional muscle for Molly. And she always had her eye on

Guy, who seemed almost not to care about his so-called best friend. Tamara's life goal was to protect and defend Molly, no matter the cost, even when it had led to their day drinking and confrontations with tabloids. Even when it had eventually led to the dissolution of that friendship, Tamara had always hoped to do right by Molly. But she was never sure the girl could learn to do right by herself.

The thought of Molly stopped Tamara in her tracks. She pressed her weight against the kitchen counter with the palms of her hands and felt nausea creep into her throat, thick with guilt. She saw what couldn't be unseen: Molly's body hanging from a tree. Then came the thought of Guy, likely snorting his way through his pretend grief over losing his "best friend." It made Tamara's blood boil. He should've been at the funeral. He should've done more for Molly. She should've done more for Molly.

The smell of cooking egg whites caught her off guard, and she leaned over the sink, watery thin saliva pouring from her mouth. She spat it out, hoping to keep her guts at bay. Sweat beaded on the back of her neck. She turned on the faucet and splashed cold water on her face.

It was supposed to be a beautiful day.

The loan to expand her dance studio to a second location in the Valley had been approved. All that was left was to cross the t's and dot the i's, and they could start to remodel the existing run-down studio they had bought for cheap. She'd fought tooth and nail for its prime location on Ventura Boulevard against a group of twenty-somethings with piles of their parents' money who'd wanted to turn it into something called an "escape room," whatever the fuck that was. Yet another waste of space that would have offered craft beer at the end of what she could only assume was an overly complicated game of hide-and-seek.

The nausea settled. Sun peeked through the clouds outside. Her son, Steph, would be back from his dad's in a little while to spend the week with her. She'd teach her class that afternoon at her current

Westside studio and take photos with fans and followers, something that always helped to put a pep in her step. And tomorrow, she'd get brunch with Andrea to find out how it had all gone.

Guy would be calling at some point soon—he'd promised—with news of their fates. She let herself believe it would be news of another season. It would be good news. It was going to be a beautiful day. It had to be. She needed the money from that upcoming season to finance the new studio. She took a breath and decided she could stomach breakfast after all. She would not need a drink.

As she sat down to eat, her phone rang.

It was Guy's assistant, a young voice with a name no one bothered to remember since that job was a virtual revolving door. He said Guy wanted to talk to her and asked if he could put her on hold. She said yes. His favorite dick swing: he called her, then asked her to hold.

She changed her mind about breakfast. The call picked up, and Guy greeted her with the fake pleasantries she'd expected about what a "fucking star" she was and how "fucking amazing" she'd looked last week at the cast reunion. Then he cut to the chase. He had some news, although not the news he'd been hoping to call with. And he wanted her to hear it from him first before agents and managers started asking for heads. It was very possible she might not be returning for a ninth season of *Tamandrea*, he told her. According to Apples execs above even his pay grade, they were looking to strategize and shake up the low numbers that they thought were a result of audiences getting bored with her.

At first, her brain registered the news as a prank. But he continued that they were considering giving Andrea her own show. He knew something needed to be done and didn't want to cause too much concern but preferred that she heard this tentative plan from him before someone else leaked it. She asked him for more information and tried to sound calm, but he had to run and needed to put out fires. He reassured her that he loved her and Andrea equally, loved their friendship and their bond, and he praised Tamara for her strength and her talent. If she continued to trust him, he would do right by her, would fight for her. Then he hung up.

She did not move for several minutes, staring out the window at her backyard, fixated on a spot of yellow-brown grass. She saw Yesenia, their housekeeper, sweeping the small porch of the back house she lived in.

Tamara kept looking at her phone, waiting for it to ring again. Waiting for Guy to confirm he'd played the meanest joke on her anyone ever could. Just because he could. Because he got off on it. Another dangled carrot for a broken woman to snatch at. But the phone stayed silent. She couldn't believe it. She was being cut from her own show. And the news hadn't come from her representation or the network; it had come from him. Before all parties could sit down and negotiate, he had decided he was going to shake things up himself. And true to his nature, he'd played it off that he was her pal. He had her back. It was the network who wanted her gone.

She much preferred a knife to the heart than a knife to the back, but that wasn't Guy's MO. That wasn't how he kept the drama alive, wasn't how he kept audiences salivating over which woman was going to tear the other one down for his pleasure.

Steph came through the front door. The sound of his backpack hitting the ground snapped her out of her trance.

"You okay, Mom?" he asked, noticing the absence of color from her face.

"Yes. Fine. How's your dad?" she asked, hearing her ex-husband's midlife crisis decision of a Lamborghini roar out of the driveway and down the street.

"He's good," he said. His recently deepened, post-puberty voice still caught her off guard. She had a young man in the house now. He stepped up next to her and followed her gaze out the window. "What are you looking at?"

"Just a patch of dead grass. How was school?" She looked at him and forced a smile.

"Fine." He opened the pantry door. "Got a new book by Avery West from the bookfair Friday," he said, referring to his favorite horror author. "*The Devil You Know.*"

"Spooky." She looked over his shoulder into the void of healthy snacks, knowing all he wanted was a bag of Doritos. And after her call from Guy, so did she. "Are you hungry?"

"Kind of." His voice grew distant as he read the tense atmosphere. "You sure you're okay?"

"I'm fine!" she snapped at him, his worried eyes making her feel defensive. He shrunk a little. "I'm sorry." She hated when her energy put him in that place. "I just got some . . . difficult news."

She wished she could take back the entire moment and start over. Steph was often getting the brunt of a frustration he didn't deserve. It was the primary thing her ex-husband had used against her when they battled for custody, that her work inherently made her a temperamental mother. She thought it funny that a man who made his money as a judge lambasting others on a competition show could remove himself from any blame for contributing to her temperament.

"It's okay," he said, opening the pantry door.

"What would you like to do for dinner?" She hoped to make it up to him but felt like she couldn't promise that she wouldn't end the day drunk in a ditch somewhere.

"I was gonna go to Johnno's," he said, anticipating fury. "For pizza. His dad got a new oven and is gonna teach us to make it by hand."

"Oh." She was envious of the fun family bonding moment with the boy who had a nickname like a sitcom side character. "That sounds nice. You tell Johnno I said hi." She kissed the top of his head. "I have to go to the studio. Just going to change first."

Back in her bathroom she looked at her naked self in the mirror again, and the day finally turned to shit. Who was she kidding? She was forty-four. Body positivity was just bullshit people told themselves to make excuses for being lazy. No one actually liked their own body. If they did, it wouldn't be so fucking hard to accept it for what it was. She was just as displeased with it then as she had been when she was performing on *Dance Battle* at thirty with thirteen percent body fat.

Nothing felt better after receiving gut-wrenching news than being unkind to herself. The addict was never really gone. Outside of the voice of her dead mother, Tamara was the only person in the world who could beat herself up so perfectly. And she hated more than anything that in a matter of minutes, Guy could rip that hateful part out and show it to her as if she deserved her shame. She sat down and examined the unconquerable natural rolls of her flesh and thought again about having a drink.

THE WESTSIDE STUDIO was opulent, with three large rehearsal rooms and a smaller fourth for private instruction. All four rooms were on the second floor and could only be reached via the studio's café downstairs by either spiral staircase or elevator, forcing all students to consider juice, matcha, or coffee on their way in and out. Tamara loved the glamor of a spiral staircase—like something from an old movie—that glowing, sweaty bodies would descend after class.

Most of the group classes she offered were held at night, and her daytime hours were used for private instruction or for rehearsals for television shows or movies. Signed headshots from actors and choreographers who had come and gone lined the halls, dozens upon dozens of scribbles featuring the feigned, "Thanks a million, Tam! Love you! XOXO, so-and-so."

Despite what she knew was undoubtedly false sentiment, she was grateful for owning the space. It had not only kept her dancing career at the forefront of her public image but also her face and name on a legacy that could not be destroyed with age. No one could take the foundation of her fame away from her. Not even Guy Maker.

In 2006, after she'd signed her contract to join Molly's show, Tamara had heard that Guy had excitedly told a room full of executives how she would help the network access the urban audience. Just like Molly, Tamara had only been a commodity to him or to them. *Dance Battle* had built a box for her, a place she could be kept, an image she would be required to uphold. After it ended, she worked harder than anyone she knew to break out of that box and build her studio, something entirely her own, in its place. But somehow it had ceased to be enough. She had thought a second location would continue to push her away from the person others expected her to be, but her time with Apples made escaping the confinement of her type almost impossible, especially now. She felt mocked by it. Like no matter how hard she tried to be something else, she was always just some Black conduit to an audience that networks otherwise could not reach. She was to deliver a white message to Black ears and Black eyes and make them pine more and more for a whiteness they could not achieve.

Now Guy was waving a brand-new threat over her without there having been a single discussion between her and Andrea. All as if to say that Tamara was not responsible for what she had built. That Guy and Apples had built it for her. That *Dance Battle* had been responsible for discovering her before them. That she should be grateful. That she should grovel at various feet to save her show and reputation. That now she was unconsciously being pitted against her younger costar. That she genuinely loved Andrea, and how the fuck would that look? That there was a spike of hate clearly being driven between them. That no matter how hard she insisted, the audience would believe it was her fault. That there she was, surprise, a bitch—just another angry Black woman. Frustration mounted at the thought that it could all drive her toward relapse, and then they would be right.

As she entered the café on the ground floor, every head turned to look at her, not because they saw her enter but because they felt her. She said nothing, creeping up to wait in line, silently waving off customers who wanted to make room for her to cut.

Outside of formal occasions, she dressed exclusively in her own athletic wear brand. If she had ever been caught in something she did not design, the photos would've been the dirtiest blackmail anyone could have gotten on her. As a point of pride, she was never anything but true to her brand and her word. Betraying trust had been the primary accusation lodged against her by Molly when it had broken that she would be getting her own show. Molly had said that Tamara was a "backstabbing, two-timing, Cunty McCunterson."

Tamara stared up at the menu board. Her mind wandered back to Andrea. Why shouldn't Tamara call her? Or text? What exactly had Guy told *her*? She knew Andrea was always in the position of giving Guy what he wanted. Theirs was a relationship that seemed not to cause any bad blood or affect Andrea's good-natured demeanor. And as much as Tamara had wanted to safeguard Andrea since she had met the girl, she had to let her make her own choices.

Then she had a sudden fear that she had been played. If it turned out that Andrea was just as duplicitous as Guy when it came to making moves on the metaphorical chessboard, not a single soul would have seen it coming. That would be the ultimate deceit. And a part of Tamara felt that, if it was true, she'd have to acknowledge what an impossibly delightful fuck-over that would be.

Tamara had always been looking for the chink in Guy's armor, but the women he continued to cast and the people he surrounded himself with invariably fell prey to his charms, to his stoking fires. Then, standing back, he watched as if he had no idea his oxygen was the fuel.

People always blamed the casts for starting drama among themselves; pointing fingers at messy whores was the easiest way for the audience to prevent themselves from feeling bad for them. They believed that the fires they started were theirs and theirs alone. But they were lit with what Tamara called the "Applause Starter Kit": a box of matches and a bottle of wine. Then came the pushes from producers, whispers of devils on shoulders, strings pulled by off-screen hands. After that, the cast members were in the hands of their fans. When they were on their side, they were more committed to these women than one could be to Christ. And they would fight tirelessly on their behalf. But there was no room for living in the in-between. It was all extremes. All reaction. All expectation. Fans either loved them or loved to hate them. If you were on Apples, when it came to a fan's opinion of you, none were lukewarm. You were a queen, or you were a cunt.

"Tam?" A barista named Marissa touched her shoulder. Tamara's head whipped over to her, and Marissa recoiled. "Sorry," the girl said immediately.

"No, no," Tamara said, seeing Marissa turn slightly yellow with fear. "It's just . . . been a long day, and it isn't even noon yet." She tried to laugh it off.

Marissa held up an already-made drink because she was Tamara Collins, and it was her café and her studio, and why on earth would she be looking at the menu as if she didn't know what she wanted, when she'd always known what she wanted and had gotten it every day without the slightest bit of fucking consideration?

"Thanks," Tamara said, taking the mug of plain black coffee and heading for the stairs. She dreaded the meeting awaiting her in an hour. A design team working on the new studio would show her lavish, beautiful ideas one after another, none of which she was now sure she could pay for.

She saw a young man on his laptop working, a paper coffee cup beside him. She was not proud that she needed to let off steam, but if she didn't, there would be a much larger explosion later. She decided he was worth making an example out of, if only to assert whatever dominance she had left in the small kingdom she had built.

"When you're going to order a beverage and drink it here, get it in a mug. Like this." She showed him hers. "Not like that." She took his empty cup and dropped it onto the ground. It landed with a hollow thunk. Everyone could have heard a pin drop.

"We don't want to create more pollution in a world that's already littered with assholes and idiots. Do we understand?" she asked.

"We do," he said, which was the common response for anyone studying or training with her or any of the staff. "We" was their motto. "Not you. Not I. We." Because dance, even when performed by the self, was a pursuit that required the inspiration, guidance, and training of others. To Tamara, all art, no matter how solitary or isolated, was a collaborative effort. There was even a Billy Idol "Dancing with Myself" poster pasted on the office wall with a big red *X* spray-painted over his face.

Because of her strict adherence to this way of thinking, and for making examples out of her students, a lot of people had accused Tamara of running what was akin to a dance cult. In defense of the belief, she insisted that it was an integral part of her drive. The same drive that had pushed her toward her addiction and later to her sobriety. She could be committed to her failure or committed to her success. But it was her choice.

She ascended the spiral staircase and slipped into the office, staring at Billy and sipping her coffee. She remembered what Guy had told her when she was at her lowest—that an artist or public figure in recovery was always a more potent flavor of celebrity, especially when it came to women like her or Molly. Not because they had done the impossible and kicked their habit, but because for most audiences of shows like theirs, there was the palm-sweating thrill of the thought that someday they might fall off the wagon. And the audience got to watch. It was the virtual-contact high of the drama that reminded them that, despite all reality stars' successes and accomplishments, drive and determination, deep down they were more broken than their viewers. Which was why women like her needed to remember the reason they did what they did, why they put on the makeup and did the shows and got through the recoveries and ran the studios and did the dances: to prove the audience wrong. Because the bright side of this, Guy had once told her, was that, not unlike matter, stars like her could not be destroyed. Rather, they were merely repurposed. And it would be up to her to find out what that new purpose might be.

3.

FIEVEL/ELLIOT

"**B**E HONEST, BRO. Good?" Fievel said as he walked in a tiptoe fashion over the tiled floor of their suite at the Tropicana. His clothes were soaking wet, dripping onto the floor.

"What'd you, jump into the pool? Where's your towel?" Elliot asked.

"Didn't want one. I wanted that cold rush to wash over me," he said through chattering teeth. "Felt good."

"I thought it was good," Elliot said soberly of Fievel's first completed poolside DJ set.

Fievel stared down at his treacherous friend. "You're a shit liar. I saw you, dude," he said.

"What did you see?"

"You left like fifteen minutes in. I know you try to stand at the back for everything, but I watched you duck out, you fuck."

"You've demoed the set for me a dozen times. I told you I thought it was good the first time. I still think it's good."

"Wow." Fievel nodded, his mouth tightening and turning slowly down. "Well, you know what? You know *what*? You weren't even down there, so you couldn't feel the full force of it. So, you wouldn't even know. You were up here in your castle. Rapunzel. Watching this." He motioned to the TV.

"All right," Elliot said. He knew Fievel wanted to bait him into an argument, but he didn't have the energy to push back. Instead, he sat motionless in an oversize armchair, an eleven-year-old episode of *MML* playing in the background.

It was a darkly fond memory for both of them, when Molly and Tamara had helped Ryann, a former cast member, buy a wedding dress for her upcoming nuptials. The episode then cut to the boys out for the soon-to-be husband's bachelor party. At the strip club, Elliot was, once again, at the back while a very excited Fievel couldn't get over the fact that Tamara's stuffy British husband, Winslow Philips, had decided to join them. Fievel took it as his solemn duty to get such a prim and proper gent so thoroughly shit-faced that he'd never forget who the life of the party really was. Fievel insisted on calling him Dubs and paid for floor dances for the guys, as well as a round of blowjob shots they took between dancers' legs. It had caused a fight later when Molly, Tamara, and Ryann, feeling threatened by strippers, asked the men if they had done other things with them too, like fuck them. Then they made thinly veiled jokes about why four grown men would guzzle down blowjob shots together. After the heat died down, Fievel pulled the other three men into a small embrace and said, "Good times. Love you guys. No homo."

"Turn this shit off," he now said, before the scene could be entirely replayed.

Elliot sat unmoved.

"I said turn it off!" He stormed toward Elliot to snatch the remote but slipped in the puddle that had formed beneath him, hitting his head on the tile floor.

Elliot rushed to him. "Shit! You okay?"

Fievel sat up slowly and pushed his friend's help away. "No, you asshole."

Elliot pulled a nearby blanket off the couch to sop up the water around Fievel, who struggled to get to his feet. "Why are you watching this?" he asked, wincing.

"I don't know. It was just on, I guess. They've been doing this Molly flashback celebration thing on Apples all month."

"Were you watching this while I was spinning?"

Elliot was quiet.

"You're a fucking asshole, man," Fievel said, and shoved Elliot. But the force of the shove and the newly formed, smaller puddle beneath Fievel caused him to slip again, and he sat down hard onto his tailbone. "Motherfucker!"

"What do you want me to do here?" Elliot didn't know how to respond.

"Help me up!"

Elliot hoisted Fievel to his feet. "You should've gotten a towel."

"I am aware. Thank you," Fievel said as he hobbled slowly toward the bathroom, his feet slipping every few steps until he was safely inside, where he slammed the door.

"I'm surprised they let you walk through the casino and the hotel all wet like that!" Elliot shouted after him. But Fievel didn't respond.

Elliot plopped back into his chair. He unlocked his phone and opened his texts. He stared down at a six-month-old conversation with Andrea that ended in him saying, "I'm sorry."

She'd never replied.

They hadn't acknowledged each other at the funeral, which had sent Twitter into an uproar, one popular fan saying, "I hope @ElliotThuhMan and @NotTHATAndreaBocelli rage fuck in the bathroom at the Hollywood Forever Cemetery."

The rage-fuck would've been because Elliot and Andrea's last encounter before the funeral had been at a bar called Laurel Hardware on Santa Monica Boulevard as they filmed a crossover episode of *FGE* and *Tamandrea*. After the *Holy Matt-Trisha-mony* special, they'd spent their respective previous seasons in a will-they-won't-they back-and-forth. It had been messing with his head. In one of his rare on-camera moments of brashness, Elliot had gotten blackout drunk and told Andrea he was in love with her. At the bar, he kept drunkenly trying to kiss her as she dodged his overt advances, insisting she was committed to someone she had been dating for a few weeks named Kyle. Kyle, buying another round for everyone, witnessed Elliot's behavior and weakly punched him in the shoulder. Elliot registered the punch and shouted, "You punch like a little bitch, Kyle!" Then he tackled Kyle into a crowd of people, spilling drinks.

Security broke up the fight, and Elliot called Andrea a cunt and said Kyle had a small dick and was nobody but a fame whore trying to siphon off some free exposure from her. Andrea told Elliot she thought *he* in fact had the small dick and that Kyle was a gentleman who had an excellent beard. Fievel had to shove Elliot into a Lyft to send him home. He then threw up inside the car and later had to pay a cleaning fee.

Prior to all that, Elliot had been texting with Guy after being a guest on *WHH,S!* He had wanted his advice on what to do about Andrea, and Guy had said, "You should absolutely tell her how you feel!"

Now in his oversize chair, he sat with his regret. "I'm sorry" was never going to be enough. He'd spent the last six months wondering how he might repair whatever it was they had. Seeing her at the funeral had stirred up a lot of things he thought had simmered down, and the bitter reality of the mortality of one of their own made him feel like he was losing time to go after the things he really wanted in life.

He typed, "It was good to see you a few weeks ago. Wish it was under better circumstances." Then his finger hovered over the send button. He thought about the old cliché of missing a hundred percent of the shots he didn't take but wished maybe he hadn't listened to Guy and confessed his love to her in the first place.

The bathroom door opened, startling him, and he dropped his phone.

Fievel walked out wearing a suit. "Get up," he said.

"Why?" Elliot asked, leaning over. His fingers curled slightly under the phone's edges to pick it up, their heat brushing the screen. He flipped it over. The text had been sent.

"Because we're going out. That's why. I want to find some K."

Elliot's palms automatically got sweaty at the mention of the drug, his brain recalling the fun of the high but also the danger. "I don't want to," he said and wondered if an accidental text sent to a former lover was akin to the risk one took for a dopamine hit.

Fievel turned off the TV. "Don't be a bitch," he said. "Put some acceptable pants on, man the fuck up, and do some drugs with me."

"It's four forty-seven." Elliot squinted in the Vegas sun out the window. "And it's hot outside."

"You sat up here sad during my big debut. You owe me this. I met some girls after, and I told them I was coming back down once I changed. Now I'm changed. So, we're going to hang out with those girls."

Elliot double tapped his phone to bring the screen to life, curious if he'd gotten a response, but there was nothing. As he often did to Fievel's obnoxious charm, he conceded and got cleaned up, and they went out.

IT WAS THE off-season for most Apples shows, a time when cast members rarely hung out with one another outside of the few real-life bonds that formed while filming. Mostly, even when they swore they all loved one another, they didn't want to see the same stupid faces they were forced to see during production when they didn't have to. Aside from Tamara and Andrea, Fievel and Elliot's bond was the rare exception. They'd been together so long that most people compared their relationship to that of a bickering, elderly married couple. They never left each other's side. Even when one was mad at the other.

Fievel had hired Elliot almost twenty years prior. Fievel's previous driver, Christopher, had been his father's driver. When Fievel's dad died, he'd wanted to keep Christopher employed because he'd always been like an uncle to him. But having been a part of the family so long, Christopher had gotten a DUI while reeling from the loss of Fievel's father, and his license had been suspended. So, he'd recommended Elliot, a kid Fievel's own age, whom Christopher had met at an International Brotherhood of Teamsters, Chauffeurs, Warehousemen, and Helpers Union event. Thinking therapy was for weak people and girls, Fievel started confessing all his woes to Elliot.

After Fievel met and began dating Molly, his and Elliot's odd, seemingly one-sided friendship was caught on camera during the filming of *MML* and was one of the primary things that endeared fans to them—so much so that a lot of people had their fingers crossed the two of them would end up romantically involved. The flames of this wish were further stoked one night after Fievel and Molly broke up. He and Elliot, both drinking away their woes at a bar and caught on camera, confessed that if they had been gay, they absolutely would have had sex with each other.

"Where are they?" Elliot asked now, peeking down at his phone again.

"I said I'd meet them at the bar." Fievel looked around over the tops of heads but did not see the girls.

"*Gatman!*" a voice boomed, and a middle-aged man in a WWE hat stumbled toward them, trying not to spill his full beer.

"Oh Christ." Fievel grabbed Elliot's arm. "Hey, man."

"What happened?" the man asked, grabbing the back of a bar chair to keep himself upright.

"What do you mean?" Fievel said.

"I'm Jeff by the way," the man said.

"Hey, Jeff," Fievel and Elliot said in unison.

"Yeah, man, what happened to you?"

"Well, I just crushed my first DJ set at the poolside lounge outside like an hour ago, so that happened," Fievel said.

"No, no. I mean the wrestling career! I loved you. 'Gun him down! Gun him down!'" Jeff shouted as Elliot and Fievel worked to quiet him and avoid suspicious looks in response to the violent catchphrase.

"It didn't work out, okay? Listen, how long have you been at the bar?" Fievel asked.

"Pretty much all day," Jeff said. "Wait, you're a DJ now? Shit."

"Did you see two cute girls here a minute ago, Jeff, two brunettes?" Fievel asked.

"I've seen a lot of cute brunettes here today."

"Do cute girls even hang out at the Tropicana?" Elliot said passively.

"Hey, man!" Jeff said, taking offense. "This place has really upped its game these past few years."

"I'm sorry," Elliot said. "I didn't realize."

"Yeah, dude, don't shit on the 'Cana," Fievel said as he patted Jeff on the shoulder. "Jeffrey, it's been great. We're gonna try to find these girls." He grabbed Elliot's wrist and attempted to pull him away, but Jeff stopped them with his hand on Elliot's opposite wrist.

"Wait, wait," Jeff said. "Will you do the Gatling gun for me? Just once! Do the move!"

"Jeff, we're in a public place. A very crowded public place. I'm certain that is a terrible fucking idea, so I'm sorry, but we have to go." Fievel again pulled on Elliot as Jeff did the same.

"Just one time," Jeff said. "Come on, Gatman!"

Fievel made eye contact with the bartender, who waved to a security guard.

"Okay, okay." Jeff started to whisper. "Just say, 'Gun him down' one time for me."

"No, Jeff!" Fievel shouted.

"I need one of you to let go of me!" Elliot said, the sockets of his shoulders getting tense.

"Just say it! Say it one time, Gatman! 'Gun him down! Gun him down!'" Jeff chanted at the top of his lungs.

"How the fuck do you even remember my wrestling career, Jeff?" Fievel shouted, desperately waving at the security guard running toward them.

"'Gun him down! Gun him down!'" Jeff continued, doing a chop motion with his beer hand, sloshing liquid everywhere.

"Ow, you fuck!" Elliot said as Fievel let go of him and used his newly available arm to shove Jeff, who sat perfectly back into the chair behind him, dropping the rest of his drink into his lap.

"Aw, no," Jeff said softly to himself. Then sadly, as he stared at his beer-soaked clothes, he said, "No, Gatman. No," like he'd just gotten news over the phone that his parents had to put down his childhood dog.

"Sorry, Jeff," Fievel said as security reached them, putting Jeff's arms behind his back, and restraining him.

"I love you, man," Jeff said. Then he started to cry. "I'm sorry, guys."

Fievel and Elliot stopped dead in their tracks. Fievel glanced over to the bartender, who just shook his head, then back to Jeff. Then Jeff vomited on the carpet in front of them, and it splashed onto Elliot's shoes.

"Ah, God damn it!" Elliot shouted.

"I'm so sorry." Jeff continued to sob as security forced him upright and walked him across the casino floor.

"Jesus fuck," Fievel said, out of breath. "Where are those *girls*?"

THEY TOOK FIEVEL'S Porsche 964 north up the strip. Fievel was behind the wheel, his rigid stop and start motions driving Elliot insane. Even after decades of trying to master it, the clutch still evaded Fievel.

"I don't like it when you drive," Elliot said.

"I gotta blow off steam." Fievel shook his head like there was water in his ear.

"Where are the girls going to sit if you ever find them?" Elliot asked. "Which you won't." He checked his phone.

"Let's just go somewhere else," Fievel said, rolling down the windows. "We can get drugs wherever."

"How do you not, like . . . have 'a guy'?" Elliot decided to power down the phone to prevent himself from constantly checking it and sitting in anxiety.

"I got guys in New York and LA, but I don't have any Vegas guys."

"I'm sure the New York and LA guys have Vegas guys. It's called networking."

"Where do you think they went?"

"I don't know why you're stuck on these two specific girls when this place is bursting at the seams with a metric fuck ton of them."

"It's a lot easier when they're way more into you than you're into them," Fievel said. "That's like half the work already done for you. Plus, the sex is always better because they're desperate to please you and your feelings don't really have to get involved."

"You mean *your* feelings. I don't really desire to meet or fuck either of these people."

"Let's go to the Palomino," Fievel suggested as they waited in traffic.

"That's so far," Elliot whined.

"I know the door guy. He probably has a *guy* guy. And he'll let us in for free."

Elliot sighed, head half out the window in the hot breeze.

"Is that a yes?"

"Sure," he said.

At the Palomino Club, they were met by Rodney the door guy, a wiry six-foot-two emigrant from Haiti who had formerly worked as the doorman at Fievel's building in New York. Rodney had been Fievel's biggest supporter as an aspiring musician himself, going by the name 19Haiti7.

Rodney's face sank when Fievel pretended to park the 964 directly in front of him. "No, no, no. You gotta move this shit, bro!"

Fievel hopped out, grinning. "I thought I was VIP."

Rodney's eyes lifted. "Oh, shit!" He beamed and pulled Fievel into a handshake hug. "Where you been?"

"New York still," Fievel said. Rodney tousled the hair on the top of his head as if he were ten years old. "Was in LA a few weeks ago, and now I'm doing some shows out here on the weekends for a while."

"You made it?" Rodney asked.

"I don't know if this is making it, but they're paying me money to do a thing I want to do, so I suppose that's making it in some capacity."

"You fucks can't leave this here," Gene, the bouncer, thundered behind them.

"Gene. It's cool," Rodney said.

"I like your 'Stone Cold' Steve Austin cosplay," Fievel said.

"What did you say to me?" Gene lurched forward.

"I'll move it," Elliot said as he stepped out of the car and hopped in the driver's side, pulling away.

"I don't do, 'Gene. It's cool,'" the bouncer said grumpily, walking away.

"How about you?" Fievel said to Rodney, ignoring Gene. "You doing any shows out here?"

"Haven't had time. I've been working as much as I can. My brother's been getting worse."

"Shit." Fievel rubbed his forehead. Rodney had moved to Vegas to help his brother's family after his brother had been diagnosed with young-onset Parkinson's disease. "It sort of feels weird to ask you about a drug connection now."

Rodney laughed. "You don't change."

Fievel grinned. "Is that good or bad?"

"Good." He slapped Fievel on the back and guided him toward the front door. "At least you're real."

"Can't be anything but." Fievel smiled.

"Hey, you talk to Josh anymore?" Rodney asked.

"Morris?"

"Yeah."

"Nah, not for a long time. He's doing this influencer, YouTube, music-producing shit. Kinda lame."

"I sent him some tracks a while ago. He said he was gonna pass them to a connection at WMG."

"That dude's a fuckin' joke. You can't trust him."

"Shit." Rodney surrendered to another artistic dead end. "All right, well, I got you, bro. I'll talk to some of the girls inside."

"Thanks, brother. Keep hustlin'!" Fievel said with a smile as he entered the club.

Elliot parked the Porsche and sat motionless for a long moment. He stared at his turned-off phone and couldn't remember the last time he'd let himself disconnect. He thought about turning it back on but enjoyed the minor fuck-you of being unreachable. It wasn't that he ceased to be anyone's target—the whole world could talk about him no matter where he was and what he was doing—but it would be up to him whether to care about what they said. It was always hard not to.

Apples shows rarely spelunked the depths of their casts' inner lives. Empathy for talent was not their brand. Even when they did, the exploration turned up little more than a few shiny, embarrassing rocks to polish and show off. As a result, Elliot felt trapped by a surface level image he was never in control of: shy, quiet, and sweet, like his Italian mother, running whenever she called. His constant need to attend to her had made its way into both *MML* and *FGE* as a major storyline played mostly for laughs. He had been nicknamed "the good son." Only now his primary job was running whenever Fievel called.

Fievel's biggest goal in life was to get everyone to have fun exactly the way he thought they should. He had the uncanny ability to turn a no into a yes at the prospect of there being a potentially thrilling reward for taking a risk. Why pass up the party when the party could lead to a networking connection or a potential business venture or, more importantly, an even better party?

Elliot could count on one hand the number of times he'd tried any other drugs besides alcohol. Being a good friend, Fievel rarely pushed them on him. However, he did not like doing them alone, and Elliot was an apt babysitter. Once he'd sat on a lifeguard tower near the

Santa Monica Pier for close to eight hours, supervising Fievel and Molly after they had taken too much acid and made sand angels on the beach, intermittently spraying sunscreen on them to keep them from getting burned.

"Where the fuck were you?" Fievel asked as Elliot finally joined him inside at the tip rail.

"Talking to Rodney," Elliot lied.

"Oh, cool. He said he's gonna talk to a few gals for me," Fievel said, raising his voice over the music.

"Great," Elliot said, doing the same.

"Hey, you think I could play Hakkasan?" Fievel asked of the popular nightclub.

"For sure." Elliot kept his eyes locked on the dancer to avoid looking at Fievel.

"Are you gonna fucking loosen up or what?"

"I don't really want to be here," Elliot said bluntly. He absent-mindedly hot-dog-bun folded one-dollar bills and rested them on the rail.

"The journey of a thousand miles begins with a single step." Fievel patted his friend on the back. "Let me buy you a dance."

"Don't want one."

"Don't be a bitch."

"I'm not a bitch."

"It'll help you relax."

"Would you stop?"

"Why don't *you* stop? Look at how many gorgeous girls are here!"

"I can see."

Fievel felt a hand on his shoulder and turned around.

"I know that face," a girl said. "Fievel!" She sat in his lap and ran her fingers down his back.

"Me!" Fievel said enthusiastically, unsure if he had seen this girl in person before or if she only knew him from TV. "And . . . you!"

"You want a dance?" she asked.

"I want my friend here to have some fun is what I want." He raised his hand and waved over another girl, who started to play with Elliot's hair. "But be careful!" Fievel reached out to stop her. "He's a greasy Italian. Keep that hand sani handy!"

Everyone laughed except Elliot.

"What's that smell?" The other girl asked.

"A drunk dude threw up on his shoes!" Fievel laughed.

Elliot blinked slowly, annoyed.

"Rodney sent me over," the girl on Fievel's lap told him.

"Ooooh." Fievel understood.

"You want a dance?" she repeated, her ulterior motive now clear.

"I think I would like a dance, yes." Fievel let himself be guided away.

"What's wrong?" The girl playing with Elliot's hair leaned in against the chairback behind him, talking into his ear. "Even with your puke shoes, I think I can help."

"I don't think so," Elliot said, tossing a one onto the stage. It fluttered down like a sad paper airplane. Fievel had forced him to come along, then left him alone like a father leaving a little kid at a soda shop while he was off having an affair. He would much rather have been in the hotel bed with room service, rerunning memories of his dead friend on TV.

"Let me try." Her hand slid down his chest and abdomen. "Ooh, someone works out."

Just as her fingers teased his waistline, he grabbed her wrist. She looked at him and saw that tears were welling in his eyes.

"I'm good, thanks," he said. "Sorry."

She watched him for a moment before leaving. He ran the back of his hand along his nose, then slapped himself on the cheek and sipped from a glass of water. As he looked up, he saw the dancer onstage was directly in front of him, on all fours. She made a pouty face at him, so he put another one on the stage.

4.

ANDREA

ANDREA LIVED ALONE. She had spent the better part of five years deciding whether or not she liked it. It was spooky sometimes. True-crime podcasts late at night didn't help. For whatever reason, she fell asleep to them. Often she had nightmares about her body being discovered in some gruesome way. Not a woman with a life story, just another victim whose life was summed up by her brutal ending, all in celebration of her killer.

She had lived with roommates her first seven years in LA. She called home once a week because it was an undying habit, but she had grown to dread doing it. Afraid of what they might see of their daughter after she'd joined the cast of *MML*, she told her parents never to get on social media and they listened.

Initially she'd struggled to pick up the lingo of the new city, but now, twelve years in, she found herself just as able to recite key words and phrases in a repetitive manner like everyone else. One of her costars, Milan, tirelessly said the word "supposably" in place of "supposedly" and would so frequently say that she was "manifesting" something that the cast once kept a tally. The final count was sixty-seven times in less than twenty-four hours.

Andrea's current words for describing herself, which she dropped into the writing of her book were "introverted extrovert" and "empath."

Just before her move to LA, as her young marriage had failed, a friend had loaned her a copy of the popular self-help book *The Daze of Whine and Rosé*. It outlined author Sonya Shure's escape from a similar situation: bad marriage, bad man, bad habits. It pried Andrea's eyes half-open to her father-controlled, mother-suppressed upbringing, and she carried her copy everywhere she went. Its tattered, noted, highlighted pages still rested on her bookshelf.

It took her five years to escape the nickname "Rodeo Queen." She'd worked hard to lighten her accent. Not so much as to sound just like any other girl in LA, but enough so that crew members on *MML* would stop referring to her as "the hottest hick" they had ever seen.

She paced her kitchen floor. It was 5:45 a.m. Her first-ever book signing that evening loomed. She was reading from note cards she'd filled out with key words and was holding the card that said *introverted extrovert*.

"I don't know about you, but I'm an introverted extrovert," she said, delivering the line like part of a bad monologue.

"Not familiar with that term?" she continued. "It means I love to work, and I love to play, but at the end of the day, I need you to stay away!" Then she laughed, as if she anticipated an audience laughing with her, only there was no one there so she flipped to the next card which read, *bad bitch*.

She sighed and chugged a tall glass of water, then whispered, "Fuck me."

Andrea was a team player. Andrea was a talented makeup artist. Andrea was a good friend. And she had worked hard in therapy to become self-aware. She knew she was not a public speaker and, despite having grown to like living alone, knew she did not perform well without someone she felt was a fellow stooge on TV with her. The joy of being part of an ensemble cast was that she was given just enough spotlight to shine but not so much that she bore the brunt of the entire limelight. She did not envy Molly for that one bit. Only now she was facing the biggest moment of her career so far, all on her own. And even though she'd learned to drink and dance and swear and laugh in front of cameras like the rest, the thought of standing up in front of people holding up their phones without the ability to edit her mistakes terrified her.

Looking at her next card, she said, "I know why I'm here. And you know why you're here. Because we are bad bitches!" Then she pumped her right fist into the sky as if this were a rallying cry, only there was no one there. She trudged on and flipped to the next card and said, "Let me tell you something. Your *worth*"—she glanced down at the card—"is not determined by anyone else but you. Understand? Let me see some nods." Only there was no one there, so she imagined the nods.

"*You* determine your worth. *You* are responsible for you. It's as simple as that. And there isn't a man in the world who can tell you how to feel, how to fight, and how to fuck. Got it?"

She started to imagine the cheers and hollers. She smiled. She flipped to the next and glanced casually at it, less obviously now, knowing if she looked down too much, the imaginary heckler in the back would give her hell for it.

"I'm an empath. Which means I tend to take on people's problems as my own. And I have a hard time saying no. It's why I got married so young. It's why I stayed longer than I should have. And it's why you see me get into so many fights on TV. I think I can fix everyone. Luckily, my therapist reminds me that isn't my job." Then, like it was a little secret, she said, "That's why I got divorced too."

The audience laughed. She didn't need to glance at the next card.

"So, believe me when I say, 'Bitch, your single body is your best body!'"

She knew that part by heart. Everyone clapped. She smiled again and waited for them to quiet down before continuing.

"Now, I know a lot of you here are probably haters of mine. And I get it. But the truth of this whole thing, this whole book"—she held up a copy—"is two parts. One, I just want to help a few gals and gays in need!" she joked, knowing the bulk of her fan base. "And two, I'm not interested in pleasing or changing the minds of every single one of you because, remember: That. Is. Not. My. Job."

The last part she punctuated with individual claps, and everyone chuckled, even one of the haters. She was reaching them.

"I've already gotten shit on social for the title. I get it. It sounds judgy. I know I'm on TV. I know I have money. I know I get into arguments too often and drink too much. But contrary to what you might think, I'm not here for *you*. I'm here for *me*. I wrote this book for me. And if it helps a bunch of you along the way, then that's all I've ever wanted." Her Texas tonality started to peek through.

"When I say, 'Your single body is your best body,' I don't mean breaking up with your man and getting skinny just to spite him." Then she covered her mouth halfway with her hand and said, "Although that's not necessarily a terrible idea," as if to subvert the whole theme of her speech, and the imaginary audience laughed and loved her for it.

"What I mean is, relationships can't fix what's already broken going into them. We have this tendency to say, 'You complete me' or 'You are my better half' or 'I'm helpless without you' or 'I need you!' Especially for us girls, we are told from the beginning that without a man we have little to no value. And without a relationship, we have even less. No one ever told us we can stand on our own. No one ever told us we didn't have to have kids. No one ever told us we could just have casual sex. And no one ever told us that a healthy relationship only works when a healed heart enters into it and finds another heart that's done the fucking work."

She was beaming now. The crowd was on the edge of their seats.

"Actually, I guess . . . no one ever told me that."

She sipped her water, electrified by her momentum.

"So, I'm telling you now. You are worthy of love. You are worthy of happiness. You are worthy of success. But the only way you're going to find those things is by giving them to yourself. You don't *need* anyone.

A healthy choice is a choice you want to make; not a choice you have to make. The title of this book is supposed to be funny, guys. I play a part on TV." She risked that wording, even though she was instructed not to suggest at any point during media or press events that what she presented on TV was not real. "And no one is going to tell me how to be Andrea or who Andrea is. Except maybe my godfather, Andrea Bocelli." She kissed the pair of her left forefinger and middle finger and raised them to the sky as if in a blessing. "Thanks, D!"

Everyone laughed, part of the inside joke.

Then she sat down, winding down, serious. "This book was for me. This life is for me. And my only hope is that reading it gives you the courage it takes to remember your life is about *you*."

She put the note cards down; she didn't need them. "No one can fix you but you. Nothing and no one can change your life but you. If you finish that last chapter, and you set this thing down, and you think to yourself, 'This book changed my life,' then I failed. There are no life-changing events. Only door openers. But it's up to you to step through them."

She waited for the slow clap, finally feeling alive. Finally feeling connected to herself. To her message and to her authenticity. Finally feeling like her struggle could help heal the hurt of the people listening. She hoped they had heard that. She hoped they would hold on to it. And she hoped it would help them. Only there was no one there.

"BUT YOU'RE LIKE my other therapist," Andrea said. It was 6:36 a.m., and she was stretching in her living room with CNN on mute in the background.

"You need to stop calling me that," Essence said on the other end of their FaceTime. "I'm your coach. There's a big difference."

"I know, degrees and whatever."

"No," Essence said, defending herself. "We do so much more than therapists. We listen. We learn. We help you build the tools to help yourself. But ultimately, we're mama birds. And one day you're going to fly, and you won't need us anymore. A therapist wants you to keep going back to them."

"Right," Andrea said, feeling briefly at odds with Essence. "I practiced the big speech like an hour ago and it felt amazing," she said, changing the subject.

"Then close your eyes, and practice your grounding exercises," Essence said, halfheartedly as if she hadn't wanted to be woken up this early, but fuck it, here she was. "Are you on your mat?"

Andrea pressed her palm into the yoga mat she stood on and looked at a small Earth-shaped logo indicating that this particular brand was designed to ground her energy. "Yep," she said, then asked, "When are you going to write a book, E?"

"Don't want to." Essence breathed evenly and deeply on the other end of the line, encouraging Andrea to do the same.

"Why not?"

"I don't know. I guess it's that mama bird feeling. I feel a little like the tools are free, so I'd rather give them away than make people buy them in a book."

"Oh. Like me?"

"No, no, not like that." Essence calmed Andrea with a cool hand she could see on the screen. "You know what I mean."

"I guess." Andrea couldn't fully work it out. "But you helped me build these tools and I pay you."

Essence was quiet, closing her eyes, continuing her deliberate breathing.

"I mean, I know I'll be okay," Andrea said. "Just nice to hear an affirming voice."

She had been a client of Essence's for almost five years but could feel the end of their journey together drawing near. Essence had slowly begun making the move many people in Andrea and Tamara's lives made, asking when they were filming, wanting to pay the set a visit, wanting to be noticed more often with them, always wanting to do lunch on their dime in bougie places. All in hope of squeezing into a frame somewhere, standing out just enough so that a producer might notice them and ask them to join in on the fun. Essence had certainly spent a lot of time cultivating the clientele. Only now Andrea felt she was outgrowing Essence.

Writing her book had been self-administered therapy and made her feel like she had real power. She was effectively learning to put herself first and seeing more and more that her lifelong giving nature had created around her a culture of need and a community of takers, of those just wanting to be seen. Unlike her old self, her new self was starting to see and feel the reality of being taken advantage of. In one way, she couldn't blame them. It had been her unconscious fault. She wondered if Essence even knew she was doing it.

"Let's have lunch then," her coach finally said. Andrea felt her head bop in a minor knowing nod. "Maybe a little real-life face time would help. What time is the signing?"

"Five," Andrea said.

"Soho House at two thirty?"

"That sounds great." Andrea smiled, wishing she had said no, but the default switch was hard to reset. "Okay, I've got yoga at seven."

"Okay, have fun!"

"See you soooooon!" Andrea felt awkward, upset at herself for committing to plans so soon before the signing. She dragged out her last word with a big cheesy smile, trying to seem enthusiastic, despite the pit in her stomach.

SHE CHANGED HER clothes and walked the short distance from her bungalow apartment on Sierra Bonita Avenue down Hollywood Boulevard to the entrance of Runyon Canyon off Fuller Avenue. Here fit, shirtless Angelenos hiked daily, and free yoga was offered in a small fenced-off area where a donation was not required but strongly encouraged. Like the rest of the cast members of Apples shows, when Andrea wanted to be seen, she wanted to be the most seen. The pick-me-up of attention was the best distraction from dealing with whatever problem was presenting itself. Waving hi and taking pictures was the fastest way to feel that work was being done to make others well. She had taken the free yoga class so many times that seeing her there was a reliable bet, and often half the population of any class were people hoping to meet her.

At the entrance to the park, her phone buzzed with a text from Guy. "Break a leg today. First signing of many. So exciting! Call me after yoga. Want to talk about something. Might be big!"

Her relationship with Guy had only recently begun to change. She had always been aware of a brewing tension between him and Tamara but had never fully been brought into whatever it was about. Tamara hadn't completely hidden suspicions she'd had about Guy but also didn't want to say so much that something could be used against her in the future. As much as she encouraged Andrea to trust her, Tamara played a lot of things close to the vest. Her life on TV, especially in recent seasons, was less about being in the moment and more about calculations. Despite the entire cast insisting their network-created friendships were real, they all knew they could blow up in an instant. Particularly with a little push from production. And most certainly with a push from Guy. Though they'd had small dustups, somehow Andrea and Tamara had made it over a decade without their relationship truly facing a major fire.

Guy was almost too caring with Andrea. Early on, as he got to know her, he actively tried to project a fatherly quality in their relationship. He checked in on her, liked to know where she was and what she was doing, obsessively talked about her skin complexion, and talked to her in a way everyone talked to Asian women—as if they were children. Never not delicate dolls. Or some easily excitable, cute-when-she-was-grumpy anime character. In the beginning, it had been familiar to Andrea. That was like all the relationships she'd had with men in Texas. It was the way her father talked to her mother. It was all she knew. But now she stared at the words "Call me after yoga" and felt like she was being watched. Wanting to talk about something sounded like a prelude to a breakup conversation. Whatever it was he wanted to talk about, he just had to present it to her today. The day she had meticulously planned and worked to have as her own, the start of something big she didn't have to share, the day to conquer a fear and speak of an authenticity she'd spent years building. Despite knowing all that, in a single instant, with a simple text, Guy had found a way to make the day about himself.

What had felt like protection and support was beginning to feel like manipulation. Especially since she'd learned that it had been Guy who'd encouraged Elliot to confess his love for her last season. Only she was the one who'd had to deal with the fallout and Fievel being an absolute asshole to her the next day at brunch. As they continued to film their shows' crossover, after taking full advantage of bottomless mimosas, he screamed at her, saying, "If anyone's going to fuck with my friend's emotions, it's going to be me!" Then he lied and said Elliot told him she was a pillow princess.

That moment was the beginning of the boys being pitted against the girls. Fans of *FGE* said the *Tamandrea* cast was used up this far into their run. On the other side of the aisle, detractors of the boys said the episode made them both look like childish chauvinists who had not been loved enough by their dead fathers.

"There she is!" someone shouted, and she looked up. It was a fan.

"Hey!" She smiled genuinely, not remembering his name despite having seen him at yoga more times than she could count. "How are you?"

"Oh my God, you look fucking amazing this morning," he said, snapping the strap of her sports bra against her shoulder.

She playfully swatted his hand away, smiling to mask her discomfort. He had a way of acting overly familiar with her. A lot of fans did.

"Oh stop," she said. "Where's Michael?" She could remember the boyfriend's name but not his and felt awful.

"He's not coming today. He went out with some friends last night and did too much coke."

She nodded along, smiling as if she understood. But she'd never tried cocaine or any drug except alcohol, and the one time she'd accidentally eaten three weed brownies from a plate at a friend's birthday party in high school, she'd thrown up on the dog's bed.

"Shit," the fan said, patting his pockets. "I forgot cash."

"I got you," she said. It was not the first time she had covered him.

Then he smiled and said, "You always take care of me."

5.

NIXON

NIXON SAT IN her father's car parked in his driveway, desperate to unhear his diagnosis.

Bill always used to joke about not letting her sit in the front seat because she could be killed by the airbag. At fifteen she had started to adopt his dark sense of humor. Only today wasn't a joke.

"When did they tell you?" She caught a brief chill, her body shaking.

"Last Monday," he said.

On her twelfth birthday, when the unofficial parenting handbook had suggested she graduate to shotgun, he threw her a car party. Then, after they went for a long drive with the top down, he'd pulled over, turned to her, thought about her recent growth spurt, and said, "I wonder if your feet will reach the pedals."

He let her drive a very cautious quarter mile home, but she panicked when pulling into the driveway and, instead of pressing the brake, she stomped the gas, sending the car into the garage door. Her instincts finally found the proper pedal, and her father yanked up the emergency brake, and they sat in the stopped car for a moment, staring at twisted aluminum. Then he looked at her and asked if she was all right, and she said she was, and instead of getting angry, he laughed.

"Mom is going to kill me," she said.

"I'm not going to tell her if you don't," he said, comforting her. "I'm not going to say it was a mistake to let you try. Okay? But maybe we don't do this again for a while."

He always treated her like she was his buddy. Because he had her for less time, it was easier for him to let her break the rules and act like an adult every other weekend than it was to enforce the ones her mother had set. It made him look cool to her friends, and it made him feel cool. Like parenting wasn't so hard. Like friendship before fatherhood was a sustainable model. It seemed to work in the movies, where kids acted much too mature for their age, unlocking wisdom through their earnest, inexperienced points of view. Only she was a teenager and couldn't fathom the way forty-year-old minds worked.

Now, at fifteen, she couldn't be sure if he was confiding in her as his daughter or as the adult in their relationship. They sat in the same convertible in the same garage, only she was confident this day would not end with his laughter.

"I don't know what any of this means," she said, as if she'd been told a big lie.

"Me either," he said. "But you're grown up now. And I don't know why, because it probably goes against the handbook, but I wanted to tell you first."

"How long have you felt sick?" she asked.

"I probably should've gone in a lot sooner than I did." He looked forward, avoiding her eyes. "But I didn't. And now I'm at, uh . . . stage four. And I guess they say, you know, that's pretty bad." He waited, but she didn't have anything to say, so he filled the silence. "I'd like to tell your mom myself, if that's okay with you. I just don't know if I can right now."

Her lower lip tightened; she wanted to say something profound, like if they could remove all doubt from their minds, maybe the resulting good will could cure him. But all she could manage was to again say, "I don't know what any of this means."

She didn't want to be an adult anymore.

HER DEMEANOR WAS cold at their polite family breakfast at Denny's. It had been an agreed-on activity, as it had seemed worth fighting for some form of civility between Bill and Samantha. In their separation, through their divorce, and now for many years as two people who used to be married but paradoxically shared a perfect gift, they'd tried to be polite for Nixon's sake.

Samantha was keeping track of her and Nixon's day on her phone, a schedule which primarily revolved around driving to LA to shoot with the photographer Todrick Kidd. His eye would be capturing the image for the cover and various promotional material for her upcoming debut album, *No Girl's Land.*

A month prior she had released her first single, "Switch Me On." The album envisioned a sort of dystopian cyberpop future where boys would fall into depravity and chaos and, because her audience was largely preteen, implied murder. In the grand story of the album, it would be up to her to lead a girl uprising to reclaim the power boys had taken from them and abused.

Samantha was also ecstatic about their recent relationship with Apples. The network had become such a fan of the free publicity Nixon had given their shows over the years that when they'd started looking to branch into scripted content, it had been a no-brainer to offer Nixon the lead in a family-friendly movie. It was called *That's So Social* and was loosely based on her real life. She was playing a girl named Cece who finds internet stardom overnight but doesn't quite know what to do with it. The spoiler-filled ending Apples producers had relayed to company executives was that she and her incredibly supportive parents, and her inoffensive-looking boyfriend, would manage to work it out together, after a brief period of letting it all go to her head of course, and then everyone would be fine in the end.

Through her new agent, Victory Valance, Nixon had also signed with her first manager, Murphy Beck. The idea that he also represented Hector Espinoza, and that she might someday meet him or maybe even work with him, overwhelmed her in the best way possible.

She had fallen for a teenage Hector by streaming old episodes of the show where he'd gotten his start, *The Fallen*—a young adult, science fiction/fantasy show about aliens posing as what humans understood to be vampires. His awkward, shy, I-have-no-business-being-here-with-all-this-fame attitude were otherworldly qualities she related to. More than his good looks and talent, Nixon was drawn to Hector because she always felt a little alien herself. Her gangly post-puberty limbs and big teeth exaggerated those feelings.

Since she'd spent the majority of her life under her mother's insistence that she quote lines from a show she had grown to hate, Hector was Nixon's escape. But rather than write his name in her diary countless times, she daydreamed of standing next to him on a poster for a movie. She didn't want to be his muse; she wanted to share top billing.

"Love you, punkin," Bill said after breakfast, kissing the top of her head, an action that required her to bow just slightly as she was taller than him now.

Feeling cast out into space like an alien on Hector's old show, she did not know what to say in return.

"CAN YOU BELIEVE they're finally closing this down?" Samantha asked as they drove by the San Onofre nuclear power plant. "It's going to be so weird not seeing this anymore. Like, what do they do with it? Just demolish it? That seems dangerous."

They were making the trek along the I-5 North to Los Angeles up from Carlsbad, near San Diego, where Bill lived.

"What's wrong, honey?" Samantha looked over briefly at Nixon staring out the window.

"Nothing."

"Your tone and use of the word 'nothing' means it's something."

"Yes, it is something. But it's not something I want to talk about right now." Nixon's sighs fogged up the glass in front of her.

"Well, I really hope you can get over whatever this attitude is, because Murphy worked really hard to get us Todrick."

"It's a moody album. I feel moody. I'll look moody. It's all on-brand."

"That's clever. You're very clever." Her mom was trying to pretend she was ending a fight when Nixon knew all she wanted to do was start one. That made Nixon laugh. She thought again about her dad laughing after she'd destroyed his garage door, a secret they'd kept to this day. She thought maybe she could keep this new one too.

"How was your weekend with your dad?" her mom asked.

"Fine."

"Good." Then they sat in silence for a long while until they reached traffic just past San Clemente. "Why don't they extend the carpool lane down here? This is always so ridiculous." It was the same complaint every time they made the drive. "Let's go back through your mixes again."

Nixon needed her to be quiet, but she knew the only thing her mother was good at was filling a silence that made her uncomfortable.

"If I say I don't want to do that, you're going to get mad at me," Nixon said.

"I'm not going to get mad at you. Who says I'm going to get mad at you?"

"Me. I'm saying you're going to get mad at me."

"Well, I'm not. And you know what happens when you *ass*-ume," she overenunciated.

"I don't want to listen to my songs on the drive to a photo shoot for the same songs. Because he's going to be playing them the entire time I'm there, and I'm going to lose my mind and hate all of them by the time we're done. I hate them now, honestly. So, I'd either like to listen to nothing or listen to Jonathan Richman."

Samantha made a sound like she was going to vomit.

"Exactly," Nixon said.

"I don't know why you like him," her mother said. "Actually, no.

I *do* know why you like him. Because your dad likes him, and any opportunity you can take to spite me, despite how hard I work for you, you'll take."

Nixon rolled her head back and looked at the ceiling of the car as if she were watching a space shuttle blow up and wondered about all those poor people on fire, plummeting toward earth. "I like music you like too," she said, trying to keep the peace.

"Like what?"

"Whitney Houston."

"Everybody likes Whitney Houston."

"I don't think that's true."

"Name one person who doesn't like Whitney Houston."

Nixon couldn't. "Fine."

"See? So, besides Whitney Houston, name music I like that you also like."

"Jesus, Mom," Nixon said instinctively, only she wasn't supposed to say that.

"Excuse me?" Samantha wanted to stare daggers at her daughter but was bumper to bumper with the car in front of her and had to glare at the traffic instead. Nixon knew her mother loved nothing more than to pretend to be pious.

Samantha took great pride in other people thinking she took her religion seriously. Bill had pointed this out enough times for Nixon to see it too. It hadn't helped that everyone discovered her daughter's singing talents when she did a solo for their church choir's Christmas pageant when she was six. The faith of their daughter had been a source of many fights between her parents, especially when Nixon was eight and Samantha found out that when she was at her dad's every other weekend, they didn't go to church.

"So, it's fine for me to say 'fuck' and 'bitch' a bunch and pretend to throw fake wine, but I can't say 'Jesus Christ'?"

"What are you even doing right now?" Samantha looked stunned.

"Poking holes in your logic."

"What does that even mean?"

"It means you don't make any sense half the time we talk about stuff!"

"All I wanted to do was have a nice drive with you and mercifully try to get through traffic so we can get to where we're going, which I guess I have to remind you is something that is costing us a lot of money."

"You think I don't know how much money we make?" Nixon diverted her attention to her phone, checking for updates and deciding to take this time to respond to DMs from fans.

"I think you don't know how much money we *can* make."

"Cool." She ignored her mom, phone screen tapping as she typed.

After a frustrated pause, Samantha scoffed and shook her head. "Apathy is not a solution, sweetheart," she said.

"Oh my God, who told you that? Did Tony tell you that?"

"Tony is a gentleman!" Her mother was offended. "You remember how good he took care of us when we flew out to Palm Beach for your Date with Destiny."

"That was for cross-promotion. He was getting paid!"

"So were you!"

"And so were *you!*" Nixon slammed the rump of her fist onto the glove box in front of her.

"Okay, so I'll just call Murphy then," Samantha said sharply, like she had to sneak it past her daughter before it could be detected. "Tell him to cancel with Todrick. Tell him he's fired."

"Mom."

"And then I'll call Applause and tell them to go fuck themselves and that we won't support the release of your movie one goddamned bit, because you think it's absolute garbage, and then they'll sue us, and they'll call Guy Maker, and he'll fly into a rage and be sure as shit that you. Will never. Work. Again."

Nixon stared at her.

"What do you think of that?" Samantha asked proudly.

"Be my guest," Nixon said, sucking all the air out of her mother's balloon.

Samantha was nearing tears, sensing that for the rest of her life she would never win in a fight against a fifteen-year-old girl. "I don't know what you want from me," she said.

"I don't want anything from you. I just want you to let me do what I want to do."

"You're fifteen. If I just let you do what you wanted to do, you'd be having sex all over the house and doing drugs and drinking."

"That's certainly the story we're trying to tell, isn't it?"

"I hate whoever taught you to talk like this."

"I wonder who that was." Nixon went back to her phone.

"It's called playing a part, sweetheart. You want to be an actress. This is part of acting."

"I don't want to be an actor, Mom. I am an actor."

"You're right. I'm sorry. You are."

The traffic eased and Samantha felt like the acceleration was an escape from whatever hell they were in. "So why don't you start acting grateful for everything God and the world has given you?"

"I'm so glad God gave me sex appeal." She scrolled through her feed, past pictures of girls looking just like her.

"You say it sarcastically now, but you better mean it. Todrick won't put up with your childish bullshit. Pros don't put up with bullshit. So, you'd better do what he says and be grateful," Samantha said with finality.

Nixon thought about her dad. "Can I listen to Jonathan Richman, please?" she asked.

"No," her mother said. "I think silence is all you've earned."

6.

HECTOR

ECTOR HATED HIMSELF for thinking, *What would Matt Source do?* Taking that approach was certainly the worst idea. But it was the only idea he could think of when it came to casting a net wide enough to help him better understand Molly's suicide, why Guy had no-showed her funeral. He needed leads. He needed to talk to the people who'd known her best, who might've known Guy even better.

He was still sitting in his car. To escape the onlookers on Santa Monica Boulevard, he'd driven a few blocks up and parked on the sloped side of a residential street.

It did not occur to him that the strategy he was considering in that moment might not be appropriate. He was forty-five but no one had ever let him believe it. Being on his own and without anyone telling him what to do almost felt against the rules. He knew the questions he wanted to ask, but he didn't know how to ask them. He did not have a lot of conversations with people about things other than work and, now apparently, his sexuality. Suddenly, everyone liked to tell him about that friend they had who was bi and how they always thought it was beautiful and that they were kind of jealous because, technically, bisexual people had twice as many options.

Essence had once told him that with the death of his mother, his emotional development had likely been arrested in his teenage years. The other secret he was keeping, the one he and Murphy had held on to since his first years in LA, had him loathing the fact that she was right. Who was he kidding? Deep down, he was just a scared little boy.

Hector took a deep breath and went to find Molly's Instagram profile. He made sport of going as long as humanly possible before getting on social media for information. Except for the purpose of posting announcements and pictures of his dog or occasionally enacting subtle revenge, Murphy discouraged him from using it on the grounds of it being a cesspool of misinformation and pain. He followed only fifty-six other accounts, of which Molly's was not one. He would scroll through her page from time to time, but that only resulted in continuing to chip away at the glass case he'd held his childhood image of her in.

Through the cracked glass of his screen, he could see the last photo she had posted, from a week before her death. Flashback Friday. Her and Tamara at a red-carpet event for *MML* from years prior. She had captioned it, "Sending good vibes to this bitch for a season 8!!!" He knew, at the very least, that at the end of her life, her and Tamara's friendship could've been described as rocky, if not nonexistent. But he knew too well the desire to post pictures and feign friendliness to save face, especially when hurt. Maybe she had hoped for reconciliation. Maybe this was part of the reason she'd ended it all.

He scrolled through the comments and saw that she must've been up late the night she made the post, engaging with fans.

"how u can stil be friends wit her idk. she fuced u big time," one commenter said. Hector sighed. Deciphering the different varieties of grammar felt like detective work enough.

"she had to do what she had to do," Molly said.

"even tho it hurt u?" the fan responded.

Molly's final response on that thread was the shrug emoji.

"Fuck dis bitch!" someone else wrote.

Molly's response was the laughing-so-hard-it-was-crying emoji.

"I was talkin bout u ho," the commenter's response.

Molly did not reply.

"Why do you think Guy doent ask u to be on his show anymore. Yer a fucking drunk." Another.

"Molly, for god sakes, get it TOGETHER girl! You're done. Stop trying to stay in the spotlight. Get a real job." And another.

"jesus christ, stfu nd kill yourself all ready." And another.

"cunt." someone simply wrote, using a period to make their point.

"with pride bitch," Molly said. And then there was the hand-making-a-peace-sign emoji.

There was "Love you Molls!!!" from someone nice. "Ignore the h8 do u."

"Lady, Tam is NOT your friend. When are you going to accept she used you!?" from someone not nice.

"Who hasn't?" Molly said.

Hector looked up. A headache pulsed through the left side of his forehead behind his eye. He thought for a moment, then googled "Tamara Colling." The first hits were photos of a middle-aged white grinning realtor in a mauve skirt and blouse standing next to several large Hollywood Hills homes. He stared at the results, unsure what they meant. His brow furrowed. Was this part of the puzzle? It was odd someone of her celebrity wouldn't be the first major result. Then he realized he had misspelled her name.

"Oh," he said aloud to himself, like his Halloween Dick Tracy mask had been ripped off. He corrected the mistake.

Photos of Tamara from red-carpet events replaced the imposter woman, along with the official website for *Tamandrea* and the website for Apples just beneath it. Third in line was the site for her studio, We Are One Dance.

He hadn't known she ran a dance studio. He'd kept his nose so far out of Molly's world that he felt like he was searching for a sister separated at birth.

He tapped on the Apples link. He navigated to the "Shows" tab and scrolled a small drop-down menu to "Molly's Messy Life." He clicked on it. The page's graphics displayed a looped video of Molly, hand on hip, glass of wine in hand. She winked at the camera, then took a swig. His options were, "Cast," "Episodes," "Schedule," "Clips," "Let's Get Lit Hos!" and "About."

His finger lingered a long while over "Let's Get Lit Hos!" before finally clicking on "About."

The next page showed Molly sitting on top of the bold-faced type of her show logo, legs kicking, obscuring the words "Messy Life." She took one stiletto heel off and threw it at the camera. Then the video played again.

He scrolled down to scan the section about the premise and origins of the show. It read like a Wikipedia summary.

After she reconnected with her best friend from her teenage years, Guy Maker, at an industry holiday party, they'd set out to chronicle what was then Molly's troubled marriage to movie producer Wally Rhoades. Guy, who had been struggling as a story producer at the fledgling Applause network, remembered their wild partying days, which he'd documented on his Panasonic AG-450 while he was in community college. Now Guy was inspired to further document her life. Molly, bored and out of work, decided her marital woes and troubles with alcohol were the perfect material to trudge through. She feared nothing and no one. She wanted to shine a light on what can become of people like her in the industry, of what happens to child stars. To show that the struggle isn't so much chosen as it is given.

The initial material was meant to be one part of a longer documentary about her life, but with the amount of footage Guy had shot, he began to shape it into something more. One day, he was discovered by an Apples executive while working on an edit for the documentary instead of doing his job. But the executive recognized Molly's face as that of the former child actor and asked to watch some of the footage. Despite most of the material intentionally showing Wally Rhoades in a negative light, it also illustrated Molly's temper and wild ways. The executive asked Guy to share the rough cut of the film with a room full of suits, who saw potential gold and a dramatic shift away from real-estate and renovation content.

Wanting to avoid involving her husband and focus entirely on the character Molly was, they decided to call her in and pitch a new idea: a television show about her life, executive produced by Guy. Its first limited run of ten episodes aired in 2004 and began with Molly getting out of rehab after the finalization of her divorce. It followed her desire to reinvent herself as she worked to stay clean. Originally, it was simply titled *Molly's World.*

Hector nodded to himself and ran a hand thoughtfully across his stubble, like the clues were coming together—despite this all being public information that millions of people already knew like the backs of their hands.

He searched "Wally Rhoades."

He learned that the man had produced films for a company called Lionel Pictures under the direction of Lionel Stamp, a Sam Arkoff or Roger Corman type. Horror pictures made for quick profit with C-level celebrities starring in direct-to-consumer D-movie scares. Wally had gotten into a drunk driving accident in 2005 and wrapped himself around a concrete lamppost on the Pacific Coast Highway near the Santa Monica Pier, paralyzing himself from the waist down. This, the page said, had led to his wife's relapse. "Wife's relapse" was colored blue and underlined, insinuating a somber hyperlink. Hector clicked on it. It took him to Molly's page and a section titled "Personal Life and Substance Abuse Issues."

He exhaled, not sure he wanted to go further, but read on. The show was rebranded as *Molly's Messy Life* after her relapse. It had made her ongoing battle with alcohol and drugs the focal point of its plot, moving away from her desire to get clean. It became a major ratings success only when she struggled to tread water.

Tamara had been her best friend for so long; he wondered what had broken up their band. He navigated back to her search results and tapped the link for the dance studio, going to its contact page.

He stared at the phone number, unsure how else to find the answers he was looking for. If he'd had a lot of extra paper, Post-it Notes, printed photographs, pushpins, and string, he would've started trying to connect the dots the way movie and TV detectives do. Randomly writing expository notes like "GUILTY!?" and circling them several times before looping a bit of yarn around them and tying it to someone's headshot.

Apples cast members had more information on Molly's character, but the amount of radio silence from them in the past two weeks outside the obligatory "thoughts and prayers" posts made it feel like no one really cared. It was not often someone like Molly died by suicide, let alone in as public a way. To Hector, it didn't feel like she'd been running away. It seemed almost like she'd been trying to send a message.

He looked back down at his phone. He had no choice. He called the number. It rang twice.

"Studio," a girl said on the line.

"Hi," he said. "Um, this is Hector Espinoza."

"Hey, Hector," she continued, as if it were no big deal.

"The actor," he said a little more firmly, assuming she hadn't known and that his identity gave him some kind of shining authority, like a rhinestone cowboy or something.

"Uh-huh," she said. "What can I do for you?"

"Oh," he said. "I guess . . ." He thought about the Instagram picture. "Is Tamara there?" He was in high school again, nervously calling a girl's house.

"She is. Would you like to speak with her?"

"Please," he said, chuckling at the fact that getting in touch with someone famous was sometimes as easy as googling them.

There was the sound of someone fumbling with the phone before Tamara got on the line and said, "Hey, Hector," in the exact same tone as the girl before, and Hector honestly had to wonder if he had met both of them at some point.

"Hi, Tamara. This is Hector Espinoza," he said again, like pretend Superman. "I was calling about . . . well . . . I wanted to ask you about Molly."

There was a pregnant pause.

"Why?" she said flatly.

"Well, as you know, she died," he said, then gritted his teeth at how fucking stupid that sounded, and it reminded him of the time he'd taken improv classes, and everyone had been very kind to him because he was so famous, but it had also been unequivocally clear that improv was not his thing.

Tamara did not respond.

"And I would like to know why," he said, swallowing the words.

"This feels like a prank call, but I know it's you," she said.

"It is me, yes."

"Listen, Hec," she began, and then he thought about how only Cyd had called him that, and he wondered if it had been some inside joke on *Tamandrea*.

"I know you were a big fan. Jesus, it's really weird to have this conversation with you," she said.

"I know," he said.

"Listen, I've got a big meeting in fifteen—"

"I don't want to keep you. I just wanted to know. Or maybe we can meet up and talk about it."

"I'm not going to meet up with you to talk about my friend's suicide."

"Okay, then I can call back at a better time if that's easier."

"I guess we all have our demons," she said sharply. "Good?"

"I'm not a reporter." He gained a little confidence. "There's no record here."

"I'm aware. Why don't you talk to Guy about it?"

"He wasn't at the funeral. That's part of it. Do you know why he didn't go?"

"No. He and I aren't exactly holding hands at the moment."

"Did she give any indication that something was wrong?"

"Did she give any indication?" she repeated, chuckling, seeing the scene she was in. He could feel the temperature of her tone change through the phone. "Fuck, you really think you're that movie guy, don't you?"

"I'm sorry?" He was caught off guard.

"This isn't a mystery. She fucking killed herself."

"I know—"

"No. You don't. It's why you're calling me instead of talking to your fucking therapist. You'd probably realize how fucked up this is if you'd come down from your tower and slum it with us housewives from time to time."

"Tamara, I didn't mean to—"

"This shit ain't so rosy," she cut him off again. "And we don't need you rubbing our noses in it." Then he heard her move the phone away from her face and, just before she hung up, distantly say, "Fucking fanboy."

He sat in stillness. He wondered how he could get better at not overstepping boundaries, but he'd spent a good portion of his career going unchecked in that regard. He tried not to beat himself up but felt bad for dredging something up for Tamara on what he assumed was a stressful workday.

He thought about calling Essence again but got angry that she'd dropped his call to clown around on some other celebrity's dime. He hated that she was right about what his mother's death had done to him and hated even more the parts of his story she didn't know. The things that made him the little boy who ran and hid when Hollywood's shit hit the fan.

His own past was part of the reason he felt like he'd locked Molly away in his mind. He'd locked a part of himself in the same box and buried it twenty-seven years in the past. Only Murphy had been there, helping him discreetly mark his pain with a pile of stones. A buried body no one could find but them.

He thought about the message Molly had been trying to send.

There had to be more to it. She was trying to tell him something. He had failed his idol in the past. He had to do right by her in the present.

"I NEED NUMBERS," he said on the phone.

Murphy hesitated. "What kind of numbers?"

"I need to call some people." Hector wiped his sweaty palms on his pants, now pacing outside his car.

"You know, sometimes I wish you weren't so successful so I didn't always have to answer your calls."

"Funny."

"Who did you call already?"

"No one." Hector spoke rapid fire. "I did call Essence, though; you should know that. And she gave me God-awful advice, and I threw my phone, and I'm gonna need you to ask Lyle to get me a new one or fix my screen or whatever, but not right now. Probably not today. Tomorrow, though."

"Je-sus," Murphy said. "You got some bad coke, pal."

"I'm not on drugs!" Hector's head whipped over his shoulder to look at the house behind him, making sure no one was watching. Then he caved and said, "I talked to Tamara."

"Oh my God." He could hear Murphy running his hand through his thin hair, making contact mostly with scalp. "This little vision quest is gonna get you killed. How did you get hers?"

"I called the dance studio."

"Fucking—God damn it, Hector."

"What?"

"Now she's going to tell everyone she got this weird phone call from you, and . . ." He stopped and took a deep breath. "You know how these people are. I'd like to find a way to spin this into a positive when they all start talking."

"I'll post a picture of me as a kid with my mom, lying next to her in bed, watching Molly's old show, and remind them why it matters."

"Whose phone numbers?" Murphy groaned.

"Fievel Geitman," Hector said quickly. "Maybe Andrea Bocelli too."

"They're both with Victory. You know that."

A woman with a name like a 1960s Marvel character, Victory Valance was the head of the Valiant agency, who represented a pile of Apples talent.

"I guess I'm not thinking straight," Hector said.

"I guess you're not. You could do this legwork yourself if you were."

"Maybe someone has kept me in a position of not being able to," Hector snapped back.

"What is that supposed to mean?"

"I just need some closure."

"Closure from someone you never met in person?"

Hector didn't respond.

"Protecting you is my job," Murphy said.

"No, it isn't."

"It wasn't called *Molly's Messy Life* because it was about her doing really well, you know."

"No shit."

"If legitimate rehab shows about washed-up celebrities getting better and actually improving themselves made money, people would make them. But they don't. So, they don't."

Hector was quiet.

"You know this industry fucked her over. What is it you can't believe about that?"

"It's not that I can't believe it—"

"Oh, really?"

"I just want to know why," Hector said.

"Why it happened to her?"

Hector drew in a sharp breath, now feeling the anxiety of the secret he'd buried years ago. "Why it happens at all," he said.

"Listen," Murphy began again, slowly. "If this is . . . I mean, these past few years with the women and the actresses . . . if the hiding inside your house is about what happened to you, maybe you—"

"Should talk to Essence?" Hector said defensively.

"No." Murphy's voice got shaky. "Maybe you and I should finally talk."

"We're talking."

"About *it*."

"You're saying you're ready to?"

"I'm asking if you are."

There was a long pause before Hector said, "I don't know."

"Okay." Hector heard Murphy breathe in quickly and blow his air out just as fast, trying to change the mood. He dodged elephants in the room the only way he knew how, by trying to make Hector laugh. "All right. Fine. You do what you gotta do, okay? You want numbers? I'll get you numbers. Hey, listen, does this mean you're making me the guy in the van? Running your tech and operations?"

"I don't know. That's a sizable promotion," Hector said grumpily, hating how Murphy's humor always seemed to work.

"Come on. It'll be like old times. You workin' for me, me workin' for you. Hustlin' and bustlin'! Makin' money moves!"

"If you don't want to appear over the hill, you need to stop saying everything you're saying right now."

"I'm just saying . . . I can get on board with this if you say I'm the guy in the van."

Hector sighed. "You can be the guy in the van, Murph."

Then Hector heard the sound of Murphy's suit jacket swish on the other end of the line as he undoubtedly pumped his fist like he was Tiger Woods sinking a putt.

HECTOR'S PLAN FOR making calls was met with voice-mail boxes. He left a short message for Fievel. But after talking to Tamara, he didn't have the heart to leave one for Andrea. Then he took a drive to a small cash-only burger joint off Pico Boulevard toward the Westside called the Apple Pan to get some comfort food.

Inside, his phone rang as he sat at the counter eating. He recognized Fievel's number returning his call.

"Hello," Hector said hurriedly with a full mouth.

"Hey," said a nervous voice on the other end of the line. "Is this really you?"

"Yes. It is." He swallowed. "Not that big of a deal."

"I mean, it's kind of a big deal. This is really weird."

"Listen, Fievel, I was—"

"Oh, no. This isn't Fievel. This is Elliot. His driver. Well . . . his friend. I'm on the show too."

"That's really great." Hector wanted to sound supportive but had no idea who Elliot was. "Is it possible to talk to Fievel?"

Hector could hear Fievel shout in the distance, "Who is that?" The phone muted briefly. Then Elliot returned, speaking in a hushed voice.

"Listen, Hec," Elliot began, and Hector knew he was the last in on whatever fucking joke that nickname must have been. "He's about to perform. He's debuting his set at the poolside lounge at the Tropicana here in Vegas."

"The Tropicana has a poolside lounge?"

"Yeah."

"Huh."

"Yeah. He's freaking out a decent amount, so I'm not sure it's a great time to talk to you."

"Me specifically or anyone in general?"

"Mostly you. Specifically. I mean, not just because you're you. But because of what you said in your message."

"Right."

"He doesn't really like to talk about her," Elliot said. "I mean,

I do think he should talk to somebody about it. I'm just not sure that's you."

Hector heard the earnestness in the man's voice as he tried to protect his friend. "You're a good friend, Oliver."

"Thanks." Elliot chuckled.

Then Fievel's distant voice shouted, "Are you gonna stop being a pussy and come do this shot with me or what? Oh shit. Are you talking to your mom?"

Hector laughed.

"Bye," Elliot said.

"Bye." Hector hung up.

He looked at his half-eaten burger and prodded it with a French fry. It seemed all he was capable of that day was poking a bear. He didn't like knowing he was responsible for making others relive their hurt. He wouldn't want the same done to him. He would have to find another way.

He recalled the only connection he shared with *The Family That Stays Together*: its casting director, Sarah Kline. Hector had gotten in the room with Sarah and booked *The Fallen* because of a fluke encounter between a very young Murphy and her associate at the time, Wendy Miller.

Thinking about the transition in her career from network sitcom star to Apples godmother, he was fascinated by the genre Molly had helped invent, the behemoth it had become. When he was young, in the eighties and nineties, being the star of a reality show had meant one of two things: either you were someone in your early twenties living in a house with eleven other yous, getting shit-faced and fucking anything that walked, or you were the old narrator of dry nature documentaries. Or, if you were really lucky, you were Bob Ross.

Always inspired by Molly and *The Family That Stays Together*, Hector had barely been eighteen when he'd moved to Los Angeles to pursue his acting career in 1992. He'd wasted more money than he should have on a hotel room his first night in town and decided to ask the concierge where he should look for housing. She had told him his best bet would be living with other actors, splitting rent multiple ways, because that was what she was doing. He asked her how many other actors there were in LA, and she said, "Everyone."

He took a bus to North Hollywood, where the concierge had said she lived, because he didn't know where else to start. He got off at a stop just past a building that said, *Acting Studio*. He met the owner, its only employee, inside a shoebox-sized lobby that opened up into an almost equally small black box theater. Hector said he wanted to take acting classes.

Because he didn't have either a headshot or résumé, the owner was hesitant. But he liked Hector's look. At that age, he seemed cut from stone. The owner complimented his bone structure and the forever tan of his brown skin. He had a free afternoon and gave Hector a short scene, which they ran through together. The owner asked if he could buy Hector a meal that night. He was nice to him. It was a relief.

The owner then put him in touch with a few other students who might be looking for roommates or housemates. He found one in a girl named Meghan. When he moved in with her, he had only two trash bags full of clothes, two pairs of shoes—one tennis and one dress—one suit, and a small box full of books and VHS tapes.

After a few weeks of classes, he started to work part-time for the owner, and the two became close. The owner was always exceedingly kind. Hector rarely paid for anything, even his rent when times were hard and he hadn't the courage to call his dad. The owner said it was his honor to help. The occasional free lunch, as he called it, was a small price to pay to help a young actor as talented and handsome as Hector. Sometimes Hector got a little embarrassed by how often the owner talked about his looks. His hair. His skin. His lips. His eyes. Even his teeth, which Hector thought was strange because no one really complimented anyone's teeth. Not that he'd ever heard.

Then Hector came to work one day and found the owner sitting in one of the theater seats, naked. When Hector asked what was going on, thinking this was some kind of practical joke, the owner told him a lot of things he said Hector must have wanted to do with him. Told Hector what he must have been feeling all those months as they got closer. Told him everything he was going to do to him. Told him it would be like fireworks. Told him it would be their secret.

Then the owner started undressing him, and he froze because he didn't know what else to do and thought maybe this was normal for people who liked both. He knew how to have sex with a girl, but he did not know how to have sex with a man. That desire he'd always kept secret. Maybe this was how it was. Maybe the owner was right. Maybe Hector did want these things. The owner had been kind to him. He had given him a job. He had helped him find a place to live. He had given him free lessons, fed him meals, paid for headshots, paid his rent. Maybe he should just do these things and have them be done with so he could go home. And the owner told Hector a lot of things he'd never imagined a man would say to another man, especially because the owner used to say only nice things to him. But these things made him realize he'd never known the man at all.

When Hector returned home that evening, blood lined the inside of his underwear. He told no one and continued to be bound in a secret relationship with the owner for nearly a year. He felt trapped. He'd been told it was what he wanted. When he was growing up, everyone he talked to had said if he did things with other men, that made him gay, and he knew people weren't nice to gay people in the industry. He never knew where he stood, wanting both. He just knew he couldn't be gay, couldn't let anyone discover his confusing secret.

During that year, the owner introduced Hector to a young man in his twenties who had been a student in his class. The man's name was Murphy Beck. Murphy was working at a large talent agency and had been to see one of the plays the studio had put on a month prior. Hector had impressed him, and he proposed they meet about possible representation.

Murphy liked Hector. But Murphy, much as in the present, did not like to bullshit anyone. He told Hector that the agency he worked for was a scam and that they had so many actors they couldn't have possibly known what to do with all of them. He was thinking about going out on his own, hoofing it in the industry independently. He wasn't sure if something like that would interest Hector, but Hector had met no other agents, and it didn't seem like such a bad opportunity. Then Murphy jokingly asked if the owner had come on to Hector the way he'd come on to him years ago. The owner was a nice enough guy but had always seemed a little pervy, Murphy had said. Hector hadn't known it could have all just been a joke if only he had said no, and he broke down in the middle of the sushi restaurant.

Murphy's stomach knotted. He promised to keep Hector's secret. Murphy had a lot of actor friends, a lot of them holding similar secrets: secrets were par for the course. Murphy said he and Hector could work together. They could be partners, so long as one didn't try to fuck the other over. He would protect Hector, no matter what.

Hector felt up against a wall when it came to trusting Murphy. He had no one else. He had no other choice.

For a while, Hector avoided speaking to anyone who wasn't his new agent and the occasional casting office when he went in for auditions. He folded himself inward and perfected his shy, quiet demeanor. He mastered the art of being a lost boy, never leaving Neverland.

One night at a party in the valley, Murphy met the casting associate Wendy Miller. He made a hard pitch to her on Hector, whom he described as a "Mexican James Dean." She was only an associate but said to send over Hector's headshot and résumé, and she'd see what she could do.

Hector's info made it to her boss, Sarah Kline. When it came to casting their young adult network show *The Fallen*, she said the studio was looking for "some color" and that Hector's Mexican-sounding name might look good on a billboard next to a few white-sounding names and one Black-sounding name and maybe a smart-looking Asian kid in a wheelchair. She said the nineties were all about diversity. Despite having very few credits outside one commercial for charcoal briquettes, one single-line co-star role on a short-lived cop procedural called *Police Line: Do Not Cross*, and parts in independent plays at the studio owner's theater, Hector landed a series regular role on the show.

At the height of the show's popularity, from the outside looking in, he was an overnight sensation. His luck was incredible. His story was told in teen magazines. He was Lana Turner in the soda shop. Hector Espinoza: Zero to hero. Nobody to somebody. He was a miracle. Only now, at forty-five, sitting solemnly on a small stool inside a cash-only burger joint, he didn't feel like one.

7.

TAMARA

TAMARA HURRIED OUTSIDE to catch her breath. Hector fucking Espinoza. Was he kidding? Afraid of looking like she was losing her mind in the parking lot, she rushed to her car and sat inside, turning up music.

Her rage settled. She realized the day's clouds and chill had blown off as predicted, and she felt resentful that the perfectly nice day she'd been promised had now been ruined by two men determined to upend her entire existence.

She thought about the picture of Molly published a week prior on the website of *Applause Magazine*, of her lifeless body. Tamara's fist instinctively slammed against the wheel.

Applause Magazine had formerly been a tabloid known as *Hollywood Inside Out*, but a decade prior, when it started making most of its money from exposés on Apples stars, it had switched its name to match the network's. Legally, the hijacking of the magazine was permitted because a judge ruled that the trademark for the network belonged only to entertainment programming, specifically film and television. The magazine's lawyers made the case that its print and digital content constituted journalism and news, not entertainment. It was reporting the facts, stretched thin as they may have been. Casual fans had no idea the network and the magazine were separate entities and assumed what the magazine printed was God's word.

Someone had sent in a photo of Molly snapped before her body was taken down. This meant someone must have seen her, recognized her, claimed their prize, and left without alerting anyone. They had let her hang there until someone else had the decency to call the cops. That thought sent more shivers down Tamara's spine. She'd never be able to unsee it, remembering that in the photo it had still been dark outside, and the nearby streetlight lit Molly's body in contrasting red and green like some horrific Christmas display.

After incredible outrage, the magazine had removed the photo. They claimed it had been posted by a foolish intern who thought he was getting a hot tip, so they took swift action and fired him. But everyone knew their story was bullshit. The network filed a lawsuit immediately. Despite the magazine's muckraking press often helping to drive more traffic to its shows, the publication of the photo had been a step too far for Apples. If anyone was going to capitalize on the death of their biggest star, it was going to be them.

Tamara looked at the clock. Barely 2:00 p.m. She took her phone from her bag and swiped it open, going to her texts to see her last messages with Andrea. They were from four days prior. Tamara again wondered at the plausibility of her being played by the girl she thought was her best friend.

Tamara closed her eyes and considered the chessboard. Guy's king moved one calculated space at a time, now possibly wielding Andrea's powerful queen against hers. As much as she hoped to constantly keep him in check, she wondered which role she was playing and which had been Molly's. What power had she now lost in the game?

More than anyone, Tamara wanted to find a way to tip the network in her favor. From the moment she'd been cast, her and Guy's unspoken and unacknowledged animosity had driven them both. It made her irate, the way he could pull the strings of so many women with ease. She wondered if he got off on it, if he liked knowing that somewhere out there a storm was now brewing between two of his heaviest hitters. That they might come to some sort of emotional blows. That he held the financial fate of her new studio in his hands. The fate of her image, of who she was.

Tamara was the only Apples cast member never to have appeared as a guest on *WHH,S!* Even has-beens from *Hard Knock Wife* made their way onto the show, bottom feeding for a little bit of extra exposure. She thought it was gross. Watching her costars grovel at Guy's feet for table scraps made her insides twist. Pretending she couldn't see through his fake fatherly attitude for the ones who didn't know any better was even worse. The ones like Andrea and Elliot. When Guy had used Fievel's infidelity against him, driving him and Molly apart and ratings up, that had been the last straw. Tamara didn't care about the little fuck Fievel all that much, to be honest. But knowing the shock and pain it had caused Molly after she'd lost both her and Andrea as castmates, Tamara hadn't been able to bring herself to watch those sad six final-season episodes of *MML*. All the other content of Molly's life had been used up. The only thing that remained was her pain.

The new casts of characters in the spin-offs had been a fresh change of pace, and watching Molly destroy herself had ceased to be fun or funny for the audience. People liked their stars having problems so long as those problems didn't remind them of their own. Molly had put viewers in the position of willful ignorance of their own tragedies because, on TV, hers were so much worse in comparison. To have been so young and successful and to wash it all away in a torrent of booze and pills was like the bitchy prom queen finally getting her comeuppance. Only the longer the prom queen stood on the stage and endured the jeers of the crowd, the harder it was to argue with why she turned to the bottle to silence them. They had finally dumped the bucket of blood on Carrie's head.

Once that reality could not be rewritten by producers for the fiction of reality TV, it was impossible for the audience to bear witness to it without feeling bad for Molly. Because she was making them feel bad about themselves.

Tamara thought about that goddamned picture again and hated herself for not trying to find some way to let water wash beneath her and Molly's bridge and bring some small measure of peace. Then she thought about the pleasant burn of gin gliding down her throat.

Her finger shook above the call icon beside Andrea's name, wanting to call her as any normal person would do. That had always been the audience's biggest question: Why didn't cast members just talk it out? If they were friends, why wouldn't they just pick up the phone and hash out the truth? But the casts overall were more gaggles of arranged marriages than they were circles of trust. If Tamara had learned anything from the network since the moment she signed her contract, it was that, excluding gravity and Sunday Funday, truth was a construct.

If she called, she risked exposing herself. What if Guy hadn't talked to Andrea? Maybe he had fabricated the entire thing just to throw her day to the wolves to see what would happen. If Andrea wasn't aware and Tamara asked her about it, the question would send her into a spiral and ruin her book signing. Her big day. The day she'd fought to have to herself.

Livid as she was, Tamara swallowed her pride in order to spare her friend and tucked her phone back into her purse.

There was a rap on the car's window, scaring her half to death. She looked out to see a sobbing Cyd staring in at her.

"Christ," she said under her breath as she lowered the window, pausing the music. "Cyd." She tilted her head to one side, feigning sympathy. "What's wrong?"

"What's *wrong*?" Cyd said sharply.

"I'm going to be honest. I'm just down here taking a bit of a breather, kiddo." Tamara tried to keep herself calm despite Cyd's manic energy. "So please don't shout."

"I didn't want you to be able to just . . . send me to voice mail." Her mascara was running.

"What do you mean?" Tamara asked.

"That's why I didn't call." She sniffed.

"I see."

"You must know what happened. It's everywhere!"

"I'm afraid I don't," Tamara said, praying to God the word wasn't out.

"Hec broke it off." Cyd's head dropped.

"Oh." Tamara was relieved.

"But that's not why I look like this!" She suddenly waved a hand across her face, indicating her disheveled look, her tone escalating. "I'm assuming Guy told you?" she choked out.

Tamara's stomach sank. She couldn't fucking take it anymore. She felt the warmth of her mammalian blood drain from her face, turning her cold and reptilian.

"What?" she snapped at the sniveling girl, then quickly tried to regain her composure, ". . . did he say?"

"That . . ." Cyd began. "That . . ." She hiccupped. "That . . ." Her face tightened. "That . . ." Tamara was about ready to lose it. "That . . . I'm fired!" She wailed in an almost cartoonlike manner. Tamara could practically see emoji tears spraying from her face. She really had learned from the best. Then her shriveling posture buckled her knees, and she fell to the ground, the back of her head making a worrying *thok* on the pavement.

"Jesus, Cyd!" Tamara rushed from her car to help the girl sit up.

Cyd held the back of her head with her left hand and kept bringing it in front of her face, checking for blood. Tamara could smell the alcohol on Cyd's breath, and even the bacteria-clad scent of fermented depression captured her and made her think about having that drink.

"Are you all right?" Tamara said, helping her to her feet.

"You didn't know?" Cyd asked.

"Apparently there's a lot I don't know," Tamara replied. She suddenly felt cast in some mysterious plot she hadn't asked to be part of or drawn into some conspiracy revolving around her own show that she somehow could not control or see coming.

"What did you tell him?" Cyd asked.

"I didn't tell him shit." Tamara was offended at Cyd's implication.

"Then why did he fire me?"

Tamara had known Guy and Apples were reconsidering what to do with Cyd. She'd been relatively sweet fodder for a fistful of years but didn't bring a whole lot of gravitas to the drama of the show. Mostly because, despite not always appearing to be the brightest bulb, she was boring. She didn't have many interests outside of simply being on the show. There were no more places to take her storyline. She had let becoming a cast member define her to the point of having nothing to do in the off-season except flutter over Twitter like a fretful pigeon.

But social media never lambasted Cyd for being vicious, even though she tried to keep up with the rest of them. That's why they had a field day with her; meanness didn't suit her. She was always in their firing line when it came to her intelligence. Even if it didn't reflect the truth, audiences delighted in how moronic her edit in the show made her look. Nothing, sadly, looking worse than the time she'd drunkenly exclaimed to her costar, Milan, "I have a degree in criminal justice, you fucking dodo!"

Guy felt bad that the camel's hump of her content had dried up. Continuing to have fun at her expense felt like beating a dead horse. There was little left to do with an Applebrity who ceased to entertain other than cut them loose.

"Cyd," Tamara began. "I'm sorry." She hung her head slightly, amazed this encounter had managed to help subdue her earlier anger. Tamara certainly liked and wanted things the exact way she liked and wanted them, but her loyal-to-a-fault nature meant she got no pleasure out of watching innocent people get hurt. She knew what it had been like to watch Molly melt down before her eyes, like a witch and a bucket of water. Now Tamara had gotten her own questionable call from Guy, and it made her wonder if at the end of this story was also her screaming doom.

"I know just about as much as you do," Tamara said, as Cyd continued to rub her head. "Are you okay?"

"I'm fine. I don't know. I had a few glasses of wine and I think that was a mistake." Cyd blinked, trying to bring her point into focus. "The show is named after you, Tam. How do you not know what's going on with your own show?"

Tamara wondered the same. "Let's get you inside, and we'll have a cup of coffee," she said.

"So all those people can see me like this? No thanks." She brushed a few strands of hair from her face with her long nails. "What did he tell you?"

"Nothing."

"He's just doing this all by himself? You don't get to make any decisions for your own show?"

"There are more of them than there are of me," Tamara said.

"But not than there are of us!" Cyd exclaimed, and Tamara was surprised to realize she hadn't ever really considered it that way; she'd been trying to fight the war all on her own.

"I'll call him and get more info," Tamara said, turning around to grab her purse from the passenger seat of her car.

"Let's call him together then!" Cyd grabbed Tamara's shoulder and cut her fuse in two. She whipped around and smacked Cyd's arm away from her. Cyd stared at her, dumbfounded.

"I will call him on my time," Tamara said sternly, locking her car. Cyd continued to stare. "*What?*" Tamara snapped.

"You're scared too," Cyd said.

"Oh, Jesus." She wouldn't hear any more of this and started to walk around the building to the front entrance of the studio. Cyd chased her.

"What did he tell you, Tam? Are you in trouble too? Is the show even coming back?" Her questions mounted, then she hiccupped and tripped slightly, and Tamara turned so their eyes would meet when Cyd regained her balance.

"I'm sorry," Cyd said, now looking at Tamara's face, taut with anger. "You let a few glasses of wine loosen your mouth enough to run it. I understand," Tamara said. "But you do not come down here and demand anything of me, understood? I don't owe you shit, girly. No one does. Least of all Guy. You were just a fucking barista here until we plucked you from obscurity and gave you your fifteen minutes. But I guess they're up. So, you either figure out what the fuck to do with yourself now that no one cares, or you keep drinking and find a way back in, just like the rest of us."

As nice a girl as Cyd was, all she wanted to do was sucker punch Tamara. But Cyd knew how that scenario would play out. She bit her lip and tried not to cry in front of the woman who had a reputation for reducing people to tears, then she about-faced and walked away without another word.

TAMARA WAS FORCED to reschedule her meeting about the new studio designs. She couldn't imagine trying to keep her composure around everyone while the back of her brain shouted "fire" in a crowded theater.

She called in a substitute to teach her class. It was something she rarely did because people came to the studio to learn from her, to meet her, but she wouldn't have been any good to them today. She'd have snapped at everyone, and that would've looked worse than bowing out. She thought about going home but knew the headspace she was in might result in her taking it out on Steph, which was the worst option of all.

She defaulted to getting lunch alone at the Formosa Cafe, her happy place. If she was going to chance being seen by anyone at least it wouldn't be on an empty stomach.

On the way, a call lit up her phone in its little air-conditioner dock. *Hips.*

Tori, another supporting cast member on *Tamandrea*, had been on the show since its beginning. After Tamara, she was the most popular instructor at the studio. Inevitably, she was folded into the drama. Everyone, including the producers and Tamara, referred to her as Hips. There was no question as to why.

Tamandrea was a show chock-full of pretty faces, but there was only ever going to be one Hips. Tamara hated to acknowledge it, but if someone had put a gun to her head, she would have admitted that Hips out danced her, even when she was in her prime. It was cause for a lot of tension. But despite Hips liking to challenge Tamara from time to time, and producers egging her on, she also knew who buttered her bread. It was the biggest reason Tamara kept her around; Hips was one of the few whose loyalty lay with her and not with Guy.

"Hey, Tam," Hips said before Tamara could speak.

"Hips. What's up?" Her stomach sank again as she wondered if everyone was going to call her with some new development from Guy.

"Hey," Hips repeated, and there was a long pause. She often called Tamara when she was high to talk about nothing, except during the off-season, when she called to subtly ask if Tamara knew about rate increases for primary cast members. "I'm watching that weird horse documentary on Netflix."

"Oh yeah. I hear that's the rage." Tamara winced at her dated word choice.

Another long pause. "Hey, have you talked to anyone at Apples recently?"

"That depends. Is this about money?"

"Maybe."

"Then no, I haven't talked to those people." Tamara breathed a sigh of relief.

"'Kay," Hips said.

"Hips," Tamara began, "how's Miles?"

Miles, Hips' husband, had also become a prominent character on the show. He was a rich young lawyer with a worrisome penchant for party favors. It had become cause for concern in their previous season.

"Fine, I think. Just working," she said lazily.

"Okay," Tamara said.

"Hey, Tam . . ."

"Yeah?"

"Guy wants me to go on his show next week."

Tamara took a deep breath. It was probably nothing. But she did appreciate the little soldier she'd trained, always reporting in when she thought Tamara should be aware of something.

"Oh, good. Good. That'll be good." Tamara paused, thinking that if Hips was going on Guy's show, they couldn't possibly be pulling the entire plug. Unless the plan was to shift the cast from *Tamandrea* to whatever a new show without her would be called.

"Are you okay?" Hips asked.

"I'm fine. Have you talked to Cyd?"

"No one talks to Cyd," Hips said flatly.

Tamara almost laughed but then felt a little bad considering her parting words with the girl. "Okay," she said. "I'm going to the Formosa for lunch. Want to join?"

"I'd love to, but . . . this horse documentary."

"You be safe," Tamara said awkwardly.

"Always." She could hear Hips's mellow smile on the other end of the line.

TAMARA SAT ALONE in a small booth at the Formosa Cafe and hated herself for waiting. Not because of slow service; the Formosa was her Cheers. She loved a taste of old Hollywood wherever possible. But she felt she'd made a mistake by going to a public place. She wasn't thinking clearly. All eyes seemed to make their way toward her, whether their owners knew who she was or not. She was chum in the water.

She held her menu as if she were a spy behind a newspaper. She felt a figure approach on the other side of it.

"You know, I've always wondered," a voice said. "How do you manage to be out at all these places and not be tempted?"

Her face fell with recognition. Simon Hudson, head writer for *Applause Magazine*. She lowered the menu. Even in the dim atmosphere, she despised his face more than anyone who had ever wronged her.

"*Tiger Beat*," she said. "Back at it."

"Why do you always come here alone?" he asked as he sat opposite her.

"Because I hate people," she told him coolly, looking back at her menu. "Don't sit."

"And why do you pretend to look at the menu every time you come in here like you don't always get the General Tso's cauliflower?" he asked, flexing his ability to track her every move, know her every whim, report on every shit she took.

"I'm aware you think of yourselves as journalists, but stalking and reporting on reality TV stars is hardly cutting-edge content anymore, Simon." She shut the menu in front of her. "I can smell the desperation, and it is not a flattering scent."

Simon waved over a server. "Heard some interesting news today," he said, and Tamara's insides were yanked at opposite ends. "Cyd got let go, huh?"

"Oh, that," she said as the server arrived.

"She'll have the usual," Simon blurted out. "I'll have a Negroni, please."

The server paused.

"Is there a problem?" Simon asked.

"Ms. Collins?" the server asked, having a rapport with her.

"Yes, yes. General Tso's," she said, waving the server off, hating Simon for knowing her go-to.

"Care to make a statement?" he asked her.

"No, not at the moment," she said, pulling her phone from her purse, screen light illuminating her face in the dark ambiance.

"Also heard something else." He waited for her to acknowledge him. "You know, I come by myself to this place to be left alone."

"We all know that's not true." He laughed, looking over his shoulder at a group of girls staring at her and smiling.

"How much do they pay you?" she asked.

"Enough," he said.

"I imagine you and your little bullpen full of Woodward and Bernsteins must really be up to your ears in drama today if you've been here waiting for me."

The brief period between a season's finale and filming for the next season was always when the muckrakers lay in wait for them, looking for stories anywhere they could find them. It was like the thrill of going to spring training with the hopes that something exciting might happen even though everyone knew it wouldn't.

"Don't you want to know what my sources told me?" Simon smiled at the server who brought his drink. He sipped it as a little victory.

She looked up at him from her phone, her expression cold and unfeeling, not wanting to give any hint of knowing what he knew. "By 'sources,' do you mean those little newsies standing on the corner of Twitter and Instagram, hocking headlines like 'Read all about it! Hector Espinoza! Was he fucking Molly Mandrie?'" She mocked him with an old-fashioned tone, not afraid to raise her voice for emphasis.

"Were they?" He smirked.

"You are so sad," she said, scoffing.

"Do you miss Molly?"

"Yes," she said, phone back up.

"What would you say to her if she was still here?"

"She's dead, Simon. There's no need to answer that question."

"Do you wish you'd worked to repair your friendship?"

"We remained friends."

"On paper."

"In life."

"And in death?"

She watched him take a swig now and had the sudden urge to smash the glass against the side of his head.

"Am I going to have to politely ask you to get the fuck out of my face? I'm starting to feel harassed," she said.

The gaggle of staring girls slid up behind Simon. Tamara turned on her charm and acknowledged them, grateful for the distraction.

"Ladies," she said.

"Ms. Collins," one of them began, fumbling with her phone. The other two were beaming, smiles glued to their faces in a perfect mixture of fear and adoration.

"Oh, God. Not 'Ms. Collins,' please," Tamara said. "Would you like a photo?"

They nodded and squeaked.

"Simon, be a sport and take the photo." She encouraged the girls to sit next to her in the booth.

Simon limply took the phone and snapped a few pictures.

"Do you want to check them?" another of the girls asked.

"I'm gonna look how I look, sweetheart," Tamara said, as if there were nothing she could do about it. To her, forty-four might as well have been fifty, and looking for and obsessing over minute details and flaws exhausted her. She was either going to be happy, or she was going to be unhappy. However she felt on a particular day, that was how she was going to look.

"I've been in love with you since I was like thirteen," one of the girls said.

"Thank you," Tamara said with a small bow of her head. "Hard to believe you aren't still thirteen. You tell Michael behind the bar that your next round's on me, okay?"

Their little Santa's-elf faces lit up in the low light like a Thomas Kinkade pastiche, and they scuttled off. Simon sat back down as they headed for the bar.

"I heard Andrea's getting her own show," he said, going for it.

Tamara was already on her phone, ignoring him, but he watched her hand squeeze it instinctively.

"Did you hear what I said?" he asked.

"Is that what someone told you? I hadn't heard."

"She's having her book signing today at the Grove."

"I know."

"Are you gonna go?"

"Well, let's see . . ." She tapped her phone and checked the time. "It's three thirty-seven now. I guess if I finish here around four thirty, I'll still have time to make it by five."

"So, you're going?" he asked.

"Why don't you meet me there?" she said with a smile.

"Is that a serious offer?"

"I don't think you're going to know unless you get the fuck out of my face, keep your nose out of my business, and slink down there to wait in line with everybody else. Will you?"

"Your tone is pretty telling, Tam."

The overhead light lit her almost like she was being interrogated. But she leaned forward, tired of his game, the shadows moving to bring out her bad side. "My friends call me Tam," she said. "Those little girlies over there—they can call me Tam. But no one at your low-rent Hearst publication, least of all you, is going to call me *Tam*." She overpronounced it, mocking him.

"I'm sorry, *Tamara*." His tone followed hers.

"No, no," she corrected him. "Until you've done a lick of legitimate work to prove yourself as a friend and not a foe, you're going to have to show a little fucking respect. Presently, you can call me Your Highness. And once your hackneyed, clickbait, bullshit career ceases to sell in Sodom and Gomorrah, maybe then I'll let you come back here and kiss my feet and beg for forgiveness. But for now, you can fuck right off."

Her food was set down in front of her.

"I'm done with him," she said to her server, shooing Simon like he was an unwanted appetizer.

Simon knew he couldn't be forced to leave, but he wasn't about to make a scene at Tamara's favorite hangout and risk upsetting his bosses. Even though he liked to push and poke and prod, he still had a job to do. He needed the story.

He stood, flashing a grin, then started to walk away.

"Simon!" she called to him.

He turned, and she threw a handful of salt at him.

"Oh no," she said blandly. "You looked back."

8.

FIEVEL/ELLIOT

FIEVEL SAT BOLT upright in a private room at the Palomino Club, watching the dancer in front of him, his knee pulsing up and down like a piston. She rubbed her tits against his face, clad delicately in a thin top. He knew he wouldn't get the glitter off his skin for days.

He remembered the first time he'd dragged Elliot to a strip club, before *MML*, when they were in their early twenties. Elliot was approached by two girls on the floor who told him they wanted to show him something and to come with them. He did. Then Fievel looked over his shoulder to see both girls grinding on a rigid, nervous Elliot. A floor dance.

When he returned, he lamented to Fievel that whatever it was they had wanted to show him had cost him a hundred dollars.

"Then why did you go with them?" Fievel asked.

"Because they said they wanted to show me something!" Elliot said, his innocence persisting.

Fievel smiled at the memory.

"I don't want to say I'm a big fan, but, well . . ." The girl slid her hand down over his groin and cupped it.

"I am also a fan," he said, breathing faster.

"How far do you wanna go?" she said, biting her bottom lip.

"To tell you the truth, I thought we were gonna do drugs back here. Is that not what's happening?"

"Anything can happen. How far do you wanna go?" she repeated.

Fievel thought maybe she hadn't heard him the first time, so as she spun around and slid down him, he shouted, "I thought we were going to do drugs back here!"

"We can do whatever you want, baby." She reached a hand into his pants.

He grabbed her forearm gently and stopped her, feeling put on. "Drugs. I want to do drugs. You said Rodney sent you over."

"You want to do that first? You don't want to warm up a little?" She pushed past his resistance, and her hand gripped his cock, and he scooted back a little, surprised, then said, "How much does a warm-up cost?"

ELLIOT WALKED TO the bar and leaned against it, setting his empty pint glass down. A dancer made her way to him and began to compliment him, but he brushed her off with, "I'm good, thanks," and she walked away.

He took a seat, and the bartender refilled his water. Elliot dropped a one on the bar and spun around on the stool like a little kid, sipping the water through a paper straw. If he couldn't get himself into a sexy mood, he could at least appreciate that this establishment was environmentally conscious.

He had retreated to the bar so as not to look cheap sitting at the rail for too long. That first time he had gone to a strip club, Fievel had also bought him a proper lap dance. He was twenty-four and drunkenly kept asking the dancer what she really wanted to do career-wise. Afterward he sat alone up front, as he'd been doing now, again fumbling his way through proper etiquette. A girl approached him, but rather than whisper sweet nothings to him, she shouted, "If you're not gonna tip, get off the fucking rail!" After that he tended to stay in the back of most places to avoid confrontation.

He was tempted to turn his phone back on but knew there wouldn't be a text from Andrea. He decided against it. He wondered how her book signing had gone.

At forty-two, Elliot had never been in a long-term relationship. He didn't count anything that had occurred before he turned twenty-one. His time with Andrea, if he could fool himself into thinking it had been a relationship, would've been the longest. Though he struggled with the idea of ever really being in a relationship. For the most part, all he had ever known after high school was his relationship with Fievel.

Fievel had inherited piles of his father's money and had never been required to consider having a real job. Elliot was amazed at how, until Fievel began to date Molly, being rich allowed him to trick himself into feeling busy because he could afford to be boring. His schedule was always packed. And he was paying everyone around him to make him feel like he had a purpose. Music producers, videographers, DJs, shamans, spirit guides, personal trainers, even girlfriends. Fievel's idea of a healthy relationship was one he paid for. He liked his idea of fun the most, assuming what he liked, others would also. Mostly, he wanted everyone else to have the good time that he didn't have growing up and wanted to give the love he never got.

If he were asked what the nicest thing was about Fievel, Elliot would have said that at least he always paid. On time and without hesitation. He tipped generously. He freely gave bonuses and bought everyone nearly everything they—especially Elliot—wanted. Early in his life, because of his father's take-no-charity-keep-your-hands-dirty-and-your-blood-on-the-streets-of-New-York attitude, Elliot never could have imagined accepting the kinds of gifts Fievel showered him with. Shoes, watches, suits, haircuts, frequently random salary raises. None of it came because Elliot had asked; it came because Fievel had wanted to give it. There were certainly worse things he could do. But after a while, Elliot began to wonder about ownership. Outside of being paid for his driving, he didn't need Fievel's money. But his job had been a blurred line for twenty years, and he wasn't even sure what the money meant anymore. There was no distinction between work and friendship. Work was friendship. But friendship was also work.

"Gawker," a girl's voice said, startling him.

"I'm good, thanks," he said, not looking at her.

"I don't work here, shithead."

He looked over. She didn't look like she worked there.

"Shit. Sorry," he said.

She sat next to him. "You are a picture-perfect asshole right now, you know that?"

"I am aware."

"You should really buy a dance. Or tip the dancers, at least. Or drink a fucking beer. Christ. Water?"

"Hey." He turned to her. "I'm here with a friend, okay? He's getting a dance. Probably a lot more than that. From what I hear, those things are very expensive. And . . . I sat at the tip rail for fifteen minutes and have already spent fifty dollars. Not all in ones, mind you. So please pardon me for not wanting a perfect stranger to rub their naked body all over mine."

She stared at him for a long moment, then smiled. "So, you really are like this in real life?"

"Like what?"

"Like how you are on TV."

"No, we're all caricatures," he said, sipping his water through the softening paper straw.

"God, what crawled up your ass and died?"

"Molly Mandrie," he said. And she got very quiet.

"Fuck," she finally said.

"Yeah."

"Sorry. I forgot."

"So has everyone else, apparently." He placed his empty glass on the bar behind him. She didn't leave. He could feel her presence squashing him, but he refused to look at her.

"I'm Brit."

"Hey, Brit."

The bartender refilled the water. Elliot dropped another one.

"I guess I didn't really know how to come up and talk to you," Brit said.

"You could've asked me how I was doing."

"How are you doing?"

"Fucking phenomenally."

"Can I ask you something else?"

"You're going to anyway." He didn't mind being a dick when he wasn't in the mood to deal with fans.

"Are you and Andrea talking?"

He looked at her, his mouth drawn in a straight line. "Why are you here, Brit?"

"I'm here with my boyfriend," she said, and pointed to a skinny dark-haired, tattooed man watching the dancer on stage.

"You come to strip clubs with your boyfriend?" he asked.

"Sure. You came here with Fievel. Two dudes at a strip club together is weirder than a couple."

"Huh." He had never considered it that way.

"It was my idea," she said.

"I see." Elliot watched the boyfriend try to coolly throw a handful of ones out onto the stage, an attempt to make it rain like he was some sort of a baller. But half of the bills stalled midair and fell pitifully to the ground, so he picked them back up and refolded them, saving them for later.

"What're you guys up to, tonight?" she asked.

"Not sure." He checked his watch. Only 6:49 p.m. The darkness of a strip club always played tricks on his mind. "It's early."

"Well, we're going to a party in a friend's suite at the Bellagio."

"That sounds like fun. You stay safe."

"Do you guys wanna come?"

"I don't know. I'll have to check with Fievel. We'll come find you."
He hoped she'd take the hint.

"Okay. Lotsa pretty girls. A cornucopia of drugs," she said, thinking
that would entice him. But the idea of that strange Thanksgiving
conch overflowing with illicits didn't quite tantalize him the way the
image of a cornucopia had when he was a kid and normal things like
squashes and apples and cinnamon sticks were tumbling from it.

"IS THAT GOOD?" the dancer asked Fievel, his breathing keeping
pace with her hand.

"Yeah. Yeah, that's good," he said, looking up at the ceiling.

"Good," she said. Then she kissed him.

"Tell me—" He paused.

"Tell you what, baby?" In her hand she could feel him retreating,
burying himself inside a head full of thoughts. His eyes were closed.

"Fuck," he said, knowing his dick was failing him.

"What do you want me to tell you?" she asked. "I'm here for you."
She straddled him and pressed her fingers into the nape of his neck,
massaging it lightly.

"It's stupid."

"I can bet whatever it is you want me to say isn't nearly as crazy as
some of the things I've done."

He cupped a hand around the back of her head and pulled her
face close to his. "Stay like this," he said. Her body ground against
his. He got a flash of that brutal final image of Molly in his mind
and tried to erase it.

"Okay," she said. "And what should I tell you?"

"Keep eye contact with me," he said. "And tell me you love me,"
he blurted out.

"I love you, baby," she said in a sexy tone, not skipping a beat.

"No, not—don't just say it like that back to me." He felt himself slipping.

"I love you," she said an octave lower, and it almost sounded like she meant it.

He had a short-lived sensation of what it might feel like to finish. But he retreated again. He pushed her off him, not able to unsee Molly dangled over the street below like some cheap party store piñata.

"What did I do?" she said.

"Nothing," he said. "Fuck. Nothing. I'll still pay for the warm-up, or whatever. And the K."

She stood and looked at him, reading him.

"What?" he asked.

He felt the weight of her gaze assessing him.

"No," she finally said.

"What do you mean, 'no'?" He took a wad of cash out of his pocket.

"I'm not selling it to you."

"I said I'd pay for the warm-up."

"Just pay for the dance," she said. "But I don't know if K is a good idea for you right now."

"What are you, my fucking mom?" he said. "I thought you guys did fucking anything for money."

"Well, we don't," she said sternly.

"Fine. Fine. Just sell me the drugs, and we're square."

"How about I don't sell you the drugs, and we're square?"

"That doesn't make any sense."

She sighed. The act was gone.

"Are you okay?" she asked.

"I'm fine. Are *you* okay?" He felt like he had to shove his impotence back onto her.

"You just seem so sad."

"Hey—"

"No." She held up a hand to stop him. "I just . . . fuck."

"What?" he said.

"The 'tell me you love me' thing."

"Oh, well, *fuck me* for having a fetish!"

"Yeah, but, like . . . your ex-girlfriend just died," she said. "So, is it a fetish?"

"I cannot believe I'm having this conversation with a stripper." He started to pace.

"Dancer."

"Whatever!"

"I'm sorry, okay?" She gathered her things.

"I don't want 'sorry'; I want the drugs you promised me!" he shouted, and there was a knock at the door.

"I don't have them," she confessed.

"You what?"

"I told Rodney I did because I wanted to fuck you. But it's clear that's not going to happen."

"Oh Jesus, you're just another fucking fan!"

She opened the door, revealing a bouncer. "I guess so. But you're clearly going through something. And I'm not sure drugs are the best idea."

She left and the bouncer blocked Fievel's exit.

"Fucking *wow*!" he yelled as she disappeared. "Wow, lady! You are *hilarious*!" But his words fell like stones to the bottom of the pool of blaring music.

The bouncer took two lumbering steps forward.

"Yeah, I got it, Colossus," Fievel said, handing him a wad of cash.

He swept out across the club floor looking for Elliot so they could leave without any further embarrassment. He was certain the dancer would have spread the word about his inability to get hard and that all eyes would be on him. And that if she wanted to, she could talk shit about him on social. About how Five-El came into her club and couldn't get it up, because he needed his dead ex-girlfriend to coddle him and tell him how loved he was, and how he was a fucking pussy.

He saw Elliot talking to Brit and slid up to them, very out of breath.

"What's up?" Fievel exhaled. "Who's this? Hey, how are you?"

"This is Brit," Elliot said.

"I'm Brit," she said.

"Cool, cool, cool, cool, cool," Fievel said rapidly.

"Did you do coke?" Elliot asked him.

"What? No." Fievel's eyes darted around the floor, a bead of sweat falling down his face. "No. No, man. Hey! You wanna get outta here?"

"What happened back there?" Elliot asked.

"Nothing. Literally nothing. I got a half chub and told her to fuck off. She was a bad dancer. I don't trust drugs from bad dancers."

"We're heading to a party at a friend's suite soon," Brit said, gesturing to her boyfriend.

"Dope," Fievel said. Then to Elliot, as if she were not there, he said, "Who is this?"

"Brit," Elliot repeated.

"Yeah, I'm Brit," she said again.

"What, have you guys been practicing this fucking routine out here?" Fievel asked, unnecessarily incensed.

"No," Elliot said, gritting his teeth, trying to send Fievel a sign that he did not want to go anywhere with Brit or her sinewy boyfriend.

"If you're looking for party favors, we have them," she said.

"Then that's where we're going!" Fievel said loudly, clapping. "Let's go!" Then he laughed because people were looking at him and he didn't know what else to do. "Let's go now," he said quieter but still laughing.

"Yeah?" she asked. "Seriously?"

"Brit"—Fievel placed his hands on her shoulders—"I have never been more serious about wanting to get the fuck out of a place in my entire life."

"I'll tell Nevin," she said. "Holy shit, he's gonna be so stoked to party with you guys. He fucking loves you."

"Cool, cool, cool, cool, cool," Elliot mocked Fievel.

She scuttled away.

Outside, Fievel took a deep breath as if he'd had the wind knocked out of him.

"What the hell did you do?" Elliot asked him.

"Nothing. I said, 'Literally nothing' inside. I'm using 'literally' literally, okay? Not like people who say it and don't actually know how to properly apply it."

"Okay, okay. Jesus." Elliot could tell something had gotten to Fievel. "And you're sure she didn't slip something into your drink?"

"Positive."

"Did she say her boyfriend's name was Nevin?" Elliot asked.

"Sounded like it."

"Huh."

"Bro, what happened?" Rodney's voice came from behind them as he stepped outside the club.

"What do you mean?" Fievel asked, panicked. "Nothing happened!"

"She said you bailed on her."

"What?" he asked incredulously. "That is patently false!"

"She said you changed your mind. Didn't want them," Rodney said.

Fievel felt a wave of relief wash over him. He'd never thought he'd feel gratitude to a stripper for not blowing his emotional cover, but there he was. "Yes. That—yes. She's right, Rodney! She. Is. Right. I did change my mind. I did. I—you know, I've got another show tomorrow at the 'Cana—"

"Don't call it that," Elliot said quickly.

"At the *Copacabana*!" Fievel overcorrected. "And I'm tired."

"Bro, it's not even seven yet!" Rodney teased him.

"I know, I know." Fievel put his hands and arms up as if he'd been caught in the act. "But that's the thing about being in your forties, man. Those nine p.m. bedtimes!"

Brit and Nevin walked out.

"You guys ready?" Brit said. "Want me to text you the room number?"

"Nine p.m. bedtime, huh?" Rodney said.

"Ha! Rodney! Such a jokester!" Fievel shouted.

"Who's this?" Rodney asked.

"Brit," Fievel and Elliot simultaneously answered for her.

"I'm Brit." She reached her hand out to shake Rodney's, but he just looked at it.

"Dude, this is fucking unbelievable," Nevin said walking up to Elliot and Fievel. "Are you fucking *serious* right now?" He vigorously clapped twice. "We gonna get fucked up or what?"

"Nevin, please stop shouting," Fievel said.

"Keep it down, bro," Rodney said.

"Yes, thank you, Rod," Fievel said. "And no, Brit. Just tell us the room number, and Elliot will write it down."

"Let's meet at the casino bar for a drink first," Nevin said.

"Yes, better plan," Fievel said. "We'll see you there."

Brit and Nevin almost skipped away from them, hand in hand like they were going down the yellow brick fucking road.

"What are we doing?" Elliot asked, confounded.

"We are going to party with Brit and Nevin," Fievel said matter-of-factly.

Rodney laughed.

"Okay." And Elliot relinquished himself yet again to his fate, remembering that for Fievel, Guy and Apples producers did not have to work hard to come up with story lines for him or his show. They simply had to wait for the wind to change.

9.

ANDREA

YOGA DID NOTHING to relax her. She wanted to check her phone but knew if she did, she'd be *that* girl. People checking their phones during class did not have good reputations.

She ran through a sort of to-do list in her mind to walk herself backward from the fear Guy might slip her some bad news just before she had to get in front of a room full of people and talk about her book. She had woken up early. Practiced. Eaten breakfast. Checked in with Essence. Showered. Done her makeup, gym look. Gotten to yoga on time. Despite having been awake for only three hours, she felt monumentally accomplished, but she always tended to take on more than she could handle to convince herself she was productive—also in the hopes that she would never upset Apples and lose her job.

Was that why Guy had told her to call him? Would she be losing her job? The show hadn't technically been renewed yet. This was her least favorite time of year, when all the women on the show questioned their value.

Her stomach bucked and she burped, tasting oatmeal and blueberries.

The gentle touch of the instructor reminded her she was a few seconds late to the next pose. She had forgotten to breathe. She adjusted her body and decided Guy had nothing but good news. That was much more comforting than the alternative. Maybe she would be getting a raise. She had fought last season to make the same amount of money Tamara had been making but still managed to fall just under her.

In an attempt to keep up the illusion that what happened on the show happened in real life, Apples was constantly trying to dissuade cast members from writing books. Andrea in particular had a habit of letting the public know via Twitter that the way she was edited in the show was not always the way reality had played out. She had been in hot water after posting screenshots of texts and emails and even her own iPhone videos of certain events to prove that she hadn't been crazy or stupid or drunk or being a bitch, as viewers might claim and as haters might attack her for. She had wanted the truth to be known. That made the network look like liars. And they did not like looking like liars.

But often, no matter the evidence she presented, viewers who had negative opinions about her would not be swayed by things they felt could be easily photoshopped or faked. Sometimes she doubted anyone would even believe she was dead, should her story line come to that horrible conclusion.

Even though Guy appeared like a benevolent father, deep down, like everyone else, she was scared of him. He had the power to run his thoughts all the way up the food chain of the network and make or break anyone. An invitation to appear on his show meant one of two things. If he liked someone, it could mean increasing their visibility and improving their image. If Guy Maker told America that Andrea was his favorite, many would echo that approval. But for a lot of cast members, it meant that if he wanted to fuck with them, they would be at his absolute disposal. Talking back was frowned on. And defending oneself to try to present the truth was considered talking back. If a guest was in his cross hairs the day they appeared on his show, they had no other option but to take the hit, all the while smiling and laughing as if the humiliation was their idea.

The last time Andrea had been a guest on *WHH,S!* the other guests had included the young actor Brando Keates and Cyd. At the time, Brando had just done some promos for the Splice dating app alongside Fievel, and after a bit of teasing, Guy had asked Cyd to pull out her phone to sign up for the service on live television. She balked, and Guy asked her to be a good sport. Then she confessed to everyone that she already had a profile and the audience erupted in laughter, and she went red. Guy then asked for her phone so he could hold it up to the camera and show the world her profile. She nervously complied. Inevitably, the details of how she presented herself on the dating app became the butt of everyone's jokes for weeks after.

Andrea felt bad for not saying anything against the invasion of Cyd's privacy. But at the end of the day, even Cyd knew what Andrea also knew, what they all knew—if you wanted to keep your job, you had to play along. Bullying masked as playful ribbing came with the territory. So Cyd smiled and leaned into it and called herself the names others had always called her. Acknowledging on live television that she was just a basic bitch.

Andrea had managed to block the incident out of her mind for the most part, but she was nauseous thinking of it now. Cyd was always getting chewed up and spit out for sport. It was the only way the network could turn someone who was otherwise boring and regular into good television. That was the way it was. Only people who were crazy enough to already be fully formed characters got instantaneous fame—big personalities like Molly and Tamara and Fievel. Even Andrea had had to spend a few years on *MML* becoming someone of substance before audiences took her seriously enough to think she deserved her own show.

After class, the fan from before tried to talk to her again, but her nerves and inability to remember his name had her politely brushing him off as she walked quickly away and back toward her apartment. Her stomach kept creeping up into her throat until, eventually, the anxiety dam broke and she threw up behind a parked car. As far as she knew, she had avoided anyone seeing her. The last thing she needed was someone's cell phone video of her hurling her guts out onto the steaming-hot blacktop.

She took a moment to catch her breath and wiped the corners of her mouth with her thumb and forefinger, then took a swig of her water and spat it out onto the street. Then the fan's voice came from behind her.

"Oh, God, are you okay?" he asked.

She spun around to meet his gaze, but he was staring at the fresh pile of puke in the street. She would have rather he walked in on her naked.

"What happened?" he said.

"Nothing." She tried to play it off. "Think I just got a small bug from whatever I ate this morning."

"The worst," he said. "What did you eat?"

"Oatmeal," she said, looking around and seeing no one else. She could have sworn she hadn't seen him behind her just prior to her throwing up. Had he been hiding somewhere? She let her mind wander to the worst place, that true crime place.

"Listen." She tried to remain polite. "I've got a huge day ahead of me. I've got to get back to—"

"I know, I know! I'm sorry. I just . . ." His voice trailed off. "It sounds crazy because I know I see you in class all the time, but—" He stopped himself and suddenly looked wounded. He tapped his foot and folded his top lip tightly under his bottom in an effort not to cry.

"Do you remember my name?" he said through a choked-up throat.

"Of course I do," she lied, not knowing what else to say.

He waited patiently for her to tell him, but he could see in her eyes how sorry she was as she plumbed the depths of her mind and came up empty.

She panicked and said, "Michael."

His face fell and he looked hollow. "That's my boyfriend's name."

"I'm sorry." She hung her head a little. She hated being put on the spot or in a position where she couldn't help but look bad, as she often was on her show.

"I see you like twice a week," he said.

"I'm so sorry. I just—I meet a lot of people, you know?" she said helplessly, knowing he was now another crestfallen fan with a story to take to *Applause Magazine* or to post on Twitter about how he'd been mistreated and how she'd actually just been a huge bitch all along.

"I know you do," he said sadly. "I guess I just thought, I don't know, since we see each other regularly, maybe we were becoming friends."

Although she felt bad, this wasn't her first rodeo with this type of situation. Fans, especially on social media, tended to confuse interacting with reality TV stars with the building of a legitimate bond. If a handful of DMs were exchanged, fans felt seen in a way they'd never expected to. Here their idols were, like Michelangelo's cherub-supported God, reaching gently out to deign the exposed and unworthy Adam with a touch of life.

Like any cast member on an Apples show, Andrea simply met too many people, saw too many faces, and heard too many names. Without scrapbooking them all with corresponding photos, remembering them was impossible. She had forgotten this fan's name long ago, but because she saw him regularly, she hadn't had the heart to tell him or ask for it again. She hadn't anticipated seeing him as often as she did. And she'd dreaded this moment more than most. It would have been a simple ask. But she'd chosen not wanting to look forgetful over admitting he was just a drop in her bucket.

"I'm sorry," she said again, her guilt honest. "Do you mind telling me again?"

He stared at her for a long moment. The color drained from his face, and his hands tightened into fists. She worried he might hit her. It wouldn't have been the first time a female cast member had been assaulted by a fan—far from it. Molly had practically egged it on as a sport.

"It doesn't matter now," he said. Then, almost as immediately as it had taken him over, his rage released him, and his disposition brightened, as if a cloud had briefly blocked the sun. "I'm sure I'll see you again sometime." Then he playfully plucked her bra strap again, turned, and walked up the sloped street to the right.

She watched him walk away for several paces, then turned and jogged home faster than normal.

SHE STEPPED OUT from a cold shower and stared at her phone. She did the math in her head to ensure she could make all her obligations on time. People could say what they liked about her attitudes and behaviors on the show, but she was nothing if not perfectly punctual. Something that often became a point of conflict between her and Hips, who was routinely, if not intentionally, late. The reason Andrea and Tamara had gotten along so well in their early days, even before Andrea became an *MML* cast member, was that Tamara was someone who held others to her standards. She lived by the three *p*'s: purpose, professionalism, and punctuality. Andrea, new to LA and eager to please, had been happy to oblige wherever and whenever she could.

She remembered her first lunch with Tam outside of work, how she'd felt like she was sitting across from a legend who was willing to grace her with what spare time she had. Andrea had felt desired as a new friend, which was nice, since she had found friendships harder and harder to make as an adult.

Tamara saw in Andrea the salt of the earth. She knew there was little of that in her city. She also knew how quickly it could be spoiled if it wasn't fostered by the right people. When Apples asked Andrea if she'd like to be brought in for a few scenes while they were filming season six of *MML*, she asked Tamara's permission first. Grateful her instincts had identified Andrea's loyal behavior, Tamara said yes. In her eyes, Andrea had yet to be tainted with the intoxication of being on TV. It could be fun for her. And they could have a lot of fun together. But it was important that Tamara tell her something no one else would, especially not Guy.

"It is worse than any drug," Tamara said. "So, you've got to make sure you keep your wits about you when the cameras start rolling. Because it can be five, six, seven years before you know it, and if you give yourself over to it completely, it will take you. Once you become a part of this, to the rest of the world, you cease to be you."

"What do you mean?" Andrea assumed she was trying to talk her out of going on the show.

"There's a lot of people who come and go on these shows. Even for the ones who stay, they all think they've got *it*. Even if they've got money like Fievel where the I. T. factor doesn't really matter; most everyone lets this go to their head. But the truth is, unless you're smart with your money and your image, inevitably when all this comes to an end, you will be no one."

"Do you think you've got 'it'?" she asked.

"Sweetheart, I had it." Tamara chuckled. "There's a difference. This is my second shot. There isn't a lot of fame and fortune on the road ahead for a worn-out choreographer from *Dance Battle*."

"But you were amazing on that show."

"Thank you. But why do you think I opened the studio? Started a clothing line?" Tamara patted Andrea's hands. "TV fame with a network like Apples is Diet Coke. Don't forget that. Nobody thinks it's bad for them. Tastes great. No sugar. What's the harm? They guzzle it down. Then it turns out the ingredients are all fake and it's rotting everyone from the inside."

Tamara waved their server over to order another glass of wine. "You're going to be a big deal right now, but you're not going to be a big deal twenty years from now unless you're a movie star or a mess," she said. "So, don't put your everything in Apples' basket. This isn't an Easter egg hunt. It's a dog and pony show. We can have years' worth of fun doing the song and dance, but eventually our knees will give out, and we'll get ugly, and enough time will pass, and unless we also worked to establish ourselves outside of this thing, nobody will give one single fuck about us. And that's a promise. This isn't your end goal. This is your stepping stone."

Until writing her book, Andrea had spent much of her eleven years with Apples floundering, wondering who she would be if the curtain was suddenly pulled back and everyone saw the wizard. But Guy's behavior while they were filming their most recent season had started her thinking in new directions. And when he didn't go to Molly's funeral, her doubts began to snowball. Few things pissed Andrea off. She and Molly had never been particularly close, but Molly had made them all. Andrea had to give credit to her for being the first. Guy should have done the same with his presence at her send off. But he didn't. And that pissed her off.

She used to wonder who he might be if his curtain had been pulled back. Now she was starting to understand his greatest trick. By starting his own talk show, he had pulled back the curtain on himself and the network. He flaunted the levers and gears and strings pulled in plain sight. That was the true sleight of hand. By showing the audience the mechanics of how the watch worked, he got everyone so focused on the cogs that cranked the machine that they never really knew what time it was.

Andrea stared again at the text he had sent. That he couldn't let her have her day without making his omnipotence known irked her. She was working to fully realize the advice Tamara had given her long ago: To create something for herself outside the show. To be her authentic self. But as soon as she'd started pushing back against the system, Guy had started to elbow his way in to take partial credit for what she had written. She didn't want to think about him. She just wanted to go about the rest of her day without throwing up her nerves in the street again. But the anxiety of not responding to something work related, of not answering the expectations of those in power, forcibly brought her finger to the screen. She lightly tapped the call icon, pressing the phone to her ear. With each ring, her heart beat faster. She was unsure if the beads on her body were water or sweat.

Guy answered, and after a handful of pleasantries and well-wishes, he took a calm, even tone like he was going to break the news to her that someone had been in a terrible accident. Only he told her exactly what he'd told Tamara. The details, of course, were yet to be determined, and there were fires he needed to put out before anything could be said for certain. But he'd wanted her to hear it from him just in case anything leaked to the press. She asked him if she should call Tamara, but he warned her against it. She knew how Tamara could be. She had a tendency to overreact. She could get angry. This was so stressful, he assumed, that it might even drive her back to drink. He would handle her. He wished her a broken leg at her signing and promised if there were any further developments, she would be the first to know.

After they hung up, Andrea wondered if she'd be branded a traitor. She wondered what would happen to the show and if it could sustain breaking the band up. She knew, no matter how he phrased it, this news would not sit well with Tam. It was only a matter of time before they would have it out over this. Now Andrea was torn between mother and father. She owed everything at present to both of them, but it was Tamara who had brought her gently and supportively into the fold. Guy had taken it from there.

10.

NIXON

Nixon and her mother arrived at the downtown studio of Todrick Kidd. It possessed the same aesthetic charm everything in downtown did: well-worn but timeless, classic but modern, upscale but a stone's throw from Skid Row.

"Remember what we talked about?" Samantha asked Nixon, who slung a small backpack over one shoulder.

"Yes."

He came out to meet them.

"The once and future queen!" he shouted, raising his arms in excitement. His high energy and handsome face broke through Nixon's mood, and she smiled. "Amazing fucking album," he said. Then he said, "Ohp!" and covered his mouth. "Sorry, Mom."

Samantha smirked, knowing he was displaying a deliberate coolness to put her daughter at ease.

"How was the drive?" he asked.

"Oh, you know," Samantha said with a smile, a subtle dig at her daughter's attitude. "Just swell!"

"Traffic not too bad?"

"Same as usual."

"What games did you play?"

"I'm sorry?" Samantha said.

"You know, like car games." He was trying to be chummy. He looked at Nixon. "Twenty questions and I-spy and stuff."

"We don't really play games," Nixon said quietly.

His eyes drifted between the two of them, sensing tension.

"Okay! Well, let's take a look at the space together, and then we can look at your wardrobe options," he said.

That was Nixon's least favorite phrase. Even though she had a new, high-profile manager and was working with one of the most sought-after photographers in LA, she was still required to drag her own wardrobe around. Since this was her first album and they felt they had overpaid for its production, the label had decided that when it came to hair, makeup, and wardrobe, the little starlet would be left to fend for herself. Nixon didn't exactly know what "making it" meant. But she knew she'd have made it the moment she wasn't required to bring a single stitch of her own clothing to fittings and shoots.

The three of them wandered the large open space. There were several wall facades that could be used to emulate specific backgrounds or to bring in a light texture as a backdrop. The building's actual walls were classic exposed red brick. And at the space's farthest point was a traditional white cyc wall. With a gentle curve at the bottom, it met the floor in an effortless slope, an architectural truce.

"I know we're going postapocalyptic with all this, so we'll spend most of the day here," he said, kicking his shoes off and taking a few steps in his socks onto the white floor. "Mom, I do ask that you stay off this if you don't mind." His head gestured to Samantha's feet, hugging the pristine white edge. She hopped back suddenly, like the floor was lava.

"Sorry!" she said.

"Just want to keep it clean," he said.

"Of course, of course." Samantha's head kept twirling as she looked around the studio. She couldn't shake the feeling that it wasn't really all that special. They'd worked with plenty of photographers before.

To a large degree, it was always the same. But she'd let herself get caught up in Todrick's name, which meant more than most.

"I think we'll also want to venture outside a little and capture some of the authenticity of the neighborhood," he said.

"Outside, like outside this building? Like out there?" Samantha asked.

"Mom." Nixon tried to shush her, not wanting to be embarrassed in front of the Kidd.

"I'm just saying, is it . . . like, is it safe?" Samantha peered out the windows at the grunge of their surroundings.

"Junkies are people too," Todrick kidded.

Nixon laughed. Samantha did not look pleased.

"It's perfectly safe," he continued. "I wouldn't have the reputation I did if my talent got stabbed every time they shot with me."

Samantha pursed her lips but forced them into a smile. "Yes. Right. Okay!" She clapped as if she was psyching herself up. "Wardrobe options, yes?"

"Sure." He chuckled. She was not the first of her kind that he had encountered. As the industry continued to shift, shooting with influencers Nixon's age was becoming half his business. And Mom was always in tow.

Outside, Samantha opened the back of her car, revealing a stack of clothes neatly tucked inside garment bags.

Nixon's heart sank. "Mom."

"Yes, honey."

"Where are my boots?"

Samantha could feel the cold steel of a gun in her mouth clattering against her teeth as she prayed for death.

"Uh-oh." Todrick sort of laughed, as if it didn't really matter.

"Fuck," Samantha said. Then her head whipped over to her daughter. "Why didn't you remind me?"

"I did," Nixon said. "Last night. I told you to put the box next to the front door and put your keys on top of it specifically for this reason."

Samantha wanted so desperately for this not to be her fault, but there wasn't any way around it. She would have to make the nearly three-hour round trip to retrieve them.

"It's okay," Todrick said. "I've got some loaners if needed. Or we can do this barefoo—"

"No," Samantha said sternly, taking the heavy stack of garment bags and handing them to her daughter. "We're not paying you all this money for her album cover to look like it's a day at the fucking beach." She slammed the back of the SUV shut. "We spent six hundred dollars on those boots specifically for this. I will go get them. Can you shoot anything in the meantime?"

"Of course," he said confidently. "I'm serious. We can make this work without—"

"Mr. Kidd," she said, stopping him.

Nixon felt a quick jolt of panic, of what it would mean to be alone with a stranger for several hours but recalled the fight with her mother in the car and decided three more hours of that was a worse alternative.

Samantha said no more, got into her car, and drove off.

Nixon and Todrick watched her go.

"Well, all right," he said, smiling. He put a hand on her shoulder. "Is she always like that?"

"Yes," Nixon said.

"Do you say more than one word at a time?" he asked her, trying to break the ice a little further.

"I do." She smiled, bashful, trying to hide the teeth she had been told were too big.

Then he touched her chin, and her face nervously shot up, and he looked her in the eyes and said, "Let's go through what you have."

He led her inside. Even though Nixon hated her mother on most days, without her there the space suddenly felt ten times as big.

She and Todrick slid the clothes from their garment bags and hung them one by one on a wardrobe rack. He began to look through them, eyeing each piece intently.

"Your mom lets you wear this stuff?" he asked.

"She buys most of it," Nixon said quietly.

"I'm kidding," he said, trying to reassure her. Then he pulled a pair of leather pants and a studded black blazer from the rack. "Let's start with these. And yes, we're going to do a few barefoot."

She smiled and held the clothes in her arms, looking around the enormous space.

"Bathroom's that way." He pointed.

"Right," she said and scuttled toward it.

Inside she moved to put the pieces on but realized they had not picked out a shirt to go beneath the blazer. She popped her head out.

"We didn't pick a shirt!" she called.

"What?" he yelled back, still mulling over things she had brought.

"To go under the jacket!"

"People don't wear shirts in the apocalypse!" he said. "We'll just do whatever bra you have on!"

She shut the door. In the mirror she looked at herself and wondered about her dad and whether to call him. Then she remembered she was still mad at him. She removed her shirt and put the blazer on over her nearly naked skin, staring at how much it revealed. She had been mocked by Lindsay Carlisle for having small tits, and her fifteen-year-old insecurities stared back at her, screaming through the mirror. She had worn plenty of revealing outfits throughout her career. But they had always come with the safety net of mom nearby.

Her nerves fluttered in her chest. She closed her eyes and remembered her usual escape. She was an actor. So, she would act the part. Influencer by day, lonely girl by night. She would be all right. She always was. She was otherworldly. An alien, like Hector. She could transcend her fears.

She took a deep breath and buttoned the blazer. There was a light knock on the door.

"You ready?" he asked, sounding like he had better things he could be doing with his time than photographing a child. She opened the door. His eyes did not bounce downward but instead met her gaze.

"Looking good," he said. "Let's test some of the light in here."

He walked and she followed.

"Hit that little mark for me," he said, pointing to a small blue X on the ground.

She did as she was told and watched him watching her through the camera. But his energy remained cool. Like this was just a job. Like he was not emotionally attached to its outcome the way she was. The way her mother was. The way her father hoped to understand but never could.

"Just want to see how natural light plays in here first. Every shoot you've done is probably nothing but bright lights and flashes, I bet. Everything over exposed," he said.

"Mostly." Her one-word answers had returned, and she kicked herself inside for sounding stupid.

He smiled behind the camera. Then the shutter flapped, and he looked at her unassuming pose on its small screen. He continued to adjust.

"Are you okay with there not being any props?" he asked.

"Yeah," she said. "Everything's digital anyway. Even my voice."

That got a big laugh out of him. "Most kids your age wouldn't admit to that. And even if they did, they wouldn't believe it," he said. Another snap. More adjusting.

"Our record producer seemed like a talented drug addict," she said.

"Twozie?" he asked playfully.

"You know him?"

Todrick lowered the camera, a big smile on his face. "He and I go way back. Back to when he was *DJ2Z*," he sounded it out to make fun of the lame pun. *A to Z.*

"Oh, really?" She was excited. It was like they were finally connecting.

"I shoot all his talent. Lotta kids like you. This is good," he said, the camera rising back up to block his face. "Gives me some direction."

"What was it like working with Nina Cardone?" she asked of her pop idol.

"She was a bitch, honestly," he said nonchalantly, snapping one more photo and looking at it closely.

"Oh." She deflated.

"Did I just ruin her for you?"

"I mean, everyone has a reputation, I guess."

"That's the best part about being fifteen. You don't have a reputation yet." He laughed.

"I don't?" she said a little sternly, not interested in someone twice her age but still young treating her as if she were a dumb tween.

He looked at her. "Keep this, whatever this is," he said, raising the camera, firing away rapidly behind the lens.

She fell into a routine she was familiar with, turning on her typical look: pouty mannerisms, smiling only with the eyes—the smize—periodically changing the angle of her face but never the intensity of her stare.

"Stop," he said, letting the camera fall. She was instantly self-conscious. "I don't do what you're used to."

"What do you mean?" she asked.

"Not all photographers are the same."

"I know that."

"Well, don't do this model thing," he said bluntly. "I'm going to work with your theme, but it's not about the theme. It's about you. I want to capture you. Does that make sense?"

"I guess." She wished they could go back to their joking rapport.

"This album is about, like, a fucked-up future without boys, right?"

"A girl uprising," she corrected, despising its hokey premise.

"Okay, well, when you get pissed at me like this, your face has real emotion. That's what I want. You're already sexy. Trust that that will do the work on its own. But I want you to open up to me, okay?"

"Okay," she said.

He stared, not believing her.

"Do you want to wait for your mom?" he asked.

"No," she said immediately, feeling chastised. The last thing she was going to be in front of someone with his reputation was a little girl who needed her mother.

"Great, then let's cut the bullshit and get to business." He raised the camera back up.

She was torn between hating him for talking down to her and trusting him for pushing her. Her face couldn't help but express her conflicted feelings as she started to give him what he wanted.

II.

HECTOR

HECTOR PARKED HIS car in front of Sarah Kline's small Sherman Oaks home. If phone calls had turned up nothing, he thought a face-to-face conversation with a real person could better his odds of getting answers. He looked himself over in the rearview. He could not remember the last time he'd seen her. If he was being honest with himself, moving up to the big time of franchise blockbusters had made him forget about a lot of the little people in his life. But there was no one more important to his success than Sarah. She had given him his break and, by extension, given Murphy his.

He remembered the first time he'd auditioned for her. He was filled with dread. She had bluntly asked him why he had so few credits. He told her he had only been in LA two years by that time. He had been asked to audition on a recommendation from Wendy. She liked his look, but she hadn't heard of his agent. No one knew a "Murphy Beck." Whoever he was, he sounded like an asshole.

Hector stumbled his way through the audition as badly as anyone could, at one point dropping his sides and losing track of which page was which, forgetting his lines. She told him to stop. He looked up at her, shaking. His mind had drifted back to the black box theater, and he suddenly felt caged. Desperate. Terrified.

Although sure he hadn't just blown but incinerated his chances, she called him back to read again. He came overprepared the next time but still his fragile self.

After booking the part, he asked her why. Why the risk? What had she seen in him?

"You remind me of Molly," she said.

Hector understood now what she'd meant. It was what had pulled him back to her. Why he felt she would have the answers he needed. She knew the abuse Molly had suffered better than anyone. She had seen the same thing in his eyes.

To protect his image of her, he kept his eyes blind to the damaging details of Molly's story, as he did to his own trauma. He tried not to think about the fact that when she was fifteen, she allegedly had a relationship with one of *The Family That Stays Together*'s directors and executive producers, Reg E. Wilson. Reg had always denied it, and it was hard to prove without her saying it was true. But Hector knew better than most that those kinds of clandestine affairs were almost always more than just hearsay. He had assumed that in the wake of Me Too, she would disclose the details officially, seeking restitution for what had happened to her. But she'd stayed silent till the end. He wondered if being a mess in front of the world on television had been easier than being honest with herself.

He got out of the car and looked both ways down the sidewalk, seeing no one. He was used to fans following him, but now he felt like he had an emotional tail. Like he was on to answers others didn't want him knowing. He knocked on the front door of the house.

Sarah peeked out from behind blinds in the bay window. Then she opened the door and looked at him as if he were the only one of her sons who ever came to visit.

They sat inside, had coffee, and caught up, but the pleasantries faded quickly, and his awkward, leg-shaking demeanor suggested his ulterior motive. Seeing such a sweet, almost mythical face at her door, thinking of the bright spots in a career gone by, for a moment, she had let her heart be taken away from her reclusion. But she knew why he was there. She felt a tinge of betrayal before taking a stab.

"I saw you," she said.

"How do you mean?"

"At the service. On TV."

"Oh," he said. Her eyes bored holes in him, and all the niceties dropped out from under them. His reason for being there hadn't been a secret, he supposed, but he felt exposed.

"It is nice to see you, Hector. But this is the first time in almost fifteen years. So, I very much doubt you're here just for coffee and to rub my sore legs."

He dropped his head and ran a hand nervously along the back of his neck. He'd heard a slight break in her voice, and now all the certainty in his forthcoming questions was gone. "Listen, Sarah, I'm sorry if—"

"Fans do have their ways, don't they?" she said, as if she had known ten thousand gallant but emotionally paper-thin men like him.

"I just want to know why."

"You mean you don't already?"

Clouds overhead cleared, and sunlight suddenly leapt through the window. She sipped her coffee as a defense mechanism, then put the delicate cup down onto its saucer with a shaking hand.

"Why do you think Guy skipped her funeral?" he said, trying to recover.

"He was her best friend when they were both teenagers," she said.

"I know that."

She almost scoffed in response. "If you'd known everything he knew, and you'd used all that to make a money machine fueled by her hurt, and then she killed herself, would you be able to bring yourself to go to her funeral as it was broadcast to the world?"

Hector felt punched in the face.

"Do you remember how often you would ask me about her after you booked *The Fallen*?" She smiled at the memory. "'What was she like? Is she that funny in real life? Is that the way she really dresses? In episode seventeen of season four, when she kissed Kevin Ross . . .' You were like a love-sick puppy."

"I guess I was." He blushed.

"Well, since you're here, I'll tell you . . . Molly wasn't a very nice kid," she said, popping all the balloons of his childhood at once. "She was difficult. But for whatever reason, that's what the producers liked. That's what Reg liked."

Then she stopped, chewing nervously on the delicate skin of her lip.

"She was written as a spunky kid; she *was* a spunky kid," she said. "But when we met her parents, we knew where she got it."

Hector saw a thought suddenly strike her. She stood.

"Hang on," she said and walked down a thin hallway.

He could hear her rooting around in a distant room, then she returned with a photo and showed it to him. It was of Molly, her parents, and Sarah at a mall in front of a step and repeat. It featured the logo for *The Family That Stays Together* collaged in various nineties neon colors on a vinyl background with a small red carpet for people to stand on and pose for pictures.

"Do you remember these?" she asked. "Those mall tours and signings?"

Popular teen shows back when he was growing up would put on cast meet-and-greets at malls. He remembered wishing Molly would visit his hometown of Redding, California, but it was much too obscure. These small, makeshift tours only swept through major cities, and his parents were not about to drive him to San Francisco.

"This was here at the Beverly Center," she said. Then she pointed to Molly's parents. "Do you know how drunk they were that day?"

Hector leaned in and gazed into their lazy, half-open lids.

"As if I wasn't busy enough, I was recruited to go on this little adventure with her because the network didn't trust them not to get into a car accident with her in the back seat and kill their star," she said. "I'm sure that's something very few people know."

"Why'd they pick you?" he asked.

"She did." Sarah sat back on her love seat.

"Why'd you keep it?"

"I was shocked, honestly. She wasn't ever particularly nice to me, or anyone. But that photo, that period, was the only time in my entire life that that girl was sweet to me."

"I'm sorry," he said.

"We spent every day together for a month. And at the end of every day, when her parents went back to their hotel room at five o'clock to get blasted and she still wanted to horse around, that's what we did together. Arcades. Comic-book stores. Shoe shopping. Then we'd have dinner. We'd talk, almost like peers. It was astounding how adult this teenager seemed. Like her parents needed her to take care of them. And it started to make sense why her wits were so sharp."

She laid the picture on the coffee table.

"I was like an accidental therapist. The cool aunt. For a moment, at least. But after thirty days, I had to give her back. It was like some kind of brutal trial run—to know all this about a fifteen-year-old and have to keep it in here." She tapped her chest with two fingers. "A lot of kids like Molly have parents who had no idea they could be so talented. No idea. They sort of just decided at some point to go along with their kid's cockamamy scheme, and when the kid strikes gold, it's more an accident than anything. And so, there's no plan. There's no plan for the money or the fame or the success or the recognition. With stage moms, at least they have a strategy. I wish some of those parents' kids would make it more often, but usually those parents are certain their kid is way more talented than they actually are. Most of *those kids* are downright bad.

"But Molly, kids like that, talented like that, their parents think they're no good until they suddenly make them rich. And it's usually because the kid believed they were no good that they're so talented. Because there's something unconscious they're fighting against, something they're trying to prove. And so now that the kid is famous, she's like the pearl, you know? They're a thing the parents found by accident when they were out looking for food. And that kid becomes a cursed cash cow. They're milked dry. And then the parents resent them after it happens. Because they never really knew where the money was coming from or why. For her life to culminate in this—in you sitting here, curious why she might've done what she did . . . what happened with Reg . . . I saw it coming, and I couldn't do anything to stop it."

"Sarah." He leaned in instinctively. "None of that was your fault."

"I know it wasn't my fault," she said angrily. "I don't carry guilt with me. I carry shame. There's a big difference."

"Why?"

"Because it wasn't like I didn't try to help her. But every time I did, no one gave a shit."

Seeing what he had dredged up made Hector wish he'd never been born.

"She was fifteen years old." She choked briefly, then took a moment to compose herself, and swallowed her emotions. "No one, least of all the studio, wanted the headline saying that their star had been taken away from her parents by CPS," she scoffed. "So, they ignored it. It would've been too much of a mess to clean up and a lot less profitable. Besides, they always thought she was a mean little bitch. I'm sure they felt she got what was coming to her."

"Her dad was at the service," Hector said.

"And you think that means he's absolved?"

"I guess not."

"Listen, whatever happened to her parents after the show ended, I have no idea. Her mom was on a suicide mission, it seemed like. I don't even know if she's still alive. I wouldn't be surprised if she ended up dead in a gutter somewhere." She tilted her neck from side to side, stretching it. "I heard her dad got into AA and got sober long enough to see the Edvard Munch painting he was in. So, who knows? But he was never *not* going to be a creep to me."

She picked up her coffee cup.

"The whole world is asking themselves the same question as you, I bet." She put on a silly, over-the-top voice. "How could someone famous and rich like Molly do such a terrible thing? How could she not have been happy? She had all the money and fame in the world! Why would she do it?" Then she laughed to herself as if it were all a sick joke. "Do you want to know what my question is?" she asked.

He waited.

"When does the world *really* care about a woman like her?" she said.

He opened his mouth to speak, but she gave him the answer instead. "When it's too late."

A breeze kicked through an open window and knocked over a picture frame, startling him. She sat perfectly still.

"You think Reg was the only one? He was just the shithead who felt big enough to whisper it to his buddies. I bet he's sweating now. I wish someone would take him to task, honestly. But he got off free and clear. She took his damnation with her to the grave. But I know about the others. The ones no one else does. The family members. The things she told me when we were on that little tour together. That's why I kept the picture. Because in that month, I saw how incredibly special that kid was. How infinitely talented. And how deeply broken. She trusted me with a lot of information. Not just what happened to her when she became a name. Before. At home."

He wrung his hands, wanting to stand and run but held firmly to the couch by his guilt.

"Why don't you come out with it now, then?" he asked. "People would corroborate the story. I would back you up."

"It isn't my story to tell," she said plainly.

Hector wanted to scream. How could it not be? How could no one, none of Molly's friends or family, want to see justice done in her name?

"Would it be right of me to suddenly paint this picture of her? Against her will?"

"You don't think she would support you?"

"I think she's dead. And what difference would it make?"

His anger bubbled up.

"It's not so easy to be some hero who tries to tell a world full of people who watched her destroy herself that they should feel bad for her," she said.

"Why not?"

"Because you can't bring yourself to do the same thing."

Dogs barked across the street. Then a leaf blower started up and ripped apart any serenity they might have hoped to find. She raised her voice to speak over it.

"You might be a middle-aged man now," she said, her face suddenly showing a spark of compassion, "but don't think I don't know a broken little boy when I see one."

"I didn't . . . I didn't mean to come here and . . . I feel like whatever friendship we had I just threw into the fire," he said, his volume gradually increasing as he spoke.

"What does it matter?" She laughed. "It's not like I can give you any more parts!"

He laughed too as the sound of gas-powered yard work broke the tension. "I feel like an asshole!" They were near shouting now.

"You're not an asshole!"

"Are you sure?"

"Jesus, God!" She leapt to her feet and shut the window. The noise dropped to a murmur. She watched the worker walk several paces down the sidewalk before turning back to Hector.

"You know I've always loved you," she said. "Same way I loved Molly. But with you, you were shy. She wasn't. I always knew I could give you some tough love to push you because you wouldn't push back. Molly I always felt was going to rip my head off if I got after her."

He laughed again and pinched the tears in the corners of his eyes.

"So, if I can offer you anything, it's to stop making her death about you," she said.

He stared at her. There was no one else in his life who could see so clearly through him. It was the reason for his career.

"Whatever this is really about," she said, mercy in her voice, "whatever it is going on underneath that you're trying to fix—I sincerely hope you find a way. That's your story to tell. Not this one." She smacked him hard on the shoulder, resuming her tough but fair nature. "But you've got to promise me something."

"Anything," he said.

"That you won't use any more women as emotional stepping stones to get you to wherever it is you need to go."

Seeing how hard Sarah had tried to put the past behind her, Hector wondered if his recent isolation had really done him any good at all. He hated that he'd used Molly's death as the crowbar to pry open his own vault of anguish, fumbling through phone calls to Apples talent like an idiot. Showing up on Sarah's doorstep like the prodigal son who was only kidding. She had made it clear: he was finally on his own.

AFTER THE FALLEN ended, Murphy had made the switch from agent to manager. Hector had been his most successful client, and he had safeguarded him so long he felt that his skill set was better suited for managerial duties. Now in middle age, he wanted to protect his most important relationship as best he could and foster that same safety for the occasional new talent as well.

"Hey, what do you think of this Nixon Bryce girl?" Murphy asked Hector on the phone.

"Who's that?" Hector said, concentrating on driving.

"One of these *influencers*," Murphy said, as if it were a dirty word.

"Oh," Hector said. "I guess I don't know. Is she talented?"

"I'm not sure yet. She's got a lot of followers. I signed her the other week."

"Then why are you asking me my opinion now?"

"Because, I don't know, I'm just asking. Jesus. Are you still in your car?" Murphy could hear the mild background whoosh of Hector's driving. "You're just bopping all around town today looking for clues or what?"

"I talked to Sarah."

Murphy sighed, and Hector could hear the gentle scratch of a palm pensively running over stubble.

"I've been thinking a lot about our last conversation," Murphy said. "I talked to Essence—"

"What did you say?" Hector cut him off, worried about what he'd always felt was Essence's gossipy nature.

"Not about you," Murphy reassured him. "Just about, like, how to talk to people. People like you, maybe. I don't know. The feelings."

"The feelings?"

"Talk about my feelings, yes! God, are you going to make me feel bad about this? I knew this was a bad idea."

"Stop," Hector said. "I appreciate you saying it."

"Hector, as you well know, I am now over the hill." Murphy's discomfort moved him into his reliable sarcasm. He had just celebrated his fiftieth birthday a month and a half prior and liked to use his middle age as an excuse not to do things he didn't want to do.

"Now that I'm fifty, I don't know. You know, life happens, and then you die, I guess," Murphy said.

"Life happens, and then you die."

"Yeah."

"Okay."

"You are . . . important to me. I guess is what I'm trying to say," Murphy squeaked out. "And I would like to help you. Just, you know . . . let me know how I can do that."

"You want to have a drink tonight?" Hector asked.

"When you say tonight, you mean six?"

"Can you be flexible?"

"Your yoga instructor is flexible. You talk to her about flexibility.

I'm a fifty-year-old man now, remember. I like a nine-p.m. bedtime and a Netflix. Let's go to the Phoenix."

"You only like going to the Phoenix because it's in walking distance from your office."

"Hey, Hector," Murphy began in a higher pitch. "You see that hill? Out there in the distance?"

"Yes, Murph. I see it."

"Good. 'Cause I'm over it. Come back, Odysseus. Let's have a drink now. I'm tired of being your van guy."

"You got me two phone numbers—"

"*The hill, Hector!*" Murphy shouted.

Hector had a much-needed laugh. "There's one more person I'd like to talk to," he said. "If he'll talk to me."

"Oh God."

"Why don't I come by the office tomorrow afternoon? We'll have a drink, and I'll catch you up."

"Fine!" Murphy relented. "Tonight works. But no later than seven!"

They hung up.

12.

TAMARA

WHEN TAMARA FIRST met Guy, she was drunk. It had been at Molly's birthday party soon after her guest appearance on *Dance Battle*, and Tamara had bought a round of shots for the group, which was dancing on the second floor of Micky's in West Hollywood.

Over the years, much of the cast of *MML* and all subsequent spin-offs had partied in WeHo. Gay men were their core fan base, followed very closely by middle-aged white women, who, for whatever reason, hated every single one of the women in the cast almost as much as they hated themselves and, although they would never admit it, their children.

Guy rarely socialized with the casts of the shows he produced. He didn't want to blur any lines, as everyone was quick to try to curry favor with him, something he detested. A fact he had let slip when speculation began about his possible drug use as he hung out with Cyd's ex-boyfriend, Josh.

That night, Tamara had spun around at the bar, a shot glass in each hand, spilling them both on Guy's vintage Fiorucci jacket. They had stared at each other for a long moment as loud music shook them. He waited for her to apologize; she waited for him to get angry. But neither did either, and Tamara said, "Why the fuck would you wear that here?"

Even intoxicated, she had known precisely what she had ruined and refused to feel bad about it. Then she pushed past him, making her way to the bathroom to wash her hands and try to clean brown liquor from her dress.

The following day he called Molly and asked her to formally introduce them. Guy met with Tamara for drinks, and her brash attitude and blunt honesty was everything he knew *MML* needed to give it a ratings boost. He pitched her to the network as "cool," "tough," and "a bad bitch." He described her attitude as "like a rapper's girlfriend." Despite her being married at the time to a white Englishman.

When she originally met Molly, Tamara had been looking for the enabling kind of friend who wasn't going to tell her to slow down. Together, they had lived up to the name of Molly's show. It had been fun forming a wild bond with her. More than anyone else in Tamara's life at that moment, Molly was trustworthy, even though she didn't always say the right things. Many times, she put both feet in her mouth, but at least she said what she said to people's faces. Tamara appreciated direct, offensive candor instead of insincere flattery while a knife was slipped between her shoulder blades. But beneath the mess, Tamara could see Molly's confusion and vulnerability. She watched the way she clung to and kissed up to Guy like he was simultaneously her aloof boyfriend with his eyes on another girl and her distant, careless father.

The salary Tamara was paid never stopped feeling like blood money. But it had its purpose. She knew she could dump it into building her dream, her studio. It continued to be a sore point for her, always feeling like she was living in the house that Guy Maker had built. That morning, yet again, he had reminded her of the power she still did not possess. That his one single phone call could throw her entire world into chaos made her feel helpless. She tried to remind herself he needed her more than she needed him. In fact, he needed both her and Andrea. Who the fuck did he think he was dealing with?

Still in her booth at the Formosa, she had given the server her credit card and sat quietly, staring down at the half-finished drink Simon had left on the table. He hadn't even had the decency to order a silly themed cocktail at the pretend Chinese restaurant. He'd deliberately ordered a Negroni. Her favorite. Although she was proud of the way she'd gotten rid of him, he had intentionally released a slow poison by leaving the drink in front of her. Just to let her know, to remind her no one knew her as well as he did. For everything she had accomplished in her life, that this man could simply place a drink in front of her and make her question her sobriety filled her with righteous anger.

One weekend shortly after joining the cast of *MML*, Tamara had proposed a girl's getaway, just her and Molly, so they could get to know each other better. They had gone to Palm Springs to day drink by the pool and tell everyone else to fuck off, even if only for forty-eight hours. But what began as an emotional release turned into a lot more when the two of them got so drunk, they stumbled to a 7-Eleven to buy boxed wine and got the bright idea to take a joyride in a stranger's car. They stole one left idling with a small dog inside while its owner popped in to buy cigarettes. They crashed it into a telephone pole a few blocks away. The man gave chase on foot and caught up to them. The front hood of his car had caved in a foot, and the airbags had deployed, breaking Tamara's nose and bruising Molly's sternum. The small dog had broken its front leg after being launched into the driver's seat from the rear.

The man was Simon. He had been following them for an early assignment as a young writer for *Hollywood Inside Out*. It was the first of many encounters he'd have with both of them and the beginning of an intentional career path that veered toward trying to ruin Tamara's reputation for destroying his car and injuring his dog. After that, the only story he published about her that appeared half-kind had been when Guy had called his magazine's editor in chief to leak news of the *Tamandrea* spin-off before any other outlet had learned about it.

"Say what you will about Tamara Collins's rocky road to super-stardom," the piece concluded, "but this writer waits with eager anticipation to see this multitalented and multifaceted woman finally shine as bright as she deserves and outshine the woman who's been holding her back for so long." He could write something nice about her only if he also used it as an opportunity to drag Molly, knowing the piece would add to the turmoil their friendship had already undergone.

Still, for all his conniving and two-facedness, Tamara hated Simon as a person less than she hated his writing. Even with all the truths made up or stretched, she would've been less incensed if he had actually been talented. Instead, she felt like he wrote as well as a child in a middle school English class. As she'd told another news outlet, his paragraphs were as basic and simple as the juvenile construction "concrete detail, commentary, commentary, concrete detail."

Outside of her and Molly having injured a dog that had gone on to live an otherwise full, happy life, she could not understand why one man would spend nearly fifteen years covering the same type of content. Perhaps she had underestimated how much a man could love his dog. Although she'd always suspected it was driven by a type of hatred he would never admit to. For several years, she had been the only Black cast member on Apples.

The cocktail was a time bomb in front of her. A small bourbon cherry was submerged at the bottom, its thin red stem like a tiny fuse. Simon's pushing and prodding about the tragedy of her dead friend, and the fear he might know things about her that even she was unaware of, made her sweat. She realized he was willing to stoop to a new low. She wondered how long the waiter would be before he returned with her card.

She stared at the group of young girls, suddenly furious that a picture of her looking haggard was being injected into the social media vein. All those little pop-culture-heroin chics lying back, looking at it with their tongues lolled out, drifting off into the freedom of being nobodies yet somehow feeling sorry for her.

She thought about calling Guy and asking him point-blank if he'd manufactured all this drama. She knew he'd leaked the details of the

Tamandrea spin-off to *Applause Magazine* all those years ago because he'd told her as much.

"You keep your enemies closer by leaving the hope alive that someday you might be their friend," he had said.

The ice in the cocktail shifted, clinking softly, and her sense memory recalled the smooth bitterness of the Campari and how much she hated sweet vermouth but hated even more that only in this drink did she love it.

She'd been tempted back toward booze plenty. By exes. By fans. By castmates. Even by her own son when she found Smirnoff Ice bottles hiding beneath junk mail in the recycling bin after he'd told her he was throwing a small party for his friends. The evidence of his pubescent taste buds had made her want to buy him a good bottle of gin and teach him how to drink like a man. But she refused to cave. Who would she be if Guy Maker broke her with a snap of his fingers? If his little turd Renfield, sent to do Guy's dirty work, got the satisfaction of drawing her blood for his master?

The waiter returned with her receipt. She tipped thirty percent and signed her name with a small smiley face at the end—a habit born of hoping servers everywhere would collectively say she wasn't cheap.

She stepped outside onto Santa Monica Boulevard, where two photographers started snapping cell phone pictures, trying to be sly but failing.

"You might as well be watching me through a newspaper with eyeholes cut out of it," she said, putting on her sunglasses.

"Sorry, Miss Collins," one of them said.

She stared at them. They waited.

"Would you like to smell my breath?" she asked.

One put his phone down. The other was now taking a video.

"Tell Simon it didn't work," she said. "And tell him that if anyone catches me relapsing, it's certainly not going to be the magazine."

"Who would it be then?" one blurted out.

"Hector Espinoza," she said with a smile, hoping maybe that

suggestion would turn Hector's day of playing Magnum, P.I., upside down.

She walked down the boulevard to an escalator that took her to the parking garage. She stood for a long moment next to her car, watching others exit, and could feel herself being pushed as usual. By unseen hands and outside forces. They wanted her to react in a big way. Guy wanted her to go to Andrea's signing; she was sure of that now. If she did, and Simon published the story just prior, the crowd there would be expecting a fistfight. Exactly what Apples was hoping for. Not just to find reason to sever the tie between her and Andrea, but also to put an end to Tamara's ability to push back against Guy's influence. She knew he was banking on her going in swinging. As of late, he'd been getting tired of what he felt was her shit attitude. She made him aware of everything that made her unhappy. She wanted accountability for past wrongs. She wasn't quiet when it came to telling the network what was on her mind. Times had changed. She wanted representation, more cast members of color. She also wanted producer credit on her own show, a show that, along with her face, had made them millions. That she still needed permission to live her life from a council of men—and two women in pantsuits who she felt tried simply to blend in—made her fists clench.

In contrast, Fievel seemed welcome to do whatever he wanted. Even the men on *Tamandrea* weren't subjected to the same kinds of scrutiny the women were, weren't held to the same standards or requirements. Fievel and Elliot certainly weren't. Boys got to be boys. If the girls weren't perfect, they were trash. Tamara wondered how cunty she must have seemed the past few years. Her mother's voice rang in her ears every time she was on the receiving end of any kind of criticism, warranted or not.

That voice was the one that had driven her to self-medication. That and the memory of her brother's death, of what it had taught her about what happens to Black faces in white seas. The fear of never being good enough, because being good enough still hadn't been enough to save him. And then there was the stigmata she'd felt emblazoned on her palms when sobriety led her to realize what a sacrifice he'd been, what lesson he'd taught her from beyond the grave.

She felt his hand in hers now, breaking the tension of her balled up fist with a warm reminder of what happened when she let others get the best of her. When she let others tell her story and paint her picture. As with Molly's, no matter how hard Tamara's life begged the audience to ask who she was and why she did what she did, the fiction was always much easier to swallow than the truth.

Tamara's mother had run their family home like the headmistress of a conservatory. She had grown up being taught that her dreams were not a Black girl's dreams and therefore had to be surrendered. As an adult, she tried to squeeze everything she had wanted for her young self like blood from a stone out of her children. While she'd been able to resist at first, Tamara had gradually learned that the only way to earn her mother's love was through movement. Through losing herself and surrendering her identity to her mother's stolen dreams of dance.

Tamara's brother had been three years her senior. He had started with tap before her. Before she found her own reason for dancing, she had spent the first several years of her life living in his shadow. As a kid, she had mainly wanted to screw around the neighborhood, playing and getting yelled at for crawling through the neighbor's bushes and coming home smelling like rosemary.

At that point, she was too young to be left alone while their father was at work, and her mother saw it as unnecessary to pay a sitter, so she took Tamara to her brother's classes, rehearsals, and recitals. Her mother was even gracious enough to eventually bestow the nickname "Tagalong" on her.

She'd wander the studios looking at pictures of aged, nondescript dancers on walls; signed photos of perfect strangers thanking the owners for some moment under a spotlight long since passed. She made up stories about who they might have been and what their lives amounted to, assuming most of them had died. There was always something about old people and dance, she thought. As if the gradual acknowledgment of expiration meant finally freeing yourself to doing what you'd always dreamed of. As if deep down, everyone wanted to dance.

Back then, it had been next to impossible to get her mother's attention. Tamara had at first responded by acting out so she could be reprimanded, which was better than no attention at all. But she struggled with her focus. Her brother, as far back as she could remember, had always been driven to dance. She wondered whether it was by choice or design. Sitting in the back of their family Volvo, even she had grown exhausted with the way her mother would chastise him after every rehearsal, after every performance, critiquing his form and execution down to the millionth digit of pi. Often, he would cry when they returned home, trying to hide himself in his room. Tamara remembered being barely old enough to see the top of the kitchen counter the first time she'd instinctively slipped her hand in his to comfort him, asking how she could help.

Their childhood bond had lasted until he hit puberty. Pressured by his father to do something masculine once he was a teenager, he split his body and devotions between dance and football. Tamara watched him agonize over being pulled in two directions by the parents he wished would one day tell him that he was doing enough. That he was good, decent, and okay. Having no one else to turn his frustrations toward, he picked on his sister and her friends with a growing ruthlessness. She hated the bully he became.

As a senior in high school, once after a Friday football practice, he brought home a handful of his friends to go swimming. Their parents were away on a rare trip to recover some passion. The boys brought alcohol. Gradually her brother's eyes and lips wandered, and he retreated with a girl to his bedroom. Left alone as the only freshman in a sea of seniors, Tamara tried to keep up. It was the first time she blacked out. She woke up naked in the back seat of a car, not close to home. A snoring boy sat next to her, pants around his ankles. She dressed and walked home. Her brother laughed when she told him what had happened. Tortured by the memory of who he used to be, she said she hated him.

Competition was the most valid form of payback she could exact from him. If they could not share their parents' spotlight, she would take it from him. If they could not be friends, they would be rivals.

When she said she wanted to take classes, her mother questioned her motives. But if she had learned nothing else from the woman by then, Tamara at least knew how to be stubborn. She began working part time to pay for her own lessons. She started with jazz.

Motivated by bad memories, she practiced at home, sometimes until her feet bled. She was forced to take three weeks off when an open wound on her left foot became infected and swelled up with enough puss that she couldn't fit it into her shoe.

Because of his prowess, her brother was accepted to the Boston Conservatory at Berklee. He was required to leave his love for football behind, something his mother did not mind and his father accepted as inevitable. Tuition was expensive enough that they could not justify visiting him often. The distance between them and him became Tamara's greatest ally. She could take up the space he had left.

But not being physically present did not mean his mother was not ever present in his life. She called him daily, asking him to mail home tapes of his rehearsals and progress, then would call back with critiques.

Tamara began to stand out, although still not to her mother. The vacancy left by his son endeared her to her father, and she found him a trustworthy ally. While he could not connect with his son, and while her mother was still so desperate to control the boy, they could finally have their father-daughter dance.

When her brother visited home during holidays and over the summer after his first year away, Tamara saw a deep change occurring in him. Mercifully, he was no longer a bully. But worse, he bore no resemblance to who she remembered. Something precious had left his body. He looked and seemed tired all the time. He no longer objected to his mother's criticisms, when once he had at least put up some facade of a fight. He did not talk about school. He did not talk about his friends. He only danced, as if a gun were always being fired at his feet.

After he returned to Boston for his sophomore year, a continuing fear of failing to fit into an industry of pale pink faces and a desperation to find his place in a dream that was not his own left him constantly running out of steam. Then he found the remedy. At a party, a friend gave him Adderall. He found the energy it provided helped him stay up on nights when he needed to study after rehearsal had drained his natural supply. When he found himself dragging his feet at practice, he discovered the drug could be used to bring them to pointe. When he needed to be affable and hoped for nothing more than to belong, it delivered him there. When he needed to rally as per his friend's requests so they could party, it led him to that realm too.

The more he took, and the more it allowed him to accomplish, the more pressure that mounted. Those who did better were expected to do more with less recognition. The requirements of his body and mind, of what was needed to pass muster under his own and others' standards, fought for dominance—the standards of his mother, father, sister, choreographers, professors, coaches, partners. He didn't need to try hard to stand out. Every day held the weight of new requirements placed on him. Of needing to prove why he deserved to be where he was. On that stage. In that shape. In a league next to ivy, which always favored ivory.

That fall semester, his body finally stopped placing bets against his mind that he would let it rest, and it folded. He collapsed during a rehearsal and fell off stage, breaking his leg in two places. The doctors said he would likely never dance professionally. Despite all his hard work and the will to get to where he was, he took them at their word.

One month later, he took his life.

A week prior he had called Tamara. Feeling trapped in his wheelchair, lips loosened by pain pills, he'd apologized. She'd asked what for. He'd said, "Mom."

Despite his body being the final offering of all that he gave to others, his end wrote a legacy that became just another rubber stamp on a document. His life boiled down in a report that sought to find justification for ending such a promising, young life. Why had he done it? The answer came easily: drugs. The story of Black boys' dreams broken by the expectations of others. Of their being shoved into prechecked boxes. Of the ease with which the finger could be pointed to the supposed culprit. His college friends talked about how he had been hooked on Adderall. Maybe even something more, they speculated. "When he got drunk, he got real ghetto," they said.

After that, her mother's grief mutated into brutal disappointment. Her son's legacy became a cautionary tale for everyone, including her. His story was not about the rigors of suffering under the weight of everyone else's demands; it was about the drugs. It was always about the drugs. To the outside world, a suicide could only make sense if it was summed up in big, bold lettering. Easy to read, easier to digest.

To keep herself from feeling too deeply, Tamara's mother turned that story into her own pill to swallow. The type of intoxicating fiction that stops people from caring for others, halting empathy with a veneer of entertaining inebriation. The story was the salve. She had not been too hard on her son. He had been too weak. And the drugs had taken him. That was her new reality.

At seventeen, after her parents divorced, Tamara completed high school, but determined not to repeat her brother's journey, emancipated herself to pursue her dance career full time. She wanted completely to leave behind who she was and where she lived. She moved to Los Angeles. She called her father once a month. Every time, he would ask her if she had spoken to her mother. Tamara would say that she had not.

One day, he called her. He had heard about her mother. She had been in a car accident and had been killed.

Steadily working but saddled with guilt, she found solace in fulfilling the prophecy she resented. The one foretold by her brother's story. About all of the caged-in anguish of Black girls and Black boys who had the audacity to dream. It was why they deserved to be assigned prechecked boxes and locked up in prisons. Why they deserved to die. Why there was a war waged against them. Why else would she turn to drugs?

Sitting now in her car, surrounded by the screeching of tires and shouting of voices arguing over parking spaces, Tamara could still feel the ease with which she might relapse. She felt it every day. Just because she had gotten sober didn't mean she had defeated her demons. They merely possessed different faces now. Wore different suits. Danced to the beats of different drums. Still they danced around her, their chants boxing in her brother's memory, boxing in Molly's. An audience of the cruel, thumping their chests to the rhythm of their desire to be entertained.

As her car exited the garage, she slipped her validated parking ticket into the machine, and the fee flashed: $5. She gave the machine her credit card. Then she waited. Here she was again, waiting for permission. Permission to exit, to be free. Permission dependent on Guy. On a network. A system. And now permission from a fucking robot arm.

Across the street she saw a billboard with Hector's face on it. He was wearing a large diver's watch. An attractive woman stared longingly from the blurred distance behind him. The tag line for the watch company read, "Only time will tell." And Hector was giving a little smirk like, "We're definitely gonna fuck."

It was so silly. Such a dumb notion. Timepieces selling sex. Hector Espinoza, watching her.

She started to laugh. Then the laughter tightened in her chest, and she gripped the steering wheel as if she were going to snap it off, and the laughter became labored, panicked breathing, and tears started to roll down her cheeks, and she couldn't unsee the image of Molly's body, swinging lifelessly from the tree at the end of Mulholland Drive over the Cahuenga Pass.

The robot gave its permission, processing her payment and surrendering her card. She took it, and a small smiley face displayed as the arm lifted, with the words *Have a nice day.*

13.

FIEVEL/ELLIOT

"**Y**OU GOING TO tell me what happened in the champagne room?" Elliot asked as he drove.

"Chris Rock was right," Fievel said, looking out the passenger window.

"It's okay, you know. Whatever happened."

"It's really not, though."

"So rather than do a stripper's drugs, you're going to do ones that belong to fans? What if they kidnap us and tie us up in their room and try to do weird shit to us?"

"They're perfectly harmless. Why are you so scared?"

"I'm not *scared*. I just don't love partying or hanging out with complete strangers."

"That is exactly what partying is!"

"And I don't like it! Plus I'm tired."

"It's 7:29. Can you power through to midnight? Then you can leave."

"I can leave whenever I want because I'm my own person," Elliot said, trying to stand up for himself.

"You're right. I'm sorry. You're becoming a man now. Coming home from school, taking long showers. Leaving mysteriously crispy socks on your floor for your mom to wash."

"What?" Elliot often had trouble following what Fievel felt was his excellent wit.

"Forget it. I'll pay for valet," Fievel said as they pulled up to the Bellagio.

"Do you want to just go somewhere else and talk?"

"Fuck's sake, for the last time, no." Fievel pushed open his door. "And don't ask me that right here. Hey, man!" He immediately shifted his energy and smiled at the valet.

"Oh shit, Five-El!" said the twentysomething kid who looked like he'd borrowed his dad's uniform.

"What up!" Fievel slapped money in the kid's hand, then grasped it and brought him into a one-armed hug. Fievel had a way of acting like fans had friendships with him stretching way back when.

"When do you start filming again?" the valet asked.

"Our season just finished airing, brother." Fievel patted him on the shoulder. "We need to take breaks from time to time. Plus, I've got my residency at the 'Cana."

"Are we calling it a residency?" Elliot chimed in. "You know how to drive stick?" He withheld the keys briefly.

"Don't get hired unless we do," the kid said.

"Would you stop harassing him?" Fievel said, taking the keys from Elliot and handing them to the child. "But be careful. That was my dad's car."

"I've driven way more expensive cars than this. Don't worry," the kid told them as he took the keys, thinking he was saying something reassuring but insulting them instead.

"Cool," Fievel said as they watched the Porsche be driven away in jerky stops and starts. Then his phone buzzed. It was Guy. Fievel hesitated for a moment before swiping to decline the call.

"You don't want to talk to him?" Elliot felt legitimate concern. A call from Guy wasn't just a call from Guy. It was either going to send you to the moon or put you in a personal hell for weeks.

"Fuck him," Fievel said as they walked inside the casino.

"When was the last time you talked to him?"

"Couple weeks ago. Before the funeral he didn't have the guts to go to."

Elliot wanted to press further but knew it wouldn't have done any good. In the past, Fievel had not usually been one to decline calls from Guy. Fievel loved to schmooze and act like a big shot with his boss, mostly because Fievel didn't need Apples money and Guy loved to watch him put his foot in his mouth on a regular basis. But even though he rarely admitted it, Fievel always stayed vigilant in protecting Molly and her image. No one had ever caught him saying a dirty word about her, despite how things had ended between them. For him, a slight to her was worthy of a fistfight. Skipping her funeral would warrant having a hit put out on you.

"You know there's more than one bar here, right?" Elliot asked.

"Of course I know that."

The last time Fievel had been to the Bellagio was eight years prior, with Molly. They had planned a romantic getaway weekend to celebrate wrapping season eight of *MML*. Only season eight had ended with the bomb drop of Tamara and Andrea getting their own show, which had turned Molly's mood inside out.

He looked around the casino floor and remembered the scene she had caused. What had begun as a little innocent gambling and the tossing back of free drinks had eventually spun into her shoving a blackjack dealer and being detained by security. Fievel had bribed them to let her go.

They had been staying in a suite and were supposed to see some kind of circus show but had missed it when Molly threw up in the elevator on the way back to their room. Their relationship had always been entertaining, but it was at its unhealthiest then, always tipping in a seesaw fashion as they traded blame and spite. Much as with everyone else in his life, Fievel had wanted to take care of Molly. When she was sober, she hadn't minded his chivalry. But when she was drunk, she resented it. Many of their fights began with Fievel telling her to calm down, but the rage she could fly into in response sometimes saw her disappearing for days at a time.

After he'd bailed her out and cleaned her up that night, he went back down to the casino floor after she had passed out. He threw away $3,000 at a blackjack table in half an hour and continued working on drinking himself blind. Feeling like he'd finally had enough, angry that Molly had fucked up what he'd planned to be a fun weekend for her, he went out to a strip club and had sex with one of the dancers after her shift was over. She ended up shaking him down for more than he'd imagined he would ever have to pay for sex, and he regretted what he'd done in more ways than one. Worst of all, he'd gotten no satisfaction from it. He felt dirty, and not because of who it was with but because of the things he had said to her and the aggression of the act. The rage meant for Molly. He had done it out of some petty form of revenge. He had hoped someone might feel bad for him. But no one seemed to care.

When they were happy, no one had been able to make him laugh like Molly could. But by season eight, the bright spots were farther and fewer between the dark ones. She used to joke that her yin and yang temperament was the result of her being a Gemini, but after a while he learned that a lot of people used astrology as a justification for bad behaviors they simply did not want to change. He also had the high-tide-low-tide misfortune of seeing her when she alternated between sobriety and insobriety, which became harder to watch happen and even harder to see played back to them after the cameras stopped rolling and the episodes aired.

Their four-and-a-half-year relationship moved fast. His courtship of her became a major plot point when filming for season five began. He'd met her by accident at a Mother's Day brunch in San Diego. Fievel's mom had been out to visit from New York, and Molly had been engaged in the never-ending effort of keeping some kind of relationship with her parents alive. Despite it always being the unstoppable force versus the immovable objects, she continued to try.

Inevitably, what always started as a pained but polite catch-up would end in both parties drinking too much. Then the screaming would start, something would be thrown, and her parents would guilt her into giving them money.

The day they met, Fievel fell completely head over heels for her. He watched her alone at her table and finally worked up the courage to excuse himself from his mother's company and ask Molly if she was all right. She laughed and said through a snotty nose, "Do I fucking look all right?"

Not subtle at all, Fievel told Elliot to take his mom back to the hotel where they were staying so he could have a drink with Molly. Her gravitational pull had the effect on Fievel it did on most men— he would become Dudley Do-Right. There she was, tied to the train tracks, an emotional locomotive barreling toward her. He had to save her. Even if it killed him.

Cheating on her was the first time he let himself be so angry that he did something to sabotage their relationship. If it was ever going to end, it wasn't going to be her leaving him. She needed the emotional punching bag he was good at being, even if she resented him for it. Her version of pushing people away was to drink and use to a point of near oblivion, forcing them to make the decision to hurt her instead. Then she would point fingers and make speeches in search of vindication for invisible wrongs, exclaiming, "So, fuck you!"

Sad and sorrowful for having done what he'd done, Fievel called Guy the next morning to confess his infidelity. He couldn't keep it to himself. He needed someone who knew Molly as well as he did to help talk him off the ledge. Guy was her best friend. He was the only person who would know how to properly come clean with such a volatile lover. But Guy had always had a way of trading the secrets of others in exchange for a false sense of security and protection. That was his gift. The only other person Fievel told about the encounter was Elliot.

When the penultimate season nine of *MML* started filming, word of his scandal conveniently started spreading, and it became the primary story line. The season ended in the termination of Molly and Fievel's relationship. As if it had all been part of the plan, Guy made it up to Fievel later by giving him his own show.

Now Guy tried calling Fievel a second time as he and Elliot made their way across the casino floor, and a second time Fievel sent the call to voice mail.

"I feel like it's important if he's calling you twice," Elliot said.

"If it were important, he'd leave a voice mail," Fievel said.

"No one leaves voice mails anymore, even if it's important," Elliot said.

"No, they record voice memos and text them to you, like it isn't the exact same fucking thing."

Elliot could see Fievel's frustration radiating off him like heat off summertime pavement. "I think you need a drink," Elliot said.

Fievel's phone then buzzed with a text from Guy. "CALL ME. NOW. URGENT."

Fievel showed it to Elliot. "More urgent than going to your so-called best friend's funeral?" Then he laughed to hide his anger. "Let's have that drink instead."

They saw a pair of arms flailing in the distance and joined Brit and Nevin at the bar.

"You actually came." Nevin was beaming.

"Yeah, man. We're not assholes." Fievel patted him on the back. "Let's get some shots! I got this first round."

"I'm good," Elliot said.

Fievel shot him daggers. "Stop trying to be my girlfriend and be my best friend."

Elliot's brow furrowed, but he knew that Fievel wasn't going to have a good time unless he thought everyone else was having a good time. So, Elliot did what he always did—he caved.

The shots barreled down their chests like liquid fire. Then Elliot sipped a light beer slowly in an attempt to seem like he was actively enjoying himself. But he was outpaced by Fievel, Brit, and Nevin two to one. He thought about turning his phone back on but had finally made it over the emotional hill of not wanting to check it constantly.

"What are you fucking doing?" Fievel said when he noticed Elliot mindlessly watching the TV behind the bar.

"Watching this game," Elliot said.

"What *game*? You don't like sports. Stop being a bitch and have some fun." Fievel shoved him a bit too forcefully and Elliot's instinct was to punch him, but he refrained. Then Fievel cowered slightly and said, "I'm sorry."

"It's okay," Elliot said.

"Will you please just do this for me? Just tonight?" On a typical night, Fievel would have sounded like a nag, but in this moment the desperation in his voice was clear.

"Fine." Elliot sighed. "But I'm not paying for shit."

"Fuck yeah!" Fievel did a little jump for joy, and the two men in their forties were committed to being the life of the party, perhaps for the last time.

14.

ANDREA

INSIDE HER BUNGALOW apartment, Andrea stood wrapped in her towel, staring at a spider on the wall. Her instincts told her to crush it, but she hadn't moved in what felt like an hour, and she wondered for the first time how the spider might feel. Some thundering hand of a titan coming down on its brittle little body, popping it like a black cherry, smearing its tiny, insignificant memory against the wall in a brown streak. She was not one to feel paranoid, but the day was getting away from her, and she hoped maybe it was a bad dream. Living a life she was not in control of felt like being haunted. She decided on a truce with the spider.

As she was doing her makeup, she got a call from her publicist, Toni.

"Eeeeee! Are you so excited?"

"As I'll ever be," Andrea said solemnly. No matter how hard she had tried, she could never prepare herself for the exclamatory nature of Toni's mile-a-minute dialogue.

"What's this?" Toni said, her tone shifting. "You sound upset."

"I'm not upset." Andrea leaned back slightly, checking her work in the vanity.

"Dre." The pitch of Toni's voice rose slightly as she got nervous.

Andrea didn't respond.

"Andrea!"

"What?" she finally snapped back.

"Will you tell me what's going on? Should I be worried? Is this coming from somewhere? What happened?"

"Toni, I've got to get to lunch with Essence in a bit." She started shuffling through her things to make herself sound busy.

"You're getting lunch right before the big event? Shouldn't you be practicing?"

"It's part of the practicing." Andrea paused. "I think."

"Let me guess. Soho House?"

"Is there something specific you wanted to ask me?" Andrea stood and crossed her bedroom to the hanging dress she'd steamed.

"No, I called to, like, I don't know—get you pumped up. This is such a big day. So exciting!"

Andrea appreciated what Toni represented but didn't particularly care for who she was. She was a fill-in for Andrea's original publicist, Mark Allen, who'd had a heart attack and needed to go on sabbatical. He'd been in the business with his wife, Christine, for forty years. He spoke almost as slow as he worked, but given her hesitancy about entering the literary space, Andrea liked his pace. Toni had been a new hire at the agency meant to liven up the place. They had been signing new talent and, with that new blood, had figured they needed someone who spoke the same language as the kids. Toni spoke that language very fast.

"Do I need to call Christine?" Toni asked. "Do you want her there too?"

"No, no. Would you—Fuck," she said, stopping herself. "You're stressing me out. I've got a lot on my mind. I need to get dressed, okay? Just . . . I'll see you there."

"Okay," she said. "Okay, okay, okay. I'm sorry. You do you! I just think you're the greatest, and I think you're gonna kill it, and I think this is the beginning of something really special for you."

"Thanks."

Then there was another pause. Toni didn't want to be the one to hang up.

"Bye, Toni," Andrea said, giving her permission.

"Okay, bye!" She disconnected.

Once she was fully dressed, Andrea slipped on wedge pumps and stood looking at herself in her body-length hallway mirror. She looked the part but didn't feel it. The people who would be there were expecting exactly what they saw on TV, were expecting the person they imagined her to be. She felt complicit in presenting an image she now wondered if she could uphold. All she had to do was get up there, give her little spiel, and answer audience questions. Then she'd sign some copies and take some pictures and call it a day. Tons of former Apples talent had held book signings at the Grove. It couldn't be all that bad.

She regretted choosing Milan as her moderator. She had originally asked Tamara, but not wanting them to share the spotlight, as they did on TV, Tam had encouraged Andrea to do this entirely on her own. Toni had suggested herself, but Andrea had politely declined. Cyd was a hard pass. Hips would've shown up stoned. Milan was the only person Andrea knew who liked to talk as much as she'd need to as moderator. She was good at talking, often talking at people rather than to them.

Andrea wondered if Apples had sent a small crew to film Fievel's poolside debut at the Tropicana. She felt jilted that they didn't seem interested in sending anyone to shoot B-roll footage of her signing to be used next season, to have on file just in case. But now with a potential offer on the table for her own show, she realized maybe there was some other plan playing out. More than anything, she hated feeling kept in the dark. Especially when it came to the direction of her life. She felt without agency, which was why she wrote the stupid book to begin with, and the reason she was working with Essence, whom, deep down, she resented for being a freeloader and always suggesting they go to goddamned Soho House for lunch. And now she was being pitted against her best friend and thrown into a drama she had not created, asked for, or wanted. She could feel her misery being manufactured by others and was up against the wall, not fast enough to escape what felt like the hand of God coming in with a little wad of toilet paper to crush and flush her.

The thought of being up there alone in front of countless faces in only a few short hours made her palms sweat. This wouldn't be like the childhood beauty pageants she'd been forced to participate in, where she'd just had to smile and wave and curtsy or whatever. She worried about looking like an amateur if she had to reference her note cards; it wasn't a fucking open mic. She tucked them tightly into her bag and headed out the door.

Being careful not to let her nerves get the best of her and buckle her ankles, she walked slowly down the stairs toward her building's carport. When she got there, she saw she had a flat tire. Her lips went white as she held in her scream. She knew how to change it, but no way was she going to get dirty in what she was wearing. And she didn't have time to change her clothes or touch up her makeup. So, she called a Lyft.

She walked to the end of her building's long driveway and stood on the sidewalk near the corner of Hollywood Boulevard and Sierra Bonita Avenue. She watched on her phone as the little car on the map inched closer to her location. It was strange that she had a flat tire. She'd had everything checked when she got an oil change a week prior.

Her hands shook as she thought about the fan with no name, his eyes and his fists and her reveal that he was nobody to her. She had seen him at yoga an awful lot. Had he been elsewhere in her life all this time without her even knowing?

With five minutes until her ride arrived ticking down, she walked back to her car and inspected the wheel. There was a thin gash at the bottom, almost covered by the overlapping rubber where the pavement pressed up against it. She fingered it lightly, then rubbed her fingers together, trying to smudge the dirt out of existence.

Her phone buzzed as her driver arrived, and she didn't have any more time to think before hustling to meet him on the street, trying not to trip.

LUNCH AT SOHO House felt like adding insult to injury. Nothing made her feel more simultaneously ungrateful and accomplished than meeting with her life coach at the most to-be-seen-at location after receiving the news that she might be getting her own spin-off just prior to her first-ever book signing. On the way, her panic had mounted as she thought about the tire.

"And you've practiced your grounding exerci—"

"Yes, I've pressed my hand into the ground ten fucking thousand times!" Andrea interrupted.

"Then why are we here, love?" Essence asked.

"Because you said you wanted to meet here before the signing," Andrea said sharply.

"Can we hit the pause button for a minute?" Essence asked, bringing her palm slowly to the table as if she were trying to coax a dog into lying down. "What's going on in that head?"

"A lot, E. A lot." Andrea looked down at the menu. "Let's not do that thing where we talk for an hour and the server keeps coming over asking us if we know what we want. Let's take a minute to look at the menu. Please."

Essence moved her hands into her lap and looked out at the Hollywood horizon.

Andrea studied the menu in a slumped-over posture, trying to emotionally retreat from her coach, but she could sense that her sensei was not also studying the menu. She looked up with pursed lips.

"You already know what you want?" Andrea asked.

"Same thing I always get," Essence said pleasantly.

"Good." Andrea sat up straight. Of course Essence had a usual. "Because I know what I'm getting too."

"Good," Essence said.

"Yeah. It is good."

They looked at each other, Essence refusing to let a client get her goat.

"Can I speak?" Essence asked.

Andrea made a gesture like *Be my guest.*

"You're not you right now. You're carrying a lot."

Andrea's temples throbbed. She nodded.

"But you're doing a lot more . . . for other people," Essence said, using a pregnant pause for dramatic effect, "when you should be doing all that for yourself."

"Is writing a book not doing enough for myself?"

"It's a start—"

"A start?" Andrea snapped in a hushed whisper so as not to draw attention.

"A start to something great." Essence finished her sentence calmly. "But it's a momentum I want you to continue. Because there's something going on with you that, honestly, even I'm having a hard time reading."

Their server came over and they ordered. Andrea watched with a smile as they walked away, then dropped it coldly and said, "I might be getting my own show."

Essence didn't move.

"Did you hear what I said?" Andrea looked sidelong at a plane passing overhead like maybe it was a spying drone.

"I did," Essence said.

"And I think someone's following me," she added, looking over her shoulder.

"Hang on." Essence ignored the last part. "When did this happen? The show."

"Like two hours ago. I got a text from Guy before yoga and called him back, and that's what he told me."

"What did Tamara say?"

"Guy said he'd handle talking to her. It makes me sick, E." Andrea chugged water and coughed a little as it went down the wrong pipe.

"Calm down, okay? It's going to be all right."

"This is, like, protected speech, right? Patient-doctor confidentiality?"

"Of course, babe. That's why I do what I do."

"Okay. Good. That's good." Andrea took a deep breath and noticed a pair of eyes on her at a nearby table. She felt watched. Followed. Paranoid. "Shit. I shouldn't be talking about this here. I think I have a stalker."

"So, you don't know if Tamara knows yet?"

"No. Do you think she's going to get fired? Am I replacing her? What's going to happen to the cast? How am I going to lead a whole show? I don't know how to do anything. I wrote a fucking book about my diet body and wrapped it up in self-empowerment I reworded from listening to you and Jay Shetty's podcast."

"Stop, stop, stop." Essence laid both her hands on Andrea's available one. The other was gripping the side of the table in a nervous fit. "You're always doing this. You're going to shoot yourself in the foot by getting jacked up on these fears right before the signing."

Andrea released her grasp on the table. They were brought bread. Andrea eyed the server warily as if they might've been a mole.

"Do you think they heard me?" she asked.

"Without risking pushing you away, will you walk through something with me?" Essence asked.

Andrea nodded.

"Look at where you are." She paused, assuming Andrea would take in her surroundings, but she just kept staring at her, waiting for the piece of wisdom that would release her from her insecurities.

"You're literally sitting on top of LA," Essence continued. "You did not get here by being nothing or no one. You got here by being you. And you've put what you've learned along the way into this book. And now you're sharing it with the rest of the world. Everyone, including me, is the amalgamation of outside influences. In many ways, we put out into the world all the things that other people put into us. So, it's understandable that you feel the way you do. But it's also selling short all the work you've done to rewrite your script and take control as the central character of your own narrative."

"I see," Andrea said, wishing she could listen to Essence's words, but instead she was thinking about her slashed tire and the fan's rage-filled face. This brought to mind a lot of little things she'd noticed over the past several months. Items she did not remember moving inside her apartment. Things she'd chalked up to her cleaning lady or her misremembering the minute details of her busy life.

"Your feelings are always valid, okay? Remember that. It's okay to feel stressed or anxious or tired or scared or happy. But whichever feelings you give fuel to, that's the fire you burn. And in an hour and a half, I don't think the blaze that you want to be burning is the one that makes you feel scared."

Andrea looked out at the skyline, at her kingdom. Hollywood, West Hollywood, and Beverly Hills all lay at her feet. She was the virtual queen of Sunset Boulevard but was still unsure what she had done to deserve such a throne.

She closed her eyes and replayed Essence's words. The person she wanted to be having lunch with more than anyone else in the world was Tamara. Thinking about her friend might have fed her fears, but she found that it calmed her. She imagined Tamara's blunt spin on Essence's perspective, giving her a little shove on the shoulder and saying, *You're being a dumb bitch. I see you shine every day. Every day. So, stop it with this attitude, and start being that girl who makes me excited to go to work every day.*

Andrea smiled and opened her eyes.

"Feeling better?" Essence asked, leaning in.

"I am." Their food was set down in front of them.

"What are you going to tell Guy?"

"I have no idea."

"You can't say no."

Andrea took a bite and nodded.

"Who's this following you now?"

"Maybe I'm overreacting," Andrea said. "This guy, a fan, from yoga. I forgot his name."

"So now he's stalking you?"

"I don't know if he's stalking me, but it felt like he wanted to hurt me. I don't know. I got a bad vibe. The look on his face when I told him I'd forgotten—it scared me. Then when I went to get in my car, I had a flat tire."

"His negative energy gave you a flat tire?"

"Not his energy. It was cut. Like slashed, I think. Maybe it's stupid."

"It's not stupid. Remember, validate your feelings."

"Mhm." Andrea set down her fork. "This was a dumb idea. Why did I order this? I'm not even hungry." She waved over the server.

"Do you want to practice anything?"

"What's there to practice?"

"The note cards. Like you said you practiced this morning. Get up on your chair and use this audience right here!" she said, trying to make Andrea laugh, suggesting what felt like a dumb summer camp activity. It didn't work.

"Thanks. But I think I just need to get in the right headspace. I appreciate you taking the time. Your words." She handed the server her credit card.

"Of course."

"Gonna run to the restroom real quick." She exited.

In the bathroom she sat, struggling to pee. As the few drops of urine inside her trickled out, there was a light burn. She hoped it was only nerves and not another fucking UTI. That would've been the icing on the whole stupid shitty-shit-shit cake. She also wondered how bad it would look if she canceled the signing last minute. Hips had done that when she had planned an EP release party but had gotten too drunk pre-gaming beforehand. It hadn't seemed to cost her much outside of a lambasting from *Applause Magazine* and a wrist slapping from Apples itself, which had been planning to film the event for the show. Maybe the turnout to her signing would be low, and even worse than looking like an idiot trying to recite a speech, she'd look unpopular because she couldn't draw a crowd. Someone from the magazine would definitely be there. Simon most likely.

She didn't want the face of the fan to get the best of her, but it created a tension in her chest she couldn't release. Had he been inside her apartment? Would he follow her to the signing? Would he be armed? Letting herself go too far down the rabbit hole would be her undoing. The bathroom door opened, and someone entered the stall next to her. She waited and listened, hoping not to hear a man's voice.

After a long silence, the sound of that person's lunch leaving their body in a liquid rush hit the water in the bowl next door, and a girl's voice sighed and said, "Oh my fucking God."

Andrea covered her mouth, trying not to laugh, never having been more relieved to hear someone shitting their guts out.

She stood and stepped out of the stall and went to the sink to wash her hands. She looked herself over in the mirror and took a deep breath. She knew the only thing she could truly control that day was giving everyone who came to the signing what they were promised. She was grateful her default was to take care of others. At the very least, she could do that for the people who showed up to support her. Aside from her detractors, fans who had met her had spread the gospel that, of all the cast members of *Tamandrea*, Andrea was the most approachable and the nicest. That brought her some comfort.

"Thanks again," she said to Essence as she signed her receipt.

"Do you want me to come with? For moral support?" Essence asked. Only it was in a way that let Andrea know she didn't really want to go.

"No, that's okay," she said. "Baby bird's gotta leave the nest, yeah?"

Essence smiled at her. "Break a leg," she said.

"I'll break both." She left.

Once she was out of eyesight and earshot, Essence pulled her phone from her bag and dialed Simon. She had the story of the century.

15.

NIXON

NIXON NEVER FULLY understood her apparent sex appeal. Every day when she woke up, she felt lanky and awkward. She'd had a significant growth spurt within the past year and stood not only taller than her five-foot-eight father but also taller than most of the kids in her freshman class. At present, she was five feet, nine inches, an inch shorter than her mother. She had turned fifteen seven months prior. The day before her birthday had also been her school winter formal. After being ditched by Dylan Shephard, she had thrown the corsage he'd bought her into the trash and sauntered outside to sit alone at the lunch tables, where she drank too much punch and got sick to her stomach.

The few friends she had made after middle school were not present. They thought that school dances were a form of patriarchy they wanted to topple by not attending in protest. After Dylan had stuck around only long enough to get pictures with her, she tended to agree. She wondered how long it would be until he posted them. He had recently cracked fifty thousand followers on Instagram and felt like a photo op with her was a sure-fire way to ten thousand more.

Despite a social-media fandom of millions, she was not popular at school. She was taller than all the guys but two, and they were teachers. Her peers felt like they didn't have access to her, in part because her mother ran her miniature empire and Nixon primarily went along with whatever was asked of her. She was social media savvy but not passionate about it. It was easier to collect the cash and make her mother happy than invest herself fully.

She wanted to act. But when she pursued theater, the other students only wanted what Dylan thought she was good for—the potential to boost their own profiles. And her acting abilities were argued against by the kids in her class who felt that they were the real budding thespians, while she was just some sensationalized social-media phony. Some wannabe Apples trash. No one would take her seriously in a play. How could they? She wasn't an actor; she was an influencer. She quit theater at the end of the school year.

She drew doodles of characters in her textbooks when bored in class, falling in love with the idea that the student who used that book the next year might be entertained by them. She signed them, "Nix."

She had only ever kissed one boy, and it had been with a closed mouth. She was at the age when her blossoming sexuality was becoming treacherously synonymous with her personhood. Everyone else seemed to care a great deal about how she looked. Beyond that, she found she was attracting more and more unwanted attention and advances by men much older than her but never the lustful eyes of boys her own age.

She was often filled with dread while scrolling through what seemed like an infinite void of likes and comments, almost exclusively pertaining to her recent growth spurt. Perfect strangers who felt perfectly comfortable telling her she needed to wear shorter shorts now that her legs were so long, and that she needed to start using creams to prevent future stretch marks. Her awkward long torso made tops that used to look cute now look like baby clothes. Sometimes she felt like she'd been shot with a ray gun, or like Alice after she drank a growth potion, her toes bursting through the fronts of her shoes. Nothing fit right anymore, not even her teeth.

No one hesitated in the comment section with suggestions on how she could grow her small butt into a larger, more desirable one.

On what injections she might be able to get if her mom signed off on them. There were more encouragements of breast implants for her A-cup chest than she could count. She weeded out as many inappropriate messages and pictures as she could, but eventually the sheer number of propositions she received, of what kinds of lewd acts people wanted to do to her wore her down. When her mom controlled her phone, it had been a lot more fun. Once she was given access to her own at thirteen to interact with her fans directly, everything had changed.

Puberty had never been kind to anyone. She abused herself by internalizing the impossibility of going back to looking and feeling like a short, innocent twelve-year-old. Not because she wanted to do that but because it seemed like it would make everyone else happy and keep them quiet. Fifteen came with all kinds of fun surprises she would have loved to trade in. She had overactive glands and spent the bulk of her days hiding sweat-soaked underarms. Acne along her chin was becoming more and more difficult to mask with makeup. She could block people on social, but she couldn't make them stop talking in distant corners of the internet or on Reddit threads about her young vagina.

She told herself that ninety percent of her life was rejection. From the kids at school. From her mother. From an audience of millions—not one that merely filled a theater, but one that could fill a dozen football stadiums. Like anonymous emperors, these people sat safely in their boxes, collectively possessing the ability to control her fate and her feelings with a thumbs-up or a thumbs-down. She felt strongly that the person who mattered least in the equation was her. Nobody wanted a fifteen-year-old who desired and requested recognition for her authenticity. She was learning very quickly that there was no more disrespected human on earth than the teenage girl.

Biweekly, she held meetings with her mother to go over content strategy: what she would wear, who her brand partnerships were with, which makeup she would review on her YouTube channel, what dance moves she would learn for TikTok, what lyrics she would lip-synch to. Now that she had so many new projects looming as she cracked into film and television too, the questions also included: Who will you say you're dating; *are* you dating? Who is your vocal coach? Who does your hair and makeup on set? Would you hold hands and kiss on a first date? If you were eighteen, would you pose nude (it is only three years away after all)? You seem insecure, who hurt you? So, you're a child of divorce, what's your relationship like with your father?

The older she got, the more she seemed distant from and apathetic to the entire experience. She hadn't always been constantly arguing with her mother. Samantha often reminded her that they used to be the best of friends. When her mother got fed up enough, she would ask what had happened to her sweet, funny little girl and who had replaced her with this monster?

Her father never fully expressed any opinion when it came to what she did. He actively avoided taking too much of an interest in that part of her life mostly because he didn't understand it, and to try to understand would have been too much work. He was happy to be her respite from it all when she stayed with him every other weekend. He was notorious for his "just relax" response to almost everything, even when simply relaxing wasn't the cure for someone's emotional ailment. As she grew, he also began to lose his ability to marvel at what a cute, make-believe grown-up she had been. She was becoming a real adult, and he hadn't the tools or experience to deal with what he assumed were girl problems. Although they had polar opposite parenting styles, Samantha and Bill agreed that she was becoming someone they did not recognize.

And now here she was, everything on paper but nothing inside. The whispers of how to end it all had begun. Despite being on the threshold of breaking into an entirely new phase of her career, she was indescribably depressed.

"Whatever's going through your head right now, this is good," Todrick said, bringing Nixon back from her daydream. "This is what I'm talking about. We capture this. We capture whatever emotional wasteland it is that this album is about."

Nixon felt vulnerable in what she was wearing. "Can we take a break?" she asked.

He lowered the camera and looked at her sternly.

"Sorry," she said.

"You finally get into character, and now you want to stop?" he said. When she didn't respond, he sighed as if none of it mattered to him anyway and said, "Okay. Fine. Take your break."

She squeezed her lips tightly together in an effort not to cry and took long strides across the studio floor back to the bathroom. Inside, she prayed her makeup would not run and she wouldn't have to walk out looking scared. But looking any other way would've been a lie. As much as she tried to float outside of her body, be the alien that was unaffected by earthly struggle, she couldn't. She was scared. She was alone. Her dad was dying.

"Hey," Todrick said softly, outside the door. "I'm sorry."

She took a deep breath as if he had finally given her permission to do so.

"I know I can be intense sometimes," he said.

What she wanted to say was that he was an asshole. What she wanted to do was go home. But what she said was, "It's okay." And what she did was open the door.

He smiled at her. "You want to change your outfit?"

"I guess," she said. For once she wished her mom were there. Not just to choose her look for her but to be the bigger threat. For all the reasons she hated Samantha, she was happy to know the biggest bitch in the room was always on her side.

"Come here," he said and pulled her into him with a hand between her shoulder blades. He hugged her tightly. She wondered if the limp arms at her sides would make him mad, so she wrapped them around him weakly.

He released his embrace and held her at arm's length with his hands on her shoulders. "You want to wait for your mom?" he said, and she felt mocked for being an age she could not help being.

"I'm good." She lightly dabbed a finger into the corner of her eye so as not to leave a streak.

"You're sure?" he pushed.

"Yes," she said, nodding.

"Okay. Good." He smiled again. "I like someone who can make their own decisions."

She kept nodding; the corners of her lips forced upward in an appeasing smile.

"Let's change up the wardrobe." He checked his watch. "Mom should be back in an hour and a half or so, yeah?"

Nixon checked the time on her phone. "Yeah."

"Okay. We'll save the stuff we're shooting outside for when she gets back so you don't have to walk barefoot over heroin needles."

Nixon didn't laugh. She didn't really know what heroin needles were.

"It was a joke," he said, chuckling and guiding her by the shoulders to the clothes she'd brought. "Just relax, okay?" He sounded like her father.

He flipped through the items and ran his hand over his mouth, considering the next look.

"Did your mom have anything specific she wanted you to use?" he asked.

Nixon pulled a pair of black shorts and a cutoff crop top from the rack. "The boots are supposed to go with it, but I guess we can wait. She bought them specifically for this," she said.

"Well, let's see. Put this on and we'll start to get a feel for how it works. Maybe she's wrong and we'll get to tell her we like another look better," he said, as if they would mischievously be able to stick it to Mom together.

Nixon took the items on their hangers a few paces toward the bathroom with her before she heard Todrick chuckle behind her.

"What?" she said, turning around.

"Nothing, it's . . . I've worked with so many people like your mom. Stage moms, you know. I'm happy to go along with whatever her plan is for this. But I also want you to feel like this is your idea too. It's you on the cover. It's you on the tracks. Twozie played some of it for me. You're good. I don't really get many chances to interact with talent one-on-one like this. If it's kids your age, they're overconfident and their parents are calling the shots. If it's people like Nina or Hector, they're surrounded by their entourage, or their manager is telling me what to do. So, while both of us have the chance, let's make this about you before your mom gets back and makes it about her."

"You've worked with Hector?" Nixon asked, opening up at the connection to her idol.

"Bunch of times," he said. "I shoot all of Murphy's clients. Even the God-awful ones. But Hector's a good dude. Kind of weird when he's not in movie-star mode. Real quiet. Like something fucked him up."

He watched her warm up.

"I came at this the wrong way, okay?" he said. "My expectation of how the day was going to go was how these days usually go, which is an annoying shit show. But you're a cool kid. You're not a brat, and your mom's not here to be a bitch."

She laughed, her exterior cracking.

"Now go change and let's see what we can do." He offered a smile.

She reentered the room looking brighter. She hadn't loved his initial approach to how they would work together, but she knew everyone in the industry had a reputation. He had been playing a part he was used to playing; she was required to do the same. With Samantha absent, Nixon could be whoever she wanted to be, and he could too. Finally, no acting.

As she crossed the concrete floor barefoot, she watched him scrolling through photos on the small screen on the back of the camera.

He looked up and his eyebrows leapt. He whistled as if she was quite a sight. The crop top had been cut to roll up slightly over her ribs, exposing the underside of her bra. The hems on the legs of her shorts were shredded, an inch below her groin, the curved W of the bottom of her butt peeking out when she turned around.

"Okay." She breathed out, hoping to take back something she felt she'd lost. "Let's do this."

She wanted so badly to sound cool, but to her he looked like what a cool person looked like, and it made her second-guess everything she said. He had managed to master the look of no fucks given. Shaved to look the right amount of unshaven. Hair styled to look like he'd woken up only an hour ago. The air around him smelled like he didn't give a shit, while she had spent hours with her mother that morning knowing they would have to prove how many shits they gave.

"Let's get this record going," he said, walking to his phone.

He scrolled and hit Play on the first track, "I Am the Wasteland." A small but powerful Bluetooth speaker gently came to life with the sound of a windswept desert, and as she walked back onto the white floor of the cyc wall, she heard her own voice whisper, "You are the beginning. But I am the end. What starts with you is finished with me. All you boys, just dust and sand. Your time is up. I am the wasteland."

Then the low bass of the track shuddered the small speaker against the metal tabletop as the song picked up. She remembered Twozie being proud of that intro, of setting that tone of the tough cool girl who doesn't need boys. A man's version of girl power.

"Sit there." Todrick pointed. She sat cross-legged. "Bring your knees up in front of your chest." She did. "Good. Let's stick one leg out." She did. "Good, good." The camera fired off round after round. "Bring that leg out a little and wrap your arms around your bent leg." She did. "Lean your head a little toward your right shoulder." She did. "Amazing." Each new pose received a burst of shutter clicks in response, a small applause. He moved behind her. "Look back over your shoulder." She did. "Hold that." She did. "Close your eyes." She did. He moved closer to her. "Okay, open." She did. "Yes, hold that. Hold that." She did. "Amazing. Feeling good?" She nodded, not wanting to break the emotion in her look with speech. "Okay, bring that other leg up now, both knees to your chest, but keep looking over your shoulder." She did. "Scoot back toward me a little." She did. "Little more." She did.

She heard him sigh, breath shaky, tension in his throat. She wondered. "Little bit more," he said. She did. "Here, like this. All the way back to me." But before she could, his hand scooped strongly beneath her legs, and he cupped her groin firmly, using it to pull her up against him. She felt him, hard at the top of her tailbone.

She froze.

He backed up immediately and began firing away again.

"Good," he said. He took a deep breath and let it out. Then he noticed she was not moving, and he said, "What's wrong?"

Every single synapse in her brain fired "Danger." And yet, suddenly, every single one of those warning signs was met with an explanation. An accident. A hand placed wrongly. Her mind made a desperate plea for him not to be dangerous.

"You in your head again?" he asked.

She hated that she honestly considered that being all it was. Then she heard herself say it wasn't. But then that same self said the alternative was a reality she could not handle. More than an hour left of being alone with him and not knowing why he'd needed to pull her into him like that for a photo he did not take.

A clamor of heartbeats punched against her chest and told her no, she was not in her head again. But then there was that reason she might be. Mentally accusing him of someone he might not be. The infinite weight of the judgment of everyone who had gotten her to where she was right then and there. The pressure to be grateful. Not just from her mom but from twenty-five million nameless, obscured faces. Football fields filled with expectations.

She had felt him against her. She didn't even know what that was that she'd felt. She'd only ever kissed a boy once.

It must've been an accident.

"Yes," she heard herself say, as if out of her body, alien again. "Sorry."

"It's okay. Shake it out," he said. "I'm gonna pee real quick."

He set his camera down next to the speaker on the metal table. As he walked off, the synths at the end of the track dropped out suddenly, the sound of the barren desert returning, and she heard her own voice whisper softly back to her, "I am the wasteland."

16.

HECTOR

REG E. WILSON's Bel-Air home was a sultan's palace, one that few would expect the seemingly benevolent executive producer of a show like *The Family That Stays Together* to reside in.

As with driving through Beverly Hills, any time Hector had reason to enter this rich enclave in the foothills of the Santa Monica Mountains, he felt strange, as if he had no business being there. Not because he hadn't earned it. Not because he wasn't *Hector Espinoza*, but because when he passed through, he never saw anyone outside their magnificent mansions. He never saw families on walks. No kids in front yards playing games, running through sprinklers or climbing trees or scraping knees. No parents in gardens. No chalk on sidewalks. He only ever saw big, empty, beautiful monuments to nothing. And the people who took care of them. The people who looked like him. The people whose hands had built the homes. Whose hands were always dirty in the gardens. Whose hands pushed the strollers and cradled and cared for the children who didn't play in the yards.

He remembered stories his dad would tell him about his grandfather emigrating from Mexico, teaching himself English by reading Superman comic books, an immigrant like himself. People were always quick to remind Hector how important it was that he was the highest-paid Latinx actor in Hollywood. Never mind that he was one of the only ones anyone knew by name. Never mind that not even he was sure if he was Latinx or Latino or Hispanic or Mexican American or just Mexican. Afraid of publicly putting his foot in his mouth, he relied on Murphy and much younger people to tell him the things he unwittingly accomplished just by being. And now he could add being bisexual to the laundry list of apparent barriers he had broken. He was the first out Latinx bisexual, maybe highest-grossing Mexican-faced actor who had ever acted.

But like anyone who wasn't white in the industry, he hadn't planned to be the first anything. He hadn't even wanted to be. Like his grandfather, like all the others who kept lily-white neighborhoods propped up on their brown-skinned backs, all Hector had wanted to do was work. Even now, with frequent headlines reminding him how much he was worth, dragging himself through Bel-Air made him feel as it always had—like a fraud.

He parked his car in front of Reg's home. He could hear Murphy in his ear, heard Tamara call him a fanboy, and he didn't know what would come of his being there, but it felt like the most logical of loose ends to tie up for himself. Sarah was right. The day hadn't really been about Molly. But there was a rage inside him he'd locked away for twenty-seven years. And rather than that rage driving him to the brink, someone else was going to catch it.

Maybe Reg wasn't even home, although he had been retired for many years at that point. Hector couldn't imagine where he'd go. His last directorial effort had been a documentary about the protopunk scene in New York in the late sixties and early seventies. To Hector, it seemed a weird farewell to the industry. Then again, Reg's reputation had preceded him. Despite the bomb going off in October 2017, the fuse to the Me Too movement had been lit years prior. It wasn't outside the realm of possibility that Reg had been able to see the storm coming and had gotten out before it was impossible to build a money shield to protect himself. By the time he retired, he was seventy-seven and his legacy of barely legal arm candy was well behind him.

Hector struggled daily with his own disgust at his not outing the black box theater owner. But the man had died. Hector had googled his name for years with his fingers crossed until one day there was an obit. Prostate cancer. *Good riddance.* Only it had brought him no peace. Thinking of Molly's story, he wasn't mad at himself just for staying silent. But also for being partly responsible, in all probability, for letting the man continue doing to others what had been done to him. He knew too well of the stories of boys much younger than he'd been, of drugs and private arrangements, their unconscious bodies being passed around in hot tubs high up in the Hollywood Hills. He gritted his teeth. More than he hated the man who had done it, he hated himself for staying silent.

He pressed the buzzer on the call box at the end of the long, gated driveway.

To his surprise, there was an answer. A Spanish-speaking woman with a Mexican accent.

"Who is this?" the woman said.

"Buen día," he said in his pained, anglicized way. He felt like an asshole assuming there would be some sort of unspoken connection among his people. But he trudged on, just in case. "Soy Hector. Espinoza."

There was a long pause.

"Hector?" she said.

"Sí," he said.

"I can see you on the camera," she said in English.

"Ah." He looked around to wave to it but couldn't locate it.

"Your accent is not good," she said plainly.

"I'm sorry," he said.

"Lo siento," she corrected him.

"Lo siento." He let himself be dragged as if he'd disappointed Rosetta Stone, whoever the fuck she might be.

He heard her speaking with someone, the garbled tin of the speaker masking their conversation. Then the box beeped twice and buzzed.

The gate opened. He walked down the long driveway and gazed up, as if he were Matt Source and out of options, so, screw it, he would just go through the front door.

Reg lived in such a way that he made even someone with Hector's money look poor and his style cheap. Because of his involvement as a director of so many pilot episodes of shows, as well as a producer and executive producer of several others, Reg had a constant influx of residual money. He never had to wonder where the money came from; it was simply there. Still, walking up to the newly renovated Greco-Roman-style home with pillars and columns that bore no real weight but the posture of man, Hector wondered about Reg's debt. Hector had learned early in his career that the richer a man became, the more money became a figment of his imagination.

Reg was dressed in a linen suit, with a powder-blue silk shirt and an ascot. He walked with a cane but not because he needed one. He was eighty-six, although no one would have guessed it. He reminded Hector of the old man from *Jurassic Park*—a sweet-looking but rich grandfather with island-time style and a propensity for playing God. He greeted Hector on his front steps.

"I must say, I've been surprised many times in my life, but never this surprised!" Reg sort of half bowed as if he were being visited by a prince.

Hector did not want to lose sight of his mission. But he could not begin with his gun on the table, so he decided to play the part instead.

"Hi, Reg," he said, turning on his charm, smile well crafted.

Reg led him through the house and outside near the pool, where his grandchildren and their young friends were swimming.

"I hate to interrupt a day with the family," Hector said.

"Nonsense." Reg waved the comment off. A member of his staff brought them a plate of cucumber sandwiches, a pitcher of iced tea, and a pitcher of lemonade. Hector wondered if she was the woman he'd spoken with.

"Thank you," he said, not risking his Spanish.

"Gracias," she corrected him, and he felt a little more at ease after she smiled.

"I make them bring it separate because they always fuck it up," Reg said, pouring iced tea into a tall glass, then following it with the lemonade, spinning the drink with a metal straw. "The secret is three-quarters tea, one-quarter lemonade. And you have to use unsweetened iced tea. None of this sweet-tea horseshit. The sugar is in the lemonade." He handed the glass to Hector, and Hector wondered if, with all his money and success, he too would become an octogenarian whose primary passion in life was mixing the perfect Arnold Palmer.

"Thanks," he said, taking the drink.

"I miss her very much, if that's what you're going to ask," Reg said, mixing his own.

Hector wondered if Reg was trying to get in front of any questions before they could be asked. "I know," Hector said, lowering his tone, as if he felt bad for the guy.

"I didn't even realize you were such a fan. Although no one would shut up about the fact that you went to the funeral."

"Yeah. Been a fan since I was a kid. I've talked about it quite a few times doing press—"

"Oh, I don't watch any coverage for anything. I do believe there is an age at which you stop giving a shit."

"Absolutely." Hector sipped.

"That's not a reflection on you!" Reg laughed. "You're Hector fucking Espinoza. What the fuck do you care if you have my devotion? I'm just another rich geezer."

"A pretty important geezer, though," Hector chided and gazed out at the extravagant backyard and watched the wet, shining skin of bathing-suit-clad kids doing cannonballs.

"I read. I write. I take walks. I eat. And I spend time with my family. It's not a perfect retirement, but it suits me." Reg offered his glass up.

Hector clinked it with his. "Sorry, I already took a sip. Is that bad luck?" he asked.

"Only if you're superstitious, which I am not. Are you?" Reg took a big swig as if he'd been desperate for that moment all day.

Hector shook his head.

"Good. Superstition is the killer of hard work and responsibility. A weak person is always looking for ways to say the universe has it out for them. Mercury in fucking retrograde. You don't strike me as a weak person."

"I work out regularly," Hector said very seriously.

"Good," Reg said. Then he took a bite of cucumber sandwich, smearing a bit of butter on the side of his mouth. He winked and said, "Me too." With a full mouth.

"Actually, feels hard to believe we've never met before this," Hector said.

"You know what? You're right." Reg wiped his mouth with a napkin. "Sarah always had a lot of good things to say about you. I'm surprised you would even think to come out here."

"Had the day off, as a matter of fact," Hector said.

"I remember those rare days. The race car of life feels like it's redlining, and then suddenly there's a day where you come full stop, and the g-forces let go of you, and it feels like you're floating in zero gravity."

"Something like that." Hector had no idea what Reg was saying.

"You want to talk about her, I assume," Reg said. If the man was scared, Hector couldn't smell it.

"You didn't want to go to her service?" Hector asked.

"God, no. And be surrounded by those tight-skinned, high-cheeked sirens wailing for show?" Reg watched the kids swimming. "I have my memories of her. That's what I'd like to hold on to, and they are what I will honor."

"Sarah said you two were pretty close."

"I was closer to her than she was to her parents."

"I heard she was difficult."

"Depends on who you ask. Kids like that, you just have to know how to handle them. She was ten when the show started and twenty when it ended. There are bound to be some difficult moments somewhere in between. Especially after she went through puberty."

"But what about the Molly she was for the past twenty-eight years?"

"God. Tragic, isn't it? I could barely bring myself to think about her little circus of a show, let alone watch it. That part of her personality shined through from time to time when she was younger. She had her temper. And when she became a little junior sex symbol? Forget it." He chuckled. "She had power and she wielded it. To anyone who doesn't know how to handle that kind of person, they seem difficult. To someone who does, well . . ."

Hector watched Reg let his last sentence trail off, as if he was implying something. Seizing the opportunity, Hector leaned in and smirked, acting like a buddy. "You get it," he said.

"What do you mean?"

"That attraction. The resistance in the push-pull. The chase." Hector clenched his hands quickly, as if he'd caught something.

"I suppose." Reg was suddenly tight-lipped.

"She was my childhood crush," Hector said.

"Whose wasn't she?" Reg coughed suddenly, clearing bits of sandwich from his throat.

"I guess. I don't know. I'm curious if the girl of my dreams was really the girl of my dreams. You know?" Hector leaned back in his chair, feigning comfort.

"How so?"

"Do you have time for a quick story?"

Reg held out his open arms. "Nothing but."

"So, when I was twelve, my mother was diagnosed with breast cancer."

"I'm sorry to hear that." Reg's face sank in obligatory compassion.

"Long time ago," Hector said, waving off the condolence, wondering what he would say next.

Reg waited for him to continue. Hector's palms sweat. He hid them beneath the table in front of him, feeling as he had at eighteen standing under a rickety spotlight in the little theater, eyes of a predator in the audience on him. Only now he was a real actor. Now he had a voice.

"*The Family That Stays Together* was, I think, going into season five," Hector trudged forward. "But they were playing reruns all the time during the day. I'd been a fan since it started, but since my dad was working and my brothers were in high school and my mom was at home, I started to ask her to watch the reruns with me. And so, one day—I think I'm thirteen at this point—we started watching them together. She wasn't doing great at this point. Chemo was pretty rough."

"I've heard." Reg nodded along, not looking disinterested.

"So, my dad and my brothers come home, and after a while, you know . . . there we are, day after day, watching, laughing. It was like our little special thing. So, then they get hooked; everyone is hooked, and we're watching this show what feels like all day, every day. I'm taping the reruns so they can catch up. It was hard to do this all in order back then, you remember. It's so easy now."

"I say this all the time. We used to have to work to appreciate something. Now it's fucking streaming somewhere for free."

"Couldn't agree more. Anyway, it's September now. I'm about to turn fourteen in December, on the twenty-third. Which was always bullshit as a kid because it's so close to Christmas, and like, do I get two days of presents, or is it all lumped into one?"

Reg chuckled.

"The show is now on season six and it's our show. You know? Everyone's caught up. We're all sitting there live, ready to go on Friday nights at eight. Popcorn ready. Pizza ready. Cokes. The whole thing. For the time it lasted, it was this incredible feeling where, as a family, we could all step through this portal and not be sad for a while. Not be afraid. But Mom's real sick, you know? And eventually we fall behind. I keep taping the episodes. But Dad has to work, and my brothers are in community college, busy with school and working too. And so those final days with my mom, it's just the two of us. No one to take care of her but me after school. I'm cleaning up puke a couple times a day. Eventually the cancer had spread to her lungs and to her brain and she couldn't walk. She could barely talk. And in between me helping her to the bathroom to wipe her and clean her and bathe her, we're watching these old tapes. It was like, even though my family was apart for a little while, somehow we were all still together."

Reg took a drink, lifting his glass with a shaking hand.

"And there was Molly, at the center of it all. She felt like my first girlfriend even though we'd never met. My best friend down the street. I can remember renting a behind-the-scenes tape from the video store about the making of the show and seeing what a goof she was 'in real life.' And little bits of her attitude would show, and I'd think, 'God, I'm going to marry this girl someday.'" Hector sipped, soothing his dry throat.

"And then the day before my fifteenth birthday, my dad wakes me up and tells me, 'Mijo. Mom's an angel now.' We had known it was close to the end. My brothers were off school for Christmas break. And we all went into my parents' bedroom, and we looked at her body lying there. I had never seen anything lie so still. I remember her skin looked pressed up against her muscles and bones in a way like I'd never seen before. Like whatever room the soul occupies in the body, it's that little space in between. And now that it was gone, her body looked sunken, like a wax figure. It was her face, but it wasn't her face."

Hector could see Reg tearing up a little.

"So, my dad tells us each to take some time to say goodbye to her, one by one, before they have to take her body away. And we do. And it's my turn and I'm lying on this bed next to her, adjusting this little cap she'd wear at night because her bald head would get cold, and her eyes are, like, partially open. So, I do what I'd seen in the movies and try to shut them with my fingers, but they won't stay closed. They remain sort of half-open. And her eyes look dead. I can see the faint blueness of her tongue in her cracked-open mouth, jaw frozen. And she looks dead. And it finally hits me that this is real. And my brothers come in, and my dad comes in, and we all cry together. And I couldn't think of anything else to do, so I get up, walk to our hall closet, and pull out an old tape and pop it in the VCR in my parents' bedroom. No one objects or tells me no. And we watch reruns of *The Family That Stays Together*, waiting for the people from the morgue to come take her away.

"And I'm looking at Molly, and even though I know my heart has just been ripped out of my chest, I feel oddly . . . okay. I feel that little warmth of love that comes with a crush. And I knew I'd be okay. I knew we'd be okay. Because we were the family that stayed together. And nothing, not even cancer, could take that from us. And that's when I knew I wanted to be an actor."

Reg's balled-up fist covered his mouth as he choked on his emotions, then he adjusted his glasses and wiped his eyes and said, "Jesus."

"That's why she was the girl of my dreams." Hector sighed, releasing the tension of the monologue. Bowing internally. Ready to finally step down from the stage of the black box he'd been trapped in for twenty-seven years.

"What a story. I had no idea. The show really meant that much to you?" Reg asked.

"More than you'll ever know," he said, sitting up, his disposition changing. "And so, I just have to say, thank you, Reg."

"God, Jesus. You're welcome." Reg got to his feet slowly and waddled over to Hector, who did not stand, and hugged his sitting body. "Sometimes you have no idea how what you do can affect someone," he said, sitting back down. "I'm honored. Truly. That's—that you would share that with me. Thank you."

"I was always so bummed the show got canceled that late in its run," Hector said. "They didn't get to tie up anyone's story lines." He threw up his hands. "A decade invested in this family, and then suddenly one day, they're just gone."

"Ain't it a bitch?" Reg nodded. "We had so many ideas for where they should go. Where they might end up. We tried to do a reunion once or twice, but Molly was off the rails at that point."

"Listen." Hector leaned in. "It sounds silly, but as a fan, I always thought I had this great ending in mind. Fan fiction, I know, kind of lame . . . but do you mind if I share it with you? Might finally feel like I can get the ending I always wanted."

"Shoot," Reg said, another bite of sandwich in his mouth.

"So that season, a new kid moves onto the block. Shy kid. Pretty sad kid. And Peg brings him out of his shell. Saves his life honestly. And over a lot of late-night conversations about being scared to go to college or moving away or facing the major dilemmas of life, she confesses something to him. It turns out when Peg was fifteen, she was raped."

Reg coughed and knocked over his glass, spilling his drink on the table. He quickly tried to stand, grabbing his napkin to wipe it up, but Hector grabbed his wrist and very sternly but quietly said, "Sit."

Reg looked around like this was elder abuse and someone was bound to come to his rescue, but the children were too loud, and the staff was inside, out of eyeshot.

"How fucking dare you?" Reg said, matching Hector's hushed, venomous tone.

"I'm not finished," Hector said sharply. "It turns out, so was the neighbor kid."

Reg stared into the blacks of Hector's eyes, dumb struck. Hector watched the old man's eyes flick desperately from side to side. Then, as if defaulting to old programming, Reg flipped the switch on his ego.

"You're just another little fanboy, aren't you?" His chest bounced as he laughed to himself, feigning amusement at Hector's idea. "Another kid in line for an autograph at the mall tour."

"I guess I am," Hector said. "But, you know, I've got a lot of fucking money now. And I wonder how much it would cost to get the ending I always wanted."

He saw Reg break a sweat but not break character.

"Hector Espinoza. Movie star turned tabloid journalist. Coming here with this," the old man said, deflecting as best he could. "That was a cute story. This is all a very cute premise. Maybe I'll write it into something this evening after dinner. I'll even give the title character a little wetback name for you. Ace reporter Luis Lane, the inquisitive little faggot."

Hector decided against violence, stood, and walked toward the back door. Reg did not get up to follow. Instead, he laughed again and said, "You know, you are quite the actor then, aren't you? What kind of kid makes that stuff up about his own mother?"

Hector stopped and for a moment watched the children swim.

"No," he said finally. "That was all true."

17.

TAMARA

TAMARA PULLED HER car to the side of the road. She sat slumped over, her brain breaking slowly. She was trapped, not just in a sedan but in an apocalyptic vision. Her fate replayed on a loop. Her show taken from her. Her identity buried in public shame. Her legacy reduced to some crippled Parthenon; precious art pillaged from her nation while it was left to burn. For the first time in a long time, she felt entirely out of control.

She wondered if this was her accepting defeat. Of falling so often back into the spirals of manufactured drama that there was truly no escape. This was no longer just for show; it was life. No matter how the day ended, she would wake up tomorrow in a story told for her, not by her. She would face a public every day who expected to be given what they wanted. There were only ever slivers of light for her to lie in when they allowed, brief sunrises through the slatted, grim window of her prison cell. She could count the hatch marks drawn on the walls, crude little groups of five, adding up the seasons until the day she might break free or die. She hated that even off screen, Guy could pull strings and swing her marionette hand toward a gun shaped like a bottle.

She put the car in drive and took La Cienaga Boulevard south to Third Street, then turned right. She felt two hands squeezing her throat as she passed the dance studio and stopped in a small parking lot at her old stomping ground—a little liquor store on the corner of Third and Sherbourne Drive. She had picked the nearby location for the studio as a sort of testament to her strength, that she could build something new and strong on top of something that used to beat her senseless. But maybe it was all just one big fucking joke.

She went inside and the doors dinged in a way she remembered fondly. It had been over ten years since she'd entered a liquor store. Beyond their selection of snacks and cheap coffee, the convenience of their quick fix was always hard for her to refuse. She used to slide small, individual bottles of wine into her purse in case of emergency. Swig tiny, shot-glass-sized bottles before events so she didn't have to show up sober.

The man behind the counter sat watching videos on his phone. Gin would get her where she wanted to go fastest. But she didn't want to overdo it. Didn't want to get sloppy. Didn't want to fail. Didn't want to despise herself. She just wanted to feel better, to feel like life was worth living. Two hundred milliliters would never be enough, but it was a start she knew she could hide.

The man looked up as she waited, her weight shifting restlessly. He recognized her.

"It's you," he said.

She looked from the bottles behind him to his mustached face. Ten years later, he was still working behind the plexiglass. She was shamed by his memory of her. But not shamed enough to flee.

"Can I get a small bottle of Tanqueray, please?" she asked, pointing to the little green monster.

He took it off the shelf. "Where have you been?" he asked.

She was hit with an odd wave of relief looking at him. He had always been like a little genie at the bottom of the bottle. Always smiling. Always granting her wish to disappear.

"I moved," she said.

Ten years of her owning and operating one of the city's biggest dance studios only a few blocks away, and he still had no clue who she was. In all that time before, she had only ever been a reliable customer. And all that time since, he had wondered where she had gone. It was the only comfort she felt all day. Someone who cared.

He placed the small bottle on the counter and rang her up. The sounds of the video blasted loud through the tiny speakers of his phone, bending in Tamara's ears like banshee screams.

She moved to insert her card, but he stopped her.

"No, no!" he said. She thought maybe he'd called her bluff. Maybe he would save her from herself, knowing who she used to be. "Tap." He indicated the symbol for her card.

"Oh," she said, knowing she was alone in her grief again.

The card reader beeped once. She waited for it to tell her she had its approval.

Once she did, she looked up and forced a smile.

"Nice to see you again," she said.

"You too," he said. "Come back soon!"

She left and got in her car and drove fast down Burton Way toward Beverly Hills to get as far as she could from who she used to be. But the studio would always stand down the street from who she used to be; that was by her foolish design. It was there now, full of bodies begging to be seen, casting an infinite shadow over her. Had it all just been ten years of self-sabotage?

Her date with destiny was then and there in her car as she turned right, tucking herself away under the shade of trees on Maple Drive. She wasn't sure how she could live now that she had twisted the small silver cap of the bottle open and risked washing away everything she had built. Her studio, that towering testament to her success and her survival, toppled by a corner liquor store.

The smell of juniper slid up her nose. The hammer on the gun cocked. She put the barrel in her mouth. All she had to do was tip her head back, pull the trigger. Prove them all right. Confirm to everyone everything they thought they knew about her. That she was just another bruised apple fallen from the tree, rotting on the ground.

Like Molly.

What would Tamara's life have looked like if she'd stuck by her friend? Her cheeks were wet with tears for having given up on her. She was one single sip away from letting the audience wallow in that sorrow too.

But where would they go when her lights went down? They had forgotten about Molly in two weeks. Tamara wondered if her own legacy would last even that long. Whose teat would the audience move to suckle suffering from next?

She remembered her last big night out with Molly, the two of them and gaggles of their fans packed in like sardines at the Abbey in West Hollywood. It had been their favorite pick-me-up—getting fucked up, feeling like the brightest stars in the sky, paying for anything their admirers asked for. Greek gods being gracious, pretending to be humble.

The next morning, she'd woken up on a stranger's couch with no memory past, give or take, 2:30 a.m.

"Where's Molly?" she asked a sleeping boy.

"What?" he said, groggy, sleeping uncomfortably in an armchair.

"Where's Molly?"

"I don't know. She went home with Trent."

"Ugh." *It would be a Trent*, she thought. Then she tried to put her shoes on, but her balance was wrecked.

"How much coke did we do last night?" he asked her.

She looked at him and sighed, ashamed but not surprised, considering her sinuses were shouting, *You stupid bitch!*

"I have no idea," she said.

Trying to find Molly after a rough night out was a needle-in-a-haystack scavenger hunt. Partying with fans was almost always a recipe for disaster. The photos they'd find of themselves tagged in on social media the next day were hardly worth the glory they thought they were letting their beloved supporters live out.

After calling her cell, Tamara learned that Molly had left her phone with the bartender. He and it had returned to the club, which was open for brunch by then. When Tamara entered, looking like the absolute end of the world, the bartender said, "Have you seen her yet?"

"No. That's why I'm here." She glared through broad-frame sunglasses.

"We went back to my place, but she disappeared at like five thirty in the morning."

"You're Trent?"

"Yeah."

"Did you two also, apparently, do an excessive amount of cocaine?" She sniffed back the thick snot in her nose and tasted iron.

"No, that was you and Petey," he said. "He loves you guys so much."

"Mm." She tried to play along but could barely hear over the deafening throb of blood pounding through her brain. "Petey's a sweetie." She smiled.

"Anyway, we didn't even bang," Trent said, and Tamara bristled at the word. Only the type of boys who dropped drugs in girls' drinks described having sex by using the verb "to bang."

"What a relief," Tamara said. "Can I have her phone, please?"

"Shouldn't I hang on to it? She might come back here looking for it," he said.

"If this is some kind of bribe, how about I don't reach across this bar and break your fucking nose," she said, still smiling.

He put the phone gently on the bar in front of her.

"Thank you."

"She said she was going to see Jay."

"Who is Jay?"

"Her dealer, I guess."

Tamara racked her brain. She didn't know a dealer named Jay. Just their usual one, Maurice, which was a fake name for a college kid from UCLA named Brandon.

"In the Valley," Trent tacked on, nervously.

"How'd she get there without a phone, Trent?"

"Don't know. She just left. Maybe he picked her up. She was pretty gone."

"You've been such a big help." She rapped Molly's phone on the bar twice and turned to leave.

"Tell her to text me!" he shouted after her.

"No!" she shouted back.

After several hours of nothing and not knowing Molly's phone password, Tamara gave up searching for her friend and decided to do what she'd done every time this had happened—wait for Molly to turn up. Usually still a little drunk. Usually embarrassed. But always acting like nothing was the matter.

What she didn't expect was a phone call from the police the next day. Molly had been arrested for public intoxication. Tamara sighed and asked them how drunk she had been, but they responded that they had found heroin on her person.

Tamara felt a prickly-cold, horrified sensation run through her.

Molly had been passed out on the sidewalk around the corner from a bar called the Chimneysweep in Sherman Oaks. One of the officers had recognized her as the star of his wife's favorite show, and to avoid the paperwork and save her more public embarrassment, they had thrown her in the drunk tank and confiscated the dime bag. When she sobered up, the first person she had asked to call was Tamara.

She picked Molly up from the Van Nuys Community Police Station, and they returned to her home in Westwood, Molly pretending all the while not to be aware of the seriousness of that phone call.

"What happened?" Tamara finally asked.

She watched every possible response Molly could conjure play across her eyes before she said, "What do you want me to say, Tam?"

"How long?"

"I don't know. On and off," she said, trying to shrug it away.

"What do you mean, 'on and off'?" Tamara's voice rose and she watched her typically headstrong friend buckle. "How long is 'on and off'?"

Molly's face tightened as she fought tears, and Tamara thought she looked like one of those silly drawings where right side up it was a haggard old lady but upside down it was a beautiful princess.

"You're shooting up now?" Tamara shook her head.

"Jesus, no. I'm not that fucking stupid, Tam. You can snort it just like everything else we do."

Most people Tamara knew, even those with substance problems, had a line they would not cross. The mere mention of something like heroin and people immediately imagined dark alleys and needle parks. Even with her own addictions, Tamara swore never to touch anything beyond alcohol and party drugs. To her, the so-called dirty drugs weren't just the end of the party; they were the beginning of the end entirely.

"No one seems to have a problem when we're on the show joking about how much Xanax we take," Molly said. "Or Vicodin. Or Ambien. Or having three fucking bottles of rosé for lunch."

"That's different," Tamara said.

"How is it different?"

"It just is."

"I fucked up. Okay?"

Tamara sat in a long silence, watching her friend do her best not to convince herself drug abuse was the only happiness she deserved.

"What if we quit?" Tamara said suddenly, desperate.

Molly got quiet and Tamara knew her friend had asked herself that same question many times. All those drunken nights spent screaming their frustrations to each other about how they were being treated like zoo animals, glamorous and caged but edited to look wild and dangerous.

Molly remained seated briefly, like a deer in the headlights, knowing the speed of oncoming death but having no clue which way to run to avoid it. Then she collected her things and without another word opened the passenger door and got out of the car.

That was their final, quiet confrontation. Tamara felt shaken enough to start nosing around AA meetings, and Molly refused to speak to her again except on the show, afraid of hearing things she didn't want to. Shortly after, Tamara learned she would be getting her own show with Andrea. Per Guy's instructions, Tamara was not to talk to Molly about it until he could inform her. After watching her shocked face while filming, seeing her quiet rage come to the surface, Tamara knew Guy's ultimate plan was to see how high he could stack the teetering emotional Jenga tower. Pulling it apart brick by brick from the bottom and adding more weight to the top so that the anticipation of when it all might come crashing down kept eyeballs glued to screens, mouths salivating.

Andrea had now been thrown helplessly into the same shallow grave as Tamara had been all those years ago but with even less agency to dig herself out. If she had failed Molly, Tamara had always hoped to protect Andrea, to keep her out of the cross hairs. Now the queen of *Dance Battle* was going toe-to-toe with the king himself—Guy Maker, sitting up in his high tower, picking off women like a sniper.

Tamara considered the game board again. The best television would be for her to toss back every ounce of gin she could get her hands on, then go to Andrea's signing and burn it all to the ground. To point fingers and scream about secrets kept and betrayal. Guy was counting on that. Counting on cell phones filming. Counting on social media. Knowing full well the cameras never stopped rolling. He was counting on Tamara being weak.

The son of a bitch was orchestrating something exciting during spring training, and she couldn't stand it. But she also knew there was something he had not accounted for. Unlike seemingly every other relationship on the network, Tamara and Andrea's friendship wasn't just for show. And that was something she would not let him take from her.

She screwed the cap back on the bottle and ran the Hail Mary through her head. Then she opened the door and delicately set the green bomb down onto the street, feeling only a little bad for littering but hoped a homeless person might find it and have a nice afternoon.

"Fuck it," she said, turning the ignition. She was going to the book signing.

18.

FIEVEL/ELLIOT

THE PARTY HAD moved to the casino floor. Fievel was feeling good about his odds. Brit and Nevin had no money. Elliot was buzzed but present and knew that a drunk Fievel, feeling like the life of the party, would spend an exorbitant amount of money on nonsense if that nonsense made him feel better.

Brit and Nevin were that nonsense. They wanted to gamble. And Fievel wanted them to gamble because he wanted to gamble. So he bought everyone a round of old-fashioneds and took out two thousand dollars, splitting it with Brit and Nevin. The group promptly lost every cent at blackjack tables in under twenty minutes. The bulk of it went up in smoke in one fell swoop when Fievel nudged Elliot and said, "Watch this" and foolishly risked a hit on eighteen.

Fievel could sense Elliot's disapproval of his frivolity and, after collecting Brit and Nevin, looked at everyone and said with a smile, "How about those five-hundred-dollar old-fashioneds, huh?"

"Let's go upstairs," Brit said, draped over Nevin, running a finger down his chest.

"That sounds like a great fucking idea, Brit," Fievel said, clapping, trying to hype himself up. "When is everyone else getting here?"

"They're on their way," she said. "They're gonna meet us in the room."

Elliot glanced about nervously. There was a vibe between Brit and Nevin he didn't trust. "I thought we were going to your friend's suite," he said.

"We are. Need to stop by our room first. Is that okay?" she said.

"What's in your room?" Elliot asked.

"The drugs," she said. "A pregame?"

"This wasn't a pregame?"

Fievel smacked Elliot on the back. "Love a pregame! Let's go!"

They got in the elevator, and inside there was a fiftysomething woman who immediately recognized them. She was wobbling in a little black dress.

"The boyss're back in town," she said, stumbling.

"Yep," Fievel said, clasping his hands in front of him, tapping his foot. Elliot looked out the glass elevator window. His attention was forced back to the woman when she started rubbing his shoulders.

"You have the nices' arms," she said.

"Thanks." Elliot shifted to get her to stop but she persisted.

"Ever time ther's an episode where you guyss're at the gym . . ." She bit her lip and made a small growl as if she were hungry.

"Yeah." Elliot laughed nervously. "Gotta get that pump in."

Then she stood in front of him and backed him into the window. She stared at the side of his face. He smiled nervously, and she poked one of his dimples and said, "Boop."

"Lady, quit," Fievel said, mashing buttons to make the elevator stop on the next floor so they could flee.

She started to rub Elliot's chest. He tensed up and stood rigid.

Then Brit reached out and grabbed the woman's hair and yanked her away from him. The woman screamed at the jerking of her neck.

"Brit, what the fuck?" Fievel shouted instinctively.

"He's obviously uncomfortable, bitch!" she said to the woman, who was struggling to stand.

Elliot turned around to help his assailant regain her balance.

"Don't touch her!" Brit yelled.

"Brit, calm the fuck down!" Nevin yelled.

The woman began crying. "My nick," she said.

"Jesus, you gave her whiplash," Fievel said.

The elevator doors dinged and opened, and Fievel grabbed Elliot, and they got off, Brit and Nevin slipping out with them.

As the doors closed, the four of them watched the woman rub her neck and slowly sink to the ground.

Elliot looked slowly at Brit. "What the fuck is wrong with you?" he said.

"She was harassing you!" Brit said.

"We get harassed all the fucking time!" Fievel said, turning to her. "Why do you think we're hanging out with you?"

Then Brit looked sad, and Nevin puffed up.

"Come on, man," Nevin said.

"No, you come on, you shit!" Fievel shoved him a little.

"I was just trying to help." Brit started to tear up.

"Oh Jesus," Fievel said. Then Nevin shoved him back, harder.

"What's your fucking problem?" Nevin said.

Elliot laid a strong hand on Nevin's shoulder as if hitting a button, stopping his robot body.

"Enough," Elliot said. "Everyone take a breath." He could see his friend fidgeting next to him, anxious.

Fievel weighed the option of leaving. Whoever these people were, one half of them was willing to assault a stranger. He recognized that was not a good sign. But he was drunk, and the sense-memory recall of the pleasure of drugs took hold of the rational part of his brain and assured him that everything would be fine. He looked briefly like he was about lose it, then gritted his teeth and said, "Is this your floor?"

"Up one more." Brit sniffled.

"Okay," Fievel said, and they all got back in the elevator and went up to Brit and Nevin's room.

Inside, Fievel and Elliot sat uncomfortably on the bed sipping bottled beers while Brit was in the bathroom and Nevin took his shoes off.

"Keep your shoes on, pal," Fievel said. "We're going to the party suite, right?" Fievel began to get nervous, wondering if Elliot had been right all along. He was determined not to get murdered by a shoeless man.

Nevin smiled. "The drugs are on their way," he said.

"Listen, Game of Thrones, you said they were already here." Fievel got to his feet. "You've wasted dear, sweet Elliot's and my time by being royal fucking spoilsports." He pulled Elliot to his feet too.

The bathroom door opened, and Brit exited wearing lingerie.

"What's this?" Fievel asked.

"Do you guys want to have some fun?" she asked. Then Nevin smacked her ass and she giggled.

"What the fuck is *this*?" Fievel felt like he was losing his mind. "Are you a prositu—sex worker, Brit? Not that there's anything wrong with that. It's just a surprise, you know. I wish I knew what this was, and I wish I were on drugs while it was happening."

Brit held up a small glass vial full of white powder, its cap a screw top with an extendable arm and tiny spoon at the end. She shook it enticingly at Fievel. "A trade?"

"We're not having sex with you," Fievel said, matter-of-factly, then looked at Elliot. "Right? You don't . . . we're not, are we?"

"Nope." Elliot stood. "I think we should call it."

"Uh-uh." Brit walked over to them and pushed them gently by their chests back onto the bed. "You want this, you have to watch."

"Wa–watch what?" Elliot stammered. "I don't even want the drugs. Can I go?"

"Fuck you!" Fievel smacked him.

"You watch us. We give you this." She unscrewed the spoon cap and offered a bump to Fievel.

"Is this K?" Fievel asked.

"Coke," she said.

"I wanted K."

"This is all we have. And no, I'm not a sex worker."

"This isn't amateur hour, Brit." He glanced curiously at the powder.

"Five," Elliot said to him, his tone full of caution.

Fievel considered the offer for another brief moment then slowly leaned forward and snorted the powder from the tiny scoop.

"God damn it," Elliot said, throwing his hands up.

Brit's face lit up.

"But we're not gonna fucking jerk each other off in the corner while we watch or whatever," Fievel said, pinching any remaining powder from his nose with his thumb and forefinger, running them over his gums.

"You really buried the lead on this one, Nevin." Elliot glared at the boyfriend.

"What's so bad about this?" Nevin shrugged.

"I mean, nothing's *bad* about it, I guess. Just, like, why us?" Fievel asked.

"Because we love you guys," Nevin said nonchalantly.

"Is this love?" Fievel said.

Elliot stood again. "How come I have to stay?"

"Because you're in too deep now." Fievel yanked him back down by the wrist, then whispered, "And I wanna see how this plays out."

"How often do you do this?" Elliot asked as Brit and Nevin sat on the bed across from them.

"Whenever we're in town," she said. "Never had celebrities watch though."

"I mean, I don't know if we're celeb—" Elliot was cut off by Fievel's finger touching his lips.

"So, you guys do this thing, we get the drugs, we can go?" Fievel asked.

"Unless you want to keep hanging out." Nevin was unbuttoning his shirt.

"I'm not gonna lie, Nevin. We've really been bamboozled by you guys. And after Brit's little eruption in the elevator"—Fievel watched her face sink a little—"we're gonna be team players for this, okay? Then we're gonna take the drugs and we're gonna leave."

"Fair." Brit was unbuckling Nevin's belt.

"Only rule is, you can't touch her. But if you want to participate, you can touch me," Nevin said.

Fievel was drunk enough to consider it. Then his mind snapped to attention, and he said, "And to be clear, there *are* no other guests coming?"

Brit and Nevin ignored him and began. Elliot let out an uncomfortable groan. Fievel looked over and saw he was clenching his jaw, sweating.

"What's wrong with you?" Fievel asked, his voice low, as Brit reached inside Nevin's underwear and took out his cock.

"What do you mean, 'What's wrong?'" Elliot said, matching Fievel's whispered tone. "I didn't want to be here in the first place, and now I have to watch these two strangers fuck." Brit put Nevin's half-hard dick in her mouth, looking up at him.

"Oh, grow up," Fievel said. "Don't insult their hospitality. Just pretend it's like a super-immersive porn viewing experience. Like VR." Nevin ran his fingers through Brit's hair and rigidly grasped a fistful at the back of her head.

"Well, this isn't virtual reality," Elliot said. "It's literal reality—"

"You're a stick in the mud, that's what you are," Fievel said dismissively.

"Don't call me names," Elliot said as Nevin yanked Brit's head from his erection and slapped her hard across the face. She screamed, then thrust his penis back inside her mouth.

"Uh-oh," Fievel said. "It's one of those."

"Should've seen this coming after the elevator," Elliot said.

They sat quietly. Nevin started ripping Brit's lingerie from her body with such force it looked painful.

"Isn't that, like, a waste?" Fievel asked. "Now they have to buy a new outfit."

"Maybe it's like tear-away pants but lingerie," Elliot suggested as Nevin buried his face between Brit's legs.

"Well, there's blood where the bra strap used to be, so I don't think it's like tear-away pants," Fievel said.

Then Nevin pulled his face up and looked over at them. "Can you guys shut the fuck up?" he asked.

Fievel and Elliot went silent like kids chastised for talking in a movie theater.

Nevin turned Brit onto her stomach and spanked her repeatedly until both butt cheeks turned hot pink. He grabbed her by the throat and began to choke her as he entered her from behind.

Fievel's phone buzzed. He looked. It was Guy again. Fievel smacked Elliot's shoulder and showed him who was calling. "Hey, how crazy would it be if I answered right now?" Fievel said.

"What a great idea," Elliot said.

Fievel swiped the phone to engage the call.

"What the fuck are you doing?" Elliot whispered.

Fievel put a finger to his lips.

Distantly through the earpiece of the phone, they could hear Guy saying, "Five. *Five. Fievel!*" He stopped talking as the sounds of Nevin and Brit's fucking took the place of a response from Fievel.

They heard Guy say, "Jesus." And he hung up.

Elliot's eyebrows were raised high enough to pass through the roof. "You're a monster," he said.

Fievel was trying to contain his laughter but couldn't. Brit looked over to them, then double tapped Nevin on the forearm, and he released his chokehold.

"Damn, that's strong nonverbal communication," Fievel said.

"What's wrong with you guys?" Brit asked, out of breath. Nevin pulled out and sat on the edge of the bed.

"What do you mean?" Fievel said.

"Can't you be a little more respectful?" she said, getting angry.

The boys went quiet again.

"Maybe you guys should go," Nevin said. Elliot watched Nevin's erection noticeably shrink and thought seeing that was like standing at the edge of space and time.

"Hang on," Fievel said as he watched Brit's face move from anger into complete dejection. "You put us through all this runaround, let me pay for tons of shit, injure a lady, and now you want *us* to leave?"

"This is special to us," Brit said, clutching a pillow to her chest, feeling exposed.

"I'm taking that cocaine," Fievel said and walked to snatch up the tiny vial, but Nevin caught his wrist. "Don't do this, Nevin!" Fievel struggled under his grip as Nevin grabbed hold of his other wrist, forcing both Fievel's arms into the air. "We earned this, you prick!"

"Stop it!" Brit screamed.

"Tell your man to let him go!" Elliot stood and walked toward them.

"No, Fievel, stop!" Brit said.

"Me?" Fievel shouted as he was wrestled to the ground by the naked Nevin. "Come on! Ew! Your fucking dick is all over me, bro!"

Elliot charged at Nevin to shove him, but Brit leapt onto his back.

"What the fuck is happeni—God, you're so strong!" Fievel struggled to breathe as Nevin put his knee into his chest.

Elliot swung his body furiously, trying to buck Brit off, but she wrapped her arms around his neck and started to squeeze.

Fievel was certain this was how they would die.

Then Elliot slammed Brit up against the wall with his back repeatedly until she finally released her grasp and slipped down onto the floor. Elliot rushed to Fievel and tackled Nevin.

Fievel immediately snatched the cocaine and put it in his pocket.

"You can't have that!" Brit screamed.

"Yes. I can," he said. Then he grabbed his half-full beer bottle and bashed it against Nevin's head as if they were in a movie. Only the bottle shattered at the neck and sliced open Fievel's hand.

"Motherfucker!" he screamed.

Everyone stopped. Fievel grabbed a pillow and yanked the case off it and used it to wrap his hand.

"If you don't want me to sue both of you into the ground, you'll let us walk out of here right now," he said, strangely calm.

Nevin rubbed his head. Brit rubbed her eyes.

"That's what I thought," Fievel said as he stormed toward the door. He threw it open and left.

Elliot huffed a few breaths and exchanged looks with Brit and Nevin, then stepped carefully over both of them, their naked bodies dripping with sweat.

19.

ANDREA

ANDREA WAITED IN a small back room on the third floor of the Barnes & Noble at the Grove as a line formed outside. She never could have anticipated the turnout.

She'd only known about book signings from what she'd seen in movies and on TV, which was usually someone making a small speech or reading a short passage from the book to about twenty-five people and then all of them coming down a line and pestering the author with dumb questions while they mindlessly signed copies of their book, looking annoyed. But seeing the line stretch down the ritzy street of the shopping center and disappear as it wrapped around a distant building, Andrea felt like this would not be as cute as in the movies.

She flipped through her note cards nervously. More than the speech, the questions were what she was worried about now. She worried about not being able to control a situation where someone asked her something she couldn't answer, with everyone's phones recording her flubbed responses. She worried about making herself, or Tamara, look bad.

Toni entered the room in a huff, bringing her trusted reputation for making an already tense situation more taut.

"Heyyyy," she said hesitantly. Her tone couldn't hide that something was wrong. Andrea looked up at the ceiling briefly, praying this was all a dream, until Toni continued, "What's . . . what's up?"

"Toni," Andrea said, stern as she could be. "What's wrong?"

"Milan, uh . . ." Toni swiped open her phone to read a text. "Milan can't make it. She said she's . . . 'concerned I have mono' and doesn't want to give it to everyone."

Andrea was silent.

"Did you hear what I—"

Andrea held up a hand. Then she tapped her phone to light up its face. Thirty minutes to showtime.

"I really should have known better," Andrea said.

"Do you want me to call her?"

"No." Andrea stood and started pacing. "She texted you so she didn't have to talk to me. Mono. What is she, fucking sixteen years old?"

"I think she just flaked," Toni said, stating the obvious.

"Of course she flaked. That's what she does. God, I'm so stupid."

"That's not true. No. That's not true at all. Milan does this to everyone. It's not your fault."

Andrea stared at a wall lined with employee awards and congratulations. This month's star belonged to someone named Greg Abbott.

Toni's phone rang. The tiny speakers blasting Nixon's "Switch Me On."

"Sorry! Sorry. Isn't this a great song?" Toni answered the phone.

Andrea watched her publicist's face absorb even more stress than it had previously carried. She couldn't fake her way out of it with a smile. Her bright, highlighted cheeks now made her look like a sad clown, desperate not to sob. After a long pause, she said, "Oh my God, what?"

There was a muffled voice on the other end, but Toni's hand fell slowly from her face. She blindly tapped the screen, ending the call.

Andrea waited for the horrifying news.

"Fuck," Toni said, looking out distantly, as if she were remembering where she was when the Twin Towers fell. Then she tucked her phone into her back pocket, forced a smile, and said, "Don't check your phone."

Andrea's stomach sank. Nothing made someone more confident that something was wrong like instructing them not to check their phone.

"Is this about what I think it is?" Andrea asked.

"That depends. What do you think it's about?" Toni asked.

"I don't want to say what it is, in case it isn't about that."

"Well, it's definitely about something."

Andrea reached for her bag, but Toni blocked her with her body.

"What are you doing?" Andrea asked.

"Saving you."

"Well, now I definitely want to check my phone."

"*Applause Magazine* just published a story saying you're getting your own show," Toni blurted out.

Andrea let her head loll back as if she were being slowly decapitated.

"Why didn't you tell me?" Toni shouted, offended she wouldn't have first shared this news with her.

"Who leaked it?"

"Simon wrote it."

"I'm sure he did. Who talked to Simon?"

"He said an anonymous source. And that he confronted Tamara on it at the Formosa and that—" Toni pulled her phone from her pocket. "Hang on. Let me find the article."

Andrea waited impatiently.

"It's gonna be like the front page. Hang on." Toni struggled with her stress.

"Toni."

"Hang on. It's right here."

"Toni!"

"Ugh, fucking T-Mobile!"

"I have to go out there in half an hour without a moderator. I'd really rather not—"

"Got it! I got it," Toni exclaimed with pride. "He said, 'Her silence and nervousness at the question all but confirmed it.'" Then she looked up from her phone, proud she'd finally retrieved the quote.

"So, she didn't say anything," Andrea stated.

"No, no." Toni referenced and read from her phone again as if Andrea hadn't heard her correctly. "Her silence and nervousness at the question all but confirmed it." Then Toni looked up again with a puppy's smile and said, "I guess what she didn't say said a lot."

Andrea begged for death. "It was Essence."

"You think so?" Toni's eyes went wide.

"Who else could it have been besides Guy?"

"You told Essence?"

"I had lunch with her right before this. Well, sat across from her while she whispered sweet nothings into my ear."

"Wow. Fat chance she's getting on the show now, huh?" Toni smirked.

"I should bring her on just to watch her get ripped to shreds by the others."

"Oooh, I like this side of you," Toni said.

"Don't get used to it." She started to pace. "Shit. Who's going to host the Q and A now?"

"I'd be happy to do it," Toni said, perking up.

"With all due respect"—Andrea's hand went up to stop her again—"I still don't think that's a great idea."

"But I love the show," Toni pleaded.

"I know you do."

"And I love your book."

"Thank you for saying that."

Andrea grabbed her bag, then moved quickly to the exit. She'd decided to leave the makeshift greenroom and walk out into the store early and get the fucking thing over with already.

"Dre!" Toni yelled after her. Then Toni's phone dinged, and she looked down and said, "Oh my God, shit."

"What are you doing?" a security guard asked Andrea.

"Greeting my fans," she said as she attempted to breeze by him.

"You can't. There's a process for this so you don't get hurt," the security guard said.

"What's your name?" she asked him.

"Marcus," he said.

"Marcus, I appreciate you. I appreciate your work. Thank you. But it's my signing. My day. Okay? So, I'm going to do it the way I want to do it. That work?" She felt bad for taking her toughest tone with him.

He said nothing at first, then dropped his shoulders slightly in a small cower and pretended to be brave and said, "Okay. But you stay close to me."

"My big, strong man." She patted him on the shoulder and walked to the escalator.

She wanted to greet everyone as they came through the door to ensure they had a more meaningful experience than if she'd walked out from behind some makeshift curtain like a dime-store magician. She figured this way she could also control the narrative better. If all else failed, she'd deny the rumor about the show and say she hadn't heard anything.

Andrea and Marcus both got on the escalator and slowly descended to the second floor.

"Work here long?" she said, filling the silence.

"Contracted. I work for a private company," he said.

"Right. Makes sense. Not a lot of bookstore security guards pack heat," she said, nodding toward his gun.

"Does it scare you?"

"Depends on who you voted for," she said with a laugh as they reached the second floor, but he didn't respond.

"Wow, tough crowd already," she said.

He regained his strong-man composure and put on a pair of sunglasses from his front shirt pocket as they descended the escalators to the first floor like he was in *The Matrix*.

"Sorry," she said.

"Just don't do anything stupid," he said.

"I wrote a book called *Bitch, Your Single Body Is Your Best Body!* Define 'stupid.'" she said self-deprecatingly.

"Is that what it's called?" he asked as if unaware.

"That is what it's called, yes."

"My girlfriend loves your show, so I thought this would be a good gig," he said.

"That's what they all say."

"What?"

"It's the girlfriend's favorite show. The wife's favorite show." They reached the first floor, and he trailed her as she crossed it briskly. "Let me guess, you only watch because she makes you, right?"

"What do you mean?" he asked as she headed for the front door, customers watching their rapid movement. Management rushed to get in front of them. Just before they reached the door, she turned to him and lightly poked her right index finger into his chest.

"It's *your* favorite show, Marcus," she said.

He looked bashful but also angry, like he wanted to tell her he could do one hundred push-ups in only a few minutes.

"We can take a photo after. Promise," she said with a wink. "For your girlfriend slash wife."

He remained silent.

"Miss Bocelli." The store manager intercepted her as she waved at people in line outside. "This isn't the protocol."

"Greg," she said, recognizing his face from the wall in the back room. *Of all the goddamn names to actually remember.* "You ever moderated a Q and A?"

He stammered. She smiled.

"Great! Thank you." She took a deep breath and let it out, warming up her charm. "Look at me. Surrounded by nothing but supportive men. My lucky day. Listen, Marcus here has my back if shit hits the fan, 'kay? He even has a gun!" She pointed suddenly, which created a minor panic among the people in the store whose ears had picked up the word.

"I'm aware he has a gun!" Greg's tone tried to shush her.

"Okay, great. So then we're changing protocol. You let him do the protecting, and I'll do the meet and greet," she said. "Then you ask the dumb questions. Deal?"

"The meet and greet is meant to be after the—"

"Listen to me." Her false cheeriness collapsed, and her lips went white with tension. "I have never done this before, Gregory. Ever. This whole day has imploded, and I am so fucking nervous I could die. Literally die. Right here. Right now. Just drop dead on the floor. And if you don't let me do things my way to try to ease that nervousness, I'm going to throw up everywhere. All over this door. All over this floor. Everywhere! Children will see it and they will scream! Is this what you want, Greg? Is that the kind of scene you want me to cause in this Barnes & Noble? *Is it?*"

"No," he said, on the brink of pissing his pants.

"Then open the doors so I can meet my adoring public," she said, putting on her big smile again as Greg did as he was told. "Teamwork makes the dream work!" She clapped.

They were met by screams and cheers from outside. The long, sunny July afternoon now sweltering at ninety degrees. Andrea paused, staring at the line that stretched out of sight, hand shielding her eyes in a makeshift visor. They must have sensed her fear because everyone went briefly quiet, waiting for her to speak. Then her shock at the turnout sobered her, and she couldn't believe they were all there for her and said, "Ummm, *hi!*"

They were bursting at their seams with excitement. Andrea's smile grew bigger and bigger as they called her name.

"I think you're all supposed to go upstairs, and I was supposed to come out from some back room where they keep all the unsold copies of *The Secret*, but I figured I'd welcome you at the door instead. That okay?" she shouted.

They applauded. Onlookers who had no idea who she was thought they must have missed some celebrity memo.

"But you have to promise not to stand around. We'll do questions after and take photos, 'kay? Just come on in!" She felt herself dipping back into being a teenager. She would treat this just like another beauty pageant down in Tyler, Texas. Show a little leg, do a little song and dance to get the crowd whooping and hollering.

As quickly as she could, she welcomed them one by one. If anything was going to ease her anxiety and save her from feeling like she would fail, it was her mom's overaccommodating Korean politeness and her dad's southern charm. She thought that was what Ranch Water, whatever the fuck it was, should've been: a cocktail of kindness and confidence. She gave a lot of hugs and shook more hands than she would have liked to but knew it was part of the gig. The idea that she might have to do something like this an innumerable number of times across the country, however, plucked a chord of deep dread in her.

People outstayed their welcome in their brief greetings, and Marcus began ushering them toward the escalators as Andrea kept catching glimpses of Greg in the distance, rolling his forearm and hand wildly, mouthing the words, "Let's go, let's go, let's go!"

Back up on the third floor, people packed into folding chairs, and many had to stand, all clutching their copies of her book to their chests like pearls. There was a small area with two large step-and-repeat banners, her book cover printed on one and a giant picture of her on the other. In front of them was a plastic folding table with a thin pink vinyl tablecloth draped over it.

Andrea made her second big entrance as she crested the top of the escalator to the third floor with Marcus. As she walked toward the banners, she was met by Toni.

"I thought the plastic table looked ugly by itself, so I had Elena run across the street and buy a little something for it at Kmart," Toni said.

Andrea looked over to see Toni's assistant Elena half tucked behind one of the banners, the profile of her nose, hands, and phone sticking out as she texted.

"Thanks," Andrea said quickly and quietly, turning to the audience. She looked at them, then turned to look at the giant picture of herself behind her. Then she looked back at them. Then back at the picture. And finally back at them.

"Hi," she said again, now a little out of breath.

"Hi," they said in unison without needing to be prompted as if they were some *Howdy Doody* peanut gallery.

"Ugh, I can see every pore," she said of her magnified face. The audience laughed. She remembered her kitchen at 5:00 a.m., remembered her note cards, which were now imprinted on the surface of her brain.

"So," she began again. "I wrote a book. And a lot of people don't like the title. But you know what?" She pointed to the other banner, which displayed the book's title, and everyone saw the partial profile of Elena on her phone. Andrea heard Toni's voice somewhere shout, "Elena!"

Elena, realizing what was happening, slowly slunk behind the banner, out of sight.

"I'm still single. So . . ." She did a minor Vanna White from *Wheel of Fortune* arm drag across her breasts like they were vowels and said, "Bitch, this body *is* my best body!"

After the laughter and applause faded, Andrea's smile dimmed into seriousness.

"I'm an introverted extrovert," she said. "Not familiar with that term? It means I love to work, and I love to play, but at the end of the day, I need you to stay away!" Then she smiled again, anticipating their laughter, but they didn't laugh. She wiped her sweaty palms on the sides of her dress.

"I know why I'm here," she restarted. "And you know why you're here. Because we're bad bitches!" Then she pumped her fist into the sky in a rallying gesture. People chuckled, but no one imitated her move. Someone coughed.

"Let me tell you something. Your worth is not determined by anyone else but you. Understand? Let me see some nods." They nodded. "You determine your worth. You are responsible for you. It's as simple as that. And there isn't a man in the world who can tell you how to feel, how to fight, and how to fuck. Got it?" That they fully understood, and in an instant she had them back.

The pendulum swing of their approval and attention was simultaneously invigorating and nauseating. She started to pace the small section that was her makeshift pulpit and looked out to see Marcus watching intently. Her eyes scanned the crowd, working to connect with it. Then she caught a glimpse of a face she knew well. The fan with the name she could not remember. He stood there, as if trying to hide behind the fiction racks, which were pushed back toward the store's Starbucks. She could feel him more than see him. He smiled at her. She moved to speak but stammered and stopped for a sip of water, her hand shaking, which she hoped no one could see.

She turned to look at Toni, who smiled too widely and gave her an over-the-top thumbs-up. Andrea began to speak again but carried an unease with her through the rest of what felt like a PowerPoint presentation for a boss who did not respect her. She heard herself hit all the beats, but she kept rubbing the palms of her hands along the sides of her dress and broke periodically for more water than she would have liked to drink.

As she spoke, she wondered if they could see her concern. If it made her words sound lackluster. Her eyes kept darting back to that face, and she was fearful the almost constant eye contact would be taken the wrong way. He might think all her words were meant for him. She was certain it had been him who had slashed her tire, had been him discreetly insinuating himself into her life over the past several months. She saw his smile again, and it was not friendly. Had it ever been? Would remembering his name have stopped whatever snowball was building as it rolled downhill inside him?

When she reached what otherwise should have felt like a battle cry for self-help, she no longer knew what she was saying. And she was fearful about how it would get distorted. Half the crowd had their phones out, recording her every word. No matter how right she want-ed to do by the audience, and by herself, she knew millions of people were going to draw their own conclusions. That here was Andrea again, the spoiled little girl from Texas who came to fame by riding in on Tamara Collins's coattails and her hefty divorce settlement.

The audience's collective face felt sinister. Even if they were rooting for her, she could not see or hear it. To her, they were nothing but a visual comment section soon to be lobbing insults and defenses. She wasn't special. She was just a makeup artist without a real job.

"Honestly," she sighed and sat down in the small folding chair behind the pink-topped table. "This book was . . . mine. Is mine." She fought to make sense. "I mean, this is for me. Okay? This life. My life is for me."

Whatever *Applause Magazine* said of this night, no one would be surprised. She felt betrayed by everyone, especially by the woman who'd given her all the advice that had led to her being there in the first place. How could she ever trust Essence again? Was the authen-ticity she'd fought for these past few years a lie? Was she still as ripe for Guy's manipulation as she'd always been?

"I'm trying to be better every day, okay? Every day. And this book . . ." She looked over at Marcus, who seemed scared for her safety. Toni was on her phone. She could see Elena standing, almost trembling, hoping not to be seen behind the banner.

"If anyone tries to tell you you're someone you're not, fuck them," she concluded harshly. Then she sipped her water and sat silently as the crowd sat expecting there to be more until she said, "That's it."

A slow clap started, but it was halfhearted. People were slowly lowering their phones. She was visibly agitated, and they could see she was sweating through her makeup.

Greg was hustling across the floor wearing a big smile, aware something was off and trying to intercept the situation before she could ask—

"Questions?"

A sea of hands went up.

"Actually!" Greg was out of breath as he reached her. "Well, first off . . . thank you! Andrea. That was . . . so great. Wasn't that great?" The crowd applauded.

"Because this is a moderated event and, unfortunately, our original moderator was unavailable to join us, um . . . I'll be filling in." He smiled again as he sat awkwardly next to her.

"Where's Milan?" a voice shouted, and she wondered how many of them had only come to see a bitch fest between the two of them.

"She's got mono!" Andrea shouted back. "The *kissing disease*." She emphasized the nickname to spite her costar for bailing on her last minute. "I'll let you draw your own conclusions as to whose dick she got it from."

Greg, who had been nervously sipping his bottle of water, did a spit take at her rare brashness. The crowd roared.

"Let's give it up for Greg!" she said, leaning into what a mess it had all become. "Manager Greg. It's not easy pinch-hitting for someone like Milan, you know."

The crowd gave him a lackluster clap.

"Whatcha got?" She crossed her legs and sat upright.

"Well, first off, I think I speak for all of us when I say this book is incredible." He cleared his throat, gaining some confidence.

"Considering I chose you to fill in not thirty minutes ago, I'm honestly shocked you've read it." She laughed.

"You know what they say." He looked at the crowd as if they were on his side and said, "Don't judge a book by its . . ." Only they didn't complete his joke for him, so he quietly, timidly whispered, "Cover."

Andrea's eyes darted to where the fan had been standing, but he was gone. She briefly scanned the floor but couldn't pick him out.

"What was the impetus for the book's conception?" Greg finally asked, bringing her back to reality.

She wanted to punch him in the face. *Impetus for its conception?*

"Well," she began.

"What kind of fucking question is that, Greg?" a voice boomed from the back of the crowd.

Every head whip panned to its source as if, at the back of the opera house, the Phantom had shouted, "Did I not instruct that box five was to be kept empty?"

It was Tamara.

Andrea went white and the entire room gasped. There was not a chance that anyone in the audience had missed Simon's story. They had read it standing in line. Their eagerness to witness the drama of the show in real time was palpable. Every single phone rose again to capture it.

"Oh," said Greg.

Andrea glanced quickly over at Toni, who shook her head to confirm she had not orchestrated this.

Marcus thought it was appropriate at that moment to put his hand on his gun, as if under her athletic wear, Tamara had an impossibly thin bomb strapped to her taut figure.

Tamara did not walk across the floor. She did not walk anywhere. She glided with a dancer's grace that belied her state of mind. Marcus walked closer.

She reached Greg and Andrea, standing in front of the two until Andrea smiled at her and nervously said, "Hi, Tam."

"Dre," Tamara said. Then she made a shooing motion with her hand, and Greg vanished from his chair. Tamara took the mic and sat down. Then she held his water bottle over her shoulder to Greg without looking at him and said, "Let's not waste any more plastic, please."

The crowd held its breath. Tamara looked at them, fed by their anticipation like a succubus. She closed her eyes, took a deep breath, and sighed heavily into the microphone.

"Are you okay?" Andrea finally asked.

Tamara looked at her. "I thought this was your Q and A."

"My moderator bailed this morning."

"Shocker."

Andrea nodded. Tamara laughed, almost a cackle.

"Did you hear that?" Tamara turned to everyone's phones. "I'm sure once Milan is maligned on Twitter, she'll be anxious to talk about her excuses on someone's stupid podcast." They laughed.

"That sounds about right." Andrea cracked a small smile.

"Well, at least now you can get a word in edgewise." Tamara kept playing to the audience. As good of friends as they were, Andrea could not read her. Tamara had stolen the show, so it couldn't be that difficult to ascertain her motive.

"Can I though?" Andrea blurted out, deciding to push back.

Tamara's face registered the blow. "Well, according to the news, you're about to get a whole lot of words in. As many as you want, in fact."

If the audience had leaned in any farther, they would've fallen out of their chairs. Marcus let his hand relax from his hip, drawn breathlessly into their dynamic. Andrea had correctly called his bluff. It was his favorite show.

"Ladies, why don't we—" Toni began, but Andrea silenced her again with a hand.

"No?" Tamara played shocked. "You're sure you don't need help?"

Andrea decided, regardless of their relationship, she was not about to let Tamara walk all over her or rub her nose in a mess she had not made. The show was called *Tamandrea*. They were equals. And she wouldn't be treated as anything less, no matter how much she thought she owed Tamara. Andrea's eyes flicked to the banner displaying the title of her book, and she remembered that in this moment, she owed herself the most.

"Would you like to ask me a question about my book?" she said.

"I will say," Tamara began as the crowd prepared for an uppercut, "your single body *is* your best body."

Andrea hadn't expected to laugh at Tamara's response, but she did. "Right?"

"To quote Craig—"

"Greg," Andrea corrected.

"Whatever." They shared a small smile. "What *was* the impetus for its conception?"

Back by a register, Greg looked devastated as he adjusted a magazine.

"After Lyle and I broke up—" Andrea began.

"Lyle or Kyle?" Tamara asked.

Andrea had to admit that in that moment, she could not remember her ex-boyfriend's name. She looked out at the crowd for their help.

"Kyle!" the mass shouted back.

"Oh, whatever!" Andrea laughed.

Tamara turned in her chair and locked eyes with Greg. "See? Just a couple'a dumb bitches."

"I wrote this book to prove that I could," Andrea said truthfully. "To prove that we aren't all actually just that—dumb bitches."

"Why do you think I opened my studio?" Tamara said.

"You and I have talked about this a lot. You know why I wrote it."

"Yes, but they don't."

Andrea could feel Tamara's intent. She was making space for her.

"I kinda fucked up the big speech about why I wrote it." Andrea laughed. "I got nervous. I'm not really a public speaker. And I think that's really part of it. Putting myself on the page like this. Because who you're looking at now isn't always who's inside."

"And who's inside?

"What are you, my therapist?" Andrea deflected with a wise-guy accent.

"No." Tamara straightened up in her chair. "But you are my best friend."

Andrea had not known the dam holding her emotions was so full of cracks. With everything that had happened that day, building to that moment, Tamara's words broke her, and she started to cry.

A few phones went down out of respect.

Tamara got out of her chair and went to Andrea's side and did something no one in the crowd, nor Apples execs, nor Guy Maker could have ever expected. She put her arms around Andrea and pulled her in tightly against her chest.

"Sweetheart, we both got played," Tamara said. "I already lost one. I'm not about to lose you too."

Andrea's anxieties evaporated into the same energy Tamara had given her when they had first sat down for lunch all those years ago. When she had offered her blunt advice about what her life might look like if she decided to come on board the show full-time. Tamara had been right. No one was going to have their backs if they could not have their own.

Andrea felt like kicking herself for thinking this might be the end of what they had worked so hard to build. Just as she had done then and would continue to do, Tam was protecting her. But Tamara was not about to be played. She had seen the dollar signs in Guy's eyes when she spilled shots on his dumb jacket all those years ago, when he brought her on to help make the show more edgy. At almost every turn, everyone believed that, at her core, she must have been too stupid not to see what was going on. Only she was playing the long game. And they had reached the final round.

Tamara rubbed Andrea's back lightly, then returned to her chair, picked up her mic, and sat.

"I'm sorry I ruined your big night," she said.

"Oh, trust me, it wasn't you." Andrea collected herself, wiping under her eyes, trying not to smear her mascara.

They smiled at each other, and then Andrea watched as Tamara did what no other human could do. It was Andrea's favorite thing about her. Tamara's eyes relaxed as the tension in her face faded and her cheeks fell. It was a cue Andrea had seen her give only a few times as it was reserved for nuclear warfare, when her stress level got so high, it broke through the ceiling into her being completely livid but in absolute control. When Tamara was mad, she was not catty; she was devastatingly collected. And when someone caught that rage, recovery was not possible.

Tamara turned to the crowd of phones and said, "No one makes money without these faces. Do you understand?"

They both stood and set down their mics, and Tamara looked at Elena, who was also filming the event in absolute awe. This was no longer TV drama. It was a street fight. Tamara pointed into Elena's camera and addressed a streaming audience of millions, knowing one man would hear her words.

"Tomorrow, there will be a reckoning," she said.

They started to move across the floor toward the back room, but then Andrea hustled back quickly in front of Elena's phone.

"Also, Essence! You're fired. And I'm going to burn your career to the ground, you little Jordan Peterson bitch." Then Andrea blew a kiss.

20.

NIXON

TODRICK RETURNED FROM the bathroom to find Nixon sitting at the metal table, jacket over her, scrolling through her phone. She was scared and unsure of how to keep herself safe, but the one thing she found the courage to do was to demand that they wait for her mom.

Rather than confront him, she tried to protect herself by defaulting to the simple story. Those boots were key to the outfit; her mother had added another three hours to her driving time that day to retrieve them. She would be livid if they shot too much with her in those clothes but not wearing the goddamned boots.

Todrick read her newly cold attitude as some sudden petulance and decided to let her have her way. As her discomfort persisted, he began by periodically asking politely if she was sure she was okay. She replied that she was fine. Then he asked if there was anything he could get her: tea, coffee, water, snacks. She continued to say that she was fine, not once looking up from her phone. He let himself be confused. All he could recall was trying to reposition her. His hand had accidentally brushed up against her. If there had been anything wrong, it had been a mistake. And now her refusal to let him be kind had him deciding that he was done trying. He had done nothing but be nice to her, and she was being ungrateful. He checked the time. Mom would be back soon. Then he exonerated himself, concluding that because of her childish, amateur attitude, she truly was what so many trolls had viciously called her in comment sections—just a tiny cunt.

Forty-five silent minutes later, Samantha arrived in a huff, Starbucks cup in one hand, precious boots in the other. Nixon's hands, holding her phone throughout the entire wait, had never stopped shaking.

"How's it going?" Samantha smiled, desperately pretending she hadn't been screaming at herself in the car for hours.

"Low-key," Todrick said.

"That's good. Low-key is good. What have you two been doing?" she asked, setting the boots down in front of Nixon.

"Nothing," Nixon said, knowing the only way out of the day was through it. So she turned her charm back on, beaming at her mom, a good little alien. It was another opportunity to act, after all.

"Where'd this energy come from?" Samantha asked.

"Just ready to get going," Nixon said.

Todrick also smiled at Samantha; a similar charm engaged.

"We've just been kickin' it," he said, shrugging slightly.

"Did you shoot anything?" she asked.

"Just tested the light and some wardrobe," he said.

"Oh, good. That's good. Can I see?"

"Sure."

He moved the camera slung around his neck so she could see its tiny screen, powering it on and scrolling through a few photos.

"Okay," she said, smiling again. "Okay!" She looked over at Nixon. "How do you feel?"

"Fine," Nixon said.

"What's next?" Samantha asked. "Boots? Boots and boys!"

Todrick chuckled in a way that told her it was a good try, Mom. "I think we should go outside," he said.

"Really?" Samantha peered out the large studio windows. "Isn't it a little warm today?"

"It's perfectly safe," he reassured her.

She looked at her daughter.

"Yeah, let's do it," Nixon said.

Now that she had a safety net, Nixon knew she could passively waste Todrick's time by striking the poses and making the sexy pouty faces he hated. He didn't have the balls to push her around in front of her mom. She'd shot with guys like him before. They were all terrified of moms. Plus, she knew all the looks he hated were what Apples execs wanted anyway. If they'd shown them pages of proofs with nothing but her looking moody, they would've told them to do it again. As Nixon and Samantha had been told early in the process, Apples was not in the business of the brooding-sad-girl, oversize-T-shirt, maybe-they're-actually-a-boy bullshit. Apples did not do emo vibes. To them, Nixon was their new way of reaching a younger demographic via the adults that watched their shows. Hoping parents who loved *Tamandrea* would also sit their daughters down to watch *That's So Social*. The network referred to this potential young audience as "Candy Apples."

They ventured outside the studio and captured the plight of Los Angeles as it was on the east side of downtown, wading into a scene too real to be production design—tents and trash and run-down corner markets. There was something almost beautiful in its destitution. In the fact that what rose up from these scenarios was not chaos but communities, courage somehow built from a disparity of class. A broken part of the city made whole by collections of the unwanted.

Confused eyes watched as they snapped photo after photo.

Samantha grew gradually more uncomfortable with the reckless-ness of Todrick's style, feeling strong-armed into his artist's vision. She feared for their safety, feeling the gaze of the unfortunate and underprivileged, inevitably sniffing them out as well-to-do prey dangling on a hook with a fifteen-year-old lure in these treacherous waters of town.

The sooner they could get out the better. Besides, she wanted to be early to their dinner with Murphy to discuss her daughter's future with Apples and how the industry would better take care of them. The album, by this point, had taken a back seat to the much-desired TV show about Nixon's life. The life of a little Molly. That had always been Samantha's dream. If the movie performed well, it would only be a matter of time.

Trying to catch her breath, she watched as Nixon stood scantily clad in six-inch leather heels, shorts, and a crop top, biting her lip. She pursed them. She bat her eyelashes. All while their backdrop was the reality of the world her album was suggesting. Skid Row. Some sort of apocalypse to the privileged.

Todrick saw the look of dread on Samantha's face and casually reminded her, "Relax. If you don't like any of these backgrounds, we can just photoshop them out."

AFTER IT WAS all over, Nixon was grateful to be back in the shotgun seat of her mom's car. Whatever courage she had mustered to power through the rest of the shoot slipped through her now in waves of sighs.

She wished she'd had the fortitude to fight back. Wished she hadn't had to be saved by her mom as if she were being picked up from the mall because she couldn't drive. Worst of all, Todrick was allowed to keep playing his part too, hiding behind the grunge of his shit-stain aesthetic. She imagined what would have happened if she had said something. She wondered why she didn't. She blamed herself for not doing it.

"Snap out of it," her mom said. "Are you going to be like this the rest of the day?"

Nixon looked at her slowly, and the thought of stabbing her entered her mind, then she shrugged.

"What happened to you?"

"Nothing."

"Well, you were fine in front of the camera, and now you're how you are when you don't get your way. Fucking Murphy!" Samantha said and hit the palm of her hand against the steering wheel. "Who asks for a five-p.m. dinner on a weekday knowing we're coming from downtown at four?"

"He's busy I guess," Nixon said.

"We're busy too."

Nixon's mind wandered back to her dad, and she wondered what he'd thought he was accomplishing by reading her his death sentence the morning of her big photo shoot. He'd known Samantha would hold over Nixon anything that went wrong with the day. She felt played.

"How do you feel about today?" her mother asked.

"Fine," she defaulted to saying.

"Everything is always 'fine' with you."

"Because things are fine."

"Okay, I just want to make sure you think we got what we need."

"Do you think we got what we need?"

"I don't know. It's not my album."

"Isn't it, though?"

"That is uncalled for." Her mother got briefly quiet, then said, "We paid for this photo shoot, you know."

"I know."

"Even though we make good money, we still have to pay for things. You understand that, right?"

Nixon looked down at her hands and wished she could wash off the day.

"You're not in the big time yet where people just do things for you for free and Apples foots the bill."

"I know."

"We cannot piss off Guy." Then she doubled down. "*You* cannot piss him off."

Nixon held her breath.

"If this album doesn't do as well as we need, your clothing line, your movie, everything we've built—we're going to lose our chance with him. We've worked too hard for all of this, so I need you to take this seriously. Understood?"

Nixon wondered if this was what it felt like to be an android losing power, where the jaw gets stuck in the open position, and the eyes blink half-lifeless as the head ticks right to center, right to center, until the voice box draws out into a low, battery-sapped growl, and the body slumps forward, ceasing to function.

"We'll talk to Murphy about it. I'm sure he can explain it to you better than I can." She felt her daughter next to her, losing steam. "So, you'd better turn it on for him."

"I will." And Nixon dreamed of outer space.

THE THREE MET at a small French restaurant on Third Street near Murphy's office called the Little Door. He insisted it would be his treat. He apologized for forcing their end-of-day, crosstown slog, but he was having drinks with Hector nearby afterward, and it saved him a trip.

If there was anything that would send jolts of life into Nixon, it was the mention of Hector. She wondered if maybe he'd arrive early, and they'd get their chance to meet him.

"So, Todrick, he's the best, right?" Murphy flagged a server over.

"Honestly, he's incredible," Samantha said after her daughter missed the opportunity to give the man praise.

"I'm so glad," Murphy said. "Such a talented kid. I met him five or so years ago by accident right here, actually."

"Oh, really?" Samantha leaned in.

"I was a little tipsy, to tell you the truth. Had a few too many lunchtime pinot grigios and saw him shooting photos of someone right outside. Stuff for social media, like your stuff." He nodded toward Nixon. "Asked to see some of the pictures right there on the street and was completely blown away. Figured I'd give him a shot with some of my clients and"—he opened both hands toward them—"here we are."

Samantha beamed. Nixon cracked a small smile.

"Are you happy with how the shoot went?" he asked her.

"Oh my God, you should see some of the shots he showed us when we got back to the studio," Samantha answered for Nixon. "This sort of urban-blight cyberpunk apocalypse. Cyberpunk?" She looked to Nixon, who gave a single nod.

"Sounds like something someone my age should know is cool, but I'm just going to pretend it is because I have no idea what any of it means," he said.

Samantha laughed at his joke much too loud. He chuckled in response and looked at Nixon, who seemed indifferent to her work with the photographer. Murphy studied her expression and wondered where he had seen it before.

The server came to their table, and they ordered drinks. Murphy changed the mood and subject.

"So much shit—" He made a face, looking from Nixon to her mother. "Stuff. Stuff in this industry changes so fast. It's good to keep an influx of young people who know what they're doing. Otherwise, it'd just be me and Hector getting old together. Not that we don't like holding hands and watching movies late at night."

"You used to be his agent, right?" Nixon finally chimed in.

"Mm-hmm." Murphy nodded. "But then I got tired of measuring dic—dramatic moments with everyone else, so I became the pack-age-it-all-together guy. And this whole Apples market continues to be a pretty ripe orchard. I'm glad Victory gave me a call about you."

Nixon had signed with the Valiant agency, run by Victory Valance, six months prior. They'd had a two-year contract about to expire with their previous agent, and Victory's daughter had followed Nixon on social media. Knowing that she had gotten famous on her Molly impressions years prior and knowing Apples was planning to dip their toes into original scripted content, Victory had felt Nixon was the perfect fit for their experiment. Signing with Valiant made Samantha feel that they were one giant leap closer to the thing she had always dreamed of. Nixon thought starring in her own movie might give her the opportunity to shine as an actor beyond the short YouTube series she'd been in, *Squad Goals*, in which she was part of an ensemble of other influencers her age. It had been about a group of young girlfriends on the same soccer team who faced varying opponents on the field and boy problems and bullying issues off it. Adult critics with nothing better to do had described the show as "a balsa-wood-delicate drama" with a cast that was "much better suited to social media moments than long-form content."

When she had gotten the script for *That's So Social*, she had been upset to find that it read similar to episodes of *Squad Goals*. She would be playing right into her stupid type—a cute kid in over her head who ended up happy in the end.

"You excited about this movie release?" Murphy looked directly at Nixon as their drinks arrived.

She felt her mother's hand on her thigh, squeezing it to prompt a response.

"Of course," she lied. "How could I not be?"

"And how do you feel about it?" He looked at Samantha.

"It feels like the first brick laid in what we've been working long and hard toward building," Samantha responded.

"I'm going to be completely honest with you. Outside of our first meeting, I wanted you both to come to dinner so we could talk more on a human level. I can throw a lot of fancy names at you like Hector, but ultimately, I think I have more to learn from you than you do from me." He looked at Nixon. "This is a new landscape."

"Applause?" Samantha asked, confused.

"No, no." Murphy dribbled his wine just slightly and quickly brought his napkin up to his lower lip. "Fucking hole in my mouth— ohp!" He covered his mouth with his napkin as if he'd insulted a saint.

"Mr. Beck, it's fine if you'd like to swear," Samantha said. "It's . . . not like we didn't build our brand off of it."

Murphy smiled, his eyes locked with Nixon's, studying her somber expression. "That is very true."

"You mean social media," Nixon said, matter-of-factly.

"Thank you," Murphy said. "I'm an old man—"

"Mr. Beck, hardly." Murphy could feel Samantha ingratiating herself, and he didn't like it.

"Mom," he said, pointing at the front of his noticeably balding head. "I got these hair plugs that didn't take last year in an effort to run away from being a 'Mr.' anything. So, it's Murphy, or you can get the fuck out."

Nixon laughed out loud for the first time in what seemed like a much-needed release. Samantha's hand squeezed her thigh again, this time to quiet her, but Nixon felt like she finally had permission not to take things so seriously.

"All right, one out of two!" Murphy said.

Samantha sipped her drink.

"I've never been in a position of talent having to hold my hand, but I'd be a liar if I said I expected to take you to the moon on a rocket ship I built in my backyard. So, you'll both have to be willing to work with me. As much as I can open doors, I'm going to expect you to know how to walk through them." He opened his menu.

"We built this from scratch," Samantha said. "Trust me, we can walk through doors, jump through windows, even break a few if need be."

"Okay. That's good. That's good. I'm glad." He held his menu up to shield himself from them. Samantha felt immediately uncomfortable, reading his gesture as a means of shutting her up. Her phone rang. Nixon looked over and saw her dad's name.

"Excuse me," Samantha said, standing and exiting.

Murphy lowered the menu.

"Jesus," he said, looking at Nixon. "Saved by the fuckin' bell, huh?"

Nixon smirked. But then she wondered if this was her afternoon all over again. Murphy had put them in touch with Todrick. Was that by design? Was this part of the organization he ran? His grooming process? Her stomach turned over as she imagined the twist ending of Hector turning out to be a villain in real life.

"She keeps saying *we*." He put down the menu.

"Yeah," Nixon said.

"What do you think?"

"About what?"

"About what I just said."

"Oh." She started to fumble as she continued to spiral down the thought of how sure she'd been of her world at 9:00 a.m. that morning and how inside out it had become in eight hours.

"Also, what the fuck happened?" He quieted when he saw the question give her a jolt. "I mean, you were a firecracker last time I saw you. How did this day get you so topsy turvy? Don't tell me it's the whole sad-girl vibe thing."

There was something familiar in her posture. In her almost-set-in-stone energy. She looked scared.

Then he remembered. He had seen that expression before, decades earlier. He had watched other eyes feign being fine in the same way when something was so clearly the matter. He had sat across from a face like hers, harboring its secret, at a hole-in-the-wall sushi restaurant in the Valley.

"I'm your manager, Nixon," he said, serious. "It sounds stupid, but in more ways than one, I can help you."

"I know." She pretended to take him seriously. "That's why we're here."

"Not *we*," he corrected her. He looked out through the open-air seating of the restaurant's front patio and saw Samantha pacing, frustrated.

"Right." She could not decipher whether he was being sincere or sinister, and it made her terrified she wouldn't know how to look at the world anymore.

"I did notice only your mom had glowing things to say about Todrick," he said.

"It's been a really long day."

"I've been working with him a long time." He sounded tired when he reiterated this information. As if he too had been holding up a heavy pretense he had to set down for a moment. "I'd be a shit manager if our relationship didn't start off on the right foot. Yeah?"

"Yeah!" She smiled big and forced a bubbly laugh, thinking she was giving him what he wanted.

"Don't do that," he said, and she got very small.

He looked at her, and a million questions ran through his mind. Then he remembered his calls with Hector throughout the day. The journey of his own Odysseus, finding his way back home amidst the siren song of relived trauma.

"I'm only going to ask you one question. Okay? I'm not going to pry, and I'm not going to force you to say anything you don't want to. I think that's important. But this whole Hollywood machine has gone tits up—fuck. See? There I go with the wrong-words thing. It's hard for me to keep track of what's okay and what's not these days." He sipped his wine to reset.

"Things have changed. Kind of. I mean, I'd like to see them keep changing. It's why I signed you. And it's why I'm saying this now, because you look like you've seen a ghost, and I made a promise to protect someone a long time ago who wore that same face. And I want to make you the same promise. So, all you have to do is say yes or no when I ask my question."

Nixon waited, rolling his words around in her head, not sure if everyone at this level was a master of deception.

"Did—" he started.

"Sorry, sorry, so sorry!" Samantha hustled a little awkwardly to sit back down at the table. "Your father." She rolled her eyes at Nixon, which told her the conversation couldn't have been all that serious.

"That's okay! That's okay." Nixon was amazed at how well Murphy could turn on warmth to cover the cold air they had just been sitting in. "I was just about to ask your daughter, with such a crazy day"— then he turned to her, and she could see he was smiling but his eyes were gravely serious, like in a family photo taken after a funeral—"if you could, would you do it all over again?"

He laughed as if he had told a joke, which prompted Samantha to laugh. But his eyes never left Nixon's. She wanted to trust him but couldn't be sure.

It didn't matter. All he needed was the telling twitches at the sides of her mouth as her lips trembled in resistance to crying and she lightly shook her head no. Then she coughed to hide the tears in her eyes from her mother and wiped her mouth with her napkin.

"Of course!" she said, looking back at him, plastering on a familiar smile, Samantha patting her thigh in approval.

21.

THE AVENGERS

FEELING LIKE REG might chase him off the property with a shotgun, Hector hustled to his car. Afraid he was being watched through security cameras, he put the car in drive and moved it down the street to the corner, then pulled over and wept.

He wondered who he could tell about this. He had grown so accustomed to being told his opinions didn't matter, to shut up and dance. To entertain like a tortured jester. This was how the world had gotten to Molly. So many had chipped away at her, then the audience had sealed her fate. When she needed them most, they betrayed her. And no one was willing to take the blame.

He did not know where to go. He thought about Murphy and their impending drinks but wasn't sure he had the strength to spend another moment in a public place. He felt like a gaping wound. Going to places like the Phoenix with Murphy made him feel like a dog out for a walk. Everyone asked the owner if they could pet it, but no one ever asked the dog if it wanted to be petted.

He thought of Essence, but the sound of her voice in his head made him angry. He was proud that he had jumped and taken this risk but now felt like he would have to learn to fly on his way down before he crashed.

His phone rang. He stared at its brittle, cracked screen. Too many times he had been burned by curiosity about unknown callers. People who had somehow gotten his number. Fans. Stalkers. Telemarketers. But there was always an allure to wondering who it might be. There was always the thought that if the call went unanswered, something important might be lost forever.

"Hello?" he answered weakly.

"Are you still on your little Cub Scout crusade?" Tamara asked on the other end of the line.

He didn't respond.

"Let's meet for a drink," she said.

"I thought you didn't."

"I don't. You and Andrea can have one, and I'll have some over-priced nonalcoholic elderberry bullshit. But we should talk." Then, almost begrudgingly, she added, "We could use your help."

"Where are you?"

"In the back room of the Barnes & Noble at the Grove."

"Why?"

"It's a long sto—listen, do you want to meet up or not?" she snapped, then took a deep breath. "Look, I'm sorry about earlier today."

"It wasn't my best idea," he said and pulled the phone away from his face to check the time. "I've got to meet my manager for a drink at the Phoenix at seven."

"Who goes to the Phoenix?"

"It's walking distance from his office."

"Ah," she said, knowing managers' and agents' least favorite thing was being inconvenienced. "We'll see you there, then."

She hung up, and Hector wondered if he was being played. The dominos, though tragic, had now fallen into a neat line. A good portion of him wanted to retreat home, to sit with everything he'd learned, have another cry, and force his dog to cuddle him. But, for him, the last step had to be cracking the emotional door open further with Murphy. It was time to exhume the body. Secrets never served anyone.

EVERY ROOM HE walked into stopped still. Even people who did not like him or his movies stared. He had precisely the magnetism needed to not be hated by anyone. Disliked but never despised.

"Oh Jesus!" Murphy liked to draw attention to Hector's presence because it made him feel similarly like a star. All eyes on Hector were peripherally on Murphy. "Avert your eyes, you fucking gawkers!"

Ellie, the bartender, had a gin and soda ready for Hector.

He sat down on a stool next to Murphy. "Thanks, Ellie."

"What a day, huh?" Murphy said, a little too loud.

Hector sipped his drink, holding it with a shaking hand. Murphy watched him set it down slowly with both.

"Can I ask you something?" Hector said soberly.

"Of course."

"How is it that Reg is still living like that?"

Murphy knew he couldn't joke his way out of this. Especially not after the dinner he'd had.

"I went to talk to him," Hector answered before he could be asked.

"Honestly?" Murphy wished there was a better answer. "He's too old."

"What difference does that make?"

"He dodged the reckoning. I mean, don't get me wrong, he was exiled to his fucking Elba estate by insiders a long time ago. They all knew. No one would hire him. But no one could technically prove it either. Anyone with eyewitness testimony said mum's the word 'cause they were creeps too and didn't want the finger pointing at them. So, he got to keep his reputation in exchange for being quietly kicked out."

"There's no one else?"

"You saw his fucking house. He lives like Scarface. What is anyone going to do to him now? The person who could have damned him the most is dead."

"Why didn't you ever tell me about stuff like this?" Hector sounded petulant.

"It's time to stop pretending like you never knew."

"I am."

"I just wanted to keep you safe. Okay?"

Hector almost never saw Murphy get flustered, but the unsteadiness of his voice told him Murphy was going through something. "What good would it have done to talk about it?" Murphy asked.

"About what happened to Molly or about what happened to me?" Hector countered.

Murphy was quiet. Then he said, "I was scared you'd end up like her."

"Dead?"

"Yeah." He looked sad. "Or all fucked up, I guess. Just another mess like everyone else."

"I am fucked up."

Murphy's gaze met the bar, no longer able to run.

"Are *you* okay?" Hector asked.

Murphy's eyes darted about. "Me? I'm fine. Super fine. Everything is fine."

"Maybe you should call Essence." Hector smirked.

"I oughta kick you in the dick, pal."

Hector laughed. "What's it like to only have one real friend in your life?"

Murphy looked surprised.

"It's really hard," Hector answered for him.

Ellie put down another glass of wine for Murphy, who was holding back tears. Hector pulled him into a little side hug, knowing that was about as far as he would get him to open up for the night.

"I appreciate you." Hector said.

"Don't touch me, peasant." Murphy's pretend curmudgeonly attitude returned as he shrugged Hector off his shoulder. "I assume you've given up on getting a hold of Guy?"

"It's not about him anymore," Hector said.

Murphy's eyebrows rose. "Oh, really? It's always about Guy Maker."

Murphy chuckled. "It always comes back to his headline. America's innocent little sweetheart."

"Why did you two stop talking?"

"Why do you think?" Murphy mindlessly looked up at a Dodgers game on the TV above the bar. "He kept asking me to get you on his show. I kept saying no."

"You didn't want me promoting Matt Source on the biggest platform in the country?"

"Truthfully, no. I did not. He told me he wouldn't ever feature any of my talent on his show again if I refused to let you go on, so I told him to fuck off."

"You didn't think I could hold my own?"

"Now, maybe. Then, no."

"I'm honored you think so highly of me."

"It would've made you look bad. That's what he revels in. You'd go on his show, and he'd make you look like an asshole. If you went on today, he'd make it about your little tryst with Cyd. Make it about why you've been virtually MIA for two years. Make you feel really weird about being bi—probably not even believe you that you are bi. Jokingly ask to see your dick pics but definitely not be joking. He'd make it about everything other than who you are as a person. Just ask those girls who had their little sob story at the bookstore today."

"What are you talking about?"

"Your little Apple Dumpling gang. Tamara and Andrea."

"Oh. Well, they're meeting me here," Hector said.

Murphy choked on his wine. "Come again?"

"She called me back."

"Who?"

"Tamara. Said they need my help." Then, as if it were an autopilot function, he smiled and waved at a group of onlookers with their phones out in the distance.

"What, do you all plan to spend the rest of the night running blindly through a hallway of open doors like the fucking gang from *Scooby-Doo*?" Murphy asked.

"Maybe."

Neither had to see Tamara and Andrea enter to know they were present. There was awe when someone like Hector entered a room, but there was perfect pandemonium when fans of Apples shows saw their icons. It was like kids crying behind the barriers outside of a Beatles concert.

Hector and Murphy watched for ten whole minutes while the girls gave everyone the attention, hug, and photograph they asked for. It was something Hector had never experienced or even tried to do. The faces of their fans melted with a particular kind of glee that left a lasting smile.

Finding the brief opportunity to break away, they sidled up next to Hector and Murphy at the bar.

"What kind of idiot comes here?" Tamara said, not dropping her smile.

Murphy raised his hand.

"Oh. Right," Tamara said. "The manager."

"Just the manager." Murphy nodded as he spoke. "That's *all* I am."

The bar was crowded. Andrea looked at two girls sitting on Murphy's right and said, "Hi, girls. I'm so sorry but . . . we have a kind of important meeting with Hec here. Do you mind if we steal these?"

Hector registered the nickname again as the strangers acted happy to have kept the seats warm for Andrea and Tamara.

"What is that?" Hector asked.

"What's what?" Andrea said.

"You all call me Hec. No one else calls me that. Cyd called me that, it's like some inside joke."

"It is," Tamara said.

"Why?" Hector asked.

"Fievel started it last season on his show," Andrea said. "The promo for your last spy thing," she continued, and Hector got a kick out of knowing that she had no clue what an entire billion-dollar franchise was called other than a "spy thing."

"There was a tag line or something you said like, 'This summer, there will be hell to pay,'" she said. "Only Fievel said you said it in a weak-sounding way, and it should've been 'This summer, there will be heck to pay.'"

"Hilarious," Hector said.

"So, we all started saying 'heck' all the time back and forth between us, and when we saw you on billboards and stuff, we'd just point and shout, 'Heck!'" Her small, satisfied laugh trailed off as she continued to be amused by the joke.

"It's actually a meme too," one of the girls who'd offered her seat felt emboldened to share. She showed him her phone, and on it was a picture of him as Matt Source making an awkward face mid-frame that someone had screen grabbed. It looked like he was orgasming. Bold white text said, "Hector Pay!"

"I don't understand," Hector said.

"Just, like, instead of 'hell to pay,' since they were saying 'heck' on the show and you made so much money the past few years, people used the rest of your name to finish the line," the girl explained.

"I see," he said, trying to comprehend.

"Yeah, like if someone gets a good deal or gets a bonus or makes a lot of money or something, it's referred to as 'Hector pay,'" she concluded.

"It's actually on Urban Dictionary," her friend added.

"That's not so bad!" Murphy slapped Hector on the back. "I like Hector pay."

"How can you go through your life and not know what a meme is," Andrea asked him, "let alone when you become one?"

"Ask him." Hector nodded toward his manager.

"We like to keep a low profile." Murphy cleared his throat.

"Yeah, but like, not even accidentally?" Andrea asked.

"I don't know. I kind of don't pay attention to a lot of things outside work," Hector said.

"Well, now we know you do!" Tamara shouted.

"I don't like this volleyball shit," Murphy said. "You all talking, with me in between."

"Then switch with Hec," Tamara said.

"But this is my seat," Murphy said.

"This isn't fucking *Cheers*, you ancient Gen Xer."

"Hey, you kiss your mother with that mouth, lady?"

"We're here to talk business with your boy. Frankly, we don't need you."

"Well, all the tucks and lifts in the world still don't change the fact that we're basically the same age."

"And that's why they invented them, old man—so no one has to know that."

"All right," Hector said, hoping to settle things down. He let one of the girls behind them take his seat and stood behind Tamara and Andrea so they could swivel to face him. "Good?"

Murphy sipped his wine in a private little victory celebration.

Andrea's phone buzzed. It was a text from Guy. She showed Tamara the name.

"What's that?" Hector asked.

"Guy," Tamara said.

"He hasn't called you?" Andrea asked her.

Tamara shook her head. "What did he say?"

Andrea opened the message and read aloud, "Do not say one more fucking word to anyone." Then she looked up at the others. "He's pissed."

"There you go." Murphy patted Hector. "You wanted Dracula? You got his brides."

"You are just *so* funny!" Tamara spat at Murphy.

"He tried to play us in real time," Andrea said.

"What happened?" Hector asked.

"Too long; didn't read: he thought Tam and I might kill each other," Andrea said.

"He was wrong," said Tamara.

"Then what do you need me for?" Hector asked.

"I'm so glad you asked." Tamara grinned. "It's not every day a big-time movie star wants to do right by his former idol. You got a big platform. We got a big story."

"First things first, you need to fire Essence," Andrea said, then chugged her entire glass of wine. "What? It's been a day," she said in response to their stares, delicately wiping her mouth.

"What did she do?" Murphy asked.

"I told her what Guy told me and Tamara," Andrea said. "That I might be getting my own show. Thought I was saying it in confidence. She spilled the beans to Simon Hudson."

"Who's that?" Hector asked.

"Head writer for *Applause Magazine*," Andrea said.

"What's *Applause Magazine*?" he asked.

"Jesus fuck." Tamara rubbed her forehead.

"It's all very bad is what it is," Andrea said.

"God damn it." Murphy sighed. "Can't trust anyone anymore."

"I wonder what she's told the tabloid about you," Tamara said.

Hector shook his head. "Man. I've wasted so many hours pressing my hand into the ground."

Andrea gave him a little back rub, feeling his pain. Then her phone buzzed again. It was a text from Toni. A link to another story from the magazine.

"I don't know if I have the stomach." She handed her phone to Tamara, who opened the link.

"The results of Molly's toxicology report," she said.

Even in a crowded bar, they felt a commanding hush around them as Tamara read quietly.

"Simon?" Andrea asked.

Tamara shook her head, continuing to read. "Only alcohol in her blood. But the cops found a bag of heroin in her pocket."

"You think someone planted it there?" Hector asked.

"This isn't a conspiracy, spy guy." Tamara gave him a disapproving look. "She was an addict."

"Right," Hector said.

"What's J2Z?" Tamara asked.

Hector and Andrea didn't have an answer.

"It says there was a stamp on the bag that read, 'J2Z,'" Tamara continued.

"Like the music producer?" Murphy spoke up.

The three of them turned slowly to look at him.

"What?" he said.

"How do you know that?" Hector asked.

"Nixon Bryce, that girl I was telling you about on the phone today," Murphy said. "The influencer girl. He produced her record. Goes by DJ2Z, I think."

"What's his real name?" Tamara asked.

"Fuck if I know. They recorded that before I signed her. Ask her mom."

"Murphy," Hector put a hand on his shoulder and squeezed. "Give me her phone number. Right. Now."

"Jay," Tamara said to herself, remembering her last night out with Molly.

"We need to get out of here. I feel like this place is collapsing in on us," Andrea said, her anxiety bubbling back up.

Murphy texted Samantha's phone number to Hector. "Hey . . . that kid is a big fan of yours," Murphy said. "The biggest, maybe. And she had a rough day too. So, say something nice to her while you're at it, will you? Would help, I think."

"You got it." Hector slapped $200 on the bar top and followed the girls outside.

Murphy eyed the tender, then got Ellie's attention by holding up and shaking his glass, mouthing, "One more!"

Outside, Andrea was pacing.

"You okay?" Tamara asked.

"Fine. Fine." Andrea suddenly lowered herself and put her hands on her knees, feeling like she was going to puke.

Hector had his phone pressed to his ear as he waited through rings. "Hello?" Samantha said on the other end of the line. He could hear she was driving.

"Hi, uh . . ." Hector forgot how to act like a person. "This is Hector Espinoza. Are you—You're Samantha Bryce."

"I am. Is this a joke? How did you get this number?"

"From Murphy. Beck. My—me and your daughter's manager."

"Oh," Samantha said. "Oh my God." He could hear her fumbling with the phone as she said, "Sweetheart, it's Hector."

"What?" he heard a girl's voice say.

"Yes," Samantha said, then moved the phone back to her face. "Hi. Uh, sir. How can we help you?"

"I just heard about Nixon's new album, and I'm really excited to listen. Murphy played me some of it," he lied. "Really great stuff."

"Thank you," Samantha said in disbelief. "That means so much coming from you."

"Hey, I was curious, what's her producer's name?" His voice cracked a little.

"Jay?"

"Yeah. Jay. What's his name?"

"DJ2Z, right, sweetheart? That's what he says?"

"No, right. I mean, his real name. His full name."

"Oh, you know what? I don't know. Honey, what's Jay's full name?"

"Why don't you put her on the phone," he suggested politely.

There was a scuffling sound, and a small, vulnerable voice said, "Hello?"

"Hey, Nixon. Hector Espinoza here."

"Hi," she said.

"Do you know Jay's full name?"

"Josh Morris," she said. "But yeah, he goes by Jay. Or Twozie."

"Twozie. Of course. Okay, well, thank you," Hector said. Then he thought about Murphy's words. "How, uh—how are you doing with everything? Careerwise."

"Oh. Good. I'm fine. Everything's fine," she said.

"Listen, Murphy says you're pretty incredible. I'm excited to check out more of your stuff."

"Thank you."

"Keep pushing, and you know, know your worth," he said in an odd chummy way.

"What?" she asked, not having heard him fully.

"I don't know. I wanted to say something encouraging." He laughed. "If there's anything I've learned doing this this long, I guess it's that—know your worth. And don't let anyone take that from you. Okay? Murphy's got your back." He made an awkward face and shrugged toward Tamara. "And I've got your back too."

"Thank you." He heard her sniff on the other end of the line, and it sounded like she was crying.

"Have a good night, okay?" he said.

"You too," she said.

He hung up.

"Who is Tootsie?" Tamara blurted out immediately.

"Twozie. That's another nickname. Full name is Josh Morris." Hector tucked his phone into his pocket.

"Jesus." Tamara couldn't believe it. "Josh Morris?"

That did it for Andrea, who threw up her full glass of wine into the gutter. Unsurprisingly, someone in line to get into the bar had been filming them while they stood there. Whenever it hit social, everyone would think Tamara and Hector Espinoza for some reason were taking care of a drunk Andrea, who must've gotten smashed after the nerve-racking night she had had.

"That's Cyd's ex-boyfriend," Andrea wheezed.

"He was on the show for a season while they dated." Tamara was rubbing her friend's back.

"Does anyone have his phone number?" Hector asked.

They shook their heads.

"You're gonna make me call her?" he said.

"Come on, Hec. I'm sure she'd love to hear from you." Tamara smirked.

"God damn it." He walked to them. "Maybe we do this in a less public place?"

"Good idea," Andrea said, standing and wiping her mouth on her forearm. As they turned around, a familiar face without a name stood at the back of the line, staring at them. Andrea went rigid.

"What's wrong?" Tamara said, sensing the change in her.

Andrea couldn't find words. Hector followed her gaze forward to the fan, who broke eye contact.

"He . . . that guy has been fo–following me all day," she stammered.

"Which?" Tamara turned around to look at the line.

Spotted, the fan about-faced and walked briskly down the street.

"Hey!" Tamara called after him, starting to jog in his direction, but he picked up his pace, sprinting.

"You want to go after him?" Hector asked.

Andrea shook her head, still out of breath. "Let's just get out of here."

22.

FIEVEL/ELLIOT

B Y THE TIME the elevator reached the casino floor, they were halfway to sober. It was ten thirty. Fievel checked his phone and saw five missed calls from Guy.

"Jesus," Fievel said, slipping it back into his pocket. "He just keeps calling."

"Then maybe you should call him back." Elliot was practically chasing Fievel as he swept across the floor.

"Why? So he can give me some back-patting bullshit about how he wants me to come on the show and talk about Molly and then we can be chums?"

"You don't want to?"

"Let's go to the MGM."

"I don't want to go to the MGM." Elliot could barely get the words out before Fievel whipped around.

"Then what do you want to do?" he shouted, loud enough to draw attention.

"I would like to go back to our hotel room and go to bed."

"Why?"

"Because I'm tired. And I've been letting you drag me around all night in search of girls and then a drug we couldn't even find. And now you're going to be doing coke all night, staying up till fucking five a.m., and I'd really rather not do that."

Fievel trudged toward the bar, knowing his friend would follow.

"We just watched two people fuck and then *fought* those people so you could steal their drugs!" Elliot tried to block Fievel from making eye contact with the bartender. "I hit a girl, dude. I body-slammed her up against a wall. Am I supposed to feel good about that?"

An older woman craned her neck halfway around to look at them. Elliot smiled at her.

"I admit that that was not how I intended the night to go," Fievel said, calmly.

"Yeah, no shit."

The older woman stood and left her empty glass, and Fievel slipped into her seat.

"Don't sit down," Elliot said.

"I'm already sitting," he said defiantly. "And if you wait long enough, one of the seats on either my left or my right will become available to you, and then you are welcome to sit next to me."

"I don't want to be here."

"So where would you like to be, Elliot?" Fievel refused to face him, making eye contact with the bartender. He ordered a shot of whiskey and a beer and threw a twenty on the bar.

"Whatever, man." Elliot turned and took a few steps away.

"Where are you going?" Fievel called after him.

"Back to the hotel."

"Why?"

"Because I can't do this anymore!" Elliot finally yelled at him.

Fievel hopped to his feet and rushed to Elliot as the bartender put down his drinks. "You're right, I'm sorry."

"Stop." Elliot pushed Fievel's hands off him. "Why can't you just let me leave?"

"Because I don't want to be alone," Fievel said. His throat swelled up, and he choked a little, looking away. "Why would they release that picture, man?" His voice cracked and tears came into his eyes. He grabbed Elliot's forearms. "It's all I see."

"I would love to talk about this. But I don't want to do it here." Elliot's default was to console Fievel, but he knew he had to stand his ground. "So, I will be in the room. And if you would like to talk about it there, we can. If not, then I'll see you whenever you get back."

Fievel stared at him. "You're just gonna leave me here?"

"No, I'm giving you the choice."

For the first time in a long time, Fievel felt the weight of responsibility. But before he could speak, over Elliot's shoulder he saw elevator doors open, and Brit and Nevin walked out of them.

"Oh Jesus God," he said abruptly.

Elliot turned around. "You gotta be fucking kidding me." He watched them scan the casino floor, looking for them.

Fievel hustled back to the bar and took his shot.

Elliot looked over at him as he started to chug his beer. "What the fuck are you doing?"

"I paid for these!"

Elliot rubbed his temples. He could try to take Fievel out of the drama, but he couldn't take the drama out of Fievel.

"Do not run," Elliot said, slowly walking toward him as he lightly set his beer glass on the bar top and gently, carefully wiped his mouth like even that motion might give away their position. They turned their backs to the elevator bank.

"Let's hide in the gift shop," Fievel said, hopeful.

"There's no place to hide in the gift shop."

"We can wear, like, 'I Love Las Vegas' hats and shirts and pose as tourists."

Elliot's face fell.

"What?" Fievel said incredulously.

"They know our faces pretty fucking well," Elliot said. "If we move calmly to the exit, which is in front of us, we can just walk out, get the car, and go."

"Okay," Fievel said.

They began to walk, cutting a path between tables and slot machines.

"You have the valet ticket?" Elliot asked.

"I thought you had it," Fievel said.

"No, I thought that kid gave it to you when you paid."

"You're the driver, dude. He gave it to you."

"Well, I don't have it, because he didn't give it to me."

"Well, I don't have it, because he didn't give it to *me*!"

"Fuck," Elliot said. "What's the worst they can do to us?" They took a left.

"Call the cops, I guess. But what are they gonna say? We stole their illegal drugs?"

"I thought drugs were legal here."

"What? No, dude. Cocaine is illegal everywhere."

"Oh." Elliot was bashful at his periodic innocence.

"'What happens in Vegas' doesn't mean you can just do whatever you want here." Fievel was suddenly the authority. "Like, you can fuck an escort, but you can't murder someone."

"Yeah, I got it," Elliot said.

Fievel looked behind him but could see no sign of Brit or Nevin.

"I think we lost them," he said.

"Where you guys headed?" A deep voice flanked them. They looked right. A security guard stood with the drunk woman from the elevator, who was swaying, in tears.

"To my car," Fievel said promptly. "We're leaving."

"This lady says two guys assaulted her in the elevator." The guard stepped up to them, looming over them. "Two guys who look like you."

"Well, actually it was three guys and a girl," Fievel said, feeling the heat of Elliot's angry stare. "But none of those guys were us," he course corrected. "The elevators have windows, see?" He pointed to the now very distant elevator bank. "So—Fuck." He stopped himself. Brit and Nevin made eye contact with them and approached.

Brit saw the woman whose hair she'd pulled. Nevin halted, unsure.

"That's the lady that pulled this lady's hair!" Elliot exclaimed, pointing a finger like Shag and Scoob had just pulled the mask off the culprit.

"She said it was some guys from a TV show," the guard said, feeling like this wasn't going to be worth what he was getting into.

Elliot saw a flash from the corner of his eye. A cell phone. Someone started filming them.

"Put that away!" he shouted, pointing into the lens.

"Why are they filming you?" the guard asked.

"Because we're not from a TV show," Fievel said quickly. "They're from a TV show." He pointed to Brit and Nevin. "They're clearly filming them."

"We're not from a TV show!" Brit yelled, moving toward them. "These guys assaulted us in our hotel room!"

"I'm starting to see a pattern here, gentlemen." The guard was tired.

"We did not *assault* them," Fievel said. "They were fucking, and we were watching, and then they told us to leave."

"After you stole our property!" Nevin joined in.

"And what property was that, *Nevin*?" Fievel said, mocking his stupid fake-Kevin name.

"What happened to your hand?" The guard nodded toward the blood-soaked pillowcase.

"Nothing. What happened to your hand?" Fievel said sharply.

"What?" the guard said.

"What?"

Everyone's eyes shifted from person to person. Elliot shared a glance with the security guard that said, *Yeah, this is most days.*

"What abut my herr?" the elevator woman slurred.

"Well, that lady sexually harassed my friend," Fievel said. "She pushed him into a corner and groped him. It was a man Me Too!"

"Dude." Elliot smacked him. One phone had become a bank of

them as a group had gathered to film, forever capturing what was surely be a phrase social media would roast him for.

The drunk woman was now smiling, as if thrilled to be part of the show.

"Sir, please. Look at this. Look at this woman," Fievel instructed of the security guard. "This is all fun and games to her. It's appalling you would take an inebriated woman's complaint so seriously."

"Hang on. Did you say you two were watching these two have sex in their hotel room?" the security guard said, wanting to get back to the good part.

"Oh Jesus." Fievel threw his hands up in defeat.

"Hey!" Nevin said, making his and Brit's presence known again. "They stole our property. We want to talk to hotel management."

"What'd they steal?" asked the guard.

A long pause. In the distance they heard a slot machine pay out big and someone gleefully shouted, "And on my birthday!"

"That's what I thought," Fievel said.

"Look, does anyone here want to file a formal complaint?" the guard asked.

More silence.

"Was it drugs?"

"No!" Elliot said immediately, fearful of the law. Everyone looked at him. His eyes darted back and forth, and he made eye contact with a distant cell phone to save his and Fievel's asses in case any of this could fuck them over and said, "Because drugs are illegal. Sir. Everywhere. Even here. And what happens here stays."

The security guard looked over his shoulder as if he were being pranked and saw the wall of phones. He sighed.

"All of you need to get the fuck out of my face before I throw every single one of you out," he said.

"I love you, Ells." The drunk woman tried to swipe at Elliot's chest as the security guard took her by the shoulders and led her away.

"Don't let her touch him!" Fievel shouted. "You take her to the drunk tank!"

He and Elliot felt Brit and Nevin breathing down their necks.

"Go away," Fievel said.

"This isn't going to look good for you guys," Brit said.

"Why's that?" Fievel asked.

"What's to stop us from spreading this all over social media?" she said.

"No one knows who the fuck you are. You think it's going to catch on like wildfire?" Fievel stepped to her. "Those people in the distance who have no clue what's going on are going to get more traction than you."

Brit looked at the anonymous group of amateur documentarians.

"We'll see," she said confidently.

Nevin took his phone from his pocket, engaging the camera and raising it in front of Fievel's red face. Suddenly, Elliot's hand slapped it to the ground. Everyone looked at him. He was huffing with rage.

"You think you're going get your chance to shine as some fucking Twitter controversy next season?" He pushed past Fievel to get in Brit's and Nevin's faces. "That Apples is going to send a production team to your mobile home and get your story? Just because you spent one night being unequivocal cunts to two guys from a show you like?"

"All right, man." Fievel put a hand on Elliot's shoulder, but Elliot shoved him away, standing inches from Brit and Nevin's noses.

"You're fucking nobodies," Elliot said as they stood frozen like scolded children. "So, the next time you go to post some opinion about us, to start some nothing argument with a few other fucks like you, remember that no matter how many of you there are that pile on, that make up stories and lies about us, that make fun of us, that shit on us, that hold ratings over our heads like we fucking work for you, it's us who take all that in and have to figure out what to do with it. Understand? We have to sit and live with your shitty criticism, have to justify it and somehow validate it, just so we can wake up the next day, go back out, and let it happen again. For you."

He jammed a finger into Nevin's chest but looked at Brit. His voice dropped low.

"People like you killed Molly," he said. "And I bet you're just giddy for the next news to break that one of us drew a warm bath and opened a vein, so it doesn't remind you of how fucking pathetic your own lives are."

The couple looked like sad dogs, unsure of what they had done to deserve such abuse.

"I don't work for you," Elliot said definitively. "I work for me. Got it?"

They nodded in rapid succession, arms stiff at their sides.

Elliot turned, plunged his hand into Fievel's pants pocket, removed the vial of cocaine, and slammed it into Nevin's chest.

"Why don't you go get high and forget about who you are." Elliot caught another glance of the wall of cameras and knew there was no taking any of it back. Then he stormed out.

Fievel stood with Brit and Nevin for a long moment. None of them looked at the others. A few phones lowered. Fievel could not bring himself to speak. Then Brit ran. Nevin looked at the vial in his hand, put it into his pocket, and followed slowly after her.

Fievel looked over at the remaining phones, desperate in a way that not even his own show could capture. Then he went after Elliot.

Outside, Elliot was pacing in the distance beyond the valet. Fievel approached him like a cornered animal.

"Do you want to talk about something?" Fievel asked, sheepishly.

Elliot was breathing deeply in through his nose and out through his mouth. He ran his fingers through his hair and pulled at the strands as if he were losing his mind.

"You don't think it fucking tears me up too?" he said.

"What does?" Fievel asked.

"Molly!"

"Oh . . ."

"I can't fucking do this anymore, man," Elliot said.

"What do you mean?"

"The show," Elliot said. "This." He pointed at the casino. Then his hand twisted into a sort of claw, and he struggled desperately to say, "*This,*" as his claw hand shook, indicating the two of them.

"What do you mean?" Fievel repeated.

"Jesus fucking Christ. You. And me. Just running in these circles to do what other people want us to do!"

"I didn't know you felt that way."

"Yeah. You did. And it's not just tonight, man. It's every day with you. Every fucking day. I spend all my waking hours reiterating to you the things I don't want to do, and I end up doing whatever you want regardless. And I'm tired of it. I'm exhausted at the thought that to you and to the entire planet, I'm not a real person."

"I've never wanted to make you feel that way," Fievel said, struggling.

"I know you don't *want* to. But you do. You just do. And I can't wait around anymore for you to work out your shit with Molly on me," he said. "This shit with people like Brit and Nevin, it's just more on top of more, and more, and more." Elliot thumped his chest, getting worked up. "And I'm done."

"You want to quit?"

"Yes."

Fievel paused. "Do you want to quit . . . being friends?" he asked nervously.

"I want to be friends where you treat me like your equal."

"I have."

"No, you haven't."

"I've been good to you, bro. I never wanted you to want for anything."

"Sometimes people have to want for things!" Elliot shouted. "I don't need your money and all the shit you buy me that I didn't ask for. I don't want you to spoil me. I don't want to be 'the good son.' I want you to respect me. To respect what I want to do. And if that means I'm broke and struggling and whatever, then maybe I need to do that to get to where I want to go. But I have to go."

"Where?" Fievel asked.

"I don't even know." Elliot hiccupped a hysteric little laugh. "Isn't that fucked? I don't even know what I want. All I know is what I don't want."

Fievel was thinking. It was the longest Elliot had ever seen him go without saying a word. Then he looked up at his friend, confused, and earnestly asked, "Then who will I be?"

Elliot felt a pang of remorse. "I don't know, man," he said. "That's up to you."

"I guess . . . it's this DJ thing right now." The words fell out of Fievel's mouth like he didn't know what he was saying.

"It doesn't have to be."

"Guy said—"

"Fuck Guy," Elliot interrupted. "You know that's how you feel. You've been dodging his calls all night."

"You really think I'm taking out my feelings about Molly on you?"

"Yes," Elliot said, matter-of-factly. "But she was my friend too."

"I know she was—"

"Then how come you've never asked me how any of this shit has made me feel?"

Elliot suddenly thought about the *MML* marathon he'd watched in the hotel room that afternoon. There'd been an old episode where Fievel had rented a Lamborghini in the hopes of driving to Palm Springs in under two hours to surprise Molly with a marriage proposal. But he'd left on a Friday at 3:00 p.m. and sat in gridlock traffic for three hours and changed his mind halfway there. He'd been so accustomed to Elliot driving everywhere, he had no concept of how to get from A to B in real time. He knew only that he always started somewhere and ended up where he wanted to go.

Elliot laughed at the memory.

"What's funny?" Fievel felt mocked.

"Nothing," Elliot said.

"Then why are you laughing?" Fievel shouted.

"It's nothing! Just a memory."

"A memory of what?"

"When you rented the Lambo and tried to get to Palm Springs in 'record time.'"

"Oh." Fievel knew he wasn't lying. "Why are you thinking about that?"

"It was on TV today." Elliot shrugged.

Fievel thought about it too and smiled. "That was pretty fucking stupid." He started to laugh. "And then I came out here instead because I changed my mind and was scared of what that meant."

"Probably that it wasn't right?" Elliot said.

Fievel's silence rivaled his previous one. Then he started to cry and looked at his friend and asked, "Was it my fault?"

"No, man." Elliot stepped toward him, but Fievel held up a weak hand to stop him.

"You know . . . just that fucking picture. Why did they . . . ? Maybe I could've done something. You know? I stopped calling her. We didn't even need to be together. We could've stayed friends."

"I know," Elliot said.

"And I didn't. I didn't do anything." His mouth pursed. "Even when we were together . . . I just let her do her thing. Even when I knew she shouldn't have. Even when I knew she needed help."

"We all did that," Elliot said.

"She was so sweet, man," he said, choking on the words. "Like, this side of her no one got to see but me every once in a while. This little kid." He drew a sharp breath in and bit his lip, then exhaled slowly. "But I couldn't bring that out of her when I wanted to."

"Then what do you want?" Elliot asked.

"I don't want to do the show if you're not doing it with me," Fievel said.

"Yeah, but you can't just chase me, dude," Elliot said. "We don't have to be together all the time."

"I guess . . . I don't want to not be your friend."

Elliot laughed at Fievel's roundabout confession. "I don't want that either," he said. "But I think I need to be my own person. For a while, at least."

Fievel nodded. Then he quickly turned away and said, "Fuck."

"What?" Elliot asked.

Fievel tried to combat the sobs that shook his body. "This is gonna sound so gay."

"It's okay." Elliot put a hand on his friend's shoulder.

"Out of all the people in my life"—he reset, made eye contact, then pushed the words forward—"you're the one I love the most."

He forced a hard sniff and looked away again. Elliot looked at the back of Fievel's head.

"At least, I think this is what love is," Fievel said.

"I think it is," Elliot said. "It isn't supposed to be easy, I guess."

"Cool," Fievel said.

After a beat, they both made awkward moves to hug each other but a voice interrupted.

"Are you guys okay?"

They looked. It was the valet. Fievel quickly wiped his tears, trying to make it look as if they hadn't been doing anything.

"You forgot your ticket," the kid said, holding it up.

Then Elliot laughed. "Record time in the Lambo. Stupid."

"You're fucking stupid." Fievel smacked Elliot's chest and laughed too.

23.
SUICIDE NOTE

ANDREA, TAMARA, AND Hector sat in Hector's car, pulled onto a side street off Third, his tinted windows giving them privacy.

"We've been taking the same yoga class for . . . I don't know. Months now, I guess. The free one at Runyon," Andrea said in the back seat, sipping from a water bottle.

"You're positive he's the one who slashed your tire?" Tamara turned to face her from the passenger seat.

"I've lived there for five years, and there's never been a problem," Andrea said. "Some homeless guys wandering around from time to time, but they never hurt anyone or break anything."

"What else has he done?" Tamara asked.

"I don't know. That's . . . .I wasn't even really aware of it until today. But now it's got me thinking about a couple strange things that have happened in the past. Stuff I chalked up to me being a ditz or to the maid moving things around when she cleans."

"Like what?" Hector asked.

"Things in different places," Andrea said. "Things I wouldn't have moved to where they ended up. There was a dress laid out on the bed once. I assumed I'd just left it there in a rush on my way out the door one morning."

Tamara shivered. "Creepy."

"It does seem pretty deliberate then. The tire," Hector mused.

"He just looked so angry when I told him I couldn't remember his name," Andrea said.

"Sweetheart, no one remembers anyone's names," Tamara said. "It's nonessential information our brains dump when we sleep. I'm sure Hector remembers even fewer names."

"It's true," he agreed. "Also, people think they're not supposed to talk to me."

"Should we call the police?" Tamara asked.

"No, no. It's fine." Andrea tried to brush it off, taking another sip of water. "Maybe after. Right now, I wanna figure out this thing with Josh."

"Right," Hector said nervously.

"Are you getting cold feet?" Tamara smirked.

"No, I'm not getting cold feet." He psyched himself up, grabbing his phone. "And what am I asking her? 'Hey, it's me. That person you hate. Just curious if your old drug dealer boyfriend is still on your speed dial.'"

"It's cute you say, 'speed dial,'" Tamara said.

"Whatever it's called."

"Tell her he gave the heroin to Molly," Andrea said.

"We don't know that yet." He straightened in his seat, pulling up Cyd's contact.

"Oh, really? What other numb nuts would stamp his same fucking music producer name on his dime bags?" Tamara dug through her purse and removed a pad and pen.

"Are you gonna take notes?" Hector asked.

"Yes. Be prepared for anything, spy guy. Jesus. Would you just call her already?"

Hector blew out a breath, then tapped the phone.

Cyd did not pick up. After only one ring, the call went to her voice mail, and fifteen seconds later she sent him a text that said, "fuck you hec."

"Real nice." He showed it to them.

"Why did you have to break up with her this morning?" Tamara said.

"How is this my fault?" he asked. "You try her."

Tamara hung her head.

"Tam?" Andrea looked at her.

"I didn't do myself any favors with her today either," she admitted.

"What happened?" Andrea asked.

"She came to the studio, drunk and in tears about getting let go. I tried to be polite, but she kept picking at the wound. I might've said some not-so-nice things to her."

Andrea sighed. "Terrific."

"I'm sorry, Dre."

Andrea didn't like being the cause of potential conflict, on the show or off, but she dialed anyway.

"Dre!" they heard Cyd virtually scream on the other end, ecstatic to hear from someone, anyone, who might be the bearer of good news. Andrea switched the call to speakerphone although she didn't need to.

"Hey, girl," she said through a fake smile.

"Are you okay? I've been keeping up with everything. You just threw up outside the Phoenix?"

Andrea slow blinked. "Yep. Yeah, I did. Little stomach bug, I think."

"And that stuff with you and Tamara, what does this mean?" Given the kind of day Cyd had had, a call from Andrea was like an answered prayer.

"We're still figuring things out. But I promise you'll be one of the first to know, 'kay?"

"Thank you. Seriously. God, what a fucking day I've had," Cyd said.

"Hey, by chance, do you have Josh's cell?" Andrea tossed it into the open hoping it would fly under Cyd's emotional radar.

"My—" She cut herself off. "Morris?"

"Yeah . . ."

"Why do you want to talk to him?"

"He's, um, he's producing an album. For Fievel," she lied.

"Oh, really?"

"Yes. And we need . . . to . . . talk to him. Rights clearances and things. Have to figure out what samples he's using," she said, grasping at straws.

"So why are you calling me if it's for Fievel?"

"Because." She looked at Tamara, helpless. "Tam is going to be featured on a track."

Tamara smacked her leg, mouthing, "What the fuck?"

"Oh, that's cool. I didn't know she could sing," Cyd said, unenthusiastic. Then, because she was feeling ballsy, she asked, "What's in it for me?"

"Gratitude," Andrea said, so over this whole thing. Tamara's tight face said this was not the time for her to get cute. "And your job back next season?"

"Don't lie to me," Cyd said.

"Scout's honor," Andrea said. "When have I ever lied to you?"

"That time you said we would go glamping in Idyllwild together but then said you couldn't because you had to get your IUD implanted, but it was actually because you went with Hips and Milan instead," she said between sniffles.

"Right," Andrea said, remembering the three of them had tried to keep it a secret until Milan had posted an Instagram story of them scantily covered with suds in vintage bathtubs. "Well—"

"And when you told Guy I was so dumb I didn't know how to swim."

Andrea remembered saying that as a way to leave her out of a houseboat trip the rest of the cast was taking for a vacation episode. She wondered if she was really as likable a character as she thought she was.

"Okay," Andrea said to stop her, knowing there were oodles more examples of this type of behavior from everyone.

Producers had told both Andrea and Tamara to find ways to slowly exile Cyd that past season because they thought she had become boring. They had sent the occasional cameraman with their phone to covertly follow her when she was alone so they could cut back and forth from everyone else having the time of their lives to footage of Cyd drunkenly dancing in bars by herself.

"Well," Andrea fumbled to recover. "Things are different now."

"Oh, really?" Cyd blew her nose.

"Yes. You saw what happened today. Tam and I are calling the shots now." Andrea puffed up a little. "We're shot callers."

Tamara rolled her eyes. Hector's body shook with silent laughter. When Andrea tried to act tough, people did not often take it seriously. It had taken her years to learn how to swear properly. Tamara had advised that, if she was going to survive, Andrea needed to double down on R-rated behavior when she was pissed at someone on the show. It would help create sizzle-reel moments. People loved to see the cast yell and point their fingers at one another in accusatory ways. Tamara had termed this specific type of behavior as "the fuck-you speech." No matter how silly the moment was or how shaky the ground seemed, people wanted to feel like cast members were desperate for vindication of something. Laying into their costars with everything they had during arguments on camera, even if they had to make it up, and ending it by pointing a finger and shouting, "So fuck you!"

When it broke live within the show that Tamara and Andrea were getting a spin-off, Molly stood abruptly from the brunch table they were sitting at, spilling her water glass, and laid into Tamara, feeling betrayed. After a slew of insults, Molly pointed her finger at Tamara and shouted, "So fuck you, Tam! *Fuck. You!*" Then stormed off. She'd organically given a fuck-you speech. And Tamara was right, it did make for good TV.

"Why didn't you call Fievel or Elliot?" Cyd said, bringing Andrea back to reality.

"That is a great question. Honestly . . . I wanted to check and see how you were doing, more than anything."

"Well, thanks," Cyd said. "Should I talk to Guy and tell him—"

"Do not talk to Guy!" Tamara shouted without thinking. Then she slapped her hand over her mouth.

There was a pause so pregnant they could see the drama crowning.

"Tam?" Cyd finally asked. "Are you guys togeth—am I on speakerphone?"

"Yep," Andrea said quickly. "We're in her car now, coming back from the Phoenix, and we're working out the music deal tomorrow." She finally lost her temper, feeling like they were running out of time. "So, give us Josh's phone number, or we're not giving you your job back!"

Cyd sighed, then recited Josh's number from memory. Tamara wrote it down.

"We'll talk tomorrow," Andrea said, retaining her sternness. "Don't tell anyone about this or we'll find you." She hung up.

"What're you, a mobster?" Tamara asked.

"Thank you for not telling her I'm with you." Hector was relieved.

"Last time we do you any favors, Hec," Tamara said as she dialed.

Then Josh's name popped up as the phone recognized his number.

"Huh," Tamara said, a little surprised. "I had it this whole time and didn't think to look."

"Are you fucking *kidding* me right now?" Andrea said.

Hector laughed.

Tamara showed them both her phone displaying his name as it rang.

"Tamara?" Josh answered, his phone apparently recognizing her number as well. Neither could remember when they had exchanged them.

"Josh," Tamara said very seriously. "Andrea and I need to see you. Immediately. Also, Hector Espinoza is with us."

"Oh shit, Matty Source?" His aloof bro tone overrode any hope of a serious conversation.

"Yes. Matty Source himself. Say hi, Hector." She held the phone out to him.

"Hi, Josh," Hector said.

"How do I know that's not just some guy saying, 'Hi, Josh?'" Josh asked.

"Fair," Tamara said. "You'll see him in person. All of us, actually. We need to talk to you before the police talk to you."

"The police? What are you talking about?" Josh sounded as if her call had woken him up.

"Where do you live?" Tamara asked

"Wait. What? I'm not telling you where I li—"

"The police, Joshua. Sorry, *DJ Tootsie*." She knew she had to show their hand. "Your little high school nickname stamped on a dime bag of heroin. Right? Does that sound familiar?"

"Fuck," he said.

THEY DROVE LIKE hell to Van Nuys, sure the wildfire that was modern technology would send the cops to his place before they could get there. Andrea was reading the comment section of the *Applause* article and refreshing Twitter and Instagram.

"They got him," she said.

"The cops?" Tamara shouted. She didn't want to lose her ace in the hole.

"No, not yet. But everyone else. They're commenting and tagging him and saying who it is. There's already a TikTok trend of people using his music and acting like they're dead." Andrea looked up from her phone. "They're just lying on the ground. Some people are pretending like they hung themselves."

Tamara tried to contain her rage, wondering if this was the man responsible for pushing her former best friend over the edge and whether she would put him through a wall with the butt of her hand when she saw him.

"Actually wait. Now those are getting taken down because everyone is saying they're insensitive," Andrea continued. "This new

Applause headline says, 'Molly Mandrie's Murderer, a *Tamandrea* Music Mogul!' Oh shit . . . Cyd texted. She just read the article."

"Dre." Tamara couldn't take it anymore.

"Sorry," she said and flipped her phone over, putting the screen against her thigh.

They arrived and Hector parked his car outside Josh's apartment building in a red zone with the hazards on. They rushed to the gate of the run-down complex. Hector moved to the intercom to input Josh's unit number. It dialed, then engaged and immediately clicked, hanging up on them.

"That little fucker," Tamara said, pushing Hector out of the way and dialing again. This time, Josh's voice got on the intercom.

"Go away!" he said.

"Josh! This is going to look very bad for you!" Tamara shouted. "We're the only ones who can help you. Do you understand?"

"I shouldn't have told you where I live," he whimpered through the speaker.

"Too late. Buzz us in, now," Tamara said.

"No!" he said petulantly, then the intercom clicked again, and his voice vanished.

Tamara shook the metal door, as if by some miracle it might open. Then a voice from an adjacent balcony said, "Tamandrea?"

All three looked up to see a girl, no older than twenty, staring down at them.

"Hi, dear!" Tamara called up to her.

"What are you both doing here?" the girl asked.

"We're . . . visiting an old friend." Andrea smiled.

"Is that Hector Espinoza?" the girl asked.

"Oh my God," Tamara said to herself.

"Babe!" the girl called. "Come out here. It's Tamandrea! And Hector Espinoza!"

"No, don't—" Hector tried to stop her, but she disappeared.

"Has anyone ever thought about what it would feel like to spontaneously combust?" Andrea asked.

The girl returned with her boyfriend.

"Holy shit!" the boyfriend said. "We love you guys."

"Yes, we love you too!" Tamara was losing her mind. "Could you—do you think you could show us how much you love us by buzzing us in?"

"Why are you even here?" the boyfriend said, dumbfounded.

"*Because we're visiting a friend!*" Andrea screamed, her brain finally breaking.

"Oh. Okay," the boyfriend said, then vanished briefly. The gate buzzed and Tamara yanked it open, exploding through it. Andrea followed quickly. Hector offered a small wave up to the girl.

"Thank you!" he said and hustled in.

Tamara pounded on the door of Josh's diminutive studio apartment.

"I don't want to go to jail!" he said on the other side.

"Then open the door!" Tamara shouted. More neighbors were starting to poke their heads out of their front doors.

"You're causing a scene, Tam," Josh said.

"*You* are causing the scene, you little shit!" she volleyed back. "Either way, the cops are going to come for you. Do you want us on your side or against you?"

"I don't even know why they would come for me. I haven't sold that shit in years." His voice cracked.

"Josh," Andrea spoke up, trying to ease the tension. "We know. And we're here for you. Okay?"

"Dre?" He seemed almost relieved, letting his guard down and opening the door a crack.

Tamara put her shoulder into it, knocking him backward as it ripped the chain lock off the wall. He tripped over his feet and sat down hard on the ground, then rolled onto his back.

The three of them entered quickly. Tamara moved across the floor to him in an instant, grabbed him by his shirt, and stood him up, shoving him into a wall.

Hector locked the door slowly behind them.

"Tam!" Andrea shouted.

"What kind of fucking idiot uses the same name to sell both drugs and records?" Tamara's growled.

Josh winced. "I told you! I haven't done that shit in years!"

"You're Jay," Tamara said. The Jay from the 5:30 a.m. drug deal that ended her and Molly's final night out. The night it had all slipped through her fingers. The night she'd known she could no longer stop Molly from destroying herself. There he was.

"It was you, wasn't it? You sold it to her," Tamara said.

"I'm being serious. I haven't hustled any of this stuff in a long time. I don't even sell weed! I don't wanna go to jail," he whimpered.

"Too late," Tamara said, suddenly feeling like she was chastising her son, and she thought of Steph and realized she'd never told him she would be out late. She let go of Josh's shirt.

"Josh," Andrea said cautiously. "How did she get the heroin then? With your name on it?"

Josh was racking his brain, panicked. "The last time I sold to her was like five years ago. Or more. I don't know. I thought she had gotten clean."

"Why the *fuck* would you use the same name to make music?" Tamara reiterated, frigid.

"It seemed like . . . I don't know. Tons of dudes talked about selling drugs to support their kids and shit. Like Biggie. I thought it would make me sound hard, I guess."

"Well, now you'll be doing hard time!" Hector had heard the scripted line in his head and thought it was a good idea to say it out loud as he tried to find his place in the group dynamic. But Tamara's and Andrea's expressions put him in time-out.

"So, you're saying she held on to this heroin for five years?" Tamara asked.

"I guess," he said.

"Why would she do that?" Tamara hissed.

Andrea pulled up a photo of the bag and showed it to him. "This is yours?" She needed to confirm what the faded red letters seemed to indicate. "She didn't Sharpie this or something to get back at you?"

He started to cry at the sight of the picture. "It was like a stamp. I had it made at Staples."

Tamara backed away from him.

"But why would she do that to me?" he asked. "We never had any fights or anything. She just bought and that was it. We weren't even friends."

"Where did you two meet?" Hector risked reentering the conversation.

"Guy introduced us," Josh said plainly.

Everyone's emotional momentum came to a sudden stop. Hector's mouth froze mid word formation. Chills ran down Andrea's arms. Tamara sat down slowly at a small dining table decorated with empty takeout containers.

"What happened?" Josh asked. "What did I say?"

Tamara stared at the floor. All those years she'd thought she was playing the long game in her war against Guy Maker. But Molly had beat her to the punch. She had held on to the heroin, waiting to make her move. Using Josh as the messenger. Waiting until the pain became too great; then she would take Guy with her. Five years. Betrayed by her best friend. Left with nothing but the mess he'd helped her make. Now he would undeniably be implicated in her suicide. He may not have killed her, but his hands had guided hers as they tied the noose together on television for years.

"She didn't put that in her pocket to fuck you over," Tamara said, breaking the silence.

"She didn't?" Josh seemed relieved.

"No," Tamara said.

"Am I . . . am I still going to get arrested?" His voice regained a little optimism as he felt Tamara's anger at him evaporate into something new.

"What do I do?" He started to panic again. "Fuck, shit! What do I do?"

Tamara unlocked the door and opened it slowly. The neighbors' faces had retreated into their homes. Without another word, she left.

"Dre," Josh begged. "Please."

Andrea stared at him, wishing she had more to say. All she could muster was "I'm sorry." Then she followed Tamara.

The forever fan in Hector had waited for this moment, some semblance of emotional restitution for his childhood sweetheart. Only instead of Molly's face, to his surprise, it was Nixon's small, shaky voice that echoed in his head. The sound of her holding back tears.

"That girl," Hector said.

"What girl?" Josh was getting angry, feeling cornered.

"That girl whose album you just produced."

"What the fuck are you even talking about?"

"She's just a kid, man," he said.

Josh's brow furrowed as if he were being accused of something he hadn't done. "What the fuck do you think I am?" he asked Hector, disgusted by the accusation.

"I don't know," Hector said, trying to read behind Josh's eyes.

"Get your ass out of here!" Josh shoved Hector, and he stumbled through the doorway, catching himself with a hand on the ground and taking a knee.

"You're piece'a shit. All of you! Why do you think I stopped selling? Huh? You think I'm so fucking stupid?" Josh shouted.

Hector stood slowly as Josh got in his face.

"You spoiled, rich assholes. You think you get to come over here and do this to me? Because you're so special? Fake ass movie star tough guy. You're a fucking joke, man. I'm not the one who stays in bed with the kind of people you work with. I'm not the one who takes their money and looks the other way, like those girls. Tell me why you're better than me, huh?"

Hector wanted to hit him but brushed the dirt off his shirt instead. "Fuck you, man," Josh said coldly, pointing a finger in Hector's face. "Fuck. You!"

24.

EULOGY

WHY DOES ANYONE ever give it up?" Tamara asked as Andrea approached her outside the building.

"Give what up?"

"Drinking."

"Oh. Because one is one too many, and a thousand's not enough?"

Tamara looked sourly at her from the corners of her eyes.

"That's what you told me to tell you when we first started going out together again," Andrea said innocently.

"I did say that." Tamara exhaled as if she were smoking an invisible cigarette.

Hector met them, then stood stoically with his hands in his pockets, staring at the building.

"We probably shouldn't linger," Tamara said.

"You're right," he said.

Headlights lit up the end of the street as a car turned onto it and faced them, creeping toward the building. It stopped and two young men got out, gazing at the apartment complex.

"Holy shit," they heard one of them say. "We got here first!"

Then the two boys looked over and saw three silhouetted figures watching them, obscured by Hector's headlights. It was hard to tell who they were, ghosts maybe. Or perhaps some specters of ancient Hollywood lore, come to lay to rest the soul they had lost.

They got into Hector's car and drove away.

The passenger from the other car ran in front of the building and called to his friend, "Let's go!"

The driver left the car running and jogged to meet him. He switched on a small light rigged to his phone, igniting the other man's face.

"What's up, guys? It's your boy Jake Lamantia, a.k.a. the Raging Fool," he said. "And we are live on IG as the first on the scene here outside Josh Morris's apartment, the dude who killed Molly Mandrie."

And in the distance, more headlights made their way to the scene.

25.

NIXON IN SPACE

TAKE NOTES, PLEASE," Samantha said on their drive back home. "We need to strategize the next few weeks now that we have Murphy's go-ahead. Jesus, it never ends," she said as they slowed into traffic.

Nixon was looking idly at her phone. "Why don't we just move then?"

"Because no one actually wants to live here," her mother said.

"I don't think that's true."

"When you're eighteen, you can move here. Or when you're twenty-one. I don't know. We'll see."

"What are you gonna do then?"

"What do you mean?" Samantha asked.

"When I move out."

"Honey, that's years from now."

"Only three."

"I'll move next door."

"And I'll kill myself."

"Stop that! Don't say things like that!"

"It was a joke, Mom."

"That's not a funny joke."

Nixon mindlessly scrolled through Instagram.

"Notes, please. This is important," Samantha reiterated.

"What if we talked about this tomorrow instead?"

"Tomorrow will be too late."

"Why can't we just talk about something else for once? Or maybe not even talk at all?"

"I let you get one Diet Coke at the gas station, and now all the caffeine is pumping through your body making you a brat."

"I'm not being a brat."

"What would you call it?"

"Being tired."

"*Tired*," her mother mocked her. "Please. I see your jittery thumbs double tapping over there. Thank God you're *not* eighteen so I don't have to see the types of people you'd be swiping on."

"Mom—"

"If you're going to be on your phone, we should be strategizing our posts these next few weeks. This is a busy quarter for us."

"Why do you always say 'we'?" Nixon blurted out.

"Because this is a team effort, honey."

"But it's my face." Nixon put her phone down. "And it's my body."

"What do you mean, your *body*? It's not like I'm whoring you out to anyone!"

"What if I wanted to quit?"

"Don't make more bad jokes, sweetheart."

"What if I said this was all bullshit and I didn't want to do any of it anymore and I just wanted to be normal?"

"You are normal."

Nixon burst into laughter.

"Stop it!" Samantha felt chastised.

"What about any of this is normal?"

"I don't know. It's the new normal. What's gotten into you?"

"Maybe I really am tired, Mom."

"Maybe I'm tired too, sweetheart."

"Then maybe I should quit."

"Stop saying that!" Samantha slammed on the brakes, a few seconds from rear-ending the car in front of them. "We are not quitting."

"Stop saying 'we'!" Nixon screamed.

"Then stop acting so fucking spoiled!" her mother said, losing it. "You couldn't do any of this without me. You wouldn't have any of this if I hadn't started posting your videos when you were—"

"I *hate* Molly Mandrie," Nixon cut her off. "Did you even realize that? I fucking hate her. She was just a drunk."

Her mother opened her mouth to interrupt, but Nixon was finally ready to let her have it.

"You want to know what I really think?" she continued. "She's just another dumb Apples cunt. And I'm glad she's dead."

Samantha's primal defenses sent a threat signal to her brain, then its response moved without a second thought back out to her right hand, which shot out and made hard contact with Nixon's left cheekbone, just under her eye, and took her daughter so by surprise that the back of her head cracked against the passenger side window as she attempted to dodge it.

Samantha retracted her hand immediately to cover her shocked mouth, disgraced by what she had done.

Nixon rubbed her cheek. She looked down and she stared at the boots she was still wearing. The stupid boots that had changed the course of her entire life.

She heard her mother sniffle. Samantha ran her forearm under her nose to wipe it like a little kid, and Nixon realized they were the same age.

"Why do you say things like that?" Samantha asked.

"People say things like that to me every day," she said. "I am tired, Mom."

Samantha was quiet.

"You make me feel so small," Nixon said.

"I don't mean to."

"Yes. You do."

"I don't know what you want me to say."

"You don't even have to say sorry."

"Well, maybe if you wouldn't push my buttons like you always do."

Nixon picked up her phone and stared at her reflection in the black screen.

"If you want to quit, then fine. You should quit," Samantha said. "But I hope you know what you'd be throwing away."

"I don't want to quit."

"Then why do you keep—"

"Because I want you to stop treating me like a kid."

"You are a kid, sweetheart."

"Don't call me sweetheart!"

"What would you like me to do then, huh? Just be more like your father? Playing a passive role in all this, looking on with vague confusion about whether I should approve?"

"This has always been about you," Nixon said. "But because I get to be the one to deal with all the hate and the comments and the—"

"Far more people love you than hate you."

"I'd like to share my opinion, please."

She looked at Samantha. Nixon had formerly been so sure of the fuck-you speech she would give if she ever got the podium. But now she got distracted by the profile of her mother's face. How they shared it. Slightly upturned noses her father had called French. She wanted to tell her mother she hated her for leaving her alone. She wanted to tell her she hated her for turning her into someone she was not. She wanted to tell her she hated her for stealing her essence, like some kind of resentful witch. But she knew this kind of love, the closest cousin to hate. She'd watched her grandparents belittle Samantha at the Thanksgiving table every year. She had watched Bill never stand up for her. She had watched his aloofness, almost intentional. She had listened to her mother sob when she thought she was alone. She had found the empty wine bottles her mother had tried to hide beneath junk mail in the trash can. She had watched her mother care so much that she cared too much and that was what she hated.

"What?" Samantha snapped, feeling naked in front of her daughter's introspection. "You have the floor; take it."

Everything Nixon had wanted to say left her. She wanted to blame her mother for leaving her. She wanted to blame Todrick. But instead, she took on the teenage task of blaming herself. Maybe she was what they all said. Puberty had ravaged her brain as it had her body. She was just a hormonal brat.

As Nixon started to cry, Samantha's phone rang with an unknown number.

"Shit." Samantha sighed. Then she looked at Nixon, seeing a wound she hadn't the tools to mend. "This could be one of the manufacturers or someone at Apples."

She answered.

"Hi, uh . . ." The dim tone of a man's voice spoke on the other end. "This is Hector Espinoza. Are you—You're Samantha Bryce."

"I am," Samantha said. "Is this a joke?"

THERE HAD BEEN an accident on the I-15 South on the way back to Murrieta. When Samantha and Nixon took Hector's call, they had been sitting at a standstill for over fifteen minutes. Samantha slowly put her phone back onto its delicately balanced air-conditioner dock, their GPS route showing their time in traffic increasing incrementally. They wouldn't be home for another two hours.

Out of nowhere, Hector was now at the intersection of Nixon's secrets and her grief. Even to share that moment, through however many G's it had taken to send their existences back and forth to each other, she had finally met him. She had daydreamed of that moment for years. She'd always wished it would be on a set for a show or movie. But as life was so good at carrying on without a care or plan, it had brought them together when she'd least expected it.

Her unconscious was still on the defensive, and she wondered what Murphy had revealed to Hector. He had certainly made a strong case for being on her side. Feeling out of her body once more, she felt she had to make the choice Hector had made in the finale of *The Fallen*—to trust in humanity, despite their propensity for their own destruction and the destruction of others.

She was an alien again, she decided. She and Hector both. They were so similar. Extraterrestrials. Thinking about how her audience viewed her, she knew he must have experienced the same many times throughout his long career, that their opinions as performers didn't matter. Her paychecks, even weighed against the trouble of her day, meant she should put up or shut up. She was fruit. And to consume that fruit properly, the first thing an audience had to peel away from any kind of celebrity was their humanity.

She thought about her slowly dying father as if he were now on the distant home planet she longed to return to. She had journeyed that day and faced hardships, sent out by the social media universe to retrieve a message of hope and bring it back to the masses that followed her. Hector's words settled into her psyche, and she thought maybe they were the revelation she had been looking for. She had a message to bring back to base with her, back to control.

Know your worth.

The earthlings, they were so funny. She had watched them in comment sections, how they communicated with one another. Strange. Sometimes the easiest way to make one's voice known was through spewing the hurtful. Saying the hateful. Harming the others. Their arguments seemed like arguments about nothing, yet they were argued as if all were of vital importance; spewing hate not from a heart full of it, but a heart full of hurt. What a strange planet. So much time spent fighting over differences when they bled similarities, everyone brittle and broken, begging to be lit up and to shine like screens, to be seen and to be heard and to be known. To be liked. To be followed. To be friended.

Humans, she thought, *always pretending*. Curious that all people could be so different in their skin but share humanity in their blood. Across oceans, maybe even across stars too. Humanity was wherever one landed. Hatred was there, but goodness and grace too. Wearing those ancient masks, it was these plays they were always acting out; one sad, one happy. People making make believe so long that life had lost its meaning, that it was not two stories but one, that only because of hurt could happiness thrive. This was where joy lived. In realizing that humanity was bound by the blood of collective trauma, by the underside of tragedy, by the frown turned upside down. A divine comedy.

She felt her shuttle finally begin to lurch forward through space. Her coordinates were true, and her path was clear. T-minus two hours to telling father and mother of what had been done to her that day. Of what now had to be done. How she would move forward. How she would learn to fly as she fell, sure she would soar before she hit the ground.

She looked at her mother, with whom she shared her pod, and knew that she, too, had been wounded somewhere in time. Nixon saw into the blood now. She saw into the pieces of the soul that give the eyes their color. She saw the "we," and she understood the "we." It was the "me" missing from identity.

In the dark of space, the lights of human fleet ships crowded their path home. In this kind of chaos, they could be incognito. They could move freely where needed. She thought of the more than twenty-five million who followed her journey across platforms. As much as some had begged to see her fall, so many had begged for her to see in them what she now saw in her mother, and in her father and in herself: their worth.

It would be a long, long time until touchdown. But she stored this new knowledge in her data banks. And she savored this, that she continued living the only way a person could after any kind of inflicted pain—by defying the odds. She bet on herself. She refused to let what had happened to her be the thing that brought her down. She was fast approaching the ground. But she could fly now.

"I'm sorry, honey." Out of the corner of her eye, she saw her mother's head hanging. "What did you want to tell me?"

That Nixon had been given the option to return to her feelings, rather than the two of them falling back into screaming, meant she had made an impression prior to Hector's call. She would take that as her win. She would choose her next words very carefully. She had no one to protect but herself and her magic.

26.

TAMANDREA

THE CAR RIDE back to the Phoenix was largely silent.

"You need a ride, Dre?" Tamara asked, solemnly.

"Please," Andrea said.

Hector's car crept slowly up to the curb. Tamara looked at him, wanting to ask what he might do next. He stared at the steering wheel.

Andrea read the room and stepped out of the car, giving them space, politely saying, "Bye, Hec."

He wondered how, even now, she could still manage to keep some pep in her emotional step.

"Bye," he said.

Tamara didn't move.

He looked at her. "Why didn't anyone help Molly? Talk about Reg. Tell her story."

"How much fun was it to be outed against your will?"

Hector's face went cold.

"Do you want someone else telling your story?" she asked.

"Maybe mine's not that interesting."

"You'd be surprised," she said, offering a small smile. "We're on the same team, you know."

"I do know that, at least," he said. Then he asked, "What did you really mean when you called and said you needed my help?"

She eyed Andrea through the window. "Everyone thinks we're crazy, you know. People just think you're quiet."

He watched her futz with her purse, an activity to hide behind.

"You wanted to help Molly. But a lot of this goes deeper. Who we are as people away from who people expect us to be. You can understand that."

"I can."

"I guess . . . I wanted to know whether or not someone like you would stand with people like us."

"What do you mean, people like you?"

"Applebrities." She wiggled her fingers as if the term deserved half-hearted jazz hands. "Big-time movie star backs us up and says we're not crazy bitches after all. Could go a long way."

"I see."

"You've got the biggest platform and the loudest megaphone in the world," she said. And for the first time that day, he heard her voice shake with nerves. "We just want to share it."

He wished he could make whatever pain was wreaking havoc inside her go away but knew that was work they all had to do themselves.

"Okay," he said, nodding. "Anything you need."

"You're a good kid, Hec." She patted his shoulder hard, as if he was a chum, and buttoned up her vulnerability, becoming Tamara Collins again.

He laughed. It was a strange sensation to make a new friend.

"Thanks," he said.

"I'll call you tomorrow," she said.

"Okay."

She leaned forward. They hovered for a breathless moment there, in the delicate space of shared grief. Then she quickly kissed him on the cheek, grabbed her bag, and left.

She and Andrea watched him drive away. They stood in silence for a while. Then they walked to Tamara's car.

"CAN I COME inside?" Tamara asked as her car pulled in front of Andrea's building.

"Of course," Andrea said, getting out.

"Where do I park?" she said, noting the overcrowded and permitted West Hollywood side street.

"Just leave your hazards on. I do it all the time," Andrea said.

"For how long?"

"You're good for a few hours. If we hear anything, just yell down and tell people you're moving."

"Okay . . ." Tamara warily put the car in park.

Inside, they sat at a small table in Andrea's kitchenette. Tamara looked around, not remembering the last time she had been there.

"How much do you pay for this again?" she asked.

"Thirty-five." Andrea poured herself a glass of wine. "You want a LaCroix?"

"Two bedrooms?"

"Yeah."

"Why don't you just buy property?"

"I like apartments."

"Said no one ever."

"I like old buildings." Andrea shrugged. "Kind of like a piece of old Hollywood, taken out of time and dropped in the here and now."

"Buy an old house."

"Old houses are creepy."

Tamara laughed. "You are fucking ridiculous."

Andrea chuckled mid-sip, the exhale of her nose spraying droplets along the inside of the wine glass. She wiped her mouth and said, "Did you want something?"

Tamara waved off the request, their brief silliness becoming somber. "We need to talk about what we'll say."

"Right."

"What's wrong?"

Andrea bit her lip. "We're being honest, right?"

"Have you ever felt like you couldn't be with me?"

"Yes and no," she said, being honest.

"Fair."

"When were you ever going to clue me in?"

"On?"

"The plan."

"What plan?"

"Whatever you've been lying in wait for with Guy."

"To tell you the truth, I didn't think I was ever going to get a shot. There's a lot I've wanted to be able to do for a very long time because of the boxes he's tried to keep me in. But it's been personal. I didn't feel like you would ever get sucked into it. It's always been my fuck-you speech to him. In my head at least."

"Gotcha." Andrea wasn't fully convinced.

"Let me be clear: I don't want to do this without you."

"I know."

"I need you."

"I know."

"Then what would you like me to say?" Tamara felt suddenly on the defensive.

"We're equals," Andrea said.

"We are." Tamara nodded.

"No, moving forward." Andrea straightened up in her chair. "We make the same. We both get producer credit. What we do outside of the show is our own thing, but inside we're fifty-fifty."

"I am not interested in screwing you over, Dre," Tamara said.

"I know. I'm just . . . sharing my requirements. Someone once told me to fight for what I deserve, so I'm doing that."

Tamara smirked.

"I don't like being used as a tool to try to take you down," Andrea said. "But I will say that if we're going into this together, it has to be one hundred percent. After tonight, the only people who're going to corroborate Josh's story is us."

"And Hector," Tamara added.

"You think he will?"

"He will."

"Then we have the dirt to bury Guy. So, let's do it."

"He's going to go down swinging," Tamara cautioned.

"I'm not always a pitcher of sweet tea, Tam." Andrea gulped what was left of her wine. "I can fight back too."

"I know you can," Tamara said, looking past Andrea and out a small window into an adjacent apartment.

"Then let me," Andrea said. "Don't treat me like everyone else does."

"Like you're made of porcelain?"

"Yes." Andrea looked frustrated. "I'm tired of it. You've been shoved into a box. So have I."

Tamara nodded slowly. "It's hard, Dre," she said. "I keep thinking about that picture of Molly that the magazine published. And I keep—" She stopped herself.

"What, you think I'm going to kill myself too?" Andrea said, raising her voice a little.

"God no!" Tamara exclaimed. "If ever there was someone certain to save the world, it would be you."

"Thanks." Andrea blushed.

"I care about you, I think, too much," Tamara said, remembering their lunch long ago. Her advice on the fragility of their fame. "I want no bad things to happen to you. Ever. All I've ever wanted to do is keep you safe. And to think that I could spend half of today wanting to smash your face in, to know that I let him play me like that—it makes me sick. And I'm sorry."

"I was really worried." Andrea laughed nervously. "I honestly didn't know what to do, and you were the only person I could think of to call."

"So, whatever you want, we get it together. Okay?" Tamara put a hand on Andrea's. "That's a promise."

"Okay."

"I need to go call my son." Tamara stood.

"Tam." Andrea rose to meet her. "Are you gonna be okay?"

"What do you mean?"

"Just . . . tonight. I didn't know her as well. So, learning about Molly and Josh. And Guy. She was your best friend."

"In the spirit of being honest, no. I'm not okay. All I can think about is having a drink. I'm really pissed off and really hurt, and all I want to do is set fires and cry. But we have work to do."

Andrea hugged her. "We'll be okay," she said.

"Outside of an act of God, I think the ball is finally in our court," Tamara said. Then she left.

She walked quickly down the stairs and returned to her car only to find a parking attendant writing her a ticket.

"Excuse me!" Tamara jogged to the woman. "This is my car."

"I'm happy for you." The attendant was in a mood.

"Thanks. I'm—I was about to . . ."

"You can't just leave it in the street for ten minutes, ma'am." The attendant tore off the ticket from her small printer, tucked it into its envelope, and handed it to Tamara.

"What kind of pleasure do you derive from doing this?" Tamara glared at her.

"More than you know." The attendant smiled, got back in her car, and drove off.

"Sorry!" Andrea shouted from above.

Tamara turned to see her and flipped her off.

"Wow, rude!" Andrea responded.

"I'm telling Apples I don't need you anymore!" Tamara called up. "Please do!"

"And that you're a huge fucking bitch!" she said, smiling as she opened the car door.

"I know!"

"Fuck off, Dre!"

"Fuck you, Tam!"

ANDREA CHECKED THE time—only 10:00 p.m.—and considered another glass of wine. The one benefit of Hector's having such a curmudgeonly manager was that everyone got to bed on time. She poured one more.

She tapped her phone again and swiped to unlock it. There had been an unread text haunting her since she had sat in the back of Hector's car. It was from Elliot. She stared at it, not sure if she should open up that particular can of worms. She did it anyway.

"It was good to see you a few weeks ago. Wish it was under better circumstances." He had said.

She knew her response would be an even bigger can of worms. But she was over the bullshit now. Elliot wasn't a bad guy. None of them were bad people. Like anyone else in the world, they were simply who they had been made into.

"Me too." She typed, then paused, thinking. "Hope you're okay." She hit send, sighed, and took her wine with her into the bathroom.

She always loved an excuse to drink wine in the shower. As she undressed, she felt she was stripping off the weight of her life's previous expectations, piece by piece. She had never even known how to fantasize about being in control of her own narrative. Others had always shaped it for her, the invented reality they lived in. Guy, Apples, their producers, the audience. Manufactured situations that became real, created scenarios and emotions and fights and fuck yous and repercussions that the casts were all left to deal with. Like her imagined beef with Cyd. Like everyone's imagined beef with Cyd. And somewhere out there was poor Cyd, not knowing what she had done to deserve such imagined beef. That may not have been her reality when she first started on the show, but it was certainly her reality now. The audience and her producers made sure she never forgot it.

Andrea poked her hand into the steaming water to test its temperature and stepped inside the shower. They were apparently bad for her skin, but she liked showers that felt like they burned a little. As if the price of relaxation was a little punishment. She washed away the idea that she would be slave to anyone's idea of who she should be and breathed deeply so that the steam opened all passages within her and could let in the person she wanted to be. All she wanted was to live authentically, to make good on the promises she had sold in her own book, to make good on the pact with Tam, to undo the knots of tension throughout her body that said her life was not her own.

Fucking Essence. Andrea should not have been so surprised she'd been selling her out all along. Who wasn't? Just another hanger-on. Just another weekend-crash-course LA life coach. Andrea couldn't wait to call her in the morning and puff up and say, "Ground this energy, bitch!"

Then she cried. Then she laughed. She soaked in the feeling of what it meant to be in control. She reveled in it. She cherished it. She promised never to lose sight of it again. Never to let anyone other than herself dictate the passages of her own story.

She shut off the water and opened the shower door, reaching for her towel on a nearby hook. She dried herself off and wiped the steam from the mirror with her wet hand and looked at the obscured image of her own face. The flaws, she decided, were with the mirror.

The door behind her opened, and she felt her blood spread out flat in her veins, an indescribable chill. Her brain only had enough time to flash the hope that it was Tamara pulling a prank on her before she was forced to accept that it was not.

He moved swiftly across the bathroom floor before she had a moment to scream and plunged her own kitchen knife into the side of her neck.

Her brain synapses fired danger but also confusion. That she could be so on top of her own game seconds prior and now so despairingly at the bottom caused a twist in her face as he pulled the knife out. It wasn't pain. The shock was too great for that. It was that no matter how much she had worked to prepare herself for her own reality, reality had plans of its own.

Her hand instinctively covered the wound, and he stabbed again, this time beneath her ribs. She watched him as if outside of her body. He wore a hat and a plain dark green jacket. Her eyes drifted down, and she thought his pants were too big for him but his shoes were stylish brown Chelsea boots, and she couldn't help but think they were an odd choice to wear when murdering someone. Then she saw him at the Phoenix. At the book signing, standing silently in the back. After yoga as she'd watched his spirit get sucked from his body when she could not remember his name. All those times she'd covered the nonmandatory but strongly encouraged ten-dollar class fee. All those times she'd decided nothing was amiss inside her home. That she must've been crazy. That she should've called the cops long ago. That the adrenaline of this night had made her forget. That all this time she'd thought she was just being nice to him.

He pulled the knife from her gut, and she dropped her towel.

Her body slumped to the floor. All she could think to do was crawl. He put all his might into driving the knife into her back as many times as he could, shocked with each movement at how easily steel punctured skin and muscle. As if, when push came to shove, the body could not resist at all. Life seemed so infinite, but death came easily. As her body slowly slithered away from him, he kept his position, stabbing her buttocks, the backs of her legs, her calves.

Then her body quit. Despite all the movies she had seen where the heroine gets by on the skin of her teeth, where the body defies reality and is able to stand and run, where the best friend comes charging back through the door, none of it was real. She was alone.

Even though her own murder was not her fault, she worried about Tam. About being taken too soon. About her losing both she and Molly. About her drinking and her son and her ex-husband and her feud with Guy, and Andrea hoped she might at least come back as her best friend's guardian angel.

She wondered how long he had been waiting outside, and then she accepted that none of it mattered. She was dying and there was nothing she could do about it. There was no way to produce it differently, to edit her story line, no way to undo what the fan had done.

He turned her over to see her face. He was out of breath, and his eyes were filled with tears, and she thought that it was strange that he was the one crying. She tried hard not to let her last thoughts be wasted on him. But she couldn't help but wonder where he had been so desperately failed that this idea had seemed like a rational one. Where had he been so hurt that causing this kind of harm was the only logical extension of his suffering?

She held on as long as she could but was permitted only the white noise that was the rest of her life. She begged her eyes to remain open long enough to prove to this phantom that she wasn't just another death by misadventure. That she hadn't willfully entered into this life of fame to bear such a burden as the hatred and judgment of her own audience. She could hear their voices telling her that if she hadn't wanted to lose her life like this, she should have chosen another career. She should've been kinder. She should've listened more. If she really cared so much, she should've remembered his name.

Her eyes made out the swift motion of his shape toward her face, then her throat felt the dulled, numb sensation of tension drawn across it, the blade slitting it. What blood she had left she had no choice but to let for him, a sacrifice to the unknown audience.

Whatever his name was, she thought, he could now rest knowing no one would forget it.

27.

ROYAL

ON JULY 20TH, 2019, at 3:00 p.m., Andrea Bocelli was interred at the Hollywood Forever Cemetery. Unfortunately for the famed opera singer, he fell prey to a social-media death scare when people who had no idea who the other Andrea Bocelli was scanned headlines and assumed it was him. He reassured fans via Twitter that he was alive and well and expressed sympathy and condolences that his homonymous female counterpart was not.

Despite her grieving parents' initial wishes, they let themselves be convinced to have an open casket so castmates, friends, and high-profile fans could say their good-byes face-to-face and lay white roses atop her body. She was dressed in a white gown with a high neck to ensure the covering of damage done. She appeared to be smiling gently, but her expression had been manipulated. Many people thought her makeup was well done considering it was the only time she had not done her own.

Her father gave the eulogy, despite Milan's hoping she might be asked to. Her mother, the former choir director for their Lutheran church in Tyler, tearfully led the massive audience in "The Old Rugged Cross," a hymn Andrea had always liked to sing as a child. And the pastor from that same church flew out to read a passage from the Bible that did not seem appropriate for a somber occasion but was to those who knew Andrea. Something about loving one another, about God abiding in humanity, and about a love perfected among those humans who dared to do it.

Despite strong encouragement and lots of dollar signs, her parents refused to let the service be broadcast. Their daughter's life, they said, had been broadcast enough. They wanted to retain one singular event to keep sacred with them when they returned home. They had no other children. They would have no grandchildren. And they would keep her picture on their bedside tables for the rest of their lives.

Too young to have considered it, Andrea had left no will. Her possessions were not many outside of her makeup, her clothes, her shoes, and an assortment of vintage and antique furniture in the apartment she'd loved so much, inside the old building she'd loved even more.

Despite there being only photographers from print publications and the occasional person recording with a cell phone at the service, her costars got themselves appropriately ready in case of emergency production. But the energy among them was different this time. When Molly had died, it had been as if she were pulling a prank. That would have been Molly, they all thought, to pop up out of the coffin and yell, "Gotcha, bitches!" Just to see the looks on their faces.

Where people may have shrugged off Molly's death, suicide being the fitting end for a mess like her, they truly mourned Andrea's. She left behind her sweet, benevolent image. Her inability to stay mad at anyone or hold a grudge. Her giving nature. Her love for her fans. The way she'd brightened every room she entered. It was hard to justify a world where such a violent act could be done to her. True-crime podcast hosts were already lining up to give glory to the man who had murdered her.

People had started to print her image on handbags and backpacks, T-shirts and jackets. An infamous artist known only by the pseudonym Loews Delancey had designed a stencil of her face, a small crown slightly askew atop her head and the word "ROYAL" at the bottom. The image was spray-painted under cover of darkness days after her death on the side of a large pink wall on Melrose Avenue that was part of the property of the designer shoe brand BB Dees. Dee Brenda Bracket, the designer, was a fan of all things Apples and said she would leave it as a permanent installation for fans to visit and pay their respects. People flocked to it to take their pictures in front of it. They offered peace signs, hands on hips in knee pop poses, smiles, frowns, tears, and blown kisses to the monochrome altar.

Milan, Hips, and Cyd were among the key cast members who spoke at the service, reflecting and remembering only the good times they'd shared with Andrea. How she had given them late-night rides after bad dates and too much booze, loaned money without any expectation of it being paid back, encouraged charitable giving not just during the holidays. How she had always looked fabulous at yoga. And how she didn't deserve what had happened to her. They worried about their careers without her. They worried for their safety.

Fievel and Elliot stood as far back in the crowd as they could. Both declined to speak. One of the many photos from the day to go viral was of Fievel holding a sobbing Elliot in his arms, Elliot's forehead pressed firmly into his friend's shoulder. Fievel had spoken privately to Andrea's parents prior to the service and insisted he foot the bill. They thanked him but declined. Guy had already done so.

Hector stood with Tamara, causing everyone to speculate about whether they were sleeping together, some believing they had conspired on a murder plot to get rid of Andrea after Tamara had found out she was getting kicked off her own show. The last known photos of Andrea alive featured both him and Tamara outside the Phoenix. Some felt that maybe Hector was a kind of Apples grim reaper. First Molly, now Andrea. Who might his cold hand touch next?

A few days prior, after being released from police questioning, Josh had begun a social media campaign alleging that Tamara, Hector, and Andrea had confronted him. He had told them what he knew was the truth, that Molly's suicide could be laid at the feet of Guy Maker. And so time should be up on the man's career just as it was for the men who'd taken advantage of so many other women in the industry. Because what was the difference?

No one believed him.

Having lost another best friend to tragedy, Tamara was a hair's breadth from burning the world down. But the game had taken her that far. There was nothing left to do but do right by Andrea any way she could. It had always been Andrea's favorite thing about her—the way Tamara's eyes relaxed as the tension in her face faded and her cheeks fell, a cue for nuclear warfare. She was livid, in anguish, but in absolute control. She saw the game board, and it was her move.

Moments before she took the stage to pay her respects to her better half, Tamara quoted Josh's tweet.

"I'm just getting started," she wrote.

Social media exploded, a collective buzzing in everyone's pockets like applause as she addressed the crowd, making eye contact with the man who finally decided to show up. Guy Maker. Guy "the People" Maker, "The Money" Maker. She smiled at him. She was going to make sure he met his.

EPILOGUE

GUY MAKER WAS born Guy Edward Maker VII. The name had been passed down in his family so many times that for a Guy Edward Maker not to name his first-born son after the family's ancestral patriarch would have been offensive.

The family took great pride in the name. Guy Maker—the maker of men. It was strong and resilient and had first been bestowed by Guy Maker VII's great-great-great-great-great-grandfather Martin Maker who, with his wife, Elizabeth, had adopted an orphaned young boy left at their home by a young woman. She had come into the small California county of Shasta and attended church services looking for a place to stay. She had traveled out from Missouri with her brother, who had been looking to cash in on the gold rush. Combining both their inheritances from their dead father, he purchased a mining claim that washed up nothing more than a payout for fools.

When the investment soured, he borrowed money from a local gambling hall owner to purchase the claim on the north side of his neighbor, certain he would have better luck there.

Having lots of free time and little to do outside of maintaining camp, the sister made contact with a Shastan man who spoke English. At first, she was afraid, but soon she became fascinated by him and his people. She had heard that they were rapists and monsters, but he brought her freshly killed mule deer, coho salmon, and plenty of black oak acorn meal. He was gentle and kind and quiet. He liked to sit in stillness and listen to his world, finding the mercy of God in gentle breezes rather than in the Bible.

The brother, drunk in town and gambling, gone for days at a time, returned home periodically to bountiful feasts. He asked questions, but his sister always found a lie.

After some time, she started to be sick each morning. No longer willing to accept that the food had been provided by neighbors and luck, her brother told her he was going into town for a few days but instead kept distant watch as the Shastan man returned each day. The brother had his proof that she had been communing with the red devil, and he brought back with him a group of men hell bent on returning to camp with a scalp.

They got what they came for.

Shortly after the brother's second claim washed up even less than the first, his debt cost him his life when it could not be repaid.

On her own, she gave birth to the half-native child. Zealots, miners, and would-be cowboys reminded her she was a whore with a bastard son, half-savage, and chased her out of town. She moved quickly to the edges of the county line and found refuge with the sheriff, Martin Maker. He and his wife, Elizabeth, took pity on her. They cared for her and the child until one morning they woke to find her disappeared, the baby left behind. She'd left no note other than a palm-sized piece of gold, the only thing her brother had ever been worth.

In the position of raising a boy destined for scorn, the Makers decided on defiance. Certain of the vitriol the child would receive for the rest of his life, they championed him as the hero of his story. Not demonic at all, but divine and rare. Through his veins pumped the blood of the land, though his blue eyes tethered him to his persecutors, who prayed God would bless him with whiteness.

This new hero, born into struggle and cast between the narratives of two worlds, would remake this world in his own image. They put their faith in him. He would be a maker of men, this Guy Maker.

At least, that was the way Guy Maker VII's grandfather had told him the story when he was a boy.

Their long lineage of proper masculinity had ended with Seven's father, Six, whose diminutive stature, poor vision, and propensity toward books and paintings rather than sports had derailed what had seemed like a legacy of hunter-gatherer football stars. Seven's grandfather, Five, harassed his son, Six, to no end. Everyone, including Six's own siblings, could not believe that he had been the first of his generation to be married and the first to have a child. For the first time in that many generations, the family considered allowing a skip so as not to permit Six's son be Seven, but after the aged and ailing Four had a premonition in his sleep, they decided rules were rules. If they broke this one, they might as well not name any more children Guy Maker at all, and that thought made them ill.

The Maker clan had moved from California generations prior to Saint Louis, where they had stayed for over fifty years. Four had come back from the great war, chased a girl there, and taken a job as a barber in 1919. Giving a shave and a haircut was a noble profession then, and Five inherited it from his father. Five took his father's talents a step further, also constructing and selling wigs. The sign outside his barbershop read, "Guy Maker. Wig Fixer. Barber too."

But Six developed an eye for the arts. He found photography in high school, a hobby that Five felt was frivolous and sissy, and took it with him to New York University. He paid his own way through college by tutoring wealthy children. He avoided the draft thanks to his asthma. He masked his insecurities by growing his hair long and found his style taking glamorous nude portraits of any young girl who wanted to rebel against her parents and the war.

After graduating, he was hired to shoot ads for a fledgling automotive company by a friend who had gone to work at his father's advertising agency. Six suggested bringing in a few of the girls he'd shot with in the past to create a *Playboy*-like environment without the nudity, using sex to sell cars. The approach was a success, and the agency hired him as their in-house photographer.

Because of his budding reputation, he gradually began to be called to shoot for magazines like *Harper's Bazaar* and *Vogue* and even flown to France to shoot for *Elle* before the US version was launched.

While shooting in France, he met a model named Isabella Auclair, the daughter of a wealthy textile family that produced garments for high-end designers, pretending their products were still in reach of the common man by naming their company Auclair Sociétaire.

This meeting, and subsequent work together, created a fast, strong bond. Six felt like a god in France, a country where artistic merit went further than athletic might. He and Isabella started a correspondence when he returned to the States, and he flew again to Paris six months later to ask her to marry him. She accepted the proposal and looked forward to her modeling work in America, where opportunities were greater, as was the allure of scenes like New York and Los Angeles.

Six's success allowed him to merrily throw his family's judgments back in their faces, especially when Seven was born. It was a source of great pride for him, knowing that in the face of his all-American family, here was high art born of something and someone beautiful. He adored Isabella. Often too much. As a model, she at first felt threatened by a pregnancy so early in their marriage. But she dedicated herself to her career postpartum, refusing to let the stigma of having a child make her damaged goods. Her face, having appeared on numerous style magazines, transitioned comfortably into housekeeping and lifestyle ones that championed a woman's ability to have both her children and her empire, despite her rarely being home.

Six's work also kept him away often, meaning Guy VII's upbringing bonded him most closely with Martha Espinoza, their housekeeper and nanny. She eventually moved into the family's back house behind their sprawling Studio City home. She prepared nearly all young

Guy's meals, took him to school, picked him up, helped him with his homework, and made sure he was tucked in. In between her duties, she found time to clean the home, skim the pool, unblock clogged drains, change the oil in Six's car, handle Isabella's dry cleaning, keep the flower beds free of weeds, and take care of the family dog, a Labrador named Lexington.

Guy was teased mercilessly at school for having what the other kids called "a Mexican *mamacita*," and they called him "the little beaner lover." He was not much of a fighter but tried to defend Martha's honor. But his black eyes and bruised cheeks were never going to put an end to their verbal abuse, and she told him to stop fighting. It was not worth the excuses they had to make to his parents.

Guy's only defense was to say they all had housekeepers. And it was true, they admitted. They all had some variation of these women, but their help stayed home where they belonged. Only Guy Maker's made herself visible. Only Guy Maker's acted as his mother.

As he got older, Guy began throwing tantrums for his parents' virtually nonexistent attention. Because of their absence, his prepubescent angst lashed out at the only mother on hand. Martha asked him where the sweet boy had gone who she used to enjoy spending so much time with. She missed holding his hand and singing gently to him. She missed all the special things any mother missed from a growing child, even the changing of wetted sheets and the telling of lies to hide the truth of his parent's lack of affection.

He was thirteen then, and he hated her for reasons he could not explain. All he wanted was for the bullying to stop. All he wanted was for his real mother to finally take an interest in him. Martha tried to explain to Isabella where Guy's pain was coming from, but Isabella believed that he was bored. She used to lash out because her father was so busy. That was what children did. She got him a tabby cat, which he named Abigail.

His father's trust in his wife began to deteriorate bit by bit as his work slowed and hers continued. She had found new markets for modeling as a successful mother and entrepreneur, having started her own fashion line with her father, "Air of Auclair."

Her frequent international trips combined with his slowing career meant that, as the young Guy Maker aged, his father was spending more time at home without his wife. He began to feel trapped with his son and the strange Mexican woman he barely knew. He had taken to drinking heavily but began at 5:00 p.m. to avoid appearing like an alcoholic, which he claimed one could only be if drinking was an activity that could not be resisted during the daytime.

He began finding reasons to blame Martha for things that were not her fault and calling Isabella to complain. He started to take out his frustrations on his son. Hoping to bond, he tried to teach the boy about how to be his version of a man and how to talk to bullies. But life lessons were not his forte, and Guy thought his father sounded foolish.

Once, when Guy didn't want to hear his father's stories of false bravado any longer, he mocked Six for his small stature and lazy posture and said he was grateful he'd inherited his mother's slender figure and good looks. His father beat him so bad he couldn't attend school for a week. Martha was forced to call the school office and, in her best English, lied that Guy was away with his father on a photography expedition.

Martha tried to comfort Guy throughout his father's increasingly violent and depressive episodes, but he was closing in on fifteen, and he felt comfortable screaming at her to leave him alone. Martha was also aging. Fifty-five when they first hired her, she was approaching seventy. Her work began to slip. She missed spots while cleaning. She didn't have the strength to jack up Six's car to change its oil. She could not reach out far enough to effectively skim the pool. She had trouble driving at night.

One evening, picking up Guy from school after drama rehearsal, she attempted to make a right turn at an intersection and did not see a jogger in dark clothes crossing quickly in front of them. She hit him with the front of Six's Mercedes and knocked him to the ground, the front left tire running over his leg.

Isabella had chosen to take no hardline stances on how her son should be cared for until his surrogate mother became a legal liability. There wasn't a world in which Martha could pay to defend herself. Isabella and Six were not about to pay for her to go to trial and sully their good name. Guy felt caught in the middle. His misplaced anger and frustration with her vanished when he thought about losing her. He did not want to be alone. When Martha offered to quit, it was decided that would be best. The Makers settled with the jogger out of court.

Guy cried and begged his parents to keep her. He apologized to Martha for his nastiness and his confusion, said that he would be different if she stayed. He swore to his parents the accident had been his fault. He should have gotten a ride home from school. He had called her. He had made her drive in the dark. He fell at the old woman's feet hoping, in some way, she could take him with her.

His parents had to pry his fingers from her dress as Martha's nephew escorted her to his car. She told Guy she loved him but could say little else between her sobs. As the car drove away, Six had to hold his son's bean-pole body tightly in a bear hug to prevent him from chasing after her.

Guy shut himself in his room that night with Abigail while his parents argued. Later, Isabella sneaked in and sat on his bed in an attempt to comfort him. He kept his back to her and made himself cold to her touch. She spoke only a few words of encouragement, trying to console him as best she could.

"Don't worry," she said. "We can always get another."

Not knowing what else to do, gradually Isabella began to take her son everywhere, often against his will. At sixteen, he was the most well-traveled of his peers. He had been to New York, Paris, Rome, Milan, Nice, Egypt, London, Edinburgh, Berlin, Prague, Amsterdam,

Barcelona, and many other places. On rare occasions, his father came along too.

Because the young Guy's mother did not know how to get close to a teenage boy, she mistook spoiling him for care. She gave him style. She walked him down runways and put him in front of cameras. His often-vacant look, slender frame, and visible, high cheekbones were well suited for fashion. One stylist favorably described him as "a quail's egg." His don't-care attitude became an iconic look, his expression always one of being perfectly willing to do nothing at all.

When he was home, he crawled through the remainder of high school, his parents offering donations in exchange for teachers looking the other way about their son's chronic absences and sudden trips to faraway places. He hosted parties at their house when they were gone and did drugs out of boredom. If someone had asked him then, he would have said he thought that it was funny to be seventeen years old with a several-hundred-dollar-a-week cocaine habit.

Having gotten his driver's license, one day he took a group of friends to a house party in Calabasas. The host was a former friend from his theater program who had been suspended a year prior after being discovered in the handicap stall of a bathroom nearly incapacitated on Percocet. Everyone made a delightful fuss when Guy arrived looking like a spectacular party monster, clad head to toe in Givenchy. He was able to live as a minor celebrity—a young brand ambassador to the world with an eye for fashion and drama and access to any drug imaginable.

But as big a fuss as kids made when he walked in the room, it paled in comparison to when Molly Mandrie did.

She was still going strong as the star of *The Family That Stays Together*, and Guy was desperate to meet her. Not because he was a fan; he hadn't seen a single second of her stupid fucking family sitcom. But because of her legendary reputation for turning what had been a party into a virtual crime scene.

He noticed she had come alone and quickly introduced himself.

She didn't seem to care who he was or who his parents were. He told her he didn't care about her show. She said she didn't respect anyone who dressed cheap. He said he didn't like cunts, but he'd be willing to make an exception in her case. Then she laughed. In a strange way, she reminded him of Isabella.

Their chaotic friendship built fast over the course of a year. They were the same age and had the same interest in giving no fucks. He envied her lifestyle. She was a bitch and he loved it. *To be seventeen and run the world*, he thought. She was remarkable.

The only people she refused to let him meet were her parents because, she said, they were drunks. And not the fun kind. Her and Guy's friendship was exhausting, but they did not let up until he entered junior college, taking an interest in film and television production. He had never wanted to be a fashion icon. He'd thought he wanted to be an actor but realized he had to care a great deal more than he did to pursue it. But being on the other side of the camera lent itself to the kind of control he liked. The ability to rewrite the scripts of his life. He could film his family and edit them as he pleased. He began to document everything—friends, school, strangers and passersby, and especially Molly.

One drunken night as the two of them floated in his parent's pool, Molly began to ramble about her life on *The Family That Stays Together*, which had by then ended. She had taken quaaludes and slipped into the safety of feeling like she could share anything with him. Guy reached for his camera at the side of the pool, holding it carefully over the water so as not to get it wet. The twin spools of tape inside cranked to life. A rare moment of not pretending entered the lens and caught the twenty-year-old Molly Mandrie in a way no one else had ever seen or heard.

She told him about a time when she was fifteen and one the directors and producers of her show had made her have sex with him. But he was very careful about it, she said, so she could not decide whether or not she had been raped because she hadn't technically said no. He made her feel, somehow, like they had had that moment planned for years. That it had always been there, lurking under the surface of their working relationship. How he doted on her and loved her and treated her simultaneously like his daughter and his whore. How he prided himself on being the only man who could put the irascible Molly Mandrie in her place. And he said that when she was old enough, he would leave his wife and they would marry, and she thought she had fallen in love with him. Only what he promised never happened. When she confronted him, he told her she was delusional.

She looked to Guy for his take on whether she was right in thinking it was all very fucked up or whether she had been making a big deal over nothing. She'd had sex plenty of times with plenty of men in plenty of age brackets. But Reg had been the only one to keep her tethered to him in the way he had. It was because she could not pull any of the tricks on him that she could on anyone else. He'd known her since she was ten. He read her like a book because he'd helped write it. She felt she could not find a way to get around him. He was rich and powerful. There would be some sort of retribution if she tried. A ruined career or a secret spilled. He was right; she was a whore. She had not said no. It was her fault.

Guy let her words run through the filter of his lens. The rage he felt at his friend's abuse recalled his own neglect, and he let bitterness take him over. Wanting to protect her, he told her what he told himself each day—not to think about it. Put it away. Don't dwell on it. Bury it. If you give them the chance, people will only find ways to hurt you. So best to cut out the ones that did. Leave the old man behind. Love the only friend that loved her back. Trust him. He was her best friend. And she was his. At least they had each other. At least both their lives were messes.

ACKNOWLEDGMENTS

CERTAINLY THE MOST important person to whom I owe this book's existence is Emily Murdock Baker of EMB Editorial. When this all began, I had a novel I loved and no clear cut path before me. No path at all, in fact. I knew absolutely zero about the publishing industry, and she has held my hand and shown me the ins and outs for almost three years. She has always taken the time to be kind, courteous, and helpful, if even just to hear me vent about how fucking difficult all this was. I have trusted her opinions, notes, and thoughts above all. Thank you, Emily.

Thanks to the wonderful group at Amplify Publishing: Jess Cohn, who got the ball rolling and said so many nice things about the book that I still have trouble accepting them; Rachel Applebach, my production editor and book-baby midwife, who told me to just breathe during delivery and whose opinion on editing, design, and esthetic helped put this book into your hands; and Lorna Partington, whose edits only made this book stronger, clearer, and more concise.

I'm grateful to Katie Herman, the woman with the most incredible brain for tracking dates, timelines, and inconsistencies or things needing clarity. I believe she knows this book better than I do. Not to mention she taught me a lot about grammar, and it is apparent I need to go back to school.

Emily Snyder's beautiful interior design brought the biggest smile to my face when I first saw it. It's hard to imagine what a book will truly look like out in the wild until you get a peek inside, and boy did she show me the one I'd always dreamed of.

Nicole Hower, my cover designer, deserves ten million dollars for somehow reaching into my soul and pulling out the perfect design. They say, "don't judge a book by its cover," but we all do. What's a cover that would make you pick up the book and turn it over and read the back copy? To then crack it open and read the first page? Nicole created that cover. Are you a writer? Hire her!

My pops, Randy Sterling, gets credit for always providing sound legal (and fatherly) counsel on both technical matters and the matters of the heart. I love you, Dad.

Heartfelt appreciation goes to my very patient spouse, Kacey Short, who has dealt with years of work, planning, depression, self doubt, and eventual joy at this final product. She rides with me when things are at their best and sympathizes with me when fear and failure cloud my mind. She's the best thing that has ever happened to me. She deserves all the nice words written in every possible world.

Additionally, there are a lot of women in my life who deserve accolades. My mother, Maria, whom Hector's heartbreaking monologue about losing his own is almost verbatim my own experience, give or take a few details. My mother's mother, Olga, who gave me all the wit in the world and taught me how to tell a great story. I wish both these women were alive today to share in the success of what they'd both likely say was not their cup of tea. To lose a mom at fifteen does a lot to a kid. I hate it. But I'm also grateful, because I like me. And I like this book very much. And it wouldn't exist without these women, without these losses, and without my hurt. I pray continuously for their rest as much as I pray for my own.

There are many women I can't mention by name for all the reasons you're aware of, but my gratitude to them is infinite. Despite all the progress we think we've made in today's world, somehow it still bears repeating: believe women.

To be honest, I've spent way too much money and time in therapy working on validating my self-worth and not kicking that same self to the curb, to not acknowledge the fact that this book would not exist had I not believed it deserved to. I shoved this thing into the world because that's where it belongs. I'm proud of myself for doing it, for taking an uncountable number of rejections and spinning them into what I will always believe is gold. So, you know, I thank me. Go me! Go therapy!

I like to tell the people I love that I love them. I love all these people. I love you for reading. And for the select few who actually read the "acknowledgments" section, if you see me out in the wild, your next round is on me.